# THE
# THIRD ANTICHRIST

*Mario Reading's varied life has included selling rare books, teaching riding in Africa, studying dressage in Vienna, running a polo stable in Gloucestershire and maintaining a coffee plantation in Mexico. An acknowledged expert on the prophecies of Nostradamus, Reading is the author of eight non-fiction titles, as well as the bestselling novel* The Nostradamus Prophecies.

# THE
# THIRD ANTICHRIST

# MARIO READING

CORVUS

First published in the UK in 2011 by Corvus,
an imprint of Atlantic Books Ltd.

3 5 7 9 2 4 6 8

A CIP catalogue record for this book is available from the
British Library.

ISBN: 978-0-85789-666-7 (paperback)
ISBN: 978-0-85789-479-3 (eBook)
ISBN: 978-0-85789-348-2 (trade paperback)

Printed in Great Britain by Clays Ltd, St Ives plc

Corvus
An imprint of Atlantic Books Ltd
Ormond House
26-27 Boswell Street
London WC1N 3JZ

www.corvus-books.co.uk

# QUATRAINS

*Between 1555 and 1558 Nostradamus
wrote 942 quatrains.*

*Only the Bible has outsold them.*

*Scholars now believe that 77 of these verses predicted
the rise of two Antichrists: Napoleon and Hitler.*

*A further 36 quatrains (three sixes = 666 = the mark
of the beast) refer to a Third Antichrist.*

*3 of these are reproduced overleaf.*

Du plus profond de l'Occident d'Europe,
De pauvres gens un ieune enfant naistra,
Qui par sa langue seduira grande troupe:
Son bruit au regne d'Orient plus croistra.
(Index date: 35, Century Number: 3)

Tasche de murdre enormes adulteres,
Grand ennemy de tout le genre humain
Que sera pire qu'ayeulx, oncles, ne peres
En fer, feu, eau, sanguin & inhumain.
(Index date: 10, Century Number: 10)

Du mont Royal naistra d'une casane,
Qui cave & compte viendra tyranniser,
Dresser copie de la marche Millane,
Favene Florence d'or & gens expuiser.
(Index date: 32, Century Number: 7)

*From deep in the Western part of Europe,*
*A child will be born, to poor parents.*
*He will seduce the multitude with his tongue:*
*The noise of his reputation will grow in the East.*
*(Index date: 35, Century Number: 3)*

*Stained with mass murder and adultery,*
*This great enemy of humanity*
*Will be worse than any man before him*
*In steel, fire, water, bloody and monstrous.*
*(Index date: 10, Century Number: 10)*

*Though born in poverty, he will take supreme power,*
*He will tyrannize and bankrupt his people,*
*Raising a thousand-year army,*
*He is called lucky, though he costs both lives and gold.*
*(Index date: 32, Century Number: 7)*

# EPIGRAPHS

*But the day of the Lord will come as a thief in the night; in which the heavens shall pass away with a great noise, and the elements shall melt with fervent heat, the earth also and the works that are therein shall be burned up.*
II Peter 3: 10

\*

*At that meeting he was struck for the first time by the endless variety of men's minds, which prevents a truth from ever presenting itself identically to two persons.*
*War And Peace*, Leo Tolstoy

\*

*Kill a man, and you are a murderer.*
*Kill millions of men, and you are a conqueror.*
*Kill everyone, and you are a god.*
*Pensées D'Un Biologiste*, Jean Rostand

# AN OCEAN WITH NO SHORE

I marvelled at an ocean with no shore
and at a shore without an ocean;
At a dawn without darkness,
and at a night with no daybreak;
Then later at a sphere with no locality
known to either fool or sage;
And at a sky-blue dome thrust high
above the earth, twirling – driven;
And at a blossoming world with no heaven
and no hell, its secrets hidden…

*I courted an eternal mystery;*
*for I was asked: 'Has thought bewitched you?'*
*I answered: 'I cannot say; my advice would be:*
*have patience with it while you live.*
*But, in essence, once thought becomes established*
*in my mind, the embers stutter into flame,*
*and are consumed by inextinguishable fire.'*
*It was then told me: 'He does not pick a flower*
*who deems himself, by rights, "freeborn".*
*He who woos a beauty in her bedroom, devoured by love,*
*will never carp at the bride-price!'*

*I paid her dower and was given her in marriage*
*all through the night until the break of dawn*
*But I found only myself. – Or rather*
*the person I married – may his affair be noised abroad:*
*For, adding to the sun's light*
*is the refulgent moon, the shining stars;*
*Reproached, like time – though the Prophet*
*(blessings be upon his head!)*
*had once declared of your Lord that He is Time.*

Ibn al-'Arabi (1165–1240)

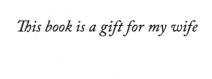
*This book is a gift for my wife*

*Cenucenca, Orheiul Vechi, Moldova*
*7 October 1982*

# 1

Dracul Lupei killed his first man when he was twelve years old. On his birthday. Thursday, 7 October 1982.

He did not intend to. But later, when he bothered to think about it, he realized that it had been inevitable. Like a boy losing his virginity. But this – the virginity thing – he had done the year before with his sister Antanasia.

As far as his sister was concerned, she had only given him what she had already given to pretty much the entire adult male population of Cenucenca at one time or another. Dracul's father, Adrian, rented her out on Friday nights when he needed drinking money for his *rachiu*. The two siblings shared a bedroom at the back of their father's ramshackle wooden farmhouse, so Dracul had been forced to listen ever since the whole thing began, somewhere around Antanasia's tenth birthday. He had listened for four years. Then, close on the arrival of his first erection, he had tried it for himself.

But killing a man was better. Much better.

In order to earn himself a little extra money, Dracul had formed the habit of setting out, early every Sunday morning, for the thirteenth-century Orheiul Vechi cave hermitage, situated six kilometres up the valley from his father's house. The hermitage was a twenty-minute uphill walk from the nearby village of Butuceni. It was positioned on top of a wild plateau dominating the Raŭt River, just a few hundred yards from the equally vertiginous parish church of St Maria.

The prehistoric cave complex was almost completely sealed off from the outside world, as was the section that housed the now abandoned troglodyte monastery, which was set high on a massive limestone buttress overlooking the gorge. The remaining hermitage, which was all that was left of the once thriving Pestere monastery, loomed over a landscape that resembled nothing so much as a slice of the planet Mars, transposed, like an alien spaceship, onto the Gaeto-Dacian plateau.

The main chapel, which formed part of a vast honeycomb formation beneath the surface of the plateau, could only be reached via a stout door, and from there down a flight of stone steps which led to the main crypt. The crypt contained a carved wooden reredos, built to the exact dimensions of the cave, and a few random pieces of furniture laid out over threadbare oriental carpets. Devotional paintings and ancient icons were scattered about the walls. The solitary embrasure let in little light, and the door that led through to the unfenced stone walkway overlooking the river, 200 feet below, let in little more, for it was covered in its entirety by a frayed set of damask hangings that some generous soul had donated to the hermitage when they were no longer of use elsewhere.

One old monk occupied the hermitage these days, and

he spent most of his time praying, reading the Bible, or painting icons, and was thus tolerated by the state authorities. So Dracul had been able, by degree, to make the exterior of the cave complex his own.

When touring parties visited – Young Communists maybe, or the Society of Cognac Workers, or members of the nomenklatura, drunk after a visit to the nearby Cricova or Cojuşna wineries and craving a breath of fresh upland air – Dracul would be there, waiting for them. Then, depending on the inebriated or non-inebriated state of the party, and on whether they had formal guides or not, he would step in and offer his services.

'You give me money. I take you places you never see. Secret places. You see views that make you sick with fear. You see snakes. You see wild boar. You see wolves. Maybe even bears.' It was all bullshit of course, but as Dracul insisted on being paid upfront, he was generally able to show the expectant tourists a clean set of heels before the promised wonders failed to appear. There were, needless to say, few repeat visits.

Dracul wasn't an easy boy to get past. From earliest childhood he had been a natural salesman. Golden-tongued, his mother had called him – her golden boy. If the visiting parties refused to employ him, Dracul would spread-eagle himself across the single main entrance to the rock-cave complex and refuse to move. This presented the visitors with something of a conundrum.

They could either remove him bodily – but there was usually some good soul around to object to grown men or women abusing a child – or they could come to an accommodation with him and be permitted inside. And the accommodation was generally easier.

Especially if one were drunk and out of one's head, like the astronaut Yuri Gagarin had been for two days, in 1966, during a visit to the Cricova winery. The Moldovan authorities had finally sent down a search team to identify and carry him out. Dracul knew this, because his father had been part of the team. The team had been dispatched into the underground winery on the first day of Gagarin's visit. They, too, had emerged, blind drunk, twenty-four hours later. As his father said – there were 120 kilometres of tunnels in that complex, situated 100 metres below the earth's surface, of which a full 60 kilometres were used to store wine. What was a man to do? During the ensuing visit to the monastery they'd had to attach Gagarin to a guide rope in case he inadvertently stumbled over the edge of the unfenced precipice, triggering a public relations disaster that would have ended Russia's domination of the Space Race once and for all.

These days it was usually government apparatchiks – less drunk, perhaps, than Gagarin, and a great deal less eminent – who reeled up the endless stone steps leading to the great cross, which sprang, like an outstretched hand, from the pinnacle of the Orheiul Vechi plateau, halfway between the St Maria church and the sunken entrance to the hermitage.

The old monk – whose name Dracul had never bothered to learn – appeared oblivious to Dracul's goings-on. He had recently taken to crossing himself, however, whenever Dracul hove into sight, so he must have suspected something, even if the exact details eluded him.

There were times when it seemed to Dracul as if he had taken on the role of penitential burden, which the monk, by default, now had to carry. This pleased Dracul. He liked being a penitential burden.

But the murder had come as a shock, even to him.

# 2

People almost never came to the hermitage alone. In Moldova, only high-up members of the Communist Party could afford to run cars, and such individuals were hardly likely to indulge themselves in a day trip to see a solitary monk going about his business in a 700-year-old glorified cave.

But on this occasion a black armour-plated ZIL-115 pulled up on the outskirts of Butuceni village. A single man got out. He was wearing a shiny suit, a red tie, and a white cotton handkerchief neatly triangulated in his top pocket. To Dracul's eyes, he looked like Leonid Brezhnev, whose picture his father kept on the wall of the outside privy. This man had two small medals pinned below his display handkerchief – exactly like Soviet General Secretary Brezhnev in his father's picture. In fact he gave the impression of having just left an important meeting, and of having decided, on a whim, to pass the time before his next appointment on a short rural visit. Maybe he had been born in Butuceni, thought Dracul, and wished to revisit the cherished scenes of his youth? Or maybe he was just slumming?

Dracul spied on the man from behind a shambling

stone wall.

First the man smoked a cigarette. Dracul could smell the tobacco drifting towards him on the icy breeze. Then he barked at his chauffeur. The chauffeur hurried out of the car and went to fetch his employer's black fur coat. This he draped around the man's shoulders, so that the coat hung down near the ground.

Dracul swallowed. It was a beautiful coat. A transcendental coat. In fact the coat was so large and the fur was so thick that it might even double as a blanket, if necessary. Failing that, the coat could be disguised – after a theft, say, leading to a change of ownership – via a trimming away of the base, instantly transforming the coat into a jacket and matching hat. Antanasia was a skilful seamstress. She would have no trouble adapting the coat to Dracul's specifications. He might even gift her some of the remaining fur with which to make a muff for her hands against the winter chill – if she pleased him, that was, and granted him certain of the additional favours that the Friday-night visitors so frequently demanded of her.

Dracul watched the man start up the rocky steps towards the plateau. The chauffeur also watched his master, his face twisted into a supercilious grin. Then he got back inside the car, which he had left running to conserve the heat, and slammed the door against the cold.

Dracul ghosted the coat-bearer's steps towards the monastery complex. It soon became apparent that the man wished, for some reason, to visit the actual hermitage itself, and not simply the St Maria church.

This decision played directly into Dracul's hands.

At the last possible moment, Dracul darted in front of the man and splayed himself across the hermitage door. 'You go in. You pay. You pay to me. Otherwise you not go in.'

Dracul's eyes played over the man's coat like a dog sizing up a marrowbone. Closer to, the coat was even more gorgeous than he had at first supposed. In fact it was the single most beautiful object that Dracul had ever seen in his life. If he had possessed a hundred rubles, he would willingly have given them for a coat such as this. But he had only eight-seven and a half kopeks to his name. Hardly enough to purchase a pair of nylon socks from the local flea market – far less an astrakhan coat.

The man punched Dracul in the face. The boy's head cracked back against the hardwood door as if pivoted on a spring. The shock was total. Dracul lurched forwards onto his knees and vomited out his breakfast.

The man kicked Dracul in the stomach. Then he wiped his shoe – which had been tarnished by some of the vomit – onto Dracul's trousers.

The man hesitated for a moment, clearly weighing up whether to kick Dracul again. Then he grunted, unlatched the door to the hermitage, and started down the stone steps.

# 3
—

Dracul lay on the ground outside the monastery entrance. No one had ever hit him that hard before. Not even his father in one of his drunken rages. Dracul felt as if his jaw might be shattered. And one or two of his ribs.

He dry-retched like a cat. Then he levered himself up onto his knees. He remained on all fours for some time, his head hanging down between his shoulders. Then he lurched to his feet and staggered towards the great stone cross, his body bent double, his hands cradling his stomach like a man with colic.

Dracul collapsed in the lee of the cross. An icy wind bit into his thin jacket. He could feel it searching up the legs of his trousers.

Despite the intense pain, all Dracul could think about was the man in the astrakhan coat. The man filled him with an intense admiration. This nameless person was clearly someone of immense importance. Someone he must learn to emulate. No one, in all the years that Dracul had eked out his living from blackmailing visitors to the monastery, had ever responded as this man had done. One or two had grabbed him, it is true, or pushed him roughly aside – but never with violent intent. They had simply been reacting out of frustration.

But this man had acted without compunction. Dracul had got in his way. So he had forced Dracul out of his way. The fact that Dracul was only twelve years old had clearly not clouded the man's thought processes in the least.

Dracul hugged himself and moaned. The pain in his ribs was spreading out across his stomach. He coughed in an effort to clear the congestion in his throat, but the pain from the movement was so great that it nearly caused him to black out. He clutched at his mouth to prevent a further unwanted spasm.

It was October, and the autumn was shaping up to be a hard one. Dracul knew that he would not be able to walk far with the injuries he had sustained. Perhaps not even as far as nearby Butuceni. Would the hermit agree to take him in? Might he lie up for a while in one of the stone cubicles the former monks had used as bedrooms? Probably not. The old man spoke to no one. And he mistrusted Dracul – that much was clear. Suspected that Dracul was misusing the monastery site.

Dracul sensed, rather than saw, the man's approach. The man still had the astrakhan coat draped across his shoulders like a cloak. He stopped at the cross, ignoring Dracul completely. Then he strolled to the lip of the plateau and peered out over the edge.

Everyone did this. It was hardly surprising. It was one of the wonders of Moldova. The river snaked below the limestone escarpment – a sheer 200-foot drop from the base of the great cross – and slithered on through the distant countryside like the retreating back of a meadow viper.

Dracul leapt to his feet and ran at the man. He did not think of the pain. He did not ask himself whether he was capable of achieving his end. He simply acted. Just like the man had acted at the monastery door.

At the very last moment the man began to turn, as if he intended to fend Dracul off with the flat of his palm. But it was too late.

Dracul struck the man full in the back, just as he was swivelling, on one foot, to face his assailant. Just as he was at his most vulnerable.

Dracul was not a large boy. But he was strong. He had been used to hard physical labour in the fields ever since his sixth birthday. He was a master scyther and a master hayricker, just as all village boys his age were. His body was as hard as iron from the summer harvest.

The man began to fall.

Dracul's last conscious act was to drag the astrakhan coat from about the man's shoulders.

Then he blacked out.

# 4

—

The pain in his side awoke Dracul five minutes later. He looked around for the man, but he was not there. The astrakhan coat lay beside him, however, like the sloughed-off skin of a reptile. Like the sloughed-off skin of the river that snaked through the valley below them.

Dracul could sense himself starting to hallucinate. Moaning softly, he dragged the coat towards him and rolled himself in it. The warmth and the smell of the coat comforted him immediately. He lay there for some time, immersed in the fur, not trusting himself to think.

The rush at the man had damaged something further inside him. This much was clear. Dracul could scarcely breathe. It was as if his lungs were filling up with soapy foam.

The chauffeur. The chauffeur would come up and look for his master. Then he would find Dracul. He would see Dracul in his master's coat. He would look down over the ridge. He would see his master's body on the rocks below. And his master was clearly an important man.

The authorities would take Dracul away and they would torture him. He had heard of such things happening to people who got on the wrong side of senior Party officials, or who fell foul of the nomenklatura in some way. His father regularly regaled him with gruesome tales of what had gone on over the border in Romania, at the notorious Sighet prison, before the powers-that-be had transformed it into a broom factory and salt warehouse in 1977.

The fact that Dracul was still a minor would have no effect on what they did to him. It would make it worse, perhaps. They would use him, just as the procession of men who came to his father's house on Friday nights used his sister, Antanasia. And this Dracul could not contemplate.

Once again he forced himself achingly slowly onto all fours. Still clutching the coat, he drifted to his feet and stood, swaying, near the flank of the great cross. One part of him was tempted to approach the ridge and look over the edge to see the body of the important man below – to see where it had fallen. But Dracul knew that this would be madness. He too would fall. Or the old monk would come out onto the stone terrace below the hermitage for a little air, look up, and see him. This could not be allowed to happen.

Dracul stumbled away from the cross and towards some nearby rocks. He knew, from his previous wanderings, where a hidden cave was set deep into the plateau floor. Perhaps a hermit had used it in the old days, before the time of the Soviet Union? Maybe wild animals used it now? Dracul didn't care. It would serve as shelter from the wind. No one would come there. No one knew of it. In all the years Dracul had been visiting the plateau, it had remained undiscovered.

And now, too, he had the coat.

# 5
—

Dracul awoke to find himself lying, not in his secret crypt, but on one of the stone cots in the communal sleeping quarters of the Pestere cave monastery. Candles were burning at his head and feet.

At first he thought he might be dead, and that the village had found his body and had laid him out in preparation for his wake. Then he realized that he was still wearing the astrakhan coat. And that he was still in pain. And dead people, he knew, did not feel pain.

He had crept into the monks' dormitory often enough in the past, when the weather had turned angry, or when he had felt the need for some, albeit insubstantial, proximity to another human being. The old monk was partially deaf. It had been an easy thing to sneak in when his back was turned, steal some of his food, and then take shelter until the storm had passed.

Dracul would pass the time by secretly watching the old monk at work on his icons – or listening to him muttering to himself and reciting his prayers. Sometimes he would entertain himself by moving some of the old man's things. Just a small movement. To a different chair, perhaps. Or onto a different bench in the chapel.

Did the monk think that this was God scattering about his possessions? Or the Virgin Mary? The prospect of the old monk's bewilderment pleased Dracul immeasurably.

Looking at the candles, a memory resurfaced of his mother's wake, four years previously. Her waxen face. The barely disguised bruises that still clouded her neck, and which a thick layer of powder and masking cream could do little to diminish.

At first Dracul suspected that his father had killed his mother in a jealous rage. These rages had been a constant of his early youth. All would be well for weeks, if not months. Then, unexpectedly, his mother would disappear from the house. She would be gone for days. His father would career about the village in increasing desperation, cursing the fact that he had married a Gypsy – cursing his wife's wandering ways – to anyone he could get to listen. Then he would start drinking.

By the end of the week he would be a walking nightmare. His hair bedraggled. His clothes unwashed. The children unfed. If one of Dracul's mother's exoduses coincided with the harvest, Adrian Lupei would simply abandon his fields in disgust.

'Zina, Zina,' he would shout around the village.

'He is hexed,' the villagers would say. 'The Gypsy *vrajitoarea* witch has hexed him. Such things always result when one race marries another. Look. Even her name is hexed. Zina means "a stranger", and Samana means "one who wanders".'

Dracul had loved his mother. She had been wild and unpredictable; as likely as not to strike him as to cuddle him. But when she turned good – when she was happy – it was a magic time for him and Antanasia. She would take them into the woods and show them herbs and roots and the medicinal bark of trees, and explain superstitions and folk myths. She would teach them about animal spoor, and the significance of each beast in the forest. And she would tell them Gypsy stories, of her ancestors, and the strange things they had done, or had done to them.

Once, she told them of Conducător Ion Antonescu, his antiziganism, and his role in the wartime purging of her extended Roma family.

'Antonescu's people took my grandmother, my grandfather, my father, and his six brothers and sisters, and transported them all to Transnistria. Then Antonescu stole the gold they had hidden in the shafts of their horse cart, and he killed them with the typhus. Only my father escaped from the camp, for the typhus spared him, and he was still strong enough, and young enough, despite the starvation rations, to be able to walk back home. But he was a changed man. On his way out to Transnistria he had seen many bad things. He had seen a pregnant woman shot, and her baby, still alive, begin struggling for life inside her. This, because she could no longer walk fast enough with the weight she was carrying in her stomach. Again, in Transnistria, he and his family were forced to eat dogs, and moles that had been skinned, and the slugs that fed on roadside weeds. If they were lucky, during the height of the summer, they might secure freshwater mussels from the River Bug, or barter for a little food with the local population. But the sickness proved too much for them, and all, save my father, died.

In this way the authorities murdered untold numbers of our people. Raped untold numbers of our women. Poisoned our future. Shut down our past. But nobody mourns us. Nobody remembers. Only the survivors. And they will not talk.'

'Why, mama? Why will they not talk?'

'A wise man once said, "Whereof one cannot speak, thereof one must be silent."'

'What does that mean, mama?'

'I cannot tell you. Some things must always remain a mystery.'

The last time his mother ran away from their father, she never came back. Or not alive, at least.

Villagers found her body near the town of Călaraşi. There was talk of witchcraft, and a possible lynching. Some even whispered of a Black Mass – a *Slujbă Neagră* – held near a willow grove. At first, his father had been suspected, but villagers could testify that Adrian had gone nowhere during her absence – and certainly not the 50 kilometres to Călaraşi. And everyone knew, as well, that Adrian loved his Zina, and had never raised a hand to her. Or at least not out of proportion to her wrongdoings. A certain amount of beating was good for a woman, and kept her in line – particularly if she was a Gypsy. This had been the village's view of the matter. And anyway, a single woman should not travel unaccompanied – what had the hussy expected?

The police had finally agreed – after the payment of an appropriate sum from Adrian in recompense for their efforts – to leave the mystery of her murder unsolved. She had been a Roma, after all – a *Lăutari,* of the tribe which traditionally supplied musicians for weddings, feasts and funerals – and therefore not significant in the greater scheme of things.

Dracul eased himself to one side. He groaned, and fell back onto the scraped-out stone plinth. How had he been transported here? Surely the old monk could not have carried him the 200 metres from the hidden crypt to the main part of the cave monastery alone? And then down the narrow flight of stairs, and all the way to the monk's dormitory? Such a thing was an impossibility for one old man. And what about the dead man? And the chauffeur? And the astrakhan coat? The police would come and take him away, and then all would be lost. He would be as his mother's family. They would find out he was half Gypsy, and they would kill him.

Dracul began to cry. He had not cried since his mother's death, and at that time he had thought that he would never cry again. But now he wept long and hard – and as he wept, pictures passed through his head. It was as if all his previous life was being wept out of his body, and he was becoming someone other – someone harder, more unforgiving. Dracul knew that in the future, if he was to survive, he must take what he wanted, just like the man he had killed. That he must force people to his way of thinking, and thereby dominate them. That if he did not do this, he would be lost – his life a worthless cipher, like his father's.

When Dracul looked up from his weeping, he realized that the old monk was watching him from a corner of the stone dormitory. And that he was holding a bowl in one hand, and a wooden ladle in the other. And that his weeping had moved the old man, whose face now bore the tracks of his own tears down the craggy runnels in his skin.

Strangely, though, the thought struck Dracul that the old monk's tears were acting as a torment for him, and not as a release. As if they were being shed, not in sympathy for the young man who lay there, injured and groaning on his stone cot, but rather in lamentation for his immortal soul.

# 6

—

Dracul remained in the monastery for ten days. The old monk tended to him, and fed him, and washed him, and saw to all his needs, but never once did the monk speak to him, or betray by sign or deed what had become of the dead man. Or of how Dracul had been transported to the monastery.

Dracul accepted this reticence on the monk's part. It was just. He suspected that the monk hated him. Even feared him. But it was also clear that the monk was being driven by his faith to act towards Dracul in a charitable manner. This weakness on the part of the monk suited Dracul. The dynamic, he felt, was solely to his advantage. He was recuperating while the monk was suffering. Which was the way things ought to be.

Whilst the monk did not talk to Dracul, it was not strictly true that the pair did not communicate. During mealtimes, the monk would sit in a corner of the stone dormitory and read to Dracul from the Bible.

At first, Dracul was minded to object. Why should he be forced, alongside the pain from his wounds, to be pained also by the tedium of the monk's biblical readings? Couldn't the monk take himself off somewhere else to read his Bible, and leave Dracul alone with his thoughts? But after a while, Dracul found himself carried away by the stories – which were either from Revelation, or, failing that, from the Gospel and Epistles of St John the Evangelist – to such an extent that he began actively to look forward to them.

In his everyday life, there had been little cause for Dracul to study the Bible. The Communist regime, which he had always lived under, frowned on all forms of religiosity. Bibles were outlawed at the school he attended. Some of the women in the village, it was true, still supported the old ways, and the men, in secret, bowed and made the sign of the cross before the old shrine in the woods when they happened to pass it on their way through to their fields, but religion was explicitly disfavoured – its teachings marginalized. Curses, however, remained biblical, and there were still priests who travelled around the local villages and held services in secret, so that those who did not care to worship publicly might do so in private, and without endangering either their Party membership or their subventions.

But religion per se had been sidelined for so many years now that a twelve-year-old boy was hardly likely to understand either the soul or the point of it. This, clearly, the old monk hoped to change. But why, then, did he read to Dracul only about the coming Apocalypse? And Armageddon? And the nature and form of the Beast? Why didn't he read to Dracul about Jesus Christ, and his sacrifice, and the translation of the world through the power of grace?

Either way, Dracul found that he far preferred the end-of-the-world stuff. When you measured God against the Devil, it was pretty clear to Dracul that the Devil won hands down every time. Good people, such as his sister Antanasia, would always be used, and abused, and stricken under their thumb by the bad people of this world – bad people like him, and his father, and those men from the village who got bored on Friday nights at the prospect of sleeping yet again with their wives, and fancied a bit of fresh young flesh. And had the money to pay for it, of course.

Sometimes Dracul wondered whether his sister secretly enjoyed what took place? Otherwise, why would she stay around for it? He tried hard to think his way into her mind, but found himself totally at a loss to understand her. If such a thing ever happened to him, he would wreak a terrible revenge on all those who perpetrated it. Perhaps women were different that way? Perhaps they didn't respond in the same way as men?

Or maybe what his grandfather had told Dracul was true, and Eve really had caused the downfall of Man in the Garden of Eden? And Eve's earthly life, and that of all her female descendants, was designed as a penance to make up for that disgrace? This would explain all that happened to Antanasia very well indeed. She, and victims like her – this stupid old monk living alone in his cell, for instance – had been specifically born to carry the evils of the world on their backs.

If the choice came down to the two of them – the old monk and his sister – Dracul decided that he would prefer being Antanasia. At least she laughed from time to time, and took pleasure in serving him. Unlike the monk, who walked around like a man who has just seen his entire family slaughtered in front of his eyes. Maybe one day Antanasia would have a child from one of the men she serviced, and fulfil herself that way? Or maybe he would give her a child himself? Stranger things had happened.

But then Dracul thought of his mother. Now there was a woman who knew how to make a man suffer. How she had goaded his father, Adrian, with her absences. However much he beat her, still she left whenever the fancy took her. In the darkest watches of the night, Dracul fell to wondering what tragedy had finally brought her down. Why had the people who killed her turned on her? And was there any truth in the rumour that she had been a witch?

Dracul could feel his brain congesting with all the thoughts that were forcing their way inside his head. He had never in his life spent so much time not doing anything. Had so much time simply to think. But the wound to his ribs made it impossible for him to move without darts of agony flaring through his flanks and chest.

When he was at his lowest ebb he fantasized a scenario in which his father would have the whole village out looking for him, fearing that he had been kidnapped or eaten by bears. But privately he knew the truth. His father would be relieved to have him out of the house so that he could have Antanasia to himself – and to the Devil with whatever might have happened to his vagabond, half-Gypsy son. When he finally came home,

Adrian would beat him just for the fun of it, and just as he had done to his mother whenever she had returned from her jaunts. Dracul closed his eyes and let the anger seethe through him.

Towards the end of his stay at the monastery, when Dracul was at last able to sit up on his cot and begin to eat solids, the old monk read to him about the Second Coming of Christ. How the Parousia was foretold in scripture, and what form it would take. This, Dracul found even more interesting than St John's gory revelations about the inevitable doom that awaited the world.

If such a doom was indeed coming, then surely it made all the more sense to make the most of the time one still had left? Surely, too, such a person as the Second Coming would have untold power over the stupid masses? To manipulate them and bend them to his will? And whenever anyone in the history of the world had exercised such power, Dracul knew from his lessons that – except in the exceptional case of Josef Stalin – they had all sooner or later come to abuse it. So the whole thing was a foregone conclusion, was it not? And didn't bear speculating about. 'Whereof one cannot speak, thereof one must be silent.'

On the very last day of his confinement, Dracul requested that the old monk reread him some of the key passages about the Second Coming, so that he could commit them to memory. This the old monk refused to do. When Dracul finally left the old monk's care, however, the hermit grudgingly gave him a tattered copy of the Bible for his very own use.

Dracul secreted it in his new astrakhan coat, alongside the three silver candlesticks, the two icons, and the golden-coloured communion tray that he had pilfered from the chapel earlier that morning.

*Diablada Cenote, Yucatan, Mexico*
*El Dia de los Muertos*
*(The Day of the Dead)*
*2 November 2009*

# 7

Despite the funereal splendour of his adoptive name, Abiger Delaigue Fortunatus de Bale, Comte D'Hyères and Pair de France, Marquis de Seyème and Chevalier de Sallefranquit-Bedeau, was not a man easily given to mourning.

Abi's twin brother, Vaulderie, was almost certainly dead. But that was just the way of things. If Abi had lost both of his legs to an anti-personnel mine, he would have viewed the loss equally pragmatically, and got on with learning to run on those fin contraption things you saw on TV ads for breakfast cereal. Or if he had contracted a terminal disease – gut cancer, say, or a fucked-up heart – he would have shrugged his shoulders and taken his medicine. Surgery. Pills. Death. Whatever it took.

But drowning whilst still in one piece, and with all his mental faculties intact, in a sheer-sided limestone sinkhole that resembled nothing so much as a prison-issue shit-encrusted lavatory pan, made Abi very angry indeed.

As far as his late brother was concerned, the two of them would meet again in either heaven or hell, depending on the luck of the draw. Abi could see Vau now, straight out of a Judgement Day painting, forging towards him in Satan's antechamber, eager to give him a personal guided tour around the River of Fire.

'Look at that, Abi. You see those couples over there? Climbing out of their graves? All dressed in white? And the animals? Each carrying a heart in their mouth? Those are the lost souls. And those animals are carrying the hearts of the creatures they killed and ate during their lifetimes. They are all heading towards God, who will sit in Final Judgement over them.'

'And what about us, Vau? Will He judge us, too? Will He consign us to the Devil?'

'Oh no, Abi. We are the Corpus Maleficus. We've already been judged. We have performed our function. So we are the righteous ones. All our sins have been forgiven.'

Abi sensed his mind starting to wander. Maybe his brain was getting waterlogged? Righteous? Him? He shook his head and increased his grip on the two dead bodies he was using as flotation devices. They weren't reeking yet, but it wouldn't take long.

Somewhere in the murky water below him lay a Suzuki, also filled with dead men. Also with suppurating wounds. But those ones weren't as fresh as the bodies surrounding him on the surface. The Mexican narcos in the car below him had been there since the day before, so God alone knew what they'd already done to the water table.

What a joke. He'd probably end up dying of thirst in a million gallons of terminally polluted Evian.

Abi drifted back inside his head. He would miss Vau.

His enthusiasm. His gullibility. His dimness. But above all his sheer convenience as a conduit for the thoughts Abi would otherwise have to keep to himself. Who could he bully now? Who could he feel superior to? Rudra? Dakini? Nawal? Christ. Fate and the whims of their adoptive mother had left him in command of a trio load of freaks.

And now here he was, mentally and physically intact, floating fifty feet down in the bowl of a Yucatan sinkhole whose sheer sides, and sheer isolation, made any thought of rescue impossible. He had no cell phone. He had no weapon. The owner of the crystal meth factory he and his siblings had inadvertently stumbled on during a compromised weapons deal had seen to that.

All Abi could do was to float aimlessly around in God knows what depth of water, the bodies of his brothers and sisters, his enemies and his erstwhile victims, half alive, half dead, first rotting, then bloating, then leaching their body matter into the piss-coloured water surrounding him. And the only emotion he could summon up was anger. A visceral, all-consuming, all-encompassing, anger.

It was the sudden extinguishing of hope that had produced this curious effect.

Just twenty minutes before, when Abi had already given up any thought of ever getting out of the cenote alive, he had unexpectedly heard shouting. Seen his enemies – the enemies who had until recently been taunting him, and calling on him to refund them ten million dollars in compensation for the destruction of their factory and the crippling of their chief – toppling off the lip of the cenote and plunging down into the pool beside him. Then he had seen his brother, Oni – still alive, still fighting for his family and for the Corpus Maleficus – appear on the cenote edge, fifty feet above him, brandishing a Stoner M63.

Oni had come back to save them all in the very nick of time. Oni the Barbarian. Oni the lemming killer. Oni the *deus ex machina*. The mighty one. His banshee of a mother's seven-foot tall, tame albino.

It was then that the not quite dead drug cartel chief had reared up from his prone position on the rim of the cenote and shot Abi's brother in the head. Oni had hesitated for a moment, as if not entirely sure that his brain really had been blasted out through the back of his skull. Then he had toppled over the edge of the sinkhole, his body creating a bow wave that had rocked the four remaining Corpus members like flotsam in the wake of the *Titanic*. And which had set the bodies of the dead and the nearly dead bobbing and jouncing like a jar full of corks.

Then the terminally perforated mafioso had grinned down at Abi, sucked on the barrel of his automatic, and blown out the top of his own skull. Way to go, *pendejo*.

But all this left Abi with one major problem. How to get himself, his remaining brother, and his two remaining sisters, out of the cenote and onto dry land before time, gravity, and pollution took their inevitable toll.

# 8

—

Abi latched onto a couple of the dead bodies and transformed them into a makeshift buoyancy device.

Dakini swam towards her brother. She grabbed one of his bodies and rested her chin on it. She twitched her lips like a horse. 'Ugh. This one's been shot in the head. I can see his brains through the hole. And he's starting to reek.' She sniffed a couple of times, her nose near the corpse's ear. 'It's sort of like a mixture between liquorice and dog's meat, with a bit of dead mouse thrown in for good measure.'

Abi fought down a retch. Dakini had always been the grossest of his siblings. As a child she had been in the habit of dissecting farm animals whilst they were still alive in order to check for nervous spasms and signs of respiratory failure.

'Exactly how long is he going to float for? That's what we need to know. You're the scientist, Nawal. What's your estimate?'

Nawal trod water in front of him. 'That's simple. He'll float until the oxygen trapped inside his lungs and the air trapped inside his clothes is replaced by water. Then he'll sink to the bottom until the bacteria in his gut and chest provide enough carbon dioxide, hydrogen sulphide, and methane to send him back up to the surface again. It's a bit like reflating a balloon. Sometimes the bodies will sink once again until they've generated more gas, and then they'll pop up for a second time – the police call those ones "refloaters". Face-first bodies, which are dead before they hit the water, tend to float for the longest, because the air can't escape from their lungs. It's obvious when you think about it. They used to think that women floated face up and men floated face down. Something to do with sex, I suppose – breast buoyancy, or the size of our arses. But that's bullshit. Everybody floats face down. Look around you. You see anyone on their backs? I know research technicians who would kill for this sort of material. Face down is good for us, Abi, because the oxygen will remain trapped in their lungs for longer.'

Abi blew out his cheeks and rolled his eyes. 'Anything else? Or are you finished?'

Nawal shook her head. 'I think I've covered it all.'

'Well if that's the case, I suggest we gather all these floaters up, strip off their belts, and tie them together. Then we cut off their shirts and stuff their noses and mouths with them to keep the air in. Then we build ourselves a variation on the Raft of the Medusa. That way, we might even be able to get ourselves out of this fucking water and halfway dry.'

'You don't think that's a bit ghoulish?'

'Dying unnecessarily is ghoulish. Floating in a cenote amongst thirty decomposing bodies – some of whom we are related to – is ghoulish. And speaking of which, how long are we likely to last in this water?'

'Last? You mean until we throw up our arms and let ourselves sink?'

'Something like that.'

'Depends if the water temperature is less than sixty-eight degrees Fahrenheit in here or not.'

'What are you talking about, Nawal?'

'A normal, healthy person, fully clothed, and using a life jacket...'

'We don't have life jackets.'

'But we've got the stiffs. Same effect.'

'Okay. Continue.'

'At forty to sixty degrees water temperature – well, you've got maybe three hours before hypothermia sets in. At thirty-five to forty degrees you can halve that. Less than thirty-five, you can halve it again.'

'What are we talking about here, then?'

Nawal glanced up at the overhanging cliff. 'The sun's already gone in. We've had it for the day. So we'll be in darkness – or near darkness – for the next sixteen hours. But I'd still call it seventy degrees or so in here. Like the man who just blew his brains out said, we could survive floating here for two or three days. Maybe more. Our main problem is going to be hunger.'

'How about thirst? Would you want to drink this water?'

'If I had to.'

'Me too.'

'Come on then. Belts off everybody. Let's make ourselves a tight core of bodies, and tie the rest of them onto the sides, like ballast. How many do you think we have access to?'

'I counted twenty-two in total. Including Oni and the doctor. But I may be short one or two. Shame that the big boss – the *cacique* – didn't topple in too.'

'That would have been too much to hope for.'

The four remaining Corpus members busied themselves constructing a raft out of the corpses.

'What do we do when we're finished with this, Abi? Switch on the TV and watch a rerun of *Prince Valiant*?'

Abi congratulated himself on having effectively set the tone for the quartet's future interactions. 'Business before pleasure, Rudi. Business before pleasure.'

# 9
—

Abi knew about the dangers of hyperventilation. Breathe too deeply and too long before diving underwater and you're liable to pass out. Breathe too little, and you won't make it more than twelve feet down before the atmospheric pressure forces you back up again, like a cork in an olive pot.

Abi tried to judge his breathing just right. He cleared his lungs of air five or six times, and then drew in compensatory lungfuls of maybe 80 per cent to 85 per cent by volume. At the same time he worked on his entire system, calming himself, and imagining a yoga session, with his usual teacher guiding him through the motions of pranayama. This made him think of Vau again, and he lost concentration for a few minutes, and had to fight to clear his head of negative thoughts.

When he was ready he jack-knifed in the water and started down to where he thought the Suzuki might have settled. He had no idea how deep the pool was, or whether the Suzuki might have paraglided through the water, ending up in a completely different location from its entry. But those were the risks of the game.

He estimated that he had five or six dives in him

at most, and then he would have to pass the baton to Rudra and the girls. But he was by far the best swimmer amongst them, and he was privately certain that if he couldn't pull this off, none of the others would be able to either. He was the senior remaining de Bale – Madame, his mother, naturally excepted. He was twenty-five years old, and in his prime. If he couldn't manage this, nobody would.

Once under the water Abi realized that he would have an additional problem. Thick weed grew in streamers from the bottom of the cenote, prejudicing visibility. At first Abi tried steering himself down via the streamers, but they simply broke off in his hands like sticks of celery. In the end he corkscrewed his way down, brushing up against the streamers, but avoiding the thicker fronds in case they entangled him. At twenty feet down he still couldn't see the bottom of the pool. At thirty feet, and having decompressed three times by pinching his nose and blowing internally, he decided to call it a day and head back for the surface, leaching oxygen and carbon dioxide as he rose through the water.

'What's it look like down there?'

'Hard to tell with this amount of daylight.' Abi was gulping in great lungfuls of air. 'The weed is so thick you can scarcely see through it. But in an hour's time it will be five times worse. Five times more murky.'

'Did you get to the bottom?'

'Nowhere near it. And I must have descended thirty feet.'

'It's a no-hoper then?'

'No. I'm going to try again. But I've got to weight myself with something.'

'Like what?'

'Shoes. Grab everybody's trainers and either tie or Velcro them together. Our friends here won't be needing them anymore, and it'll serve to lighten them up and give them more buoyancy. I'll make a sort of scuba weight-belt for myself. That should get me down another ten feet or so.'

'You're crazy, Abi.'

'You got any better ideas, Rudi? You, Nawal? Dakini? Anybody got any better ideas? Or do you just want to float in here until you croak?'

'Someone might find us.'

'You've got to be kidding me. Who? Sir Henry Morton Stanley? No one came when the tweak factory blew up. No fire engines. No helicopters. No cops. And why do you think that was? Because these people floating around us are fucking crooks. They're cowboys. They're the bozos who really run things around here. The cops leave them to their own devices in return for hefty backhanders, free cocaine, unlimited call girls, and a front-end slice of the action for the higher-ups. It's the age-old story. Have money, will travel.'

'Then at least tell us what you are hoping to find in the Suzuki.'

Abi grimaced. 'That's the fifty-thousand-dollar question.'

# 10

Abi could feel himself being swept towards the bottom of the cenote by the weight of the waterlogged trainers. He lashed out with his free hand and finned himself down even faster. In his other hand he held a penknife with which he intended to free himself from the trainers if he couldn't make it back up to the surface against their drag. He was calmer now. The first descent had given him a modicum of confidence in his abilities, and he reckoned that he had a good fifteen or twenty extra feet left in him.

This time he forced himself to decompress every five feet. Just a light decompression – enough to clear his ears and regulate the pressure inside his head. Enough to stem the panic.

At forty feet down he saw the bottom. At forty-five he saw the glint of metal, about twenty feet to his right. He struck off in that direction, the shoes sweeping against him like the skirts of a jellyfish.

When he reached the car he hooked his fingers under the lip of the partially cracked side window and peered inside. The naked bodies of the murdered *narcotraficantes* were bunched up against the roof. Their faces looked yellow in the murk.

Abi pulled open the driver's door and glanced across at the interior light. Dead. He wound the headlight switch to the right. No go. Hardly surprising after twenty-four hours in the water, but it had been worth a try.

His breath was screaming to be let out.

With his last remaining strength he yanked the bodies out of the car, clearing the cab for future access. They floated off and settled in slow motion on the floor of the cenote, head down and feet in the air, like a circle of skydivers.

Abi kicked himself away from the car. He could feel the weight of the trainers holding him back. But he knew that if he cut them free on this, his first successful descent, he would never be able to get down this far again.

Half a minute later he burst onto the surface of the cenote, coughing and wheezing.

Rudra swam across and guided Abi back to the raft of corpses. 'Did you find it?'

'Yes. It's clear as a bell. It helps that the fucking thing is white.' Abi was sucking air in through his tormented lungs.

'What about the stiffs?'

'I got them out of there. It was not a pretty sight. They'll bob up to the surface again in a few days' time as refloaters. We can use them as back-up ballast if we're still alive by then. Sort of like an assembly line of gas-filled corpses.' He caught sight of Rudra's face in the gloom. 'Only joking.'

Rudra shook his head. He was getting used to Abi's

grotesqueries by now. 'Did you see anything else useful?'

'That'll be in the back of the car. I'll get to that next time.'

'Listen, Abi. You don't look so good. And I don't like the way you're sounding. If you go on like this, you'll give yourself hypercapnia. You want me to go down instead of you this next time? Or one of the girls, maybe?'

'You wouldn't make it. Neither would they. I'm on the very edge of my own capacities as it is. No. Let me go down one more time. Then I'll rest up a bit. It's not as if this thing is time sensitive.'

Rudra gave his brother an old-fashioned look. 'Oh, yes, Abi. It is.'

# 11

This time Abi swam through into the back of the Suzuki via the rear passenger door. He instinctively glanced up to check if there was an air bubble trapped in an upper corner of the roof. Yep. There was. Then he realized what sort of filth and noxious gases the bubble would probably consist of, and he discounted it. He would simply have to manage with what was left in his lungs.

He ripped up the carpet in the rear of the car and groped alongside the spare wheel. Two tyre irons and a tow rope. He grabbed them.

Then he felt around in the side compartment for the jack. His lungs were about to explode. He fought down his panic. The jack was heavy. It was attached to the main body of the car by a thick rubber strap. Abi jammed the tyre irons into his belt and sawed at the strap with his penknife. Air was bleeding out through his lips. He was ten seconds away from passing out. He made a desperate grab for the jack, and kicked himself off from the rear seat.

It was then that he saw the fire extinguisher. It was a six-litre job. Far too big for the size of the car. But there it was. Tucked in between the passenger seat and the offside door. He didn't know why, but he knew that he needed it. He lunged down with his spare hand and grabbed it, just as the trainers he was using as dead weights snagged themselves between the two front seats.

He was stuck fast. The damned shoes would kill him. He had little or no control left over his lungs. He was losing consciousness.

Maybe it wouldn't be such a bad thing to die like this, Abi thought to himself. Just switch yourself off and pass out. He could feel his eyes turning up inside his head.

Abi gripped the fire extinguisher hose in his teeth. He sawed at the shoe belt with his penknife, his arm pumping like a man using bellows. There was a sudden wrench and he was free. But he was already dead. He knew it. There was no way he could reach the surface with what he had left in his lungs.

He kicked his way to the part of the roof space where he knew the air bubble was. If this didn't work, he was finished. He had no choice anymore in the matter.

He spat all the air he had left in his lungs into the water surrounding him. Then he thrust his nose and mouth up to where the trapped air had to be. He drew in two deep breaths. He didn't allow himself to think of what he might be taking into his lungs – the makeup of the gases he was ingesting – the quality of the mulch after two days stewing. He booted his way out of the car, leaving both his belt and the skirt of shoes still attached to the front seat. He was fighting off an overwhelming desire to gag.

He still had the two tyre irons, the jack, the tow rope, and the fire extinguisher clutched to his stomach.

He knew that their weight might prove just enough to tip the scales and hold him down. But there was no earthly point in ascending without them. Something deep inside his head was telling him that.

He floated onto his back and began to ascend. He was far too weak to kick anymore. As he rose through the water, the remaining air in his lungs bled out through his teeth in a rapidly diminishing stream. Abi closed his eyes. He was kaput. He would arrive at the surface dead. Somewhere on the way up he would let go of his burdens and watch all the prizes he had fought so hard for vanish back into the murk below him.

He contrived one final upward kick with his feet. It was more like the spasmodic movement a dying man will make than any direct product of Abi's will.

He bobbed to the surface and sank forwards onto his face, still clutching his booty. His nose and mouth were in the water. He had no strength left with which to breathe. He would die now, and that was fine by him.

He felt himself being turned over. The weight he was cradling in his arms was taken away from him. Then he was see-sawed onto his front again and slammed against something soft. His back was pummelled and slapped. He brought up some viscid liquid. Then a little more.

Abi lay half on, half off the raft of bodies.

When his senses finally returned, he found, to his astonishment, that he was still alive.

# 12

Abi spent the better part of the night recovering his energy on what his three junior siblings now insisted on calling the 'body raft', and which he, playing Devil's Advocate as usual, termed the *ratis corporum*. The reeking raft of corpses would only suffer two persons on it at any one time, so the other three took turn and turn about, alternately hanging off the sides and then catnapping on board throughout the course of the night.

First thing in the morning, just as the sun began its steady creep across the face of the cenote, the raft sank. The rot began with the outlying bodies, but soon communicated itself to the central portion of the raft. Abi barely had time to grab the jack, the two tyre irons, the tow rope and the fire extinguisher, before the raft slid out from underneath him, just as if it had been spirited away, like King Arthur's sword, by the Lady of the Lake.

Abi trod water for a few moments, his heart pounding with delayed shock. The others struggled towards him through the water, their faces pale in the early morning light. Abi thrust the fire extinguisher into Rudra's hands, while Nawal took over carrying the jack, and Dakini the two tyre irons.

In a movement which belied his obvious exhaustion, Abi wrapped the tow rope around his midriff and attached it over one shoulder with a quick-release knot. 'Right. I'm going to get on and do this while I've still got some energy left. We're already half starving. In a few hours' time we'll be gnawing at the dead. If we can still find any, that is. The whole darned shooting match seems to have sunk.' Abi's fake cheer sounded flat even to him.

'The sun's coming up. At least we can see the cliff face now.'

'That's a comfort.'

Rudra cocked his head to one side. 'Are you sure you're up to this, Abi? You still look washed out from all those dives. Your skin looks kind of grey.'

'I haven't checked in the mirror recently, Rudi, but thanks for the testimonial. You always did know how to make a girl feel good about herself.' Abi floated on his back for a moment, gathering his thoughts. The effort at producing the banter was beginning to take its toll. He fought down an urge to throw up his hands and slide beneath the surface of the sinkhole – signing off at this early stage would be a mug's game. 'The straight answer to your question is no. I'm not sure I'm up to it. But as the only one amongst us who has ever done any climbing, logic dictates that I take first shot at the summit. But maybe you have an alternative idea? Along the lines of an alien spaceship, perhaps, arriving from a galaxy far, far away, to spirit us off?'

'Stranger things have happened, Abi.'

'I don't know when.'

Abi twisted in the water and struck out for the base of the cliff. The others, after a brief hesitation, followed him. They looked like a family of ducklings shadowing their mother. The four of them stopped and trod water, their eyes fixed on the fifty-foot rock face above them.

'It doesn't look so far.'

'Neither did Mars and those alien spaceships of yours, Rudi. If I happen to drop one of the tyre irons, for fuck's sake try and catch it. With your teeth, if necessary.'

Nawal pitched some water at Abi with the flat of her palm. 'Leave Rudi alone. We're all mourning our brothers and sisters. Not just you.'

Abi felt like shouting that he wasn't mourning anybody – that he didn't give a damn about any of them apart from Vau. But at the last moment he turned onto his back and frog-swam towards the base of the cliff.

The next time he spoke, his voice was detached and formal. 'If the worst comes to the worst, we can always hammer the irons into the cliff foot and attach the tow rope to them. That would give us something to hang onto. It might even buy us a couple of days.'

'A couple of days of what?'

'*Nascentes morimur, finisque ab origine pendet.*'

Rudra shook his head. 'Jesus, Abi. I wish you wouldn't spring all that Latin stuff on people all the time. What does it mean?'

'It means "from the moment of our birth we begin to die, and the end of our life is closely linked to the beginning of it".'

'Great. That's just what we all wanted to hear.'

'It is great. I saw an old English gravestone once. Its

occupant had paraphrased Manilius perfectly: "When we to be to be begunne, we did beginne to be undonne."'

'I don't get you, Abi. Are you trying to drive us all to collective suicide?'

'No, *frater meus*. I'm simply trying to put things into perspective. Classical literature helps with that. They've been through it all before, you see.'

'What? Floating in a cenote with a bunch of dead bodies?' Nawal was holding the jack out of the water as if she feared it might rust and start to break up in her hands before she could get around to using it.

'When you get a bit older, Nawal – which I agree, at the moment, looks a little unlikely – you'll realize that there's nothing new under the sun.' Abi's eyes travelled along the tangled fissure in the rock face he was intending to use on his way up. 'Pass me the extinguisher.'

Rudra handed it over.

Abi took out the restraining pin and squeezed the trigger. A thin stream of foam jetted across the surface of the cenote.

'Christ, Abi. What are you doing that for? Isn't the water polluted enough already?'

'Weight, Rudi. I've earmarked the extinguisher jacket as a hammer, not as a receptacle to put out fires with. The last thing I need is to lug six litres of useless liquid up the cliff face with me. If we hadn't had the raft, I would have emptied it last night.'

'Oh.'

'Right. Now you can take it back. Give me the jack, Nawal.'

Abi launched himself out of the water and rammed the

pyramid jack into the crack at the base of the cleft. Then he reached up and screwed it open with the tyre iron. The tyre iron was equipped with two protuberances at the distaff end, specifically designed to slip into the winding mechanism of the jack. When the jack was comfortably embedded in the cleft, Abi launched himself out of the water again, this time with Rudra's help, and clambered onto the protruding end, until he was standing with both feet tight to the face of the cliff, maybe a yard and a half above the surface of the cenote.

'So far so good. Hand me the other tyre iron and the extinguisher.'

'Jesus, Abi. This is impossible. You're never going to make it.'

'Hand me the climbing kit, Rudi, or I'll abandon you here to drown.'

Rudra handed him the extinguisher and the tyre iron.

Abi reached above himself and positioned the tyre iron in the cleft. Then he took the hand extinguisher by the trigger mechanism, and hammered the tyre iron home. 'If I can make it as far as that cleft up there, I might be able to belay across to that little outcrop. If I can traverse as far as that, I can rest up a bit and get my bearings. That's the plan, anyway.'

'How are you going to free the tyre iron? After you've released the jack, I mean?'

'I'm going to tie the tow rope to it, Rudi. Then, when I'm safely on the outcrop, I can yank it a few times and it should come free. The art is not to ram it in too far.'

Rudra looked at the girls, who were treading water beside him. He was tempted to comment further, but he could tell by the way they were staring hopefully up at Abi that any observations he might make would fall very flat indeed. 'Good luck, Abi.'

'That's the understatement of the year.'

# 13

It took Abi more than an hour, and six near falls, to inch his way the forty feet up to the final ledge. The ledge was situated just ten feet below the upper lip of the cenote, but those ten feet might as well have measured ten miles as far as Abi was concerned, for the rock face was as smooth as Plexiglas.

Abi squatted on the ledge, with his back against the cliff face, and stared down at his brothers and sisters. His clothes, which had begun to dry off during the ascent, were wringing wet with sweat.

The sun had reached its zenith over the cenote. Abi could feel it beating against the top of his head. The unholy mixture of semi-starvation, thirst, and unrelenting heat were threatening to give him hallucinations. Twice, early on in the climb, he had fumbled and lost one of the tyre irons, but each time Rudra had either caught it on the wing, or snatched it from the water before it had time to sink. Then he had thrown it back up to Abi again, with the girls acting like the backstops of a volleyball team in case he muffed the throw.

About forty minutes into the climb, Abi had jammed both feet and his one free arm inside the cleft, fearing that he might be about to lose consciousness. He had managed to snatch a five-minute breather, after tying the tow rope to the pyramid jack and making a belay of it via a Munter hitch. The thought that he might unexpectedly black out had filled Abi with existential dread. He knew for a certainty that once he fell back into the cenote, that would be it – he'd never make it up the cliff face again.

Abi twisted on the spot and squinted at the area above his head. There was no sign of a handhold. There was no whisper of a striation. There wasn't even the faint beginnings of a crack that he could take advantage of and extend. Just the limestone equivalent of an opaque, marginally convex, sheet of glass.

'Any suggestions anyone?'

Rudra cleared his throat. 'Can't you find anywhere to hammer one of the tyre irons in? To use it like a chisel?'

'No.'

'Can you jump, then? Upwards, I mean.'

'No. I'd make it about halfway, then I'd fall back into the cenote and drown. Or as good as. The face is angled.'

There was a brief moment of silence. 'What are you going to do, then?'

'I don't know. It didn't look this smooth when I checked it out from down below. I can't believe that rock can change its character like that. This has to have been manmade.'

Nawal drifted into sight below him. 'Can you weight the end of the tow rope and swing it up and over?'

'Maybe. But what's it got to latch onto? There's no wall or anything. We were up there only yesterday.

Although it seems about three years ago. You've all seen what it looks like on the top. Just an area of flat terrain with a few loose rocks.'

'You can't be sure of that. We weren't looking at it in that way when we were up there.'

Abi sighed. 'You've got a point.'

'So what have we got to lose?'

Nawal swam closer in towards the cliff. Her face was earnest. She looked as if she was about to address a science class. 'If you were to put the extinguisher through the gap in the car jack, Abi, and then screw it down tight, you'd have a pretty effective counterweight. Then you could ram the tyre irons through the jack to give it a sort of porcupine effect. Like one of those wartime mines they blew ships up with. That way it might snag on something.'

'What if it snags on something, and when I start climbing up, it un-snags?'

No one answered.

'Okay then. I'm going to do what Nawal suggests. I can't squat up here for much longer or I'll cramp up and take the big dive.'

Abi unhitched the jack from the tow rope. He screwed the jack open to its fullest extent, and then eased the extinguisher through the middle of the pyramid. When he was satisfied with the fit, he screwed the jack down onto the extinguisher so that metal bit into metal.

'Now tie the tow rope onto the jack again before you lever in the tyre irons. Just in case. Wouldn't do to drop it.'

'Thanks, Nawal. Did anyone ever tell you what a

fearful pedant you are?'

'Next, you jam the tyre irons through from either end. If you jam them crosswise through the jack mechanism, they should lock into place.'

'Okay. Hold your horses. I'm doing it.'

'Has it worked?'

'Yes. It's worked. But I doubt it'll stand a hard knock. If this thing lands wrong, it will simply loosen up and collapse on us.'

'That's a risk we have to take.'

'*We* have to take? *We?* It's me who's taking the fucking risk, not you.'

'So you don't think we're risking anything, do you? You think we're all floating down here thinking, well, that's great – Abi's holding all our lives in his hands. But it's okay. We're easy with that. In the meantime, while he's busy trying to save us, let's all go for a doggy paddle to pass the time.'

Abi puffed out his cheeks. 'Okay. I'm sorry I said that. It was out of line. But I'm feeling a tiny bit pressured up here. If this thing doesn't work out, I'm not going to sit up here and conduct an autopsy on it. I'm going to dive back into the cenote. *Capish?*'

Abi tied one end of the tow rope loosely around his waist. Then he let the jack dangle down below him. Slowly, steadily, he extended the tow rope until he had maybe twenty feet of line swinging, like a pendulum, in a tight arc to the cliff face. The further he swung it, though, the more the rope began to swing him.

Abi soon realized that he would need to take action pronto if he wasn't to launch himself like a rocket off the ledge, with the rope, the jack, and the extinguisher acting as a convenient sheet anchor for when he struck the water and went under.

On the third swing he twisted his arms up and over in order to give the tow rope a modicum of centrifugal throw out. The jack looped up towards the summit of the cliff. At the very last moment Abi rammed himself back against the cliff face and jerked the rope forwards, timing it so that the jack would get a precious extra bit of lateral leverage. The jack pitched onto the ground above him with a dull thud, and the rope went slack in his hands. Abi stood on the ledge, breathing deeply.

'You realize when I pull on this, and when the jack doesn't snag on anything, it's going to topple off the edge of the cliff, hit me on the head, and pitch me into the water?'

'Not if you pull hard enough. That way the jack will fall clear of you. Then all you have to do is not let it unbalance you when the rope tightens on the way down. It'll give you a second bite of the cherry.'

'That's okay then, Nawal, is it? That's all clear? I just yank for all I'm worth, and hey presto?'

'Yep.'

'Can anyone think of a prayer?'

'Just pull it, Abi. Let's get this over with.'

Abi gave the rope a yank. The jack came skittering over the edge of the cliff and launched itself into the void.

'Fuck!'

The extinguisher missed Abi's head by a foot or so. At the last possible moment he threw himself back against the cliff face and braced himself for the shock of the rope straightening. But instead of dragging him over the side, the dead weight at the end of the rope merely scythed across below him, dissipating much of the energy of the drop.

'Jesus, Joseph and Mary. I thought it was going to jerk me off.'

'Abi, if you don't manage to swing that thing up there and get it to snag, I'm going to jerk you off.'

'But, Nawal, you're my sister.'

'Enough with the jokes, Abi. You know what I mean. Don't be so gross. We're living on borrowed time down here. At least you're free of the water. Believe me when I say it's getting harder and harder to keep ourselves afloat. If you don't succeed with this, I shall drown myself. It's a better bet than slowly starving to death. Or dying of exposure.'

'Okay, Nawal. I get the point. I'm going to give it another shot.'

'Check the tyre irons first.'

'To hell with the tyre irons. This time it's going to work.' Abi began the second swing. The tow rope jerked into pendulum effect. Abi gave it a lot more elbow grease this time around, swinging as hard as he could on each extension, and forcing himself tightly back against the cliff face so that he wouldn't overset.

At the last possible moment he hauled upwards and outwards. The weighted jack twisted at the end of its extension, and drifted over the lip of the cliff.

The moment he heard the jack landing, Abi dragged downwards with his hands. He expected the jack to come swooping over the edge of the cliff again, but this time the jack snagged onto something solid. Abi didn't know what it had snagged on. A body, maybe? But the rope felt taut in his hands for the very first time.

'Right. We've got a response. I'm not going to jerk it anymore. I'm not going to test it. I've only got so much strength left in me, so I'm going to give it my best shot before I lose faith.' Abi swarmed up the rope. He could feel his crotch tightening in anticipation of the fall he figured for a near-to-odds-on certainty.

Six feet into his final climb, the rope slipped a little, as if whatever it was biting into had moved.

'Oh, Christ.' Abi hung for a second in mid-air. Then he restarted his upwards ascent. He could see the lip of the cenote maybe four feet above his hands.

'Go on, Abi. You're nearly there.'

'The fucking thing's moving.'

'Ignore it, Abi. Keep climbing.'

Abi scrambled up the final four feet. He made a wild grab for the cliff edge just as the rope and anchor broke away from whatever it had snagged on. Abi was left with one hand gripping the ledge, and one hand still on the rope.

He dropped the rope and lunged for the cliff edge with his free hand. He was now attached to the cliff by the tips of six of his fingers.

'Grab the rope again.'

'I can't. It's come free.'

Abi tried to drag himself the final few feet, but he had no strength left in his hands. He just hung there, attached to the cliff edge by his fingertips.

'If you fall, we're all dead. Just one more effort, Abi. Come on. Don't give up on us now.'

Abi dragged air into his lungs. He knew he was finished if he let go. He tightened his grip and lunged upwards with his left knee. This put extra pressure on his fingers. He knew he had only seconds to go.

He scrabbled with his feet against the flat surface of the rock. Slowly, painfully, he made a little headway. At the very last moment he broke connection with his previous hold and threw both hands forward, lunging with his knees and feet. His shoes were the only dry thing left on him, and he was counting on their rubber soles to give him a little purchase.

This time around he managed to apply a bit of extra leverage with his forearms. Lunging upwards, he got his chin onto the edge of the rock. Now he had both forearms and his chin in contact with the ledge. He shunted himself forward like a lizard. Then, using the traction afforded by the dirt, he got his elbows onto the ridge. He could hear shouting from below him, but he couldn't make out what anyone was saying through the buzzing in his head.

He dragged himself forward, using one elbow, then the other. First his chest was on the ledge. Then his stomach. Then his thighs.

Once he got his knees onto the ledge he knew that he was home free.

# 14

Abi lay on top of the cliff and tried to snatch his breath back. The shouting continued below him, but he ignored it.

His hands were bleeding, as were his forearms and elbows. The rest of him felt as if some sadist had given him a full body massage with a belt sander.

When his breathing steadied, Abi eased himself onto his knees and checked the surrounding area for movement. Nothing. Not so much as a swaying blade of grass. The sun was beating down on the blue agave plantation so hard it was putting a crease into the light.

He turned his head and checked out what his botched jack-and-extinguisher device had snagged on. Yes. Just as he thought. The narco-*cacique's* body. Which had then snagged onto another body, slowing down its movement towards the cliff edge. He'd been absurdly lucky that the two bodies hadn't simply rolled over each other and across the edge of the cliff, taking him with them. Rigor mortis had set in during the night, leaving both cadavers a jumbled mass of protruding arms, legs, and knees – perfect for slowing down a roll.

Well. You needed luck sometimes. The Corpus had

been having a bad run of it recently, and now maybe things were set to change.

Abi lurched to his feet. He took a few steps and then stood swaying, as if he had vertigo. Hunger was making his stomach clench – it felt as if someone had caught him unawares with a rabbit punch.

Abi's mind was cutting loose on him too. He caught himself wondering how Aldinach and Athame were doing over in Europe, following up on his orders. Whether they'd managed to find and execute their sister, Lamia, for her betrayal of the Corpus with that motherfucker Sabir. Whether they'd identified and killed the Gypsy girl who was meant to be the future mother of the Second Coming. All these things had seemed so damned important a day or so ago. The central facts of his life. Now he found he didn't care much either way.

Abi laughed and shook his head. He sucked air into his lungs like a man getting his first taste of the sea, and lurched forwards. Talk about a dysfunctional family. God had really messed up when He'd allowed Abi's mother, the Countess, free rein in choosing her adoptive children. Still. Even freaks had to have a place to call their own.

Abi focused on the problem in hand. The dead *cacique's* Toyota Roraima was parked twenty yards back from the lip of the cenote. Abi stumbled across to it and looked inside. No keys. But there was a three-quarters full bottle of water stuck into the service tray. And a box of half-eaten tacos on the passenger seat. And the passenger door was open.

Abi ate the tacos and drank the water.

The shouts from below him were getting louder. Abi pushed himself away from the Land Cruiser and walked to the edge of the sinkhole. 'Can it for a minute, will you. I'm just working out how to get you all back up. There are no keys in the Toyota so I'm going to have to find them. Then I'll attach this length of hosepipe I've found to the tow bar and lower it down. You can attach yourselves to it somehow or other, and then I'll ease the car forward and haul you out. None of you will be strong enough to shin the fifty feet up here on your own otherwise.'

Abi didn't wait for their reply but walked directly over to the *cacique's* body. He was feeling stronger by the minute. Just so long as the *cacique* didn't have a chauffeur who had pocketed the keys, and who was now lying at the bottom of the cenote with the rest of the skydivers, thought Abi.

Abi felt around in the *cacique's* pocket. The man was already ripe, thanks to the action of the sun. Swarms of blowflies were busy in the collection of bullet holes scattered about his body.

No keys.

Abi shook his head. The Corpus's rental cars had been parked too near to the crystal meth factory. They would almost certainly have fried when the place went up. And the Hummer in the basement would have fried too. Abi didn't feel like walking out of the plantation and then another ten miles into the nearest town. And no way did he feel like bodily dragging his siblings out of the cenote via a hosepipe. It occurred to him that the *cacique's* henchmen must have arrived in cars, but he would be faced with a similar problem there – no one in their right minds would leave a car unlocked near a public road in Mexico, and certainly not a habitual criminal. With his luck, the keys would all be down in the cenote. And there was no way on earth he was diving back in there to collect them.

He grabbed a fallen hat from near one of the stiffs and put it on. Then he walked back to the Toyota and felt underneath the front seat. No go. He walked around the car and tried under the passenger seat. Nothing.

He thought for a moment and then flipped the lid for the vanity compartment. There was a pistol inside, but nothing else. Abi pulled it out. It was a Beretta 92FS semi-automatic. What the US armed forces called the M9. Abi checked the load and then slid the weapon into the back of his trousers, so that it snugged between his skin and his shirt.

Keys. No. Wait a minute. No keys. A sensor. Abi knew a thing or two about Land Cruisers. And this Roraima was a Land Cruiser under another name.

Abi remembered that all top-of-the-range Land Cruisers had Smart Entry. Meaning the doors would open at the touch of a hand if the sensor was brought close enough to the vehicle. And all these doors had opened. Meaning the sensor was still around here someplace. Meaning the Smart Start would work as well, so long as the sensor was still hidden somewhere inside the car.

Abi sat in the driver's seat and pushed the button. The Toyota thrummed into life. Abi grinned. He closed the doors and switched on the climate control. The tank was full of gas. He checked around for anything else to eat, but there was nothing.

He waited patiently for the climate control to lower the inside temperature to eighteen degrees.

Then, when he was feeling comfortable for the first time in more than twenty-four hours, he engaged the automatic shift and drove down the track and out of the plantation.

# 15

The rental car he and Vau had been driving was still intact. All the paint had been burned off and the windows had blown out, but the car had been parked far enough away from the warehouse to escape the worst of the blast.

Abi squinted into the sun. The last thing he wanted was to run into any of the *cacique's* remaining foot soldiers coming back to check on why they hadn't heard from their boss.

An old man and a young boy emerged from the woods and stood watching him from a corner of the plantation. Abi bunched his fingers and aimed a pretend pistol at them. The old man took the child by the hand and led him back into the undergrowth.

Almost gagging with nerves, Abi reached in through the back window of the rental and retrieved his leather holdall. He unzipped it. His false passports, his money, and his credit cards were all intact. As was his passport in his real name.

Abi glanced up at the sky. 'Thanks, Vau. I owe you a big one.'

He threw the carryall into the back of the Toyota.

Then he walked towards the ruins of the crank factory.

He stood for some time staring at the mayhem left by the explosion. The main fire had burned itself out long ago, but tendrils of smoke were still rising from the shell of the building twenty or so hours after the initial blast.

Abi re-imagined the warehouse in his head. It wasn't a problem for him. He'd spent quite a little time there, and he had that sort of brain. He picked his way across the wreckage to where he and his brothers had hung Joris Calque from the rafters, with Adam Sabir squatting beneath him like in that scene from Sergio Leone's *Once Upon A Time In The West*. Yes. This was the place he'd left the two of them when the *cacique* and his men had made their surprise attack.

No bodies. There were no bodies anywhere in the wreckage. And the fuckers should have been burned to a crisp.

Abi grunted. He stepped across to where the basement had once been. The source of the blast had obviously been down there. Near the crank vats. That much was clear. He stood on the lip of the crater left by the explosion and looked down. No Hummer. Not even the skeleton of a Hummer. Not even the photoplastic smudge of a Hummer.

So Sabir and Calque had got away after all. And not only that. They'd clearly caused the explosion in the first place, because it was hardly likely that the Mexicans would torch their own drug factory for a non-existent insurance payoff. And by setting the place off, they'd as good as signed his twin brother's death warrant.

Abi took a deep breath. He would have a fair few

scores to settle in the coming months. That much was clear. Calque and Sabir's survival changed everything. Everything.

Without so much as a backward glance at the cenote – or a backward thought about his brother and sisters – Abi got into the Land Cruiser and drove out of the plantation gate in the direction of the main Cancun road.

*Samois Old Quarry,*
*Samois-Sur-Seine, France*
*4 November 2009*

# 16

Less than a day after Abi made it out of the cenote, Joris Calque stood watching as the tendrils of his best friend's life unravelled themselves before his eyes. If Abi had wanted to find out what had happened to his three remaining siblings, this is where he would have had to look.

A few yards from where Calque was standing, Adam Sabir lay curled up beside the body of the woman he loved. Lamia de Bale hadn't just won Sabir's heart during their trip through Mexico – she had insinuated herself into Calque's heart, too, taking the place of the daughter his embittered ex-wife had stolen from him as a young girl, and then converted to her ways.

That Lamia had been a breakaway member of the Corpus Maleficus who may, or may not, have been on the level, was irrelevant now that she was dead. The fact remained that at the very last moment she had stepped in between her siblings and Sabir, and had given up her life for the man she loved.

A few paces away from Lamia lay the bodies of her hermaphrodite brother, Aldinach, and her dwarf sister, Athame.

'So what do we do now?' Alexi's cousin, Radu, was keeping his voice low out of respect for Sabir's obvious grief. He was addressing himself to Calque.

'How do you mean?'

'I mean, we have three dead bodies here. And we're Gypsies. I know you were a policeman in your former life, so you'll understand what I am telling you. If we call the gendarmes to this place, it will be the end for us. They will tear up our camp at Samois and scatter it to the four winds. They will pin these deaths on me, Sabir, and Alexi, and they will throw away the key to the prison. Yola will be completely unprotected when the brothers and sisters of these filth come seeking to kill her and her baby – as they certainly will.'

'But I'm a witness. I can speak for you all.'

Radu laughed. 'You are also an optimist. Didn't Alexi throw the knife that pierced the small woman lying over there? The one with the pistol in her backpack? And didn't Sabir beat the other one to death with a branch?'

'Yes. But they were both acting in self-defence.'

'But the small one had no weapon in her hand. Alexi was acting with knowledge of what she was capable of doing, yes. We all know that. But the *flics* will say that she presented no threat. Is that not so?'

Calque gave a grudging nod. He knew how such things worked. The local gendarmes would take one look at the crime scene and bag it up. To them the whole thing would be as clear as day. A bunch of Gypsies, and their American fellow traveller, Adam Sabir, wanting revenge for the murder of their relative earlier that summer, kidnap a Frenchwoman whose family they feel might be involved. The Frenchwoman's brother and sister give chase. There's a showdown. The Gypsies and the American – who has already been involved in one killing of a member of the same family earlier that summer – murder everybody. Then ex-Captain Calque, the notorious Gypsy-lover … etc. etc.

'So what do you propose?'

Radu chucked his chin towards the disused mineshaft. 'This place is so deep no one knows where the shaft ends. You cannot even hear a stone strike the base. We place the bodies in the car, then we shunt the car over the edge. Later on I will send a cousin, who knows about such things, with a small explosive charge. This charge will take the whole shaft down to the bottom. As if the rain we had a few days ago had weakened the structure of the mine and caused a landslide. No one will think to dig under such a mass of earth and rock. It would be impossible. Besides, they would have no reason to. Nobody knows we are here.'

'And this cousin of yours? You really feel you will be able to trust him not to fess up later and hand you all in? Maybe win himself a reward?'

Radu shrugged. The answer was self-evident. 'He is a Gypsy.'

Alexi stepped forward. As he did so, Yola disengaged herself from the protection of his arm and went over to comfort Sabir.

Calque was relieved that she was finally taking the initiative. He hadn't relished the job of trying to prise Sabir from Lamia's dead body.

Alexi stood facing Radu. 'Damo won't stand for his woman to be placed in the car with her killers and buried in that way. This I can tell you.' He cast a worried glance at where Yola was comforting Sabir. 'Best that we give her a Gypsy burial. Somewhere nobody will ever find her. But Damo will know where it is. This will be important for him.'

'Damo?' said Calque.

'It is our Gypsy name for Adam.'

Calque blew out his cheeks. This was great. Here he was, a senior ex-police officer just a bare few months into his premature retirement, and he was already considering prejudicing a crime scene and withholding vital evidence from the authorities. If his former colleagues ever found out what he had done, they would coat him in honey and feed him to the ants. 'This is impossible. We can't hide three bodies just like that.'

'Captain, no one knows they are here. These two filth will have covered their tracks. And Damo's woman would have done the same. The Corpus Maleficus came here to kill Yola and her unborn child, because they believe her to be the mother of the Second Coming. You told me so yourself. So they won't have left a trail. There will be nothing to connect any of them with this place.'

'But Yola and Lamia might have been seen together. In the village, say. Or on the road.'

'So what? Nobody cares what Gypsies do. *Payos* like you look through us, Captain. We scare you. We are a reminder to all you non-Gypsies that there are other ways of being. Other ways to think and act. The best answer to that is to ignore us. This is the easiest way.'

Calque chose to duck the implied insult. He sensed danger in the air. 'Where do we hide Yola, then? If I agree to your plan, that is. And Sabir? What do we do with him? The Corpus will redouble its efforts to get to both of them after this.'

Radu turned to Alexi. They spoke together in low tones, in a language Calque could not understand. Alexi nodded a couple of times. Then he glanced towards Yola.

Yola was helping Sabir to his feet – she was doing this by supporting him around the lower back, as she was far too small to reach up and take him by the shoulders. She whispered something to him, and he nodded. He looked beaten. As if the simple exercise of holding himself upright was an effort too far.

Radu touched Calque's arm. 'We have a possible place, Captain. Amongst close relatives. It is far away, though. In Romania. Alexi has agreed to take Yola and Damo there. They can hide up for a while. At least until after Yola has given birth to her child. No one will find them there.'

'But the border crossing. There will be records.'

'There is no border crossing. There will be no formal records. You may count on this. We are all in the EEC now, remember? We cross through Austria and Hungary. No one will notice us. Gypsies come and go that way all the time.'

Calque gave a Pontius Pilate sigh. 'I will want to see them. To keep in touch. There are things I must do.'

'This can be arranged.'

Calque nodded. He was realist enough to recognize a *fait accompli* when he saw one. 'Very well then. Bury them. And dynamite the shaft. No one will hear anything this far into the woods.'

Radu slapped Calque on the shoulder. 'This is very true, Captain. We will cover all the entrances with our people. It will be as if the earth has swallowed them. You have made a fine decision.'

And opened myself up to a litany of blackmail and extortion whenever the whim takes these people, thought Calque gloomily. 'And Lamia?'

'Her too. The earth will swallow her too. But somewhere else. Somewhere secret.'

Calque turned away from the shaft. 'I shall return our rental car to the hire company. Then I will revisit your camp. You will tell me where I can find Yola and Sabir if I need to. I shall give you pay-as-you-go cell phones for them. So that I may keep in touch with them. You agree?'

'We shall do this.'

'And Radu. One final question.'

Radu smiled. He rocked his head from side to side as if he knew what was coming.

'What if I'd refused to go along with your plan of burying the bodies out here?'

Radu glanced at Alexi.

Alexi held out his arms apologetically. 'Captain. I'm so sorry. It's nothing personal. I like you very much. But we would have had to kill you too.'

*Paris Charles de Gaulle Airport*
*6 November 2009*

# 17

The flight from Chihuahua/Genvillalobos to Paris/ Charles de Gaulle passed uneventfully. Abi was travelling on one of his many false passports – and they were the best that money could buy. He had used his real passport, though, and his real US green card, when crossing the border from Mexico back into the US at dead of night. One never knew when an alibi might prove useful.

The half-asleep Mexican border guard had proved predictably amenable when Abi had owned up to having lost his exit permit – an instant fine of $50, in small bills, had seen him breezily waved through towards US Immigration.

US border control had no reason to delay a green-card holder – they had neither taken Abi's fingerprints nor had they conducted an iris scan, which would have necessitated an instant change of plan. Abi was clearly considered a model permanent resident. Madame, Abi's mother, owned an apartment block in Boston, which Abi managed, and from which he derived part of his income. This he could prove. If the situation changed and anyone quizzed him about his status, he would tell them that he had been away touring, and had paid for his groceries in cash and traveller's cheques.

Once he had clearly established himself as being in the US, Abi returned across the Rio Grande illegally. US border patrols were watching for people coming into their country – not leaving it. Crossing back into Mexico with a bunch of cash-rich wetbacks had been a cinch. All it had cost him was $200 and a few startled looks. What was a gringo doing smuggling himself *into* Mexico? *Hijole*. These *Yanquis* were indeed crazy. The fact that Abi was actually French had passed them all by, which further muddied his back trail.

Abi collected the Toyota he had purloined from the narco boss and drove straight to Ciudad Juarez, drug capital of the world, and the town consistently voted the most violent place on earth outside of declared war zones. He abandoned the Toyota in a side street in the shabbiest district he could find, and left the locked and loaded Beretta in open sight on the back seat. It would be a miracle if either the M9 or the Roraima were still in place twenty minutes after he had left the area. It was an altogether more effective way of ridding oneself of potentially incriminating belongings than dumping them into a convenient lake and praying there was no drought that year.

Next, Abi took the four-hour taxi ride to Chihuahua airport and boarded the first plane out for Paris. This time he used the fake passport he had originally entered Mexico with, together with the regulation green exit permit that had come with it, and which he'd claimed to have lost passing out of Mexico the first time. Simple and legal. Well, almost.

As far as Interpol and the US Government were concerned, the real Abiger de Bale was staying in an apartment building overlooking the bay in Boston's Battery Wharf, while the fictional Pierre Blanc was returning to France from a holiday in Mexico to reunite with his family.

Of Abi's real family, left behind to drown in the cenote, Pierre Blanc thought not at all.

*Cenucenca, Orheiul Vechi, Moldova*
*14 March 1986*

# 18

Dracul Lupei endured his fifteenth birthday on 7 October 1985. Five months later, he enjoyed a belated birthday present.

The old monk who had saved Dracul's life three and a half years previously died, creating a convenient vacuum in the Orheiul Vechi cave monastery tenant list.

Dracul had visited Orheiul Vechi less often in recent years – he had other irons in the fire. But from time to time he had kept up his old trick of blackmailing anyone dumb enough to wish to visit the monastery. As a result of one of these visits, he had been the first to find the old man. The monk had died in his bed. Of old age. Or so everybody thought.

In point of fact Dracul, fearing that his father was about to throw him out of the house, had crept up one night – whilst his father was in bed with Dracul's eighteen-year-old sister, Antanasia – and had smothered the old monk with a potato sack. The monk had been due to die anyway, being sick with rheumatism and pneumonia, so Dracul felt that he was really doing the old man a favour by speeding him along to Paradise.

The fact that the monk had saved Dracul's life, and

had, for reasons best known to himself, not handed Dracul in to the authorities for the murder of the man in the astrakhan coat, counted for little in Dracul's estimation of the situation. It suited Dracul to have the monk die – therefore he made it happen. In this way Dracul felt that he was adhering to the decision he had come to whilst recuperating under the monk's care. That from henceforth he would decide his own destiny. Manipulate and bend the stupid masses to his will. Act, not react.

After the killing he returned home and laid his game plan on the line to his sister.

But Antanasia was a pragmatic girl. Despite being sexually abused by both her father and her brother – and despite being rented out by her father as a Friday-night plaything – Antanasia still felt that her place was at home. She belonged to a culture where a woman was defined by her family. If Antanasia had left home, it would have meant replacing familial prostitution with the more formal variety, in Chişinău, where she would have been at the mercy of Russian gangsters. Instead of the occasional forced encounter, she would have formed part of an assembly line of whores, serving a minimum of two dozen men a day. And if she was really unlucky, she would be sent abroad, to a country she neither knew nor understood, to service men who had no earthly reason to treat her with anymore respect than they would show their dogs.

No. Antanasia knew which side her bread was buttered on. At least, thanks to their sexual interest in her, neither Dracul nor her father beat her, as her father had done to her mother. And she received occasional kindnesses, particularly from Dracul, to whom she was devoted. She was a good cook and a better seamstress. This and her youth gave her a certain status amongst the older local women, and did something to alleviate the damage done to her reputation by her father's waywardness.

Dracul had tried to explain to Antanasia that he did not intend to remain at home forever. That he would be moving up to the monastery as soon as possible, and that he needed her to accompany him and do certain things for him.

But Antanasia, despite her affection for her brother, said no. She owed a duty of care to their father, and this she would dispatch. He was head of the family. If Dracul became head of the family, and she was still unmarried, matters would change. But until then, she would obey their father.

Dracul had scratched his head in bewilderment. Married? No one would ever marry Antanasia. Didn't she realize that? Moldovan peasants didn't marry whores. And certainly not whores whose favours they had shared with their neighbours.

In terms of both affection and sex, Dracul knew that Antanasia preferred him to their father. That much was obvious. So what was her problem? At least Dracul didn't rent her out to all and sundry in return for drinking money. And whenever Dracul made love to her, he had to thrust his fingers deep into her mouth to stop her from moaning and giving the game away. This moaning never happened with their father or with any of the other men she serviced. At these times Antanasia was silent, allowing the men to have their will of her, yes, but deriving little or no obvious enjoyment from the act. Perhaps their father had broken her in too early? thought Dracul. Or maybe she was just bored?

That night, Dracul watched his father slurping his *rachiu*.

Adrian had recently given up beating his son. The boy was far too strong now, and liable to fight back. And anyway, Adrian was getting older, and didn't have the drive he once had. Drink and the loss of his wife had seen to that.

But Adrian still took the greatest possible pleasure in fucking Dracul's sister in front of his son's eyes. Despite his alcoholism, Adrian was smart enough to realize that Dracul was bitterly jealous of him. That he wanted Antanasia for himself. So Adrian made a point of using her as often and as explicitly as he could – and also of giving away her favours for free to friends and acquaintances when the mood came upon him. He didn't know why he did this, for he loved his daughter, and would not normally have wished to hurt her. But there were times when Dracul resembled Adrian's dead wife, Zina, to such an extent that Adrian's blood would boil, and he would lash out in any way he could to hurt his son. And Antanasia was the prefect conduit.

'Lie on the table.'

'What, Papa?'

'Lie on the table, girl.'

Antanasia lay on the table and raised her skirts. She knew what was coming. Adrian emptied the *rachiu* bottle and upended it. 'Now open your legs.' Adrian was aware of Dracul watching him. But the drink had lit a fire inside him, and he no longer cared what Dracul thought.

'Leave her alone.'

Adrian turned, the bottle still in his hand. 'What did you say?'

'I said leave her alone. She is mine. I will not have you touching her anymore.'

Adrian laughed. Then he smashed the bottle against the side of the table, threw back Antanasia's skirts, and made as if he were about to ram the jagged edges between her legs. 'Then no one will touch her.'

Dracul plunged towards him from across the room.

Adrian turned and raised the broken bottle.

Dracul swept it away with one hand.

Adrian twisted round and made a grab for his daughter. His face was congested and his eyes were wild. Antanasia looked into those eyes and knew, for a certainty, that her father was about to kill her. She fell back onto the table.

Adrian loomed over her for a moment, and then his head was snatched back.

Dracul ran his father across the room, just as a footballer will bundle an opposing player across the touchline.

He smashed his father into the far wall. Then he squeezed Adrian tight against the wall with his hip. Adrian was far too drunk to put up a fight. He watched his son with lowered eyes, like a bull watches the torero he knows will kill him.

Dracul reached up onto the shelf above him and took

down a hammer and a six-inch nail.

Adrian laughed. 'What are you going to do, you fool? Nail me to the wall?'

'Yes.'

In one smooth movement, Dracul raised the nail. He brought his forearm against his father's head, pinning him to the wall.

Then he thrust the nail into Adrian's ear and hammered it home.

# 19

——

Adrian took nearly an hour to die. Antanasia and Dracul watched him from a corner of the room, fearful to either approach or to touch him.

At one point Adrian started fitting, similar to an epileptic boy they knew in the village. Antanasia stood up, intending to go to him, but Dracul motioned her down.

At the end, Adrian's legs started a running motion, as if he was trying to send himself in circles, like an injured dog. Green matter began bubbling out of his ear.

Dracul turned and faced the wall, refusing to watch. Antanasia did the same. Brother and sister held each other's hand.

When it was all over, Dracul stood up. He motioned to Antanasia that she must fetch the coverlet from their parents' bed. They covered Adrian in the blanket, and then secured both ends with twine.

'I must take him out of the village now.'

'Why?'

'So that people will think that he has left us. This way, there will be no suspicion. I know just where to put him. There is a hidden crypt near the monastery. Nobody knows of it but the old monk and I. And the old monk is dead. So there is no fear of discovery.'

'But how will you carry him there?'

'On the mule. You must fetch the animal from the stable and meet me outside the village. By the plague marker. Then I will strap our father over the saddle and take him to Orheiul Vechi. Then I will kill the mule and bury it with our father. I have been along this road a thousand times. I know it even in the dark. I shall be back before morning. Then nobody will ever think that our father is dead. Just that he has gone away and taken the mule with him.'

'But if he's buried outside consecrated ground, he'll become a vampire. That's what the priest says. He will be denied eternal rest.'

'The priest just says that to frighten the old people. There are no vampires. You are being silly.'

'What about Vlad Țepeș?'

'He was an impaler, not a vampire. And anyway, the monastery is consecrated. Monks have lived up there for hundreds of years. What do you think? That I'd dump our father in a field?'

'No. No. I know you wouldn't do that.'

'However evil the bastard was.'

Antanasia began to cry. 'He was our father.'

Dracul shook his head. 'Yes. He certainly was that.'

*Le Domaine De Seyème,*
*Cap Camarat, France*
*8 November 2009*

# 20

Abi glassed the back of his mother's house. It was three o'clock in the morning. In November. With its dark and drawn-out dawns. Nobody would be up and about until at least six – Abi knew the routine.

There were security lights at the front of the house, triggered by a motion sensor. He knew all about those too. But what were these new lights at the rear, set into sconces beneath the eaves? They had certainly not been there on his last visit. Were they security lights as well? Was Madame, his mother, becoming paranoid in her old age? One thing was certain. If he set them off, there was bound to be some sort of an alarm linked to them in Milouins's bedroom. Abi offered up a prayer of thanks that the Countess hadn't gone for the full monty and installed CCTV cameras. Milouins, he knew, had eyes like a shithouse rat.

Abi feared no one in this world. But were he to fear any man, that man would be his mother's manservant, Hervé Milouins. Ever since Abi's childhood, Milouins had been a lowering presence in his life. Both Milouins and his mother's private secretary, Madame Mastigou, shadowed the Countess wherever she went. In consequence it had been next to impossible for her adoptive children ever to see her alone. This had terminally prejudiced Abi's ability to charm and manipulate her, just as he charmed and manipulated everybody else unfortunate enough to encounter him – he wasn't named after golden-tongued Abiger, satanic pinup and hereditary Grand Duke of the demons of hell, for nothing. Tonight, Abi intended to rectify the Milouins situation once and for all.

Abi lowered his night glasses and cupped his ears. Nothing. Not a sound. Not even the wind, which appeared to have died away completely. He shivered inside his thin jacket. He listened again – for a full five minutes this time – with his mouth stretched open like an anaconda to create even more of an echo chamber effect. Same result.

No outside watchers, then. This pleased him, as he had already decided on which way he would enter the house.

Abi calculated that the new security lights were designed to overlap each other, leaving no gaps through which an intruder could pass. This was fine, except that it relied on a house that was built to a modern design, with flat walls, no rounded bevels, and without eaves.

The main structure of the Domaine de Seyème was 250 years old, but with curious growths and excrescences scattered all about it, dating to maybe a hundred years before that. There was one tower, for instance, which bulged out below the casement window, as if whoever had built it had suffered from a particularly pernicious form of astigmatism.

Abi knew that this bulge had been crafted to hide a secret room below the floor, which had been used during the Revolution to conceal the de Bale family treasures. As a child it had amused Abi to envision what might have happened to the builders of the secret room. If Monsieur, his father, was anything to go by in terms of de Bale family intolerance for the sharing of their secrets, the architect and his workmen were even now acting as unwitting additions to the very tower they had so fastidiously built.

A little like the architect, Postnik Yakovlev, when you came to think about it. Legend had it that Ivan the Terrible had ordered Yakovlev to be blinded immediately after he had finished building St Basil's Cathedral. Ivan's excuse was that if he didn't do this, Yakovlev might go on to repeat his masterpiece elsewhere, thereby diluting its effect. Abi had always liked that story. It showed true power. No wonder Russia and France had needed their revolutions.

From his fresh vantage point, Abi now estimated that the bulge in the tower would effectively mask the security lights' infra-red sensor if he were to approach it at just the right angle. Once he was tucked tight against the walls of the house, he could ease himself inside the span of the security lights and through into the cellar. The cellar lock was old, and therefore amenable to picking – plus the door was indented, providing even further cover from the lights. Once inside the cellar, he would only be faced with a conventional mortise lock leading directly through into the main house. Child's play.

Abi acted the moment he'd made up his mind. He'd

broken into enough houses as part of his Corpus training to know that inaction begat failure. He and his twin brother Vau had been old hands at burglary. They'd studied with the best.

Thrusting the unwelcome thought of Vau out of his head, Abi jogged towards the house. If the lights switched on, he would simply change course and sprint back to his car.

The lights stayed off.

Abi eased his way along the wall to the cellar door. It took him three minutes to get inside. During the three minutes he was picking the lock, Abi amused himself by thinking that he wasn't yet committing a crime. Not even an inchoate crime. This was his own mother's house he was entering. He had every right to be there. Hard luck if the inhabitants thought otherwise.

He padded up the cellar steps. He didn't even need his lock picks for the mortise lock – two twists with his penknife did the trick.

Once in the main part of the house, Abi paused for a moment to take a sense of the place. Did it feel different in any way from the last time he was here? He snorted the atmosphere in through his nose. His burglary master had taught him that trick. Rationally, there was no logic to it. Irrationally, it made perfect sense. It triggered all the latent instincts of the intruder. Switched him on to what was going on around him. Prepared him. Psyched him up.

Abi started up the stairs. He knew exactly where Milouins's room was, and he avoided that part of the house completely. He made his way past Madame

Mastigou's suite of rooms and down the corridor towards his mother's. As he did so, he checked the vial of *Antiaris toxicaria* he had secreted inside the collar stiffener section of his shirt.

The Chinese called this particular variety of blowpipe poison, distilled from the Javanese upas tree, 'Seven Up, Eight Down, Nine No Life'. Meaning that once a person was poisoned with it, they would be able to take no more than seven steps uphill, eight steps downhill, or nine steps on the level, before suffering from irremediable cardiac arrest. Abi's mother was in her seventies and had a long-standing heart condition. Which doctor would think twice? And anyway, as far as the authorities were concerned, Abi was safely tucked away in Boston. Had been for the past few days. Any calls about his mother's death would reach him via his US cell phone. Who would ever know he had been in France?

The moment she died, he would be in line to inherit a quarter of her estate, as only he and his three remaining siblings, Lamia, Aldinach, and Athame, were still in the loop. What would his share be? One hundred million? Two hundred million? His mother was worth at least three quarters of a billion euros in property, shares, and other assets. In the US she owned real estate in New York, California, and Boston. In Paris she owned an entire city block in the 8th Arrondissement, surrounding the de Bale family's town house. In London she owned choice parts of Mayfair and Belgravia, thanks to an inspired marriage by one of her paternal ancestors, who had taken time off to seduce an English heiress whilst busy fleeing the Reign of Terror.

The neat thing about French law was that, under the Napoleonic Code, it was virtually impossible to disinherit a child. But that cut both ways. That's why Abi had decided to abandon the three in the cenote. With them still around, the Countess's estate would have been split seven ways. It would have cost him tens of millions.

He'd never liked the three of them anyway. So he was profoundly grateful to fate and to the Mexican *narcotraficantes* for providing him with the perfect family get-out clause. A part of him regretted abandoning his siblings to a long drawn-out death by drowning – he would much rather have slit their throats and had done with it – but it had been best to get them out of the way when the chance presented itself. In a year or so, when things had quieted down a little, he'd arrange to have their bodies unexpectedly found and given a decent burial. What was left of them, that was.

As far as any police investigation went, what had happened would be self-evident. His siblings had blundered onto a drug-making factory. They'd been taken prisoner. They'd attempted to escape. Bang. End of story. In Mexico, cops didn't investigate drug-related murders if they wanted to stay alive long enough to welcome their grandchildren into the world.

Abi stopped outside Madame, his mother's, bedroom. It pleased him that he would be taking revenge for the death of his brother and striking the mother lode at one and the same time. Vau had been a fool. And hardly the brightest button in the box. But they'd been twins. Conjoined at birth and sharing a kidney. That counted for something, didn't it?

Well, feral cats had probably eaten the kidney long ago. But it hadn't been right of his mother to try and fool him. To pretend that his sister Lamia had gone over to the enemy, when in fact she'd been working for the Corpus all the time. It demonstrated a fundamental lack of trust. Not to mention landing them in the cenote.

From here on in, Abi would be making his own decisions. Running his own life. Empowering himself.

He tipped open the door and stepped into his mother's room.

# 21

—

Unlike the hallway, which had nightlights burning at floor level, the Countess's bedroom was in total darkness. Abi paused for a moment to allow his eyes to get used to the gloom.

He slowly began to make out a hump in the centre of the bed. The one thing he really needed was for Madame, his mother, to have her face tilted either upwards or to the side. Chances were, at her age, that her mouth would be hanging open like a cargo door. In that case he would take the vial and drip the liquid through her lips. She'd be dead before she knew it.

He would stay around long enough to make sure she had no pulse, and then retrace his steps, locking up behind him. The only problem would be the outside cellar door. But he wasn't overly concerned about that. Nobody ever used it. It might be years before anyone found that it was unlocked. And by that time he would no doubt be living in the house himself, as eldest son and erstwhile inheritor of Monsieur, his father's, titles. Not to mention Madame, his mother's, money.

As Abi approached the bed, the first prickle of disquiet ran through him. The hump at the centre was far larger than he might have assumed from his mother's size. He stopped and flared his eyes. He was beginning to pick up the glow from the dashboard of a cordless telephone at his mother's bedside. The telephone cast a luminous haze across the bed.

Abi now saw that there were two heads on the bolster.

He froze. Milouins. That whoreson Milouins. Was he in here? Was Milouins his mother's lover? That would answer a good few questions he'd been aching to ask over the years.

Abi inched closer. It was crazy, but if he could drip the poison into the Countess's mouth while Milouins was asleep beside her, things would be even tighter. There'd be no room for discussion then. He could fly back in from Boston in a day or two and make an almighty fuss. Insist that they do an autopsy on her body. Incriminate Milouins. Get rid of the bastard that way.

But then someone was bound to ask him how he had known that Milouins was actually in bed with his mother at the time of her death. It was hardly likely that Milouins would own up off his own bat, was it? No. Maybe that wasn't such a good idea after all. Just kill her and have done with it. That was the ticket.

Abi took a further pace towards the bed. He could hardly bring himself to breathe. If Milouins woke up he would be for it. His mother would never forgive him for finding out her secret. He'd be lucky to make it out of the house in less than a dozen pieces.

Yes. That was his mother's head. And beside her...

Abi stopped. His mouth fell open.

Madame Mastigou.

Jesus Christ.

Madame Mastigou was in bed with his mother.

Madame, his mother, was a lesbian.

Abi hugged himself by the upper arms. Shockwaves of adrenalin flooded through his body. For a brief moment he was tempted to burst into a fit of hysterical laughter.

What was he to do now? There they were, side by side in bed, Madame, his mother, and her private secretary, Madame Mastigou. He couldn't kill both of them, could he? Couldn't make a clean sweep. That would be a bit of a giveaway.

Abi shook his head like a dog with ear mites. Who would have thought it? He'd never have come up with that idea in a thousand years. But there had been Madame Mastigou, for near enough the past quarter of a century, brash as daylight, and always at his mother's right hand. And everybody knew that Monsieur, his father, had had his lunch pack blown off during the war. The whole thing was hardly surprising when you looked at it in that light.

No wonder Madame Mastigou and Milouins had frozen the children out at every opportunity. Because Milouins must have known the truth from the start. In a small household such as this one, secrets like that were hard to keep. That must be why he and the other children had been farmed out so early on in their Corpus careers, and only allowed home on special occasions. Within the hidebound – let's face it, even reactionary – milieu in which the Countess customarily moved, any overt recognition of her Sapphic tendencies would have been tantamount to committing social suicide.

Had Rocha known about it too? He'd been the oldest of them all – already a teenager when he'd been adopted. Maybe that was why he'd changed his name to Achor Bale, abandoned the family, and gone crazy? People rarely joined the Foreign Legion simply for the hell of it.

Abi stood over the two sleeping women and weighed up his options. It was a peaceful scene. The glow from the cordless telephone was so clear now that he could even make out their matching nightdresses in the semi-darkness.

Well. Killing his mother would soon make things right again. He'd happily give a million of his yet-to-be inherited euros to see Madame Mastigou's face first thing in the morning when she woke up beside her late girlfriend's rigid corpse. If you could call a seventy-something-year-old woman a girlfriend.

He reached up to his collar for the *Antiaris toxicaria*.

The door crashed open behind him and the lights came on.

Abi swung round, his mouth hanging open like a startled cat's.

Milouins was standing at the door. He didn't even have a gun. He just stood there, supremely confident that nothing, and no one, could reasonably get past him.

Behind his left shoulder Abi could hear Madame, his mother, and her partner, Madame Mastigou, stirring in their bed.

Abi felt sick to the depths of his heart. Like a man who has mislaid a winning lottery ticket. His recent run of bad luck was turning into an epidemic.

He dropped his hands to his sides to demonstrate that

he held no weapon. Maybe Milouins hadn't seen the movement towards his collar? Maybe he could still talk himself out of the noose?

'I'm here to see my mother. In private. I don't trust telephones anymore. I need to speak to her alone. It's an emergency.' The explanation sounded lame in the extreme. But it was all that Abi had, for the time being, in his armoury.

Madame Mastigou helped Madame, his mother, out of bed. They both reached for their dressing gowns. Watching them, Abi felt a pall of despair descend upon him. The Countess did not forgive lightly. If Milouins searched him and found the poison, he would be for it. There'd be no forgiveness. He'd be lucky not to end up as pigswill.

'How did you know I was here?' Abi tried to make his voice sound as unconcerned as possible. As if it were a common occurrence for him to be discovered lurking in someone else's bedroom, at 3.30 in the morning, clutching a vial of poison.

Milouins grinned. 'Pressure pad. Beneath the carpet at the top of the stairs. You'd have to stretch a yard or more to miss it. It's specially designed for idiots like you.'

Abi gritted his teeth and threw back his head. 'Stupid. So stupid.'

He straightened up, hoping that this would galvanize his mother into suggesting they move to another location. He felt awkward in her bedroom. As though being there further reinforced his guilt in the eyes of the others. As a child he and his siblings had never, ever, invaded the holy sanctum of his mother's private apartments. They had been inviolable. Like the House of the Vestals.

Some Vestal.

'Milouins. Search him.'

Abi raised his arms. He'd been expecting this. He kept his left arm as tight to his shirt top as possible, hoping that this would hamper Milouins from checking out his collar. But he soon came to realize, thanks to the relaxed postures of all those in the room, that no one – not even Milouins – was figuring him for a potential assassin. For the time being at least he was a familial intruder who had been caught doing something terminally dumb. I mean who, apart from Orestes, went around murdering his own mother? It simply wasn't done.

Abi wound down a notch. His position might be salvageable after all. Especially if he pretended that Madame Mastigou was not standing there beside the Countess, like the Sugar Plum Fairy, still in her dressing gown and nightie.

'I'm desperately sorry I woke you up, Madame. But I needed to speak to you privately. Without any witnesses. And I didn't want to incriminate you in any way. As far as the authorities are concerned I am not here. Technically speaking, I am over in Boston. So I didn't want anybody to see me who might later be able to testify that I was ever here.'

Awkward. Too awkward. He needed to be more fluent. Abi's eyes flicked towards Milouins and Madame Mastigou. He wasn't on firm ground with them, and he knew it. And particularly given what he had just seen.

Milouins stepped back from his work. 'He is clean, Madame. No weapons.'

Abi could feel his throat deconstricting. Milouins hadn't found the poison. He felt a sudden, irrational surge of confidence in his bargaining abilities, and in his capacity for survival. He'd managed to climb out of the cenote, hadn't he? And finagle himself back to France against all the odds? So how difficult could this be?

'And why are you over in Boston, Abiger? Technically speaking?'

Well, thought Abi, in the final analysis you might as well be hung for a sheep as a lamb. 'To protect you, Madame. And the Corpus.'

'And the others? I suppose you are going to tell me that they are in Boston too? Technically speaking, that is.'

'No, Madame. They are dead. It is a tragedy. I am the only one still alive. I am sorry to be the one to bring you this news.'

'Dead, you say? How did they die?'

Abi was getting a very bad feeling indeed. Madame, his mother, was taking all this far too calmly. He had expected his last statement to demonstrably shock her – to confirm all her worst fears. But she appeared to be taking it in her stride. As if receiving news of the death of eight of her adopted children was an everyday occurrence.

Fortunately, during his flight back to France, Abi had concocted a detailed fall-back story for just such an eventuality. In it, the *narcotraficantes* had machine-gunned everybody in cold blood from the lip of the cenote, and he alone had managed to hide out amongst the floating bodies and survive the massacre. For reasons that now eluded him, however, Abi decided to jettison that version of events and construct a new one. On the hoof, as it were.

'I mean I presume they are dead, Madame. In fact I am sure they are dead. At least Oni, Asson, Vau, Berith, and Alastor are. For I saw their corpses.'

'Explain yourself.'

Abi made a last-ditch attempt to extract himself from the hole he had just dug. 'I called you from near the cenote, Madame, as you may recall, to bring you up to date on our situation. A few minutes after I did this the *narcotraficantes* attacked us, and we were forced backwards into the cenote itself. That's when we lost the use of our cell phones.'

'Why did you behave so foolishly? Why didn't you face up to your attackers like a man?'

Abi could feel himself bridling. He forced back his outrage. This was what his mother always did. She tested him. Just as she tested everybody. It was her party trick. 'We were massively outnumbered, Madame. And they were using tear gas and stun grenades, whereas we only had the weapons we escaped the warehouse with – pump-action shotguns, pistols, and the like. Useless against larger ordnance. We made the assumption that there might be some other way of escaping through the cenote. Maybe via an underground channel. Something like that.'

'That's absurd. You must have been panicking.'

'No, Madame. We were not panicking. But we had no alternative. It was either that or certain death. We knew that Vau, Alastor, Asson and Berith must have been killed in the initial battle. Their bodies were later dumped down in the cenote so I know this to be true.'

'They killed Oni in the initial battle too?'

'No, Madame. They only got him later. He came to save us. He killed all the *narcotraficantes*. Just mowed them down in swathes. But one survived. The *cacique*. He was riddled with bullets. But still, somehow, he survived. When Oni went to throw down the hosepipe so we could climb back up, the *cacique* emerged from amongst the other dead bodies and killed him. Then the *cacique* shot himself. We were alone after that.'

'I knew my Oni wouldn't let me down.' For a moment it looked as if the Countess might even be feeling a little pain – might even be about to reach behind herself for Madame Mastigou's hand. But she pulled herself together and the moment soon passed. Her expression hardened. 'What happened next?'

'Rudra, Nawal, Dakini and I spent what was left of the daylight hours retrieving any useful objects from a car we had previously ditched in the cenote. The next day, at dawn, I made my bid to climb to the summit of the cenote. Against all the odds I made it. I went immediately to get the *cacique's* car. I intended to attach a tow line to it and pull Rudra, Dakini, and Nawal out of the pit. But just as I reached the car, fresh elements of the *cacique's* gang arrived at the plantation.' Abi allowed his eyes to grow misty. 'This is hard for me to say.'

'Please make the effort. I wish to hear exactly what happened.'

Abi was clearly fighting a losing battle with his emotions – at least so far as the onlookers were concerned.

He drew the line, however, at pretending to brush back an actual tear. Apart from with his twin brother, Vau, Abi had never pretended to have a particularly close relationship to any of his other siblings. If he started shedding crocodile tears at this stage of the proceedings, nobody would believe him. He would be as good as signing his own death warrant.

'Ever since that dreadful time, Madame, I have been churning things over in my mind. Trying to make sense of them. My feeling now is that these foot-soldiers must have been sent by an associate of the *cacique* – perhaps someone working for the local police – in order to find out exactly what had happened to their leader and his men. The timing points directly to that.'

'The timing?'

'By that I mean the fact that they arrived so early in the morning.'

'Just as you were climbing out of the cenote, in fact?'

'Yes, Madame. Just at that moment. It was an unbelievable piece of bad luck.'

'Go on.'

Abi shot a glance at Milouins and Madame Mastigou. Both of them seemed to be taking his narrative worryingly in their stride. Milouins had the ghost of a smile on his face, as if he were publicly enjoying Abi's discomfiture, and had a further series of surprises – along the lines of the concealed pressure pads and the US Navy SEAL-style assault entrance – concealed up his sleeve.

'Anyway, I immediately decided to direct the enemy away from my brothers and sisters as being the lesser of the two evils facing me. Taking to the road was the only option available to me. There ensued a high-speed chase. I soon realized that my car must have a snooper hidden inside it – there was no way they could have followed me otherwise. But I could not stop for long enough to find out where it was hidden. It was a classic catch-22 situation.'

'A what?' The Countess inclined her head towards Madame Mastigou.

'A predicament that is impossible to dominate whichever way you approach it. What the Americans might call a no-win situation.'

'Ah. I see. Continue with what you were saying, Abiger.'

Abi fantasized about calling Madame Mastigou a supercilious bitch straight to her face. He nodded his thanks to her instead, to the extent that his cheekbones actually ached with the effort. No wonder she always dressed in those ultra-feminine southern-belle clothes. It was patently obvious who wore the trousers in that little shack-up. 'My only recourse was to keep going and stay ahead of the pack. And to switch my route often enough so that my pursuers could not call ahead and arrange for someone to lie in wait for me.'

'Incredible.'

'These people tailed me all the way to the US border, Madame. For sixty straight hours. There was no earthly way I could have got back to the cenote. No possible way I could warn anybody. It was clear to me, by the time I reached the border, that Rudra, Nawal and Dakini must be dead. No one could have survived in the cenote that long. Added to which the *cacique's* remaining foot-soldiers would no doubt have discovered them and finished the job the *cacique* had started. At least that was my logic at the time.' Abi was getting into the swing of his new story. Yes. This was much better than his old story of escaping the massacre. This way he could make himself out to be a hero, sacrificing himself for his siblings, who, unfortunately, had failed to benefit from his great-heartedness. 'I finally abandoned my car at Ciudad Juarez and bribed my way across the border and into the US.'

'Without your passport?'

'No. No. I forgot to mention. The *cacique* and his men had obviously rifled our rental cars before driving to the cenote. My overnight bag was in the back of his car, alongside those of my brothers and sisters. Our passports, money, and credit cards were still intact. The *cacique* must have wished to find out who exactly he was dealing with. I think that goes without saying.'

'That was lucky for you.'

'Very. It was an incredible stroke of good fortune. Otherwise I would have had to smuggle myself across the border and then make representations to the French Embassy that I had lost my passport and my green card.'

Madame Mastigou spoke for the second time that morning. 'But in that case there would have been no record of your having ever entered the US in the first place. They would have smelt a rat, surely? And I thought you just said you "bribed" your way across the border? What is the difference between "bribed" and "smuggled"? I do not understand.'

'Oh yes, Madame, there would have been a record. Because I originally entered the US under my own name. But I passed into Mexico on a false passport. As far as the US authorities were concerned, therefore, I was still legally in their country. And when I say "bribed", I simply mean that I had to pay an appropriate "fine" for the loss of my green Mexican exit voucher, which had somehow become mislaid – probably when the *cacique* was leafing through my passport.' Abi was beginning to feel light-headed. If his nose had been wooden, it would have grown to twice its own length by now.

'What did you do then?'

'I made my way to Boston. Spent a small amount of time establishing myself back at the apartment. Then I came straight here. I didn't want to telephone or e-mail you in case news of what had happened in Mexico had been passed over to the French police. Given what occurred here last summer, they might have chosen to eavesdrop on your telephone and internet connections. My first thought, as always, was to protect you, Madame. To protect the Corpus.'

'I am touched, Abiger. Genuinely touched by your consideration for my safety.'

The Countess was sitting on her dressing-table chair. Madame Mastigou was standing beside her. Madame Mastigou had her nightgown tightly closed, with the collar turned up against the cold. It was that dead moment before the dawn when spirits are at their lowest and the body at its most listless.

The Countess, however, seemed unconcerned by either the intemperate hour or the chill in the air. She waved an imperious hand. 'Milouins. It is time for you to go and wake the others.'

Abi's throat contracted. He found it almost impossible to speak. 'The others? You mean Lamia, Aldinach, and Athame?'

'No. They are dead.' The Countess's face was as pale as marble.

'I'm sorry?'

'I said they are dead. I haven't heard from them for five days. Lamia had the strictest instructions to contact me twenty minutes past the hour, every hour, until her task was completed. Her communications stopped five days ago. It is inconceivable that she is lying non compos mentis somewhere and that the other two haven't called in and alerted me to the fact. So I can only assume that they must be dead also. The little Gypsy tart and her offspring must have been better protected than we thought.'

'Then which others do you mean?' Abi knew very well to which others the Countess was referring. But he had to play the hand he had dealt himself through to the bitter end. No wonder Milouins had been smiling.

The Countess turned towards the door.

Abi could hear footsteps approaching from down the hall. His mind seethed with survival strategies. Should he try to bolt? But that would reinforce his guilt in the mind of everybody. No. He must stay and brazen it out. Swing with the breeze like Cicero. He'd always known he had the gift of the gab – now was the time to use it.

At the very last moment Abi remembered that Cicero had ended up being proscribed and murdered by the

126

very people he had striven to win over via his oratory.

'Ah, our brother.' Rudra, Nawal and Dakini entered the room, accompanied by a grinning Milouins. Rudra was limping worse than usual, on account of his club foot. Dakini peeked out at Abi from between her two floor-length curtains of hair – her face, which looked rictal at the best of times, was now set into a sort of diabolical snarl. Nawal, who suffered from hirsutism, looked drained, and thin, and even more ferret-like than she normally did.

Abi threw his hands up into the air in a clumsy attempt to mimic unfettered joy. 'You're alive. This is marvellous.'

Rudra launched himself across the room.

Abi had been expecting something of the sort. He ducked under his brother's body like a bull beneath a Minoan acrobat. Rudra cart-wheeled over Abi's back and struck the bed frame with his head.

Then Abi's two sisters were on him.

'Milouins. For Christ's sake get them off me. I can explain.'

Nawal raked Abi across the face with her fingernails. She had been aiming for his eyes, but Abi managed to dodge her. Dakini tried to knee him in the groin, but missed, and struck him on the thigh instead.

Abi pushed out with both hands. He took care, though, not to bunch his fists or to put any real power into the push. He knew he needed to keep the girls away from him while he waited for Rudra to take his next shot, but he didn't dare damage them – such a thing would be fatal. And quite contrary to the drift of his story. Rudra was where the real danger lay. Rudra could cripple him.

'That's enough.' The Countess stood up. 'Milouins. Separate them.'

Rudra wasn't listening. He barrelled at Abi with his head down.

Abi realized that Rudra was so angry that he had completely forgotten even the basic tae kwon do moves they had all been taught as children. Abi threw off the girls and moved towards him. At the last possible moment he side-stepped, using Rudra's own momentum to straight-arm him against the wall. Rudra kicked out backwards, catching Abi's knee with his heel.

Abi doubled up, cursing.

Rudra aimed a kick at Abi's head, but Abi dodged it, sweeping upwards with his hands and catching the underside of Rudra's calf.

Rudra struck the floor with his head and lay still.

Abi turned to see what had become of the girls. All he needed now was for one of them to smash him over the head with a chair.

Milouins had both of them in a neck-grip. One under each arm.

Abi moved towards Rudra, meaning to stamp on his head.

'Abiger. Stop it.'

'But the bastard tried to kill me.'

'He thought you tried to kill him.'

Abi turned to Madame, his mother. He knew that he had to put an end to this. Now. This minute. Once people started to think for themselves, he was done for.

'Right. Well you explain it to them then. I've had it. I'm going to the kitchen to put an ice pack on my knee. Then I'm going to my room. If anyone comes in and disturbs me, I'll kill them. Is that clear? You can all apologize to me in the morning.'

# 22

Abi took his breakfast alone. He knew what was coming. Wisdom dictated that he hold his powder dry until then. He had a plan that might, just might, put him in the clear with the rest of his family.

After his solitary breakfast he made his way to the hidden chamber behind the library in which the Corpus Maleficus always held its meetings.

'Any voice-activated tape recorders hidden under the table this time, Milouins?'

Milouins pretended not to hear him.

I've got a true ally there, thought Abi. How to make friends and influence people? I could write the bloody primer.

The Countess and Madame Mastigou were, as always, occupying the head of the table, with Rudra, Dakini and Nawal in subsidiary positions. Madame Mastigou was preparing to take notes on the finely milled Florentine paper she appeared to feel the occasion demanded.

Without asking, Abi took his seat in the place set aside for the oldest male de Bale – the one currently holding the family's titles. Madame, his mother, had always been a stickler for correct form. She wouldn't dare cavil.

Strike one for the black sheep.

Rudra, Nawal, and Dakini stared balefully at him from across the table. It was clear that the Countess had read them the riot act before sending them back to bed earlier that morning. Rudra had a large bruise across his forehead and still looked half out of his wits. It occurred to Abi that if something happened to him, Rudra would become the new count, not to mention sharing in an extra quarter of their mother's estate. He'd have to tread carefully. Rudra had always been something of a loose cannon. And marinating in the cenote didn't seem to have improved him one bit.

Abi checked out his two remaining sisters. Dakini was refusing to meet his eyes, while Nawal was staring at him like a mongoose facing up to a cobra. Nothing new there, then. 'You still don't believe me, do you? That I couldn't get back to save you all from the cenote.'

'What do you think?'

'What if I were to tell you exactly how you got out? What then? Would you believe me then?'

Dakini shot a glance at Rudra. 'That's impossible. There's no way you can know that.'

Abi smiled. Dakini was the weakest link. She would be the first to believe him if he managed to call it right. The first to come back to his side of the fence. 'Yes, there is. Because I arranged it. Because all three of you owe your lives to me. Only you don't know it yet.'

'Bullshit.' Rudra fingered the bruise above his eye. 'You're fishing. How we got out had nothing to do with you. You simply abandoned us all to drown.'

'No, I didn't. And I'll prove it.' Abi mouthed a silent

prayer. He felt like a cliff-diver trying out a new plunge-route for the very first time. But without having been able to test the bottom for rocks beforehand. 'An old man and a boy found you. They arranged to get you out of there. They sent down the hosepipe.'

Nawal and Rudra exchanged loaded glances. Dakini cocked her head to one side so that her hair hung down in sheets, like the Angel Falls.

Abi caught the look that passed between Nawal and Rudra. He felt a flush of triumph. He'd called it right. 'I know this because I told the old man and the boy where to find you. They were standing at the entrance to the plantation when I drove past. I was being pursued by the *cacique's* men. But still I slowed down and shouted "Cenote! Cenote!" at them. I knew that would be your only chance.What Abi had actually done had been to bunch his fingers at the pair and pretend to shoot them, but why split hairs at this stage of the proceedings? He knew he was taking a calculated gamble by assuming that it was the old man and the boy who had discovered the trio floating in the cenote. But nothing came from nothing. He had to clear the emotional logjam. With everybody gunning for him, he wouldn't stand a chance of getting near his mother for another attempt on her life – or of ensuring that he was her sole legatee – unless he squared things with his siblings. If he needed to massage a few egos on the way to attaining his goal, he would do that too.

'Yes. It was the old man and the boy.' Dakini was staring at Abi as if he had transformed on the spot from a demon into an angel. 'That's true, Rudra. How else could Abi have known? He saved our lives.'

Strike two for the black sheep.

Abi could see that the whole thing still sat badly with Rudra. But his inspired guess had effectively whipped the carpet out from under everybody's feet. They would have to believe him now. Would have to take him back into the fold.

The Countess tapped the table with the bottom of her glass. 'We will put an end to speculation then. Abiger has just proved to everybody's satisfaction that he behaved well – or at least as well as the situation permitted. Now I intend to move on to other business.'

There were grudging nods from around the table. Abi particularly enjoyed watching Milouins's face. It was a sight to behold. Just like Richard Nixon's face when he learned that he had lost the 1960 presidential election to John F. Kennedy by 0.1 per cent of the vote.

Madame Mastigou's Mont Blanc fountain pen flew across her Florentine paper at a feverish rate. Abi wondered who would ever get to read the minutes. Maybe they would be sealed in a lead capsule and buried for posterity? Or whatever constituted posterity after the apocalypse the Countess was so intent on calling down on everybody's head?

The Countess leaned forward. Her face seemed lit by an unholy glow. 'I know the identity of the Third Antichrist.'

It was as if she had just reached inside Abi's skull and plucked out his thoughts with a pair of pliers. He felt as if he had been blindsided by a lorry. Abi gave a vehement shake of the head. 'No. That's impossible. Athame told me every word that Sabir said both inside and outside that Mexican sweat-bath. Sabir confirmed that Yola Dufontaine was the mother of the Second Coming. Yes. But at no time did he reveal the identity of the Third Antichrist. I would have told you immediately.'

'But it wasn't to Athame that he revealed it.'

Abi glanced at the other three. They were watching the Countess intently. It was as if everything were being decided in that room. Everybody's fate.

Yes. That's what this is, Abi thought to himself. The old crone is dooming us all. She wants a Götterdämmerung. Not content with overseeing the death of nine of her children, she's busy piling up the tinder beneath the remaining four. And when she's got it just so, she's going to set light to the whole damned shooting match with one final flourish of her torch.

Well, I'm not about to allow myself to be immolated quite so easily. If she wants to act like Brünnhilde, good luck to her. I'll simply find a way to slide out from underneath the shit-fall.

'To whom did he reveal it, then?'

'To whom do you think, Abiger? Sabir revealed it to Lamia the afternoon they shared a hotel bedroom. The same afternoon he stole her virginity.' The Countess's voice thickened.

The truth hit Abi like a slap in the face. Never before had he been able to get a handle on the Countess and Lamia's ambiguous relationship. Now he knew for a racing certainty.

The Countess had been in love with her own adopted daughter. It was as clear as day. But her love hadn't been reciprocated. And finally Lamia had cheated on her mother with Adam Sabir, the person the Countess hated most in the world – and a man, to boot. It was irrelevant that Lamia had not betrayed the Countess in terms of the Corpus. The emotional betrayal had been the thing.

Abi glanced at Madame Mastigou. The woman's face was gaunt but triumphant. Well. That figured.

'Why would he do that?' Abi didn't fully understand his own motives. He only knew that he needed to see his mother squirm.

'Why do you think? Why are men susceptible to women? Why do they talk in bed and say things that they would never normally dream of saying when they are in their right minds? Because they are weak, that's why. Look at you. You are a prime example. You've nearly managed to bring our entire family down with your litany of botched decisions.'

Abi shrugged. What did he care anymore? He was home free. Madame, his mother, still needed him or she would have ordered him killed on the spot earlier that morning. 'That's predictable. But it's not fair. If you had trusted me with the fact that Lamia was working for you, I would have acted differently from the start. You caused this yourself. Because you can't bring yourself to trust those you should. And because you trust those you shouldn't.' Abi only half understood what was driving him to say these things. As a rule he never talked back to Madame, his mother. But a feeling of outraged virtue now suffused him – possibly triggered by his frustration at not having brought off the financial coup of the century by murdering the she-viper in her bed.

'How dare you speak like that to me.'

Milouins, who had been patrolling the doorway like a nightclub bouncer, took a pace forward in response to his mistress's tone.

Abi knew he was treading a fine line. If his mother decided, on a whim, that she wanted him dead, he would to all intents and purposes have called his fate down onto his own head. As far as the authorities were concerned, he was in Boston, not in France. Nobody would look for the body of the non-existent Pierre Blanc out here on the peninsula. And, clearly, you couldn't be charged for the murder of a man who didn't exist. *Ubi est corpus* – wasn't that what lawyers called it? When the missing Abiger de Bale's green card needed renewing, the US authorities would simply tear up Battery Wharf instead of Cap Camarat in their search for a non-existent French Count.

'I'm sorry, Madame. Vainglory got the better of me. I apologize. It shall never happen again.'

Milouins looked crestfallen.

It occurred to Abi that his antipathy to Milouins was probably returned in spades. After all, Abi was the Countess's eldest child – not Milouins. He held all Monsieur, his father's, honorary titles. He would inherit a quarter of all Madame, his mother's, money. While Milouins would never amount to anything more than a jumped-up footman.

Abi decided that he would enjoy giving Milouins his marching orders when the Countess finally popped her clogs. Then, if he still felt like it, he would put a contract out on Milouins's head and have him killed. With extreme prejudice. Like in *Apocalypse Now*.

Abi summoned up his best rendition of a filial smile. It was powerful enough to bathe the entire room in sunlight. 'What do you wish for us to do, Madame? We are at your entire disposal.'

*Cenucenca, Orheiul Vechi, Moldova*
*21 March 1986*

# 23

Dracul let a week go by before he moved up, lock, stock, and barrel, to the Orheiul Vechi cave monastery. He let it be known that it was his father's disappearance that had prompted this move. His father's abandonment of his children. That he was grieving for both his parents' sins. That he wished to do penance in a holy place.

Meanwhile he sent Antanasia around to all the surrounding *crîşmas*, canteens and drinking dens – those, at least, where she was not known. Once there, she would dance, and tell stories. She was clearly half-Gypsy. This was not so odd, then. A normal Moldovan girl would have run a mile from such places. But Antanasia loved her brother, and wished to please him.

Later, when the men were deep in their cups, Antanasia would whisper to them of the rumours going around that a young man had moved into Orheiul Vechi – that he had become a hermit there whilst awaiting His Father's orders.

'A young man? His Father's orders? What do you mean?'

'It is only a rumour. But it is said the Metropolitan himself is interested.'

'The Metropolitan? Why should he be interested?'

'He has told the Patriarch. It is said, too, that the Roman Pope is following events.'

'Events? What events?'

By this time a small crowd would have formed around her, for Antanasia was as beautiful as she was persuasive. Men were drawn to her despite themselves. There was a knowingness about her that belied her innocent demeanour. It was a seductive combination.

'That the boy is...' Antanasia would hesitate here, following Dracul's instructions to the letter. 'That the boy is... the Second Coming.'

The men would cross themselves. Antanasia understood, perhaps better than her brother did, that drinking makes men credulous. She also knew that when men returned home, feeling guilty about their excesses, it would often behove them to have some juicy titbit of gossip with which to placate their angry wives and mothers. The fact that a person who might be the Second Coming was now in situ at Orheiul Vechi fit that bill completely.

For centuries there had been a rumour that the Second Coming would be born somewhere in Eastern Europe. Moldova had very little to recommend it. It was by far the poorest country in the Eastern Bloc. It was squashed between dominant neighbours. It was landlocked, junta-ridden, and corrupt. A rumour such as this might transform the country from a sleepy backwater into a vibrant place of pilgrimage. It might provide the country with a higher status vis-à-vis the Romanians and the Russians, both of whom despised little Moldova, and wished to engulf it. A full 96 per cent of Moldovans, despite their communist appurtenances, still considered themselves Eastern Orthodox. Still adhered to the Moscow Patriarchate. It would be a triumph.

'Why should the Catholic Pope be interested? The Second Coming is one of us. He is Eastern Orthodox.'

'Yes. Yes. Of course he is. But don't you see? His existence would bring the Churches back together again. It might heal the schism between us. But this time around, we would emerge the stronger.'

Later that night, the men would return home from the *crîşmas* intent on placating their wives. They would pass on the story of the Second Coming. The women would be sceptical.

'Who told you of this thing? Some whore, perhaps?'

'No. No. A visiting priest. He came to the *crîşmas* to persuade us to change our ways. He told us of this boy at Orheiul Vechi. That he would be an example to us. The old hermit who lived there – he recognized the boy for what he is. Now he is dead, and the boy has taken his place.'

'You are drunk. This is nonsense. There is no Second Coming.'

'Yes. There is. And he is Moldovan. You should be proud, not angry. It has almost made me give up the drink.'

'You? Give up the drink? That would indeed be a miracle.'

The women then talked amongst themselves, as Dracul had known they would. They even questioned their visiting priests, who soon learned that it was wiser to claim knowledge of the boy at Orheiul Vechi, than to profess their ignorance of such a key topic of discussion amongst their flock.

Slowly, small groups of headscarf-wearing women began to make tentative pilgrimages to the shrine. Dracul played it carefully right from the start. He took his place, daily, on a rocky outcrop overlooking the River Bug, and easily visible from the great stone cross, which was as far as the women dared to venture. Once there, he never said a word. He just sat cross-legged, whatever the weather, and stared out across the vast expanse of plain ahead of him. Occasionally, he would stand up and raise his arms. The first time he did this, and the women copied him, Dracul knew that he was home free.

Soon, large parties of pilgrims would make their way to the monastery every Sunday. Queues would form to stand and see the hermit. In the weeks running up to his first public appearance, Dracul had allowed a small beard to grow on his face. His hair, too, now hung to his shoulders – he had been growing it for nearly a year in preparation for this very moment. He now felt that he comfortably resembled the pictures, icons, and statues of Jesus Christ visible in every church and household throughout the land.

When representatives from the Metropolis of Chişinău came to investigate him, Dracul refused to budge from his rocky outcrop, ensuring that it was impossible for the clerical inspectors to reach him. The stand-off continued for five days. From the perspective of the people watching from the great stone cross, it appeared as if the priests had come to marvel at the young man, not to question him.

'What is his name? What is he called?'

Antanasia would weave in and out of the crowd surrounding the cross, whispering to those she considered the key women. 'They say He is called Mihael. The "one who is like God". That He will speak only on the Feast of Theophany. That until then He communes only with God, the Holy Father.'

'Mihael? That is a fine name. The "one who is like God", you say? But that is proof, is it not? Proof that this boy is indeed the Second Coming.'

When the first miracle occurred, no more proof was needed. The crowd was there to stay.

*Brara, Maramureş, Romania*
*10 November 2009*

# 24

An off-white Slovenian-built Renault *katrca* containing Adam Sabir, Joris Calque, and Alexi and Yola Dufontaine slid over the Hungarian–Romanian border a few kilometres south of Jimbolia at a little after 3 a.m. on a moonless pre-dawn Tuesday morning in mid-November.

The Hungarian half of the border was unmanned, and the Romanian side had only a token junior customs officer on guard. The last in a steady stream of roiling drunks had crossed over hours before, and the early morning commercial traffic was yet to begin, so the solitary border guard was passing his time downloading porn onto his cell phone for later perusal. He fluttered a weary hand at the *katrca*, and returned to his screen.

Alexi slapped Calque on the shoulder. 'You see? One man on one side of the border goes to sleep while the other man on the other side watches. This is what my cousin Simu has told me. This is why all the Gypsies cross here.' Alexi offered the unwitting border guard a Mussolini-style jerk of the chin. 'The European Union is a mighty thing, is it not? Such an occurrence would not happen in the Ukraine, Moldova, or Transnistria. There, the border vultures will steal your grandmother's milk to make rice pudding with. But here in Romania? No milk stealing.'

Calque looked pained. Alexi's endless exuberance had begun to wear him down. He glanced over at Sabir. Sabir had his eyes shut, and was pretending to be asleep – just as he'd been doing, on and off, for the past thirty hours. Calque looked at Yola. She really was asleep, tucked up in a corner of the back seat, her legs folded beneath her – look as he might, he could still see no real sign of her pregnancy as yet, beyond a slight convexity in her stomach, like one of Matisse's odalisques. Calque sighed. It would have to be Alexi or no one, then.

'So you've been to Romania before, Alexi?'

'Of course. We are part Roma, Yola and I. Our cousins visit regularly to France, where there is more money to be made than in Romania – that's why they can all speak French, so you will understand them. We last came here as children in 1992. Just after the break-up of the Soviet Union. Yola's father and my father wanted to honour the new Romani leader – the *Baro-Sero*. So they took their wives and children with them. And all our cousins. And grandparents. Like in a caravan. Except this time the border crossing cost my father the entirety of his American cigarettes. This was very bad. He and Yola's father had to steal back the cigarettes from the same crooks who stole them from him. This was only justice. The thief who is not caught is an honest man.'

Calque rolled his eyes. Nothing Alexi said had the power to surprise him anymore. During the course of their seemingly endless journey through Austria, Switzerland,

and then on into Hungary, his understanding of the Gypsy mindset had increased exponentially.

First, there had been the matter of the fake identity documents. Thanks to a recent crackdown by the French authorities, the Gypsies in the Samois camp had been forced to tweak their systems to such a degree that each of the four identity cards Alexi now waved at the border guard was in immaculate, if dog-eared, order.

Calque shook his head. Not only was he busy committing felonies – but he was even busier compounding them. With each passing day he was venturing further outside his usual comfort zone. Six days ago he had turned a blind eye to a multiple homicide. And now here he was again, knowingly travelling through Europe on a false French identity card considerately provided by his Gypsy hosts. Insanity. Sheer insanity.

The new identity card setup, however, was an oddly impressive achievement for a group of people Calque had formerly written off as nothing more than a parcel of anarchists. For a start, each fake card was fully interchangeable within the community. When one person had finished using it, the photograph was switched, re-laminated, and re-inked, and the transformed card was then ready for use by the next person in line who most resembled the previous holder in terms of height, sex, and birth date. It was a simple but effective means of communality. Everybody who used one of the cards was, de facto, guilty of deception, so it was in no one's vested interest to spoil the show by snitching.

Calque had attempted to engage Alexi in a belated moral rearguard action about the use of the fake cards, but Alexi had overridden him. 'Captain. Look at us. We are Gypsies. Nobody wants us in their country. Not the French. Not the Germans. Not the Romanians. In some countries, not even the other Gypsies want us. If we try to settle, the authorities move us on. When we agree to move on, they try to settle us. But not where we want to be. So we move on again, but always in secret. This is the way of things. You have asked to come with us. I have agreed. This makes you my guest. But as a married man travelling with his pregnant wife, I am head of this party. You must please allow me to protect Yola and our unborn child in my own way. And the way I have chosen guarantees that there is no official paper trail to guide the Corpus back towards us and to our cousins in Romania. When the Corpus try to find us, they will be talking to their own armpits.' Alexi flicked his newly made gold front tooth with his thumbnail.

Calque knew when he was beaten. The Gypsies hadn't actually invited him to come with them to Romania, after all. He wasn't, in consequence, in the strongest of critical positions.

Calque's unexpected change of heart had coincided with his final farewells to Adam Sabir at the Samois camp. Without warning, he had been overwhelmed by the conviction that if he abandoned Sabir to the Gypsies, he would never find his friend again. That the Gypsies would spirit Sabir away from the real world and transform him, somehow, into one of them. Either that, or his friend would commit suicide, just as his mother had done before him, taking his secrets with him to the grave. And Calque had far too much invested in his struggle against the Corpus to even consider letting Sabir off the hook as easily as that.

Calque had nothing personal against the Gypsies. Secretly, he rather admired the way they capitulated, body and soul, to the whims of the moment – it was, quite frankly, a refreshing change from the politically correct orthodoxies of his latter days on the police force. But neither did he underestimate the Gypsy capacity for spirited chaos. And in his opinion it wasn't chaos that Sabir needed after Lamia's murder – it was peace and quiet.

The unwitting build-up to Calque's volte-face had occurred at Lamia's funeral. Or rather, as Alexi had insisted on describing it, at the Wedding of the Dead.

On first hearing the expression – and Alexi's garbled explanation of it – Calque had thrown up his hands in horror. 'But, Alexi. Listen to me. How can you hold a wedding ceremony at somebody's funeral? This is grotesque. It flies in the face of all reason. What are you people trying to do?'

Alexi shrugged. 'Lamia was unmarried. And she came to Damo a virgin when he kidnapped her – so her *lacha* was untarnished. For a Gypsy woman, Captain, her *lacha* is her essential honour. It is her maidenhood. Her purity as a woman. Yola understood that Damo would wish to see Lamia's honour in this matter recognized. In the East, where we are going, our cousins believe that when a man or a woman is killed before their time, and they are still unmarried, they should have a wedding nonetheless. That they should not appear before O Del alone. So a bride or a bridegroom is found for them, and the wedding ceremony is held at their funeral.'

Calque grabbed Alexi's arm. 'You can't be serious, man. And what's this about Sabir kidnapping Lamia? He didn't kidnap her. She came to him of her own free will. I can testify to that. We don't allow that sort of thing in France.'

Alexi quietly disengaged himself from Calque's arm and gave it a friendly pat. 'It's not a real kidnap, Captain. It's just an expression. With us you must learn to look behind the words of things. In this sort of kidnap, the woman comes along willingly. I kidnapped Yola to Corsica in July. She didn't mind. In fact she was very pleased. I swear this to you on my talisman.' Alexi grinned, and brandished his gold Sainte Sara pendant in front of Calque's nose.

'Look behind the words of things? What the blazes are you talking about, Alexi?'

'Captain. Captain. Listen to me. It's like this. Kidnapping is *my* custom. But the Wedding of the Dead is *not* my custom. When we buried my cousin, *u kuc* Babel, we did not find a young woman to marry him at his funeral. No. This is not our way. But Yola, in her wisdom, has told Damo of this custom amongst her *Lăutari* relatives of Romania, near the village where we are going. That things are done like this. And when he heard of it, Damo insisted that we conduct such a wedding ceremony at Lamia's funeral. So that they would be married before God. This we shall do. It is no problem. This is what I am calling "looking behind the words of things".'

Calque rolled his eyes. 'But that still won't mean he's legally married. His bride is dead, for pity's sake. The whole thing's a farce. The pair of them aren't even Gypsies.'

This time it was Alexi who threw up his hands. 'Damo is my brother. He is Yola's brother too. He has the soul of a Gypsy. He has been acknowledged by the Bulibasha. He was *u kuc* Babel's *phral*. What do you mean he is not a Gypsy?'

'*U kuc* Babel's *phral*? For pity's sake, Alexi, you might as well be talking double Dutch. Speak French for a change. I can't understand a word of what you are saying.'

'It means the defunct Babel's blood brother. This is how we talk of the dead amongst ourselves. We prefer not to acknowledge them. Death is nothing special for us, Captain. Life continues on. It is the living that count. That is why we have the wedding. For the living. For Damo.'

Try as he might, Calque hadn't been able to shift Alexi's stance on the matter – in such matters, Yola's word was law in his eyes. Yet there was still something in what was about to happen that had provoked outrage in Calque's rationalist French soul. That had nagged at him like a horsefly bite. 'But why conduct a marriage that isn't legal in the eyes of the State? Or in the eyes of the Church? It makes no sense. No sense at all.'

Alexi was beginning to lose his temper. He and Calque rarely saw eye to eye on matters pertaining to Sabir, and their argument over the Wedding of the Dead was only the visible tip of the iceberg. 'Legal, you say? What is legal? Who is to say what is legal? It is a matter of each person's opinion. You *payos* always tell us what you think is legal. Then you make it impossible for us to vote unless we have a fixed address. Then you act as if you are turned upside down in surprise when we choose to ignore your laws.'

'The law is the law, Alexi.'

'No it's not. If Damo wants this thing to bring him restfulness, then we will give it to him. When he recovers from his illness of the heart, and we find him a nice Gypsy girl, it won't stop him from being able to marry her – if he can afford to pay her bride price, that is, and if her father is stupid enough to accept him as a son-in-law. But Damo is rich, and the sight of money makes even the wisest father blind.' Alexi's anger had clearly transmogrified into cupidity. 'This is why I intend to ask him for a further loan. You must help me with this, Captain. He is the baby's *kirvo*, you know. Which is like a godfather to you *payos*. With the baby coming in the New Year, there will be many expenses. Damo understands his responsibilities in this matter. I am sure he does. Doesn't he?'

Calque hunched his shoulders towards his ears and grunted. It was pointless arguing with Alexi. The man had about as much interest in rational discussion as a Rottweiler.

Now, with the dubious advantage of hindsight, Calque was forced to admit that Yola's idea about the Wedding of the Dead had been an inspired one.

It appeared to have achieved the near impossible – it had jogged Sabir out of his self-destructive spiral of melancholy. He was clearly not back to his normal state of – at least according to Calque's jaundiced view of the matter – irritating whimsicality. But neither was he teetering on the edge of suicide anymore. Instead, his mood had transformed into what Calque could only construe as a condition of mercurial gloom.

Calque now accepted that he had underestimated Sabir's resilience, and also the effect his renewed companionship with the Gypsies would have on him. He had based his view of Sabir only on what he had seen of him in the few fervid weeks they had been on the run in the US and Mexico. This had been a mistake. As far as his emotional life was concerned, Sabir had been living on the edge for years. Or at least ever since his mother's suicide. He was salted to it. Like a South African buffalo to a tsetse fly.

But to measure against this, Calque had witnessed for himself how quickly things could turn bad – how swiftly Sabir could be brought down by the tenor of his own thoughts. It was for this reason that Calque had insisted, at the last possible moment, on accompanying Sabir on his journey to Romania.

Had he been wrong? Should he have remained in France to investigate the state of the Corpus Maleficus after its debacle in the Yucatan and the Gypsy camp at Samois?

Only time, and the decisions made by the Countess back at that godforsaken chamber of hers in the Domaine de Seyème, would tell.

# 25

Over the course of the past few months, Sabir's cycle of disrupted sleep had followed a roughly predictable pattern. First would come the hyper-realist dreams, in which he was back in the cesspit again, deep in the cellar below the Gypsy safe-house in the French Camargue. In these dreams he was up to his neck in raw sewage, his head bent backwards to protect his mouth, his forehead pressed against the lid of the cesspit, which Achor Bale was sliding shut across his face. Prone to claustrophobia at the best of times, the prospect of suffocation in conditions of utter darkness had been enough to curdle Sabir's soul and turn him into a gibbering, mewling, wreck.

Then would come the dreams of dreams, in which Sabir's unconscious mind revisited the hallucinations he had experienced whilst sealed inside the cesspit. Hallucinations in which his arms and legs were torn off, his torso shredded, his intestines, spleen, bowels, and bladder dragged out of his body like offal from a butchered horse. Later in the dream a snake would approach him – a thick uncoiling python of a snake, with the scales of a fish, and staring eyes, and a hinged skull like that of an anaconda. The snake would lunge forward and swallow Sabir's head, forcing it down the entire length of its body with convulsive movements of its myosin-fuelled muscles, like a reverse birth. During this process, Sabir would witness himself becoming the snake – his head transforming into its head, his skin into its skin. It was at this point in the dream that he would normally awake, his body drenched in sweat, his eyes bulging from his face.

But since the events in Mexico that had culminated in Lamia's death, six days before, this was no longer the case. Now both snake and dream continued on with their cycle of transformation even whilst Sabir had, to all intents and purposes, regained consciousness. In this semi-lucid state, the vision became even deeper and more intense, with the snake extending its transformation by growing a second, bicephalous head, which in no way resembled Sabir's own.

This was why Sabir pretended to be dozing all the time he was in the car with the others – why every time someone turned round to check on him he snapped his eyes shut and mimicked sleep. Because he ultimately feared that if he did not, whoever looked him in the face would discern the nightmare that lurked behind his eyes, and that – once outed – the chimera would resolve itself inside his psyche and steal his identity. That he would go mad, in other words, just as his mother had gone mad. And that this madness would end, like hers, in suicide.

# 26

'This is it. This is to be your house.'

Alexi's cousin Gabor was pointing out a blue-washed Saxon house on the outskirts of the village of Brara. None of the windows had glass. Part of the roof had fallen in, affording a curious view of the sky when one looked in through the gaping doorway. But in front of the house there was a cobbled courtyard, and behind the house a small orchard, with apple, plum, cherry, and pear trees in varying stages of dilapidation, but still salvageable, Calque decided, come the spring, with a bit of expedient pruning. A small river ran beneath a bridge adjacent to the property, and the water looked clean and inviting – as if it might contain a few trout, and maybe even a grayling or two.

Inside the house the floorboards were rotten, and the plaster was coming down from the walls in strips and clutches. Calque couldn't understand why, but the house raised his spirits. It was itself. What you saw was what you got. 'Who owns this?'

Gabor shrugged. 'Nobody. Everybody. The Saxons who used to live here went back to Germany years ago. It was they who maintained the houses and the church and the village hall. Now there are only a few old ones left, and they are too frail to maintain anything. So the house belongs to anyone who lives in it. If you want it, you take it.'

'We'll take it.'

Calque cast a sideways glance at Sabir staring out over the fields. He seemed entirely uninterested in the house. Heck, thought Calque – he seemed entirely uninterested in the fields.

Calque shook his head. Sabir hadn't spoken more than three words to him in the past couple of days. For one crazy moment, Calque was tempted to shout out 'How's married life treating you, then?' That would break the deadlock if anything would. Sabir would probably come over and beat the crap out of him. Well, at least it would be a response of sorts.

Alexi and Yola were already pitching their makeshift tent in the orchard.

Calque turned his attention to them. At least they answered when spoken to. 'Look. Why don't you two take the house? You'd be more comfortable there. Sabir and I can manage in the tent.'

'Are you crazy? Yola and I don't live in houses. We prefer to live out here, and use the house for storage. You two *payos* can live in the house. That way the whole village will think you're Bulgarian.'

'Bulgarian? Why would they thing we are Bulgarian?'

'You know. Lifting of the shirt. Bicyclists. Bulgarians.'

Calque gave a gloomy shake of the head. Alexi usually telegraphed his jokes from at least two valleys away. And this was no exception. 'Don't tell me that's illegal here?'

'No. No. Not really illegal. They just ride you out of the village on a rail. Then they tar and feather you. Then they tie you to a telegraph pole with duct tape and piss all over you.'

Gabor and Dalca yelped in delight. Alexi hammered gleefully at his tent peg. Even Yola threw back her head and laughed.

Calque didn't really mind being made fun of. It meant that the Gypsies had, to a certain extent at least, accepted him. That they no longer viewed him solely as an ex-policeman, but also as a human being in his own right. It had been the same while he was in the force – like any small community, he supposed. If they ribbed you, you were okay. If they ignored you, you were dead in the water. 'Very funny, Alexi. Thanks for the testimonial.'

When the joshing had quieted down, and the evening meal had been eaten, and everyone, including Sabir, had dispersed either to bed or to the local bar, it dawned on Calque that by agreeing to come to Romania, he had committed himself to a course of action whose eventual outcome was never in doubt. Whose possible effects were not even worth quantifying.

As he stared into the remnants of the fire, he recognized, for the very first time, that he had hitched his chariot to a runaway horse. And that he had not the remotest idea whether or not he was up to the ride.

*Albescu, Moldova*
*6 January 1993*

# 27

'Did you know our country is named after a dog?'

Antanasia stared at her brother. 'A dog?' She never knew these days whether Dracul was in his Second Coming mode or being his usual self. There were times when he actively believed himself to be the reincarnation of the risen Christ, and others when he treated the whole thing like an extended joke to which only he knew the punchline.

'Yes. Prince Dragoş was hunting an aurochs.'

'An aurochs?'

'A two-metre tall cow. Weighing a thousand kilograms. Like that nun of mine who swings the incense. They died out in the seventeenth century. The cattle, that is. Not the nuns. The nuns still hang on, unfortunately.'

Antanasia felt her stomach tighten. She was scared of her brother. But it was a curious fear. If she had to define it, she would say that she both loved and feared him at the same time. It was an animal need. Without him, she would be bereft. With him, she was terrified.

'The Prince had come across into what is now Moldova from the Maramureş in pursuit of this beast. His favourite hound, Molda, was hard on its trail. But the beast was strong. It fought off all the dogs. But finally Molda killed it in the river. Only he killed it by choking off its windpipe with his teeth. And when the aurochs fell beneath the surface of the water, Molda followed him down and was swept away by the current. Prince Dragoş wept. Then he named the river after his hound. And our country after the river. Do you like this story?'

'Yes, Dracul. Yes. I like it very much.'

'Why?'

Antanasia could feel her throat seizing up. She knew all the signs now. Dracul would question her on some subject she knew nothing about. He would become angry. He would strike her. Then he would make love to her, and weep into her shoulder for his guilt at the killing of their father and at laying his hands on her. She would comfort him. He would avoid her for days after that. Days in which she often despaired to the extent of wishing to take her own life. Then, just before she made her final decision, Dracul would come to her. Bring her an expensive present. Tell her he loved her. That she must only ever be his. That she must never look at another man again.

Two days later he would be pimping her out to some minor official he needed to placate. When she came back from doing whatever it was he had ordered her to do, he would be angry with her, and force her to reveal all the most intimate details of what had occurred. Down to the very slightest intake of breath – the most fleeting of caresses. Antanasia felt bewildered, in consequence, for most of the time she was with him. But the blood tie was strong with her and Dracul – she knew it. He was a part of her. If he lived, she lived. If he died, she died. It was as simple as that. It was a marriage made in hell.

Antanasia sometimes wondered what she had done in a past life to deserve the way she felt. Now that Dracul had ten thousand followers, what did he need her for? He was the New Messiah to these people. Christ reborn. Since Moldova's independence, there was freedom in the country for those who had money and connections. And Dracul had both.

Soon after the breakaway from the Soviet Union, the authorities had granted Dracul permission to build his very own village high on the Moldavian Plateau – after he had greased certain palms and guaranteed delivery of a set number of votes. For nothing ever came free in Moldova. But Dracul could afford the kickback. He had persuaded his followers that a full 25 per cent of their annual income must go to his Church, and that their votes must come with it. For Dracul had learned one valuable lesson from the Russians – that the spiritual high ground was valueless without real political power.

And the number of Dracul's followers was indeed rising daily. Even in a country where a fair proportion lived on less than $2 a day, the sums and the voting power were beginning to add up. Add to that the donations Dracul/ Mihael now received via the Hungarian, Ukrainian, and Romanian diaspora, and the numbers rose exponentially. Only a foolish politician would risk alienating a man believed by many to be the earthly reincarnation of the Godhead.

It was a long tradition in the East to donate part of your income to the Church. The perception was that this brought you closer to God. The normal tithe was 10 per cent of income. But Mihael had to be different. His people needed to make an actual, visible sacrifice. In this way they felt that they were different from the norm. Cleaner. More spiritual. That they were suffering for their faith. Martyrs, even. The fact that some of the poorer members came near to starving in the depths of winter as a result of Mihael's tithes worried Mihael's alter ego, Dracul Lupei, not at all. If they needed help, they would get it – other people would see to that. Some individuals were born to lead, and others to follow. And he was a born leader.

To add further cement to Mihael's standing, his model village was blooming. It had its very own sawmill and forge. A village hall. Vegetable allotments for every family. And a church that Dracul had designed himself, and which looked like a cross between an observatory, a planetarium, and a football stadium. Gold leaf had been imported from India for the roof. Russian stained glass had been commissioned for the windows. The place was a marvel. Each Sunday, Dracul/Mihael would walk barefoot to the church, his hair flowing about his shoulders, smiling distantly at his adoring followers.

Every now and then he would stop and fall into a brown study, as if he were communing directly with God. His followers would surround him silently, their eyes fixed on his. The silence might continue for as long as five minutes. Then Mihael would smile and raise his hands in benediction, and the procession would continue on its way as if nothing had happened.

It worked every time. When Dracul had been

recovering from his injuries in the stone dormitory at Orheiul Vechi, eleven years before, he had had ample time to observe the old monk's idiosyncrasies. Now he based his own behaviour on that of the old man. The hermit would often drift off into a contemplative trance right in the middle of one of his Bible readings – such trances could last five, or even ten minutes. At the time they had irritated Dracul intensely – all he had wanted was for the monk to get on and read his story. But even then Dracul had sensed the possible uses to which one could put such a technique.

Yes. Everything was going swimmingly for Dracul. He had his flock. He had Antanasia. He had money in the bank. And very soon he was going to try his hand at a little enlightened chicanery.

He was going to order the most zealous of his male followers to go down in secret and torch the local mosque.

*Outskirts of Samois Gypsy Camp*
*12 November 2009*

# 28

'What's your name?'

The boy darted a sideways glance at the girl beside him. Then back to Abi. 'She is Koiné. I am Bera. Who are you?'

'None of your business.'

'What do you want? Are you a bad man? Why do you have guns?'

Abi nodded. 'Yes. I'm a bad man. This…' He jerked his head at Rudra. 'This is a bad man too. And these…' He chucked his chin towards Nawal and Dakini. 'These are bad women.'

'Are you going to sell us?'

'Not if your sister does what we say.'

'What do you say?'

Abi made a face. This one was a sassy little runt. 'That she's to go back to the camp and tell your headman to come out to speak to me. Privately. Quietly. Without making a song and a dance out of it. Meanwhile, this bad man will hold you in another place. I have a phone. When your chief tells me what I want to know, then I phone the bad man and you get to go home. If he doesn't, this man will hurt you. She's to tell him that.'

'Why you do this?'

'That's none of your business either.'

'Koiné. You don't go.'

'Listen here, you little guttersnipe. If she doesn't go, we drop you both down a convenient mine shaft. I've heard there are old mines around here. We'll drop you down and you'll break your legs. Then you'll starve to death. We'll be long gone by then. Nobody will know you're down there. It's not a nice way to die. Take it from me.' An image flashed into Abi's brain from the cenote, but he shunted it away into his unconscious. He noticed, though, that Rudra looked as pale as a fish belly beneath the remnants of his Mexican tan.

Bera turned his dark eyes onto Abi. 'You killed my cousin Babel. I know who you are. I know why you are here.'

'You're a smart little bleeder, I'll give you that much. But we didn't kill anybody. That was someone else. We need information, that's all. And you're going to get it for us. Either that, or we drop you thirty feet down an open mine shaft. It's a simple equation. Take it or leave it.'

Bera looked at his sister. 'You go tell Radu. You tell him about the mine shaft. What they are going to do.'

Abi pointed to his pistol. 'You tell no one else, mind. Only this Radu person. We don't want the whole camp in an uproar. If you don't do as we ask, we will hurt your brother.'

Koiné began to cry. Bera approached his sister and yanked her by the pigtails. 'Listen. You talk to Radu. Tell him about the mine. Only him. You understand me?'

Koiné glanced up at her brother. Her mouth twisted itself out of shape in an effort to fight back her tears. She nodded.

Abi took a step forward. 'He's to meet me in an hour. Centre of Samois. By the post office. He's to come alone. On foot. He's to wear something red. If I see anybody with him, I'll order this man to hurt you. Make Radu understand that. If he talks to me, you can go free. We don't want you. I never liked kids. Untrustworthy little blighters.'

'You are a bad man.'

'You'd better believe it.'

'Go, Koiné. Talk to Radu.'

With a backward glance at her brother, Koiné started up the track.

Abi watched her go. Then he turned to Rudra. 'Okay. Take this little brat off in the car. The girls can go with you – they're far too memorable to be let loose on a sleepy little village like Samois. I'm going to walk – that way the timings will be right. I'll call you when I need you.'

Rudra urged the boy away with the barrel of his gun. He didn't look at Abi. Neither did Dakini or Nawal.

Abi shrugged. Well. Maybe he still wasn't flavour of the month with those three. But Madame, his mother, had clearly put him in charge again, so he didn't much care what the others thought. This time around he was going to do things his way. He'd follow the Countess's agenda, sure. But he'd follow his own agenda too.

The four of them had lucked into the children twenty minutes before. Found them playing alone, three-quarters of a mile from the camp, while they were scouting the area prior to moving in on the headman. Abi didn't like involving children in Corpus affairs – not altruistically, but on principle, because children refused to behave and think like adults. They were ungovernable. Unpredictable.

But their presence had given him his idea about how to persuade the headman to tell them where Sabir and his Gypsy friends were hiding. Originally, he had intended to watch the camp until he was certain of the chief's identity. Then kidnap and torture him. But why use violence when you could use psychology instead? And not queer your back trail into the bargain?

He knew that the others weren't comfortable with him sidetracking them all the way back to near Paris. Madame, his mother, had ordered them to go directly to Moldova. Once there, they were to exert pressure on some certifiable nutter called Mihael Catalin, who claimed he was the Second Coming, and had amassed an army of fanatical followers to support his claim. The same nutter whom Sabir had indiscreetly identified as Nostradamus's Third Antichrist whilst he was still pussy-struck with their sister Lamia.

'Look. This so-called Antichrist isn't going anywhere in a hurry. We can catch up with him whenever we want to. He's got his own town. He's got his own airport. He's even got his own bank. So he's going to be busy as hell. Plus he doesn't believe he's the Antichrist – he thinks he's the Second Coming, for pity's sake. The fucking Saviour of Mankind. So he'll keep. Sabir won't. He's on the run. He knows we'll be coming after him and his Gypsy friends. And I have a score to settle with that bastard. If it hadn't been for him and Calque torching the crystal meth factory, we might have been able to bribe our way out of that cenote. So I blame the two of them directly for Oni's death. And for Vau, Asson, Alastor, and Berith's earlier. And it wouldn't surprise me if they weren't involved in Lamia, Athame's and Aldinach's disappearance somehow too. So they owe us – they owe us large. And I, for one, aim to collect.'

# 29

—

'They're in Turkey.'
  'Turkey?'
  'Yes.'
  'Where in Turkey?'
  Radu hesitated.
  Abi spoke into his cell phone. 'If this imbecile gives me one more featherbrained answer, saw off one of the kid's fingers, okay?' He glanced back at Radu. 'The man who is holding the boy is mad. He likes doing bad things to children. Once he starts, I may not be able to stop him. Now tell me. Where are they?'
  Radu stayed silent for a long time. He scanned the ground like a man searching for a lost coin. Then he looked up into the sky. 'If I tell you, what's to stop me calling and warning them?'
  Abi gave a long drawn-out sigh. 'Don't act like you're dumber than you are. You're coming with us. You and the boy. What did you think? That we'd write down Sabir's address on the back of an envelope and then leave you both to get on with the rest of your lives?'
  'Not the boy. You don't need him. I will come.'
  'You still haven't told me where they are. We'll barter

afterwards. Maybe.'

Radu continued with his perusal of the village. It was as if the walls of Samois itself might contain the answer to his problems. He spat into the dirt at his feet. 'They're in Romania. In a small village in the north of the country. With Yola and Alexi's relatives. I don't know the name of the village. This I promise. But I know roughly where it is.'

'That's cute. You don't know the name of the village, but you know roughly where it is.'

'This is true. I know how to get near there. But not what it is called.'

'Anyone else in your camp know?'

'Only me.'

'I figured you'd say that.'

'It is the truth. So help me God.'

'Have they got a phone number?'

'Yes. A cell phone. Pay-as-you-go.'

'Who else has the number?'

'Only me.'

'That figures too. Give me your phone.'

Radu handed over his cell phone.

'Can the boy square things for you with the rest of the camp? If we agree to leave him here, that is? And can he keep his trap shut?'

'Yes. Yes to both. I go away all the time. I am a musician. But I must say goodbye to my wife, or she will worry. We married earlier this summer. She is pregnant. It will be difficult for her.'

'My heart bleeds for you. But no. Get the kid to give her some cock-and-bull story as to why you're heading off unexpectedly. There's an emergency in Romania. Whatever. If you take me straight to Sabir, you'll be nappy-changing in no time. If you cross me, your wife will be wearing widow's weeds while she gives birth. Do you understand?'

Radu shook his head. 'Why you want to do this? What have we done to you?'

'Not you. They.'

'What did they do to you?'

'They killed my twin brother. Not to mention the rest of my family.'

'No, they didn't. They haven't killed anybody.'

'Caused their deaths, then.'

'No. You caused their deaths.'

'I don't think you're in a strong enough position to be lecturing anybody, Pikey. I'll call my associates to come and pick us up. You tell the boy what you need to. If he, or anyone else, tries to get in touch with Sabir or any of his cronies, we'll kill you. Is that understood?'

'That is very clear.'

# 30

—

Radu watched the two *gadjes* sitting in front of him in the car. How he hated non-Gypsies. They thought and acted differently from anything you would ever expect. They even smelled different. And how could a man so young ever call himself a leader? That was the *gadje* world for you. In Radu's world, older men always led the way. Perhaps there was an older man behind this young one, telling him what to do? But he suspected not.

The bad men had just placed Radu on the back seat of the car, between the two women. One of the women smelled very bad. As if it was her time of the month, and she hadn't cleaned herself. Radu tried to avoid touching her clothes in case she polluted him, but it was difficult in the strict confines of the vehicle. He hoped the effect wouldn't transmit itself back to Lemma and damage their child.

Radu switched his concentration to the two men in the front seat. The limping one wasn't of importance. But the leader – the young one – worried him very much. He decided that if he had met this man out drinking, he would have avoided him. He was a variety of man like his father's cousin, Badu, and his one-eyed son,

Stefan. The variety of man who would strike you when you were least expecting it. He cursed the day he had encountered him. It was an unpropitious day. Someone must have given him the evil eye – the *ia chalou*.

He thought of his new wife and the child she was expecting and he felt like crying. He was too young to die. He was yet to be the father of many children. He knew this for certain, for his grandmother had read it in the cards. Added to which, so long as Alexi was away, he was the honorary headman of the camp. Radu liked the feeling of being headman. But it also forced him to take responsibility for the others. To sacrifice himself if it came to it. Radu shook his head. *Malos mengues!* It was a bad day for him when these people found Bera and Koiné playing.

One thing, however, Radu had worked out to his own satisfaction. These men did not intend to kill him outright. That much was becoming clear. And it did not seem as if they were about to torture him. Yet.

Radu cursed the fact that he had not shared the number of Sabir's cell phone with someone else. It would have been so simple. But it had never occurred to him that anyone would come looking for information at the camp. He had made the assumption that after he and Alexi had arranged for the bodies of the brother and sister of Damo's death bride to be covered up in the mine shaft, that would be the end of it. How stupid could a man get?

Radu tested the bonds behind his back. The rope had been pulled through the seat and on into the trunk of the car.

The leader turned to him. 'The rope is attached to the spare tyre, Pikey. If you cause trouble, we'll chisel the tyre off its rim, ram it around your neck, and light it. Then you can pretend to be a Christmas cake with a single candle.'

Radu shut his eyes. His hands felt as if someone had stamped on them. If he was going to have to travel like this all the way to Romania, he would be in serious trouble. 'Please. Can I have my hands tied in front of me? I can no longer feel my fingers.'

It was the leader, once again, who took the initiative. '"Up in the north of Romania somewhere" just doesn't hack it, Pikey. Give us more detail, and we'll retie your hands for you.'

'But I can't tell you what I don't know. Only my cousin Gabor knows the exact location of the village. And he can only be reached in Sighetu. There is a bar. People know him there. Or you let me phone Damo. Maybe he tell me.'

'You've got to be kidding.'

'Yes. It was a joke.'

'I'm glad you've still got your sense of humour. You're going to need it if we don't find what we're looking for.'

Radu collapsed back onto his seat. He tried to work the circulation into his hands by squeezing one against the other, but it didn't work. They'd have to let him out to piss, though. Maybe he could escape then? Or at the border? They'd have to cut his hands free at the border. There would be too great a risk otherwise that an official or a guard would ask him to step out of the car.

The two *gadjes* in the front spoke quietly amongst

178

themselves – the two women beside him said nothing. Radu found that he could understand about one word in three of what the men in front were saying. It pleased him immeasurably when he realized that they were speaking to each other in English. They were clearly doing this so that he would not understand them. He was only a stupid French Gypsy, after all.

But Radu was a part-time session guitarist who played in the style of his distant ancestor, Django Reinhardt – or rather in the style of Django's rhythm guitarist brother, Joseph Reinhardt, and his fellow rhythmician, Roger Chaput. For three years, in the early 2000s, he had travelled to England every summer to take part in the Birmingham *L'Esprit Manouche* festival. During this period he had often made out with English girls from the audience – all of the guitarists did. The girls seemed excited to be going with a Gypsy. One girl had even followed him back to Paris to be with him. Radu had learned a little English from her on the occasions when he had stayed over at her flat. It was the best way to learn anything. Flat on your back with a girl bending over you.

In the end, though, Lemma's mother had driven the English girl away by threatening to cut her face. This was sad, as the English girl was very tight in her hips. She could make a man very happy. But Lemma had wanted him to kidnap her, so her mother had stepped in and threatened the English girl.

Radu had seen where good sense lay. His own father would have slit his throat if he had married a *gadje*. And now Lemma was pregnant he would soon be a father himself. He would have many sons and many daughters. He might even become Bulibasha one day, because Alexi was far too volatile ever to be put in charge of anything really important – everyone said so.

But first – before all that could come about – Radu had to escape these people with his life and his good health intact.

Radu found himself wishing that his grandmother was sitting beside him, at this very moment, with her magic cards.

# 31

Before each border crossing the two women took to bundling Radu out of the back seat and forcing him into the trunk. Abi had explained to them that no matter how relaxed the border procedures were, there was always the chance of a spot check or terrorism control. Once in the trunk, they twisted Radu's legs behind his back and box-tied him so that he couldn't rock from side to side and alert the border guards. Then they piled their suitcases on top of him, after one of them had gagged him with her handkerchief.

The first time they gagged him, Radu had to fight back an urge to vomit when he realized to whom the handkerchief belonged. Now that they were at the Romanian border, the whole process was about to start all over again – but even worse this time. Radu knew that, unless you crossed at the right place, the Romanians, despite their EU membership, still checked their borders assiduously. He himself knew where all the easiest crossings were, of course, and at what time you needed to cross, but he wasn't about to tell the *gadjes* this. It was bad enough that, through fear for his life, he had led them this far.

'Shame you didn't think to bring your identity card, Pikey. Maybe we would have left you sitting in the car.'

'What do you think? That I'm President of the Republic?' The riposte didn't come out as forcefully as Radu hoped. He just sounded nervous and apprehensive.

'Open your mouth, *Diddikai*. It's dummy time.'

'Can I pee first?'

'You can hold it till afterwards.'

'But I'm desperate.'

'Pee in your pants. We don't care.'

Dakini screwed up her nose. 'Then he'll stink up the back of the car, Nawal. We've still got hours of driving to do.'

Radu was tempted to tell the one with the long hair that she was already stinking up the back of the car, but he thought better of it. She didn't look like she had a sense of humour about herself. He waited fatalistically for the leader to make up his mind.

'Take him into the bushes then. You can both go with him. But keep him on a short rein. Hold his pecker for him, if need be.'

'But I have to go…' Radu hesitated. 'You know.'

'You sort it out between you. You're all grown-ups.'

They'd been driving for thirty straight hours and everybody was tired. Abi threw himself onto the ground and began to go through some yoga movements. Rudra picked his way out of the clearing in the opposite direction to the girls, unbuttoning his flies as he went.

The two women shunted Radu ahead of them and along a track. 'We'll find a fallen tree. Tie him to it with one hand. He can squat over that.'

'Thank you.'

'Why thank us? If it was up to us you'd be dead by now. There's no point to this. If I started sawing at your balls with my penknife, you'd soon enough tell us where Sabir is hiding.'

Radu swallowed. An image came to him of Sabir, earlier that summer, trussed up like a plucked chicken, with Yola standing over him and being urged to cut his balls off in revenge for their cousin Babel's torture and death. All at once he understood just how Sabir must have felt. 'But how can I tell you what I don't know? I already explained to you. Only Gabor knows. We need to talk to him. And I am the only one who knows what Gabor looks like. You could sit in that bar in Sighetu for years on end and nobody would point him out. This is a Gypsy bar. No one will talk to you there. You need me.'

'So you keep on telling us. So our brother keeps on telling us.' Dakini looked at her sister. 'We've got other fish to fry, Nawal. Don't you think so? If I killed this one now, what do you think would happen?'

'Abi would be very angry.'

'And so? We are ten hours' driving time away from Moldova. Away from what Madame, our mother, ordered us to do. What could Abi do? We are never going to find anything out from this filth. He is just leading us on a wild-goose chase. He'll end up dead anyway, because Abi can't risk leaving him around to identify us.'

Radu had never been spoken about before as if he was an irrelevance. He had been used to respect. Deference, even. He realized, by the tone of both these women's voices, that his life hung in the balance. Now. This minute. If the whim took them, they would simply kill him and sort out the problem that way. Why would they speak like this in front of him otherwise? Why would they tell him he was doomed whatever happened?

'I saw Damo kill your brother.'

Both women stopped talking and stared at him. 'Damo?'

'The one you call Sabir. I saw him beat your brother to death with a tree branch. Your brother – the one with the long hair – had just killed the dark-haired woman. The one Damo loved.'

They looked at him in silence. Radu wondered whether he had gone too far. There was something wrong with these women. They had none of the normal feminine attributes. One had hair on her cheeks, and more thick hair on her arms and her legs. The other one – the one that smelled – had a face that looked as if someone had slammed a car door on her at the exact moment she was winding up to a scream. Why did they not look after themselves? Why did they not make an effort with their appearance like the Gypsy women he knew? It was disgusting.

'And our sister. What happened to our sister?'

'You mean the small one?'

'Yes.'

'My cousin Alexi killed her by throwing his knife.' Radu could feel the danger of his position spiking up a notch with every word he spoke. But he also knew that he had to disorientate these women. Buy himself a split second's leeway. He was certain that they intended to kill him now. Certain that he had no more than a minute left to live. He meant nothing to these women. His life meant nothing to them. He must live. For Lemma and his unborn child. For Yola and Alexi. They were part of his family. He would be a worthless man if he led these people to them.

'Why are you telling us this now?'

'Because I want to buy my life from you. I know where the bodies are hidden. When I've led you to Damo and Yola, if you leave me alive, I can take you back to where your people are buried. You must speak to your brother. Tell him how I can be of use.'

The women turned towards each other. The long-haired one placed her hand on the other's arm. The hand that held the rope to which Radu was attached.

Radu ripped the rope out of her hand and began to run. It had been his only chance. That split-second loss of concentration. He had had to give them the information. Needed them to believe it.

A series of shots rang out behind him. Radu felt a numbing lurch in his right arm, high up on the bicep. He continued running.

Radu was fit. He earned his everyday money laying tarmac driveways. He had just spent thirty motionless hours in the back of a car, true. But so had the women. And something had enfeebled them. He had been aware of this for some time. They had recently been through an experience that had drained them. He had learned this much from his mastery of English. And that this had caused bad blood between them and the young leader.

Radu tripped on the trailing rope and fell to the

ground. As he fell, he could hear more bullets splattering through the trees above him. He tried to fall onto his good side, but the fact that his hands were tied behind his back deprived him of any such control. Instead he rolled over and over until he was finally able to lurch back to his feet via the downhill momentum of his fall. He snatched at the trailing rope and struck out to his left. There was a thicker stand of trees over there. They might afford him some cover.

A bullet hit him high up on his left shoulder. This time it was bad. Not like the first one, which had only shaved him. This time the bullet hit home. Radu felt as if someone had struck him across the shoulders with an iron bar. He dropped briefly to one knee, and then pushed himself forward again. It was either that or die.

He reached the cover of the trees and forced his way through, disregarding the trailing branches that cut and thrashed at his face. He didn't dare look back.

There were more shots, but none mimicked the zipping sound of those close ones. Radu's shirt clung to his back. Sweat or blood? Radu couldn't tell. He forged on through the plantation and down a bank on the far side.

He could hear a road. Hear traffic through the trees.

He needed people. He needed to find some Gypsies. What he didn't need was the police.

# 32

The road was full of trucks and cars. Rusty cars. Shiny cars. Four-wheel drives with swaying antennae. Trucks with twin parts, like beetles. Open trucks, with crap piled in the back and spilling over the protective netting. And everything heading towards the border.

Radu froze on the side of the road. How long did he have. Half a minute?

He limped down the hard shoulder, his eyes searching through the traffic. He knew what he was looking for. It was an instinct with him.

The two women emerged onto the hard shoulder 100 metres behind him.

Radu darted into the traffic flow. He could feel himself becoming weaker by the second. His bloodsoaked trousers flapped against his legs as if he'd been paddling in a river, not running for his life through country he didn't know.

Air horns honked. Brakes screeched. Cars took avoiding action. Radu ignored them. He kept on zigzagging through the traffic, his eyes fixed on the lanes ahead of him. One thing he knew. The women could no longer shoot at him. Not out here. Not with so many witnesses about.

Radu saw what he was looking for. He snatched a glance over his shoulder. The women were no longer behind him. Radu's belly swooped. Maybe they had cut around parallel to him? Maybe they were going to come at him face on?

He ran towards the cart. A solitary man was driving it, geeing-on his horse. Cars and trucks were overtaking him with only inches to spare, and still the man looked forwards, minding his own business. As if he had spent a lifetime minding his own business.

Radu recognized the man as a Căldărari. A maker of copper stills. Only Gypsies drove carts out here. And this man's cart was full of copper piping, glass bottles, distillation equipment, and round-bottomed cooking pots. The man had a thick beard and a high crowned hat and was dressed entirely in black.

With one final crazed glance over his shoulder, Radu approached the man. 'I am a Gypsy. Will you take me?'

The man stared at him. Then he twisted round and looked back down the road. The border crossing was half a kilometre ahead. 'You're bleeding.'

'I've been shot.'

'And you're tied up.'

'Yes.'

'Police?'

'No. Worse than the police.'

'Get in then.'

Radu tried and failed to throw himself onto the back of the wagon. He could gain no purchase with his arms still tied behind him.

The driver jammed his cigarette into a convenient

nook on the splashboard. Then he got down. He appeared, to Radu's eyes, to be moving in slow motion.

Where were the women? Why were they not coming for him?

The Căldărari took out a knife and cut Radu's bonds. When he saw the state of Radu's arms and back he muttered 'tcheee' to himself. He helped Radu onto the buckboard. Then he took off his coat. 'Have you your identity card?'

'No.'

The Căldărari put his coat back on again. 'Then climb under the still. I come through every day. They no longer check me anymore.'

Radu lay supine beneath the still. His shoulder had begun to hurt. Badly. So badly that he wondered if the bullet had smashed a bone. He clutched both biceps in his hands and tried to prevent the weight of them dragging his arms down to the gig's wooden floor.

The gig lurched and began to move forward.

Radu gritted his teeth. He waited for the women to throw back the copper pots and drag him out.

# 33

'He got into a cart. Driven by a Gypsy. The cart is heading through the border. We can pick him up on the other side.'

'How could you possibly lose him? What did he do? Wave his dick at you while he was pissing?'

The two sisters looked at each other. 'He told us about Aldinach and Athame.'

'What about them?'

'Sabir beat Aldinach to death with a tree branch. The other Gypsy – Alexi – the one who can throw knives. He killed Athame.'

'He told you this? And you believe him?'

'We believe him. He was too scared to make this up. He thought we were going to kill him. He was trying to buy his life from us.'

'And Lamia? Did he tell you about Lamia?'

'Aldinach killed her.'

'Good. I suppose no one killed Sabir? Or the policeman? That would be too much to hope for.'

'No. They escaped. Together with the woman who is carrying the Second Coming.'

'So tell me. You were both so gobsmacked by this

information he gave you that you let him go?'

Neither of the women answered him.

'Come on. Let's get through the border. Let's try and clean up this mess.'

'Doesn't it upset you to hear that the others are dead? Doesn't it touch you in any way? That we are the only ones of our family left?'

'Spare me the violins. We already knew the others had to be dead. The fact that your Gypsy friend dotted the i's and crossed the t's for you is neither here not there. It doesn't change anything. It just makes me more angry. More determined to skin Sabir and Calque and that little whore they're protecting, and peg them out on some convenient hillside.'

'We hit him. Twice. Once in the arm, I think, and once in the back. But these were long shots. The pistol is not powerful.'

'Bravo. Great. Perhaps he'll die of septicaemia before we can pick him up again. That would be convenient. Well done, girls. Well done all around.'

*Albescu, Moldova*
*13 November 2009*

# 34

In the seventeen years since Moldova's belated introduction of a market economy, Dracul Lupei's village of Albescu had grown into a thriving town. Albescu's civic expansion flew in the face of Moldova's actual situation during much of that period, which resembled more an economic crisis than an economic miracle. There had been rapprochements with, and alienations from, Russia. The temporary *cupon* which had replaced the *ruble* had been replaced, in its turn, by the *leu*. There had been riots. Civil wars. Breakaway republics in the form of the Turkic Gagauz and the Transnistria. Epidemics of organized crime and episodes of human trafficking. Flirtations with capitalism. Flirtations with communism. All fertile ground for the fomentation of a new religious doctrine.

Thanks to Dracul's foresight in holding his currency reserves outside the country in the form of dollars, euros, pounds, and Swiss francs, however, Albescu, in marked contrast to much of the rest of Moldova, now had factories, garages, and supermarkets. It had its own police force and its own fire brigade. Extraordinarily, it didn't have menu scams at its restaurants, as happened so often in the capital, when new menus with vastly inflated prices were substituted the moment it came time to pay. And crime rates were non-existent.

A bunch of Siberian gangsters had attempted to move in, back in 1997, and make the town their own, true – but they had mysteriously disappeared. Contrary to normal Moldovan practice, the Albescu police didn't take bribes – if an individual was unfortunate enough to get himself into trouble, a hefty donation to Dracul Lupei's Church of the Renascent Christ was usually enough to ensure both his freedom and his ticket to heaven.

The actual name of Dracul Lupei, however, had been consigned to the ashes many years before, and Mihael Catalin, meaning 'the pure gift from God', had taken its place. In the past fifteen years, Mihael – who had just celebrated his thirty-ninth birthday – felt that he had taken on many of the attributes of the man he purported to be.

His Church of the Renascent Christ encouraged clean living and humility. It also encouraged chastity for the unmarried. Mihael was considered to be a fine moral exemplar in this regard, as he had never been known to frequent women, and indeed still lived with his sister Antanasia, who, like Mary Magdalene before her, had been redeemed by her saviour from the ways of darkness. Or so it was said.

In this way Dracul/Mihael enjoyed both ends of the pleasure spectrum – the expedient reputation of still being something of a hermit, and the private joys of carnal embrace with his sister Antanasia, who had, over the years, become not only his odalisque, but also his spiritual midwife. His apostle's apostle.

When Dracul didn't want to bother himself with extraneous detail, he communicated it through Antanasia. This prevented his people from becoming tired of him. By rationing his public appearances to one Sunday a month, Dracul also ensured that his followers were gagging for him when the great moment came.

To further add to his exclusivity, Dracul had surrounded himself with what he called his 'Crusaders'. These young men – and they were all men – were tasked with carrying the word of the Risen Christ to outlying towns and villages, both in Moldova and across the border in Romania, Transnistria, and the Ukraine. Cynical souls might have viewed these men as bodyguards, but there were no cynical souls amongst Mihael's flock. One either totally believed, or one was out. And life inside Albescu was held at such a premium by people to whom $10 could mean the difference between eating and not eating that month, that utter faith was a cheap price to pay for security, protection from crime and harassment, and the guarantee of food in one's belly.

Dracul's 25 per cent rule also applied in town. In fact the figure was closer to 50 per cent for those wishing to start a business and benefit from Albescu's remarkable perquisites. Even Orthodox Christians who did not live in Albescu appreciated the presence of Dracul's Church of the Renascent Christ close by them, because, when taken concentrically – and with Albescu centre of the circle – mosques and synagogues and revivalist evangelical churches would close down in ever-increasing numbers wherever Dracul's 'Crusaders' concentrated their attention.

No one could actively pin such shutdowns on the CRC, of course. It was just coincidence that rents went up, bureaucracy increased, and schools and places of employment became more discriminating when it came to accepting those from minority religions or minority ethnic groups. The 'Crusaders' were very careful not to alienate Orthodox Christians, however, for theirs was the basket from which Mihael Catalin plucked his ripest plums.

Now in the prime of his life, Mihael had come to resemble, to a quite extraordinary degree, the TV Christ of a wildly popular Russian soap opera that had run for a number of years during the 1990s. This soap opera had succeeded where Mihael's original ministry had failed – in turning Mihael from a local star into a national celebrity.

Thousands of new believers – some from as far away as Siberia and Germany – had flocked to Mihael's banner when a documentary crew had filmed him over the course of a few weeks one summer for Russian television. The programme had somewhat fortuitously aired back-to-back with the long-running TV drama, thanks to a number of discreet cash transfers to interested parties. And Mihael's uncanny resemblance to the TV Christ – an allegedly serendipitous coincidence which Dracul had actually worked up over a period of months with Antanasia's help – was indeed extraordinary. How could a man who looked so like Christ not be Christ?

Add to that the CRC's convenient advocation of female submission to a patriarchal male blueprint – i.e. man follows God and woman follows man, and man fills woman with his spirit and woman fills man with nature, that sort of thing – and one had an equation that melded particularly well with conventional religious wisdom. The leap from Orthodoxy to Renascent Christianity was not a large one, therefore, and it was money and security that finally swung the vote. A 25 per cent tithe might seem a lot at first glance, but when one was placed in a situation where one could earn 500 per cent more than the average daily wage, feed and house one's family, and avoid government and police corruption to boot, 25 per cent no longer seemed an unreasonable price to pay.

After all, what happened to the mosques, synagogues, and temples was not so bad – these people had other places to go to, hadn't they? Other countries that would welcome them? Mihael Catalin was not advocating a pogrom, was he? He was just asking people to stand up and be counted.

Lately, Mihael had come up with a clever new idea for cementing solidarity amongst his disciples – they were all to be tattooed with a three-bar patriarchal cross on their foreheads. At first, this had caused some consternation, especially amongst the women. But Mihael had swiftly won them over.

'When Armageddon comes, you will need to be at the very epicentre of the spiritual world in order to survive it. Only my followers will be saved. The rest of the world will perish. We therefore need to be instantly recognizable – both to each other and to God. The forehead tattoo is perfect for this. It is a thing of beauty. A worthy sacrifice on the altar of vanity. Women, when your husband looks into your faces when he is making love to you, he will see the diesis that represents Christ – this will sanctify your union and make it holy. Men, when your wives look up to you when you are impregnating them, they will see the slanted crossbeam representing the balance of justice. This will reinforce God's natural order.'

So the New Messiah proclaimed. And so Dracul's followers gradually came to believe.

*Two Kilometres North of
the Romanian Border
15 November 2009*

# 35

Amoy knew they would be waiting for him. All his life he had believed in fatalism. That events were predetermined, and that prayer and supplication were pointless. He was Roma. A Căldărari. Bottom of the human shit-heap. God had made him that way for a purpose, and that purpose was to suffer.

But Amoy had outwitted God. He had made a good life for himself. Married a fine woman. He had six children. And many cousins. Slowly, he had come to realize that being bottom of the shit-heap had its advantages. Nobody paid any attention to you. You weren't worth robbing. You were invisible to most of the people you encountered in your everyday dealings. This meant that, within reason, you could make your own laws, and live life the way you wanted to live it.

Poverty was relative. You were poor, yes. But you lacked for nothing that counted. Food you could grow or steal. Accommodation you could build or requisition. Borders became fluid – because nobody wanted you, nobody troubled you. You weren't worth bribing. You were hardly even worth tormenting, as what fun was it to torment a man who already seemed broken? This was your strength. And your curse.

You knew they would be waiting for you a kilometre or two beyond the border. There were no side roads. With your wagon, and your horse, it would be impossible for you to hide. So best to face it out. If it was your moment to die, then so be it. The wounded Gypsy was your brother. He too was situated on the bottom of the shit-heap. You had recognized the despair on his face. You had seen how his enemies had bound his hands behind his back like a farmer would bind a pig he was taking to market.

When the Gypsy asked for your help you were minded to say no. And then a thought had overwhelmed you. A memory from your grandfather's time. How, during a forced march to a transit camp in Hungary, a German soldier had taken pity on your grandfather and given him a bar of chocolate for his wife and family. The German had been an older man. Not SS. The sort of man who would have managed the local post office in civilian life.

Your grandfather had bartered this chocolate for many cigarettes. Then he had bartered the cigarettes for a knife. With this knife he had killed another of his guards and escaped with his family back to Romania. Fate was a powerful thing. As was destiny. Deeds moved in circles. If the German soldier had not given your grandfather the chocolate, it might have been he who your grandfather had killed. Instead, this soldier had no doubt gone back to his village in Bavaria at the end of the war without ever knowing that another man had died in his place. Maybe he had married and had children? Fathered a dynasty? Managed a whole chain of post offices? And all for a bar of chocolate.

Yes. The car was there. With four people beside it. Two men and two women. As your horse approached them, you had ample time to sum them up.

Firstly, they were not Siberian gangsters. For this you were truly grateful. The Siberians enjoyed killing. Each had his own pick, that had been given him by a mentor. The picks gained power the more they were used. Siberians would have forced the information about the French Gypsy out of him, and then stuck him with their picks just for the hell of it.

These ones had a French registered car. So they were French gangsters. Amoy knew nothing about this variety of person. He would have to play it by ear. Also, they had women with them. Were these prostitutes? Amoy did not think so. Nobody in their right minds would pay to have sex with women such as these. One had long tresses down to her ankles and a face that would curdle milk. The other was covered in hair, like a she-wolf.

Amoy pulled up his cart. He forced himself to smile. He had spent some time in Rome as a young boy, stealing. As part of a gang run by his uncle. It was a time he was ashamed of, and which he had chosen, later on, to forget. Possessing no French, however, and supposing that these people would know no Čerhari Romani, he dredged up what little Italian he had left from the depths of his memory.

'Would you like to buy a pot? I make them myself. Recycled from copper telephone wire. Best quality.'

'Why is he talking to us in Italian? Does he think we are Italian?' It was the long-haired woman who spoke.

If Amoy did not fully understand her words, he certainly understood her meaning.

The leader ignored her. He replied in Italian. 'Get off the cart.'

Amoy climbed down. He had begun to sweat. Was this what it felt like to prepare to die? He wished, now, that he had got into the habit of prayer. Because he felt that he needed to do something – anything – to justify his life to himself and to his family.

'Where is the Gypsy? The wounded one?'

There was no point in lying. These people had seen him take the Gypsy on board his cart.

'I carried him across the border. At the first bend in the road after the border crossing, the Gypsy asked me to let him off. He was bleeding all over my pots and pans. I was happy to do this.'

Amoy watched while the remaining man and the two women checked out the back of his cart.

'There's blood in here. Plenty of it. He was hit badly. He won't get far.'

Amoy decided that they must be talking about the blood.

'Why did you take him?'

Amoy shrugged. 'He mentioned a word to me. The equivalent of making a *shpera* sign.'

'A what sign?'

'It is a secret sign to transmit information. It is only known to Gypsies. The word I am talking about acts in the same way. When it is used to a fellow Gypsy, or to a Roma, like me, it would shame his family forever if he did not respond to this. The man was injured. He needed to cross the border. Nobody looks in my cart anymore. I cross here every day. They don't even inspect my identity card. They know me. It seemed a small thing to take him across.'

'What if we kill you now?'

'That is as it may be.'

Abi stood watching the Roma. There was something about the man – some certainty – that unsettled him. Why did the man not care if he lived or died? It made no sense. But this genuinely seemed to be the case. 'Burn his cart.'

'But, Abi. It will bring the police. We don't want them in our hair when we look for Radu. He can't have got far. Not with this amount of blood-loss.'

Abi looked at the Roma. He took out his pistol. He pointed it at the Roma's head.

'Abi, for Christ's sake. There's a truck coming.'

Abi swung his pistol to the right and shot the horse through the centre of its forehead. The horse fell to its knees, its back legs splayed. Then it rocked over onto its side, jerking the wagon and making it lurch forwards. Its legs began a spasmodic kicking motion. Then they stretched out to their full extent, and fell still.

Amoy looked down at the dead horse. The mare was old. He would sell her meat to passing truck drivers and make back some of her value this way. The mare had given birth to a colt three years before, in her last year of fruitfulness. This colt was fully grown now. Amoy would hurry the colt's breaking, and use him to pull the cart from now onwards. His cousin, Stav, had a horse he could borrow while he did the breaking in – a horse he could collect his cart with. Amoy was grateful that the man with the pistol had been persuaded not to burn his cart. If it was a choice of the horse or the cart, it was better to lose the horse. Carts did not breed, even though, sometimes, they were known to cradle life in their bellies.

'Right. Let's go.'

For a moment Amoy thought the man would still shoot him out of spite. Or wound him, maybe. But once again, Amoy's poverty came to his aid. It was clear that the man thought the loss of Amoy's horse would be a terrible blow for him. And that this blow would be punishment enough.

Amoy watched the car as it accelerated back towards the border. Then he looked underneath the cart. Yes. Just as he thought. The horse's blood had disguised the dripping blood of the Gypsy, which would otherwise have been revealed for all to see when the cart jerked forward. Amoy straightened up and watched the car disappear round a bend in the road.

When he was sure that it had gone, he ducked underneath the bed of the cart and unlatched the hidden compartment he used to smuggle illicit liquor and cigarettes through the border. It was as he thought. The Gypsy inside had passed out through loss of blood.

Amoy waited for a break in the traffic. Then he dragged the Gypsy into the undergrowth at the side of the road.

Nobody slowed down on account of the dead horse. Nobody gave the pair of them a second thought. They were Gypsies.

# 36

Radu awoke in a tent. He knew it was a tent without even needing to look around. It smelled like a tent. And the light was tent-like. It reminded him of journeys he had taken with his mother and father when he had been a child.

He rolled his eyes and savoured being alive. He tried to move, but his arms were bandaged tightly to his sides. He was no longer a prisoner, that much was clear – but he might as well have been for all the chance of movement he retained.

'Hey!'

He paused for a moment to see if anyone would answer.

'Hey!'

A woman entered the tent. She raised her chin and looked at him. Then she disappeared.

Radu knew that she had gone to find her husband. That, now he was conscious, she would no longer stay alone in the tent with a strange man, however injured he might be. He waited. While he waited, he tried to sum up his position.

He had escaped from the bad people. He was in

Romania. He was injured. He was amongst friends. The bad people might now go back and find Lemma. Take their revenge out on her. Or on his cousins, Bera and Koiné. Punish him that way for escaping from them. So the first thing he had to do was to contact his family and get them away from the camp at Samois.

Then he needed to find Sabir. But he had no memory of Sabir's telephone number from the cell phone Calque had given him. He only remembered the number of the collective cell phone at Samois camp.

But he did know the name of the village Sabir was hiding in. This he had kept from the bad people by telling them, instead, about Gabor, and the bar in Sighetu. But there was no bar in Sighetu. It was simply the only town in Romania Radu remembered the name of.

Amoy took off his hat and entered the tent. He looked around, as though he was unfamiliar with the place, and then he walked the few steps towards the bed.

'I am Amoy.'

'I am Radu.'

'You speak our language?'

'I have relatives in the north of your country.'

'So you are one of us?'

'Yes.'

'Good. I am glad.'

Both men weighed each other up.

Anxiety made Radu rude. He could no longer contain himself – no longer hold back and allow his older host to dictate the flow of conversation, as, by rights, he should have. 'Do you have a telephone? I need to warn my wife and family that these people might come after them.

Now that they have lost me.'

'I have access to one. We cut into the line from the police station from time to time. We can do this, if you like, for you.'

'Thank you. And thank you for what you did for me at the border crossing.'

Amoy made a downward movement with his hand. He didn't need to respond. What he had done had been done through necessity. There were customs that governed such things. Age-old laws of hospitality. Who was he to go against them?

'How badly am I injured?'

Amoy twisted his head round. 'Maja!'

The woman came back inside the caravan. It was clear that she had been hovering outside listening to their conversation.

'He is one of us. He is part Rom. He has relatives in the north of the country.'

'Good. I am glad.'

It amused Radu that she used the same words as her husband. This was a fine woman. She had raven-black hair, and skin the colour of weathered pine. She wore eight or nine heavy necklaces wound loosely around her neck, and long golden earrings. Her blouse was of red silk, and her pleated skirt was the colour of corn cobs. She brought a scent of musk and patchouli and lavender into the caravan with her.

Radu nodded his head happily. 'Do you have many children?'

'Six.'

Radu smiled broadly. 'I want six children. My wife,

Lemma, is pregnant with our first. I am glad I am alive. This way I can have more. We were married early this summer.'

'Yes. This way you can have more. *But čhave but baxt.* Many children, much luck.' Maja watched Radu approvingly. This was a proper man. Radu had established himself as the head of a family. It was right that he had told her first of his wife and unborn child. She looked at her husband. He nodded his head. Then he turned and left the caravan.

'Your wife. She is how old?'

'Eighteen.'

'This is good. She has time for many more children. I was eighteen with my first.' Maja helped Radu sit up. She checked his bandages. 'You are not hot. You have no infection. No fever.'

'How long have I been here?'

'Three days.'

Radu could feel his face flush with fear. 'I am worried for my wife. They may go back. They may take revenge on her.'

'Amoy will organize the telephone. He will bring it in here.'

'In here?'

'Yes. It is a long line. We do this all the time. The police know, but they are scared to come here. There are many of us. There are few of them.'

'When can I move? I must go and warn my other friends.'

'You can move when you want to. But there will be a risk. And you will be weak. The first bullet tore your arm. The second bullet lodged in your back. High up on your shoulder. But it was spent. We cut it out. But you lost much blood. When you first walk you will fall. You will be very weak.'

'There is a village I need to get to. In the north of your country. I cannot tell you the name of it, or it would put you and your family in danger. How could I travel there? I cannot go in a horse and cart. There is some urgency to this if I have already been here for three days.'

'My brother. He drives trucks. If he is not going north, he will know of someone who is. We can arrange this for you.'

'How will I ever repay you for this?'

'Your wife will repay us. By having your children. This is as it should be.'

*Brara, Maramureş, Romania*
*17 November 2009*

# 37

Maja's brother's 'cousin' – known to all as 'Driver' Kol – dropped Radu off some distance outside the village. Kol's eighteen-wheeler was far too big to venture any further down the narrow, cart-friendly streets, so Radu was forced to complete the final leg of the journey under his own steam. Kol simply turned his rig round on the village football field and disappeared into the murk.

Radu picked his way through the empty, echoing lanes of Brara. He had never liked being alone – now he felt bereft and abandoned. What was he doing out here in Romania, far from his family and his people? His arms, his back, and his neck hurt, and his left shoulder had almost completely seized up. With each step he felt like falling to the ground and lying there, come what may.

The trip to Brara had meant a deviation of more than 100 kilometres from the truck's formal itinerary – but this had presented no problem to Driver Kol. He had doctored the logbook and disconnected the hubometer. Even though European law dictated that he drive no more than fifty-six hours in any one week, and a maximum of ninety hours in a fortnight, the only way to make any real money for a man owning his own rig was to expand those times by a third. If that meant driving on marijuana or Red Bull, so be it. When electronic on-board recorders became mandatory, the long-haul drivers would find a way around that, too. Or so Driver Kol had told Radu on at least six occasions during their fourteen-hour journey.

Once, because of his useless arms, Radu had had to kick Kol, who had fallen asleep at the wheel, on the calf. Kol, however, had taken the blow in good part. 'Thank you, Radu. Thank you. I am a little tired. I am seeing everything in sets of four. I would not like to wreck my truck. It is uninsured.'

Radu had felt uncharacteristically grateful when Kol had let him off at the edge of the village without insisting they both go for a farewell drink. Radu would have been duty-bound to honour Kol's wishes in this matter, even though he wanted nothing more than to find his cousins and explain to them all that had happened in the two weeks since they had been away from the camp. The way he felt now, drinking with Kol might easily have turned into an all-night affair. As well as the pain from his arms and back, Radu's head, too, ached from the noise of the lorry. The drink would have been very welcome. Too welcome. He would probably have drunk himself into a stupor and been of no use to anyone for days.

Radu breathed in the night scents of the village. Above him the stars shone in unfettered splendour. There were no street lights to spoil his view of the sky, just as there were none back at his home camp in Samois. Tears of joy trickled down Radu's face when he realized that this was the same sky that his wife, Lemma, and his sister's children, Bera and Koiné, would be sheltering under on their way out to Romania to join him. Radu offered up a prayer of thanks to O Del that his family was now safe from the bad people, and that he was, to all intents and purposes, still intact enough to anticipate their arrival.

But one immediate problem remained to be overcome. Radu had not the remotest idea where in the village Alexi and Yola were living. And the village was large and well spread out. So Radu did as he always did when he felt anxious – he switched his concentration to the sounds surrounding him. Perhaps the village would condescend to speak to him? Reveal its secrets that way?

The village's subtle clamour eddied about him in concentric circles. First came the domestic sounds – the tinkling of crockery and the gurgling of drains. Then came the rise and fall of muffled voices. After that came the animal sounds – the susurration of chickens settling in for the night, and the mutter of roosting pigeons. Then came the natural sounds – the whisper of the wind in the trees, and the distant hum of insects. Radu even fancied that he could hear the swish and whirr of the short-winged bats as they surged in predatory loops through the moonstruck sky. In the far distance, and underlying everything else, Radu was convinced that he could hear water flowing. He grinned triumphantly. The village had indeed talked to him. Gypsies loved water. He would undoubtedly find Alexi and Yola lurking nearby. He switched direction and headed instinctively for the river, no longer feeling quite so lonely.

Once Radu thought he heard wolves howling. He stopped for a second and listened. Yes. It was definitely wolves. This part of the Maramureş was indeed a strange place. He had heard stories, too, of predatory bears that would only pass you by if you pretended to be dead. Radu shivered as he imagined what it would be like to play possum with a bear nosing at your trousers, deciding whether or not to take a bite out of your rump.

Some of the houses he passed had electric lights on inside them, but Radu ignored these. Alexi would not be living in such a house. A thing like that went against nature. If Alexi was ever given a house of his own, he would probably pitch a tent in the garden and use the house to keep his animals in. And these people in the houses wouldn't know where the Gypsies lived anyway. And if they did, they wouldn't tell him. They would probably shoot him as an intruder instead, and hang him out on their garden fence like a dead crow.

When he was near the river, Radu stopped and listened again. Might the bad man and his brother and sisters have somehow worked out the name of the village from the snippets of information he had given them in the car? Radu thought back to everything he had said during the journey from Samois. No. He had only mentioned the distant town of Sighetu. And an unknown village somewhere in the north of Romania. It was impossible that they could have worked it out from that. His friends were still safe. Surely they were?

He was just about to start across the ford when he heard a noise to his left. It was the sound of a woman laughing. Radu gave a broad grin. He struck himself on the forehead with the heel of his hand to acknowledge his good luck. It was Yola's voice. She was expecting a child, just like Lemma – he could recognize this in her voice and the quality of her laughter.

Radu decided that it would please him very much to see Yola again. When Radu's brother-in-law, Flipo, brought Lemma to the village – together with Bera and Koiné and their mother, Nuelle – the three women would be able to help each other out in the run-up to the parallel births. This was a very good thing. It wasn't correct for a man to be involved in the birthing of his children. Such a thing was woman's work.

Radu screwed up his eyes. He could just make out a lighter-coloured tent, partially lit from within, pitched in the garden of a rundown house. Yes. This was where they would be.

'Yola.' Radu kept his voice low, in case Alexi or Damo or the ex-policeman might be lying in wait for him with a weapon. 'Yola.'

Yola stepped out of the tent. 'Who is that? Who is talking out here? Who is calling my name?'

'It is I. Radu.'

'Radu? What are you doing here?' Yola hesitated. 'Alexi. It is Radu. You do not need your knife.'

Alexi came out of the tent after her. Both stood squinting into the darkness.

'I am over here. Shall I come to you?'

'Are you alone?'

'Yes.'

'Then come.'

Radu walked into the circle of light thrown by the paraffin lamp Alexi and Yola were using inside their tent. He noticed that, despite Yola's pleas, Alexi was holding one of his throwing knives flat against his leg.

'I am alone, Alexi. On my oath.'

Alexi relaxed. He walked up and gave Radu a bear-hug. Radu grimaced in pain. Yola scowled and bobbed her head at Radu. Then she ducked back inside the tent.

'Help me to sit down, Alexi. I still can't use my arms properly.'

'You what?'

Yola emerged from the tent carrying a saucepan. 'Alexi. Help Radu sit down by the fire. Can't you see he has been injured? You nearly squeezed the life out of him a moment ago. Radu. I shall heat you up some of this goulash soup. The meat is good. And there is much paprika. It will give you strength. Then, when you have eaten, I will fetch Damo and Calque from the house, and you will tell us everything that has occurred. Why you have appeared amongst us – injured, without warning, and alone.'

Radu nodded his head. He allowed Alexi to help him to the ground.

Trust Yola to pick up on his anxiety. And that he was injured. And that he was pale from lack of food. Alexi wouldn't notice a duck in a hailstorm.

Nothing ever changed.

# 38

Radu, Alexi, Yola, Sabir and Calque were seated around the rekindled campfire. Radu had eaten Yola's goulash, accompanied by a plateful of *sarmale* – which is stuffed cabbage with rice, onions, and root vegetables – and *mamaliga cu brinza* – which is cornmeal porridge with sheep cheese. He had also drunk a considerable quantity of the *horinca* that Alexi kept in a glass jar outside his tent. The *horinca* was made locally every autumn in the nearby village of Rozavlea, and contained – alongside its grounding of plum mash – fruit fly larvae, worms, and the distilled essence of any insect unwise enough to venture into the fermenting tub. Alexi swore by it.

'Now you tell us why you are here, Radu. Why your arms are hurt. Why you come to us at night, without calling on the moveable phone Calque gave you. But first you tell us, are we in danger?'

Radu smiled. It was typical of Alexi and Yola to insist that he be fed first, before asking him the actual purpose of his visit. Or whether his unexpected appearance had put them all at risk.

'You are not in immediate danger. No. But bad things have happened since you left the camp. Listen without speaking. Then you must question me.'

Radu described the last five days in as much detail as he could. When he had finished he turned to the assembled company and attempted to respond to their questions. After a few tense moments he waved his good hand at them as though he were flagging down a bus. 'I think now is the time for you to stop asking questions and to start answering them. You must first of all explain to me why this is happening. It cannot be revenge. Or some sort of blood feud. These people are *payos*. They are French. Only Corsicans, Sicilians, and Maghrebins do these sorts of things in France. Or maybe I am wrong. Maybe these are Corsicans pretending to be French people? Can you explain this to me please, Captain Calque? You are the only policeman I have talked to in my whole life who is not trying to hit me over the head or put handcuffs on me.'

Calque acknowledged Radu's observations with a rueful inclination of the head. 'You are not wrong, Radu. And we certainly owe you an explanation. We have inadvertently put your family at risk, and caused you to be injured on our behalf. We are very sorry. This was not intended. The way you escaped from the Corpus was incredible. And we thank you, also, for not giving us in to them, when it might have gone easier for you if you had.'

Radu inclined his head in response. It was clear that he was gratified by Calque's encomium, and the formal language in which it was couched. 'They would still have killed me. A dead hero looks no different from a dead traitor. That is what my grandfather has told me.'

'True. Very true. But thank you nonetheless. Many would not have gone so far to protect their friends.' Calque straightened up and lit a cigarette from the fire. He squinted through the smoke at the assembled company. 'Now it is our turn to talk. There is a secret we have been keeping from you all. We thought we were doing it for everybody's good. But now it seems that we were wrong. Just as we have been wrong so many times recently.' He drew in a lungful of smoke and let it drift into the gloom behind him. 'I feel that the time has now come to bring all this out into the open. Don't you agree?' He looked first at Sabir. Then at Yola.

'Secret? What secret?' Alexi had caught the direction of Calque's gaze. He scowled at his wife. Then he switched his attention to Sabir and gave him a scowl too. 'Have you two been keeping a secret from me? I don't know of any secrets. What is this secret? Who does it concern?'

Sabir's face was lit from below by the flames from the fire. There were dark smudges beneath his eyes. His hair was unkempt. His chin was unshaven. It was some days since he had last permitted Yola to wash his clothes. It was clear to everybody that he was in mourning for something – but what, exactly, was hard to fathom. Was it for his lost love, Lamia, who might – or might not – have betrayed him? Was it for his mother, who had committed suicide knowing that her son and her husband would be the first ones on the scene to find her? Or was it for his own sanity, which had been tested beyond endurance a few weeks before in the Yucatan?

Calque had tried to pierce through Sabir's carapace on

a number of occasions in the preceding days, but he had got nowhere. Sabir was as opaque as a starred mirror – little shafts of light would reflect off him, true. But they meant nothing, disconnected, as they were, from a discernible whole.

'Sabir?'

Sabir jerked his head up from his contemplation of the fire. 'What?'

'Did you hear Alexi?'

'I heard him.'

'Then you owe him an explanation. Our silence over this matter has been putting everybody at risk. It must be clear, even to you, that this is no longer acceptable.'

Sabir nodded. 'I see that. I recognize that. I'm just working out how best to phrase it.'

'Well, I'm glad you're doing something.' Calque glanced at Yola and made a 'what if?' face.

Yola placed her hand on her heart and shook her head. Then she motioned downwards, silently indicating to Calque that he should not pressurize Sabir anymore than was strictly necessary. She knew Sabir well enough by this time to sense that he still intended to hide something from them. Something he believed might cause them pain. And that his silence covered the working out of a strategy. But Yola also knew that people only spoke when they had to. That there were lies and lies – their quality depended on the motive which lay behind them. Yola had learned the hard way not to force issues when there was no need. Sabir would enlighten them when he was good and ready. She could wait.

Sabir straightened up. He seemed completely unaware

of any hidden subtexts going on around him. 'How many of the de Bale family do we now think are dead?' His voice strengthened. 'Or, to put it another way, how many of the bastards do we reckon are left? It amounts to pretty much the same thing.'

Calque cleared his throat. Despite the change in Sabir's demeanour, he was still a little hesitant about his friend's state of mind – still a little anxious that Sabir had not grasped the full severity of their situation. 'We think there are four out of thirteen of the main group still left after their disaster with the Mexican *narcotraficantes* and their subsequent run-in with us at the old quarry. From what I can work out from Radu's description, the ones we are dealing with are Abiger, Rudra, Dakini and Nawal. There is also the Countess and her manservant, Milouins. And that secretary woman of hers – Madame Mastigou. Plus a variety of other more or less unimportant minions at the Domaine de Seyème. And the Countess's fortune, of course, which can be used to buy any number of willing accomplices. But Abiger is the real danger. He's an unpredictable son of a bitch.'

'So Abiger's twin brother is dead?'

'Vaulderie? Yes. It would appear so. Killed by the *narcotraficantes*. But you knew this, Sabir.'

Sabir ignored him. It was as if he had to work out everything afresh after a fortnight spent sleeping under the influence of unnamed soporifics. 'Abiger will hate us for that.'

'He hates us already. You may have forgotten this too, but he was preparing to have me tortured to death when the *cacique*'s men attacked their own crystal meth laboratory. I still haven't got back the full use of my shoulder. If I was required to give a Hitler salute, I wouldn't manage to get my arm much above half mast.'

Sabir smiled for the first time. 'No. I haven't forgotten. But Vaulderie's death gives Abiger a special reason to damage us.'

'You're probably right. Yes. No doubt.' Calque raised his eyebrows at Yola.

Yola gave him an even more vehement shake of the head.

This time Sabir picked up the exchange of glances between Calque and Yola. He hooded his eyes and pretended to ignore them. 'What was that you said about Moldova, Radu? About what Dakini said to her sister about Moldova, just before they were going to shoot you?'

Radu looked to the others for guidance, but no one seemed anymore certain than he was about where Sabir was heading with his questioning. 'Why is this so important, Damo? They are coming after you here. This is the place you must worry about. You are safe for now. But they will not give up looking. Maybe it takes days. Maybe it take months. But they will find you. Of that I am sure.'

Sabir shook his head. He seemed almost irritated. 'Moldova, Radu. Tell me about Moldova.'

Radu sighed. He took another sip of *horinca*. It was clear that he, too, believed that Sabir had lost control of himself – that he was no longer capable of thinking rationally in the intensity of his loss. 'Very well then.

The long-haired woman with the angry face spoke to the other woman – the hairy one – and said, "And so? We are ten hours driving time away from Moldova. Away from what Madame, our mother, ordered us to do."'

'Those were the exact words she used?'

'The exact words. Yes. I remember everything she said – each word is seared into my memory as if it was burned there by a brand from this fire. All the time we were in the car I thought they were going to kill me. To torture me, like they tortured Babel. To take me away from the world. From Lemma. From my unborn child. So I focused on these people and what they said like a frightened dog focuses on the man who intends to strike him.' Radu see-sawed his head as if he was trying to rid himself of his memories. 'But what importance has Moldova? I do not understand. This is another thing entirely. Surely it is?'

'No, it isn't, Radu.' Sabir made a cutting motion with his hand, as if he were ridding it of water. 'Moldova is not another thing entirely.' He raised his head and fixed each person around the fire with his haunted gaze. 'It is the main thing. For it is the place where, in a moment of unforgivable weakness, I told my death bride, Lamia de Bale, that the man who will become the Third Antichrist might be found.'

# 39

The church clock struck four. Despite the warmth given off by the fire, Yola had long since been forced to fetch extra blankets for everyone so that they could insulate themselves against the deep autumn chill. The first snows of the season might not yet have arrived in the Maramureş, but they would not be long in coming.

Alexi threw off his blanket and crossed himself with an extravagant, throw-away gesture. He had been feeding the fire with dry sticks throughout the night, and feeding *horinca* to himself and Radu at the same time. Both men were now rocking on the spot like old women. 'This is impossible. How can a child of mine be the Second Coming? Am I then the Holy Spirit? Or the Angel...' He hesitated, a vacant expression on his face.

Calque rolled his eyes. 'Gabriel.'

Alexi punched himself on the palm of his hand. 'Gabriel. Gabriel. Do I look like this Gabriel to you?'

It was at least the fifth time in the last few hours that Alexi had used those exact words, and ended on the same dying fall. Before then he had somehow managed to convince himself that the Corpus had been pursuing him and Yola purely for purposes of revenge.

Riding shotgun to this flight of fancy had been the idea that, before his untimely death, Achor Bale might, for some obscure reason, have felt constrained to admit to his brothers and sisters how a certain Manouche Gypsy – Alexi Dufontaine by name – had singlehandedly hijacked him at the Black Virgin's shrine at Rocamadour, courageously depriving him of both his pistol and his wallet. And this despite the fact that the hijacking had cost Alexi two cracked ribs, a fractured jaw, and various of his teeth, which had needed to be replaced with a number of handsome, if expensive, gold implants – implants which Adam Sabir had generously funded from the unlimited stash of dollars that Alexi fondly imagined all Americans held at their disposal.

It was becoming clear to everyone that Alexi – vainglorious at the best of times – had felt considerably more comfortable fantasizing that the Corpus might want him dead too, and not simply be targeting his pregnant wife to the exclusion of other, no doubt equally culpable, parties. To discover that he was to be the father of the Parousia, and, in consequence, a mere third down the list of the Corpus's intended targets, constituted a step too far. It didn't tie in with Alexi's self-image at all.

'In addition, if the Corpus knew that I, Alexi Dufontaine, had killed their dwarfish sister...' He hesitated again, flailing around for a name.

'Athame.'

'... Athame, with my throwing knife. They would not be quite so happy.'

Radu jerked out of his doze like a man who has just caught himself stumbling off a kerb during the course of a daydream. 'But they do know, Alexi.' Radu's voice was slurred from the *horinca*, so that the x in Alexi's name came out as a double ess. 'They do know because I told them. When I was trying to work out how to escape.' Radu barely managed to finish his sentence before his eyes closed and he lurched forwards again. He had been catnapping for some time now. This time he managed to achieve the full monty, as it were, on the hoof.

'Ha!' Alexi narrowed his eyes. He swept his index finger in a dramatic semi-circle around the fire. 'Ha! You hear what Radu says? This is why they mean to kill us. I knew it. Well, I will wait for them here with my knives. No one will get past me. I will be like John Wayne at the Alamo.'

Sabir gave an infinitesimal sigh. 'But he died, Alexi.'

'What? What's that?'

'At the Alamo. John Wayne died. In fact all the Texians died. Davy Crockett. Jim Bowie. Sam Houston. Even the film died. Christ, even the remake died.'

Alexi did a swift double take. He had become so unused to Sabir grasping the conversational initiative in the past few weeks that for a moment it left him speechless. 'Then I, too, will die. This will make of me a legend. Gypsies will speak of me...' Alexi tried to work something out in his head – '... many years from now.'

Sabir groaned. He, like Radu, was perilously close to exhaustion – but in his case without the aid of alcohol. He had tried to explain everything to the others as best he could, but the traumas of the past few weeks had taken a fearful toll on him. Guilt, at not coming clean to Alexi about the possible significance of his child, and further guilt at withholding details of the Third Antichrist from everybody bar the one person he should have withheld it from – his lover, Lamia – had compounded the issue. The fact that the Corpus knew the Antichrist's whereabouts clearly confirmed Lamia's betrayal. There was no room anymore for doubt. Radu was the living proof of that. Sabir had to accept the fact that Lamia had played him for a sucker and move on.

And yet. Lamia had given her life for him, hadn't she? How did one account for it? Could someone love you at the very same time as they betrayed you? Was that possible? Maybe Lamia's decision to throw herself in the way of the knife had simply been an instinctual mistake? Or had she really loved him after all?

Sabir dragged both hands down his face. He couldn't go on in this way. It was making him ill. He had to do something – anything – to clear the logjam.

Calque glanced across the fire at his friend. It was clear that Sabir was suffering the torments of the damned. Calque decided that now was the ideal time to step in and encapsulate the position they found themselves in, much as he'd done for the Halach Uinic and Ixtab following their communal, hallucinogen-induced dream journey in the Mayan *temazcal* sweat lodge a few weeks earlier. This time, however, he had a crucial new piece of information at his disposal.

'Alexi. Yola. Radu. Listen up. It is best we get this thing out into the open. Sabir. Don't you wander off on me. You're next on the list of speakers.'

Sabir was gazing into the fire with his head in his hands. He didn't look up.

Calque curbed his frustration. He had already made up his mind to play things as if he were lecturing his subordinates at the precinct on their duties for the coming week – something he had done every working Monday for the past twenty years. This, he felt, was the only sensible way to avoid presenting a disunited front to the enemy. He would therefore ignore Sabir's lowering presence, and forge on with his plan.

'Right. It must be obvious to everybody that we are all now a part of something far bigger than ourselves. Something that has been lost and simmering for 450 years. Something that, to most normal people, would seem like a bad dream.' Calque raised his eyebrows like a Marine Corps Sergeant Major. Yola seemed to be the only one giving him her full attention. Calque soldiered on regardless. 'What we are in fact experiencing is the culmination of an age-old process that no one person fully understands. That no one really ought to understand. But one which has already resulted in a plethora of deaths. All that matters now is that we recognize the forces ranged against us, and do our best to try and avoid them. That much we can do. That much is clear.'

Alexi swooped into view again. 'Yes, policeman. Yes. But tell me. Tell me about these forces ranged against us. These forces that, according to you, we must run away from.'

Calque rolled his eyes. There were times when Alexi reminded him of Cyrano de Bergerac just before the Siege of Arras. Bumptious. And a master of the bloody obvious. 'We know for a fact that our enemies, the de

Bales, are sworn to protect the world from the Devil. This is their ancient gage. This is why they were made peers of France during the reign of St Louis. The only problem is that their way of fulfilling this gage doesn't quite tally with the ways of the modern world – and neither does it tally with what passes for rational thought in the Calque household.' Calque hesitated, belatedly aware that there was no Calque household left to speak of – only him. His wife and daughter had long ago decamped to pastures new. He determined to soldier on regardless. 'The de Bales are iconoclasts. Throwbacks to the horrors of the Inquisition. Nowadays, their mode of behaviour just doesn't make sense.'

'This is true. This is very true.' Alexi hesitated. 'How doesn't it make sense?'

'Look. I'll clarify things for you, Alexi. The Corpus believe that only by placating the Devil – that is, by supporting his final earthly representative, the Third Antichrist (the first two being Napoleon and Hitler, according to Nostradamus) – can the Devil be seduced into allowing the world to play out its own manifest destiny. Once the Devil himself is tempted to intervene – once he loses patience with the machinations of his henchmen, the Antichrists, in other words – we are doomed to Armageddon. Preceded, or so we are told in the Bible, by a thousand-year Reign of Terror. It will feel as if we are caught in the middle of an electrical storm – but with no let-up and with no foreseeable end. Hardly a pleasant prospect.'

'Do you believe this, policeman?'

'Of course I don't. But the de Bales believe it. That's the important thing.'

'Then who do they think is strong enough to stand against the Antichrist? Who can weaken him? Not us, surely?'

'To the de Bales way of thinking, the only palpable threat to the Third Antichrist is via the Second Coming, and the influence for good that the Second Coming will have on the world. Because the Antichrist is the evil mirror image of Christ – Christ's dark shadow, the *antimimon pneuma,* the counterfeit spirit, or what have you – only a true representation of Christ, ergo the Son of God, ergo the Parousia, ergo the Second Coming, can possibly hope to overcome him. The Corpus Maleficus can't afford to let that happen, because then they will have failed in their sworn duty to the French Crown.'

'Yes. Yes. I see it clearly. Can this not be explained to them? That the way they are thinking is wrong?'

Calque let out a ragged sigh. 'Are you going to try it, Alexi? Please. Be my guest. I'll even introduce you to the Countess myself.'

Alexi rocked his head from side to side. He had clearly reached tipping point. It was time to pay the piper for the vast quantities of *horinca* he had been imbibing since Radu's arrival.

Yola glanced at her husband out of the corners of her eyes. She gestured anxiously for Calque to continue.

'As Radu says, these people now have a blood feud with us. They are out for revenge.'

'They are evil, that is why. They need to be stopped.' Alexi had yet again succeeded in pulling himself back from the brink. He made a face, as of a man unexpectedly forced to confront the reality of his own body odour.

'Cannot the police do something about them?'

A twitch appeared above Calque's right eye. The idea of Alexi Dufontaine blithely calling on the French police to pull his nuts out of the fire was comical in the extreme. 'For that you need proof of intent, Alexi. And the Corpus cover their tracks awesomely well. If it wasn't for their mistake in Mexico with the *narcotraficantes*, we would all be dead by now.' He glanced across the fire. 'Yola and her unborn baby too. We were handed an absurdly lucky break. We can't count on that happening in the future.' He retrieved a burning brand from the flames and lit his umpteenth cigarette of the night. He squinted at Sabir through the smoke. 'The crazy thing is that the Corpus still think of themselves as the good guys. That whatever they need to do to keep the Devil at bay is justified within the greater scheme of things. All the rest is irrelevant to them.'

Sabir gave a twisted laugh. 'The good guys. Jesus.'

All eyes turned towards him.

Calque hesitated, imagining for a moment that Sabir might be about to speak. But it was a false alarm. 'Yes. If you take the Bible literally, this crazy belief of theirs makes some kind of sense. The Devil in this scenario becomes God's evil brother – and the Antichrist bears the exact same relationship to Christ. The one, in both cases, presupposes the existence of the other. Both elements – good and evil – are crucial to the furtherance of humanity. The Antichrist is therefore Christ's dark shadow or mirror image, and can only be overcome by his opposite number, and vice versa. Anyone that gets in the way of that is expendable. That's the Corpus's shtick. That's their bottom line.'

Calque adjusted the blanket across his shoulders. He accepted a mug of coffee from Yola. She had been listening intently to the conversation over the past few hours, but had chosen not to speak. Calque assumed that this was because of some ingrained Gypsy disparity between men and women. Sabir had endeavoured to explain the subtleties of Gypsy sexual politics to him some months before, but Calque still failed to grasp the hidden dynamic between the sexes. It came as a pleasant surprise, then, when Yola squatted down near the fire and seized the initiative. Calque had a healthy respect for Yola's intelligence. Of all of them, it was she who saw the clearest.

'Damo. Look at me.'

Sabir raised his head. Yola was the only person alive who could be guaranteed to lure him away from a too solipsistic descent into morbid self-analysis.

'You still haven't explained this new Antichrist figure to us. Why Moldova? What do you know that we don't? If this person is a danger to me and to my child, I must know about him.'

Sabir squared his coffee mug precisely onto the ground. He gave a slow nod. His face had taken on a corpse's pallor so that, in the firelight's refulgence, he resembled nothing so much as a dead man talking. 'Yes, Yola. You are right. You have been very patient. Let me tell you about this man.' He was looking at Yola but his eyes were vacant, turned inwards, almost, as if he were communing, not with those around him, but with some internal demon of his own making. 'But there will come a time, I think – and sooner rather than later – when you will pray that I hadn't.'

# 40

Sabir shook himself like a horse emerging from the sea. Then he dragged a series of ragged breaths into his lungs. The sight seemed to mesmerize everybody. It was as if they were watching a freshly buried cadaver emerging from its grave. The return of the zombie.

When Sabir was satisfied that he had stirred himself into something resembling normality, he turned to Calque. 'Do you remember asking me the same question Yola just asked me, but way back in May? When I was laid up in hospital following my tangle with Achor Bale?'

Calque knew that he needed to keep Sabir focused – knew that he needed to make him feel part of the group again, and not merely a rogue satellite orbiting around it. 'Yes. I remember it clearly. You told me a lot back then. But you refused point blank to tell me about either the Second Coming or the Third Antichrist. I'm glad you've changed your mind now. I think it's very much the right thing to do in the circumstances.'

The praise washed right over Sabir's head. In recent weeks it was as if he was only able to concentrate on one thing at a time. 'Do you remember exactly what I said?'

'Of course. That you'd isolated the three key

Nostradamus prophecies by default. And that these were the ones you thought the de Bales were searching for. One prophecy described the Third Antichrist – the "one still to come" – the one Nostradamus describes as the man who will bring the world to the abyss. Another prophecy described the Second Coming, and his birth via a descendant of the Gypsy woman to whom Nostradamus had vouchsafed the prophecies for safekeeping. And the third described the location of a new visionary who would either confirm or deny the date of the world's possible Armageddon – that this person would somehow obtain a glimpse into the future and channel the information that he saw there. That only this person could tell us what awaits mankind – regeneration or apocalypse.'

Calque heard himself mouthing these words with a certain astonishment. What in God's name had managed to transform him from the cynical, rationalist, world-weary policeman he had been six months before, to a man who now believed that outcomes could be preordained, apocalypses avoided, and Armageddon contained via a process of cosy communal transcendence? Maybe his Commandant had been right to welcome his early retirement? Calque had a sudden nightmare image of the entire criminal fraternity of Paris chortling in glee while he stood above them, clad only in laurel wreath and Druid's cape like Getafix, in the *Astérix* books, and waving a hawthorn branch.

'Anything else?'

'Yes. Plenty.' Calque dragged his attention back to the matter at hand. 'You were surprisingly voluble, as I recall, at the time. Unlike recently.' Calque cleared his throat. He hardly dared look at Yola. He knew that she would be watching him like a hawk. That she would be reminding him with her eyes how carefully he needed to tread with Sabir.

How did Sabir manage it, Calque thought to himself? First it was Lamia, endlessly fighting his corner and seeing that no one overstepped the mark with her lover – even to the extent of taking a fatal knife blow for him. And now here was Yola, mothering him again, and riding shotgun for the damned fool. Did these women sense something about Sabir that he, Calque, did not? Perhaps they were unconsciously compensating for Sabir's tragic relationship with his own mother, who had first disconnected from him and his father through the fragility of her mental health, and then disconnected from the rest of the world through suicide? Or maybe it was because the bastard was so good-looking? What had Lamia called him? A mixture between Gary Cooper and Dean Martin. Christ Jesus. There were moments – and this was one of them – when Calque was tempted to hold up two fingers to the lot of them, and trudge back towards France and the joys of bourgeois rectitude.

'You then told me that mankind's survival will ultimately depend on whether or not we are prepared to acknowledge the Second Coming. Recognize him universally. As an exemplar, and not as a representative of any religion. See him as something beyond dogma, in other words – as a universal blessing. You told me that Nostradamus appeared to believe that only by bringing the world together – in the communal, nondenominational worship of one universal entity – might we be saved.'

'And?'

'And what?'

'What else did you ask me?'

Calque felt like a pot about to boil over. By a sheer process of will he forced all negative thoughts from his mind. If Sabir wanted him to play along with his little games, he would do so. The accounting could come later. 'I asked you about the Third Antichrist. Who he was.'

'And what did I answer?'

'I can't remember your exact words. But you said something like "The Third Antichrist is with us now. He was born under the number seven. Ten seven ten seven. He has the name of the Great Whore. He already holds high office. He will hold higher. His numerological number is one, indicating ruthlessness and an obsessive desire for power. Nostradamus calls him the 'scorpion ascending'." Yes. That's what you said. Maybe not down to the very last comma and full stop, but close. I remember answering "But that is nothing." And you said "Oh, but it is." Then I said "So you know his name?" You answered "Yes. And so do you." Then I reminded you that I was a detective. That numerology wasn't an entirely alien concept to me. That I would try to work his name out despite your intransigence. And you said you expected nothing less of me.'

'And did you? Work it out, I mean?'

'No. I couldn't do it. I didn't see to whom it might relate. For a while I thought you might be referring to Russia's Vladimir Putin. I really thought I had something there. His name for a start. *Putain* means whore in French. So that gave me the Great Whore. I then checked out his birth date – 7 October 1952. That's Sun in Libra with "Scorpio ascending". Just as you said. And the "ten seven ten seven" bit worked too, as his birthday fell on the tenth month, October, and the seventh day of that month – that's the first ten seven – of a year that numerologically adds up to ten and seven too, via one and nine equalling ten, and five and two equalling seven. That's ten seven again. I was pretty sure I was right by this time, especially as Putin already held "high office", in the sense of being the Russian Prime Minister, and seemed likely to "hold higher" – in the sense of a third Russian Presidency – if he managed, as seemed likely, to persuade the Duma to increase the number of terms one man was allowed to hold the top job. Plus the next Russian presidential election is due in 2012. It all fit together quite beautifully.'

'That's impressive, Calque.'

'Thank you, Sabir. That's very gracious of you.' Calque surreptitiously crossed his fingers in his lap. 'I then did a numerological study on Putin's name. Imagine my delight when I realized that the numerological value of his name did indeed add up to the "number one", just as you had suggested in the clues you gave me. I can still remember the sums I did, with V being six, L being three, A being one, D being four, I being one, M being four, I being one, and R being two, making a first total of twenty-two. Then you have P equalling eight, U equalling six, T equalling four, I equalling one, and N equalling five, making a second total of twenty-four.

Add the two names together and you have two and two from twenty-two makes four, and two and four from twenty-four makes six. Add four and six together and you have ten. And ten is one plus zero which equals one in Cagliostro's numerological system. It all seemed as clear as day.' Calque was briefly tempted to burst out laughing at his pathetic attempt at intellectual slickness.

'So you think Vladimir Putin is the Third Antichrist?'

'Of course I bloody well don't. A few minutes rational thought, after the heady excitement of the chase, persuaded me of the absurdity of that idea. Putin is single-minded, yes. He may even be a bit of a megalomaniac. But by no stretch of the imagination is he an Antichrist. I can't see him flipping the nuclear button on an unsuspecting West and bringing destruction down on his own head and that of the country he loves. He's far too pragmatic for that. Heck, I'd probably even like the man if I met him. Plus he knows that he doesn't need to engage in conventional warfare. He simply needs to grab half the Arctic Circle and then hold the rest of the world to ransom over the resources it contains. The man clearly intends to make Russia the Saudi Arabia of the West. Not another North Korea or an Iran.'

'So where does that leave us?'

'You tell me. You're the one asking about Moldova. Who is there in Moldova? It's the poorest country in Europe bar none. What can it possibly produce that's a threat to anyone? Contagious poverty?'

'No, Calque. Not contagious poverty. There are far worse contagions than that. Have you ever heard of a man called Mihael Catalin?'

Calque frowned down at his damaged shoulder – one could almost hear the cogwheels turning inside his head. After a long pause he met Sabir's eyes and gave a hesitant nod. 'Yes. I've heard the name. I believe you're talking about that maniac with his own religious cult. The one they claim is poaching adherents from both sides of the Catholic divide. Am I right?'

'The "maniac" with his own town, yes – with his own mini Luxembourg. The same "maniac" who has cleared away all competition from hundreds of square miles of otherwise sovereign territory. Listen to me, Calque. There isn't a single mosque, a single synagogue, a single evangelical church left anywhere this guy's so-called "Crusaders" have visited. This "maniac", as you call him, breeds disciples like ringworm. He is even managing to lure people away from the formerly impregnable Islam. People are risking apostasy to join him, man. They are risking hell. He's that convincing.'

'That doesn't make him the Antichrist.'

'Maybe not. But do you remember "ten seven ten seven"? The numbers you ascribed to Vladimir Putin? Well Catalin was born on 7 October 1970. So, like Putin, he ticks both that box and that of the "Scorpion Ascending".'

'That's nothing. Sheer coincidence.'

'Listen to this, then. Catalin's Roman namesake, Lucius Sergius Catilina, was known as the "Great Whore" by his arch-enemy, Cicero. After sliding out from under a prosecution for extortion in 65BC (Cicero's brother Quintus claimed that Catilina "left the court as poor as some of the judges had been before his trial"),

Catilina then engaged in open rebellion against the Roman State ("I will put out my own fire through the general destruction of all"). The Catiline conspiracy forced the Senate to issue a *senatus consultum ultimum* against him, which led directly to Catilina's death in battle. Before his death, it had been an open secret that Catilina had once drunk the blood of a sacrificed child, and had been subject to the most depraved of vices and lusts. Later, when the Book of Revelation talks of the Whore of Babylon, it is to the decadent Roman Republic, as encapsulated by Lucius Sergius Catilina, that it is allegorically referring. Both Romania and Moldova are Latin countries, Calque. Even the language owes more to Latin than it does to either the Cyrillic or the Azbuka.'

'Go on, Sabir. There's more, isn't there? There had better be.'

'Oh yes. There's more. At the same time as he is evangelizing already committed Christians, Catalin is seeking to convince the as-yet-uncommitted that 21 December 2012 is going to mark the actual day of the Rapture – the day when God's chosen people will be translated up to Heaven to sit at their Master's right hand. What's more he claims that if there are any haverers out there who still want to jump onto the bandwagon, they'd better put a spring in their step and sign up with him. Sharpish.'

'But this man is crazy, Sabir. One of many. History is littered with cult leaders and religious megalomaniacs who gull the simple-minded into following them. Look at Charles Manson, Shoko Asahara, Jim Jones – these people were past masters at mind control.'

'Yes, but none of them was elected a senator in his own country, as Catalin has been. At the rate he's going, there's a fair chance Catalin will make President if Moldova holds further snap elections in 2011. There have been two elections this year already, and a succession of bloody riots which the government famously called "an attempted coup d'état". The whole place is a volcano ready to erupt. If new elections do happen, any incoming President will have an immediate standing army of 15,000 men at his command – each of whom already holds a grudge against the rest of Europe for slowing up Moldova's entry into the European Union. Transform that army into "Catalin's Crusaders" and you've got one heck of a problem on your hands.' Sabir paused for breath. His face was covered in a sheen of sweat. 'Listen. Adolf Hitler needed just one lucky election to lock himself into power for a generation. What do you think is going to happen when a man like Mihael Catalin gains total control of his country's means of communication? A country dangerously close to the geographical centre of Europe? That's on the fault line between East and West? What effect do you think a man who maintains he is the Second Coming of Christ could have on a country of three and a half million people with a poverty rate of more than 50 per cent, and which is still largely run by gangsters?'

There was silence around the fire. Dawn was breaking on the distant horizon. The sky was tinged an angry pink, as if blood and rainwater were somehow mixed. Alexi had collapsed sideways and was snoring lightly, one hand thrown casually across his face. Radu had rocked forwards at the waist as if he were attempting some advanced yoga posture. His eyes were closed and his mouth was open. A filament of saliva was pooling onto one knee.

'Look at the horizon, Calque. You too, Yola. Doesn't it remind you of something?'

Calque frowned. Then he shrugged. 'The sky is the sky. It reminds me of nothing but itself. What does it remind you of, Sabir?'

Sabir's gaze grew distant. It was as if he were returning inside himself and reliving what had happened in Mexico – the horrendous visions he had seen whilst under the influence of datura in the Maya sweat lodge. 'It reminds me of one of Nostradamus's greatest quatrains. The one which goes:

*The Third Antichrist will soon be annihilated*
*His bloody war will have lasted twenty-seven years*
*The heretics are either dead, captive, or exiled*
*Human blood reddens the water that*
*covers the earth in hail.'*

Yola leaned forwards, her face intent. 'But the quatrain says that the Third Antichrist will soon be annihilated, Damo. That he won't win. That his followers – the heretics – will either be killed, captured, or exiled.'

Calque cut in. His expression was sombre. 'You're right, Yola. That's what it says. But only after "a war lasting twenty-seven years".' Calque teased a wooden spill from the fire and lit himself another cigarette. 'Let's put that into perspective, shall we? The Second World

War lasted six years and cost sixty million lives. What if we multiply that combat period by a factor of five? Then throw in nuclear devices. What are we talking about then? Three hundred million dead? Four hundred million?' Calque sucked on his cigarette, letting the smoke trickle out through half-opened lips. 'The Bible tells us that each fresh Antichrist is set to be exponentially worse than the last. As we know, the First Antichrist, Napoleon Bonaparte, was directly responsible for more than three million deaths. The Second Antichrist, Adolf Hitler, for upwards of thirty million. Now look at present-day Europe. It's an ethnic tinderbox in comparison with what it was even in the 1930s. This time we have Moslem, Jew, Christian, atheist and pagan all at each other's throats – and all with markedly differing agendas. Half of them don't even speak each other's language anymore, making rational communication well-nigh impossible. And each vested interest is jostling for a diminishing amount of real estate – and a diminishing share of the communal pot. What do you think this Catalin person might achieve if he became President? What sort of unholy schisms could he create?'

'Tell me. Please.' Yola's eyes were wide. She had never heard Calque on one of his intellectual jags before. His off-the-cuff historical riffing seemed to mesmerize her.

'He could set Russia and the Western Alliance at loggerheads via a putsch on Transnistria for a start. Or he could trigger a conflict with the Islamic world by influencing neighbouring countries like Romania, Hungary, Bulgaria, Macedonia, Serbia, Montenegro, Albania, and the Ukraine to turn round and eject their

Muslim minorities. People always like a scapegoat – it saves them from having to think for themselves. That's what Hitler counted on with the Jews. It worked for him. And it could work again. Or he could simply set the Churches against each other. People kill for religion more readily than they kill for any other reason. It's a classic paradox. Most dogmas exhort their followers to be peaceful. And at the same time the priests and mullahs who translate those dogmas tell their followers that they must be prepared to die for their faith, and, if necessary, to kill others in defence of it. *In extremis* only, of course. And with the best of all possible intentions.'

Yola stared from one man to the other. 'But I still don't understand. If this man has all the power you say he has – or will have – what can the Corpus possibly offer him?'

Sabir smiled. 'In a nutshell, Yola? The key to gain that power. And the most pernicious of all commodities. Money.'

*Odessa, Ukraine*
*18 November 2009*

# 41
___

Odessa looked like exactly what it was – a formerly rich town fallen on hard times. The buildings were elegant but dishevelled, as if a thin film of dust had descended over everything some years before, and now the metropolis was patiently waiting for a gust of wind to blow off the dust and reveal the wonders concealed beneath. The cars were serviceable but old-fashioned. The shops were neat, modest, but understocked. The women, however, were magnificent. Milouins watched a blonde goddess sashaying past his taxi window. She was dressed in a blue denim micro-skirt, no stockings (she didn't need them), and powder-blue suede ankle-boots with pyramid heels. Privately, he promised himself a whore that evening – a blonde whore with never-ending legs, just like the blonde goddess he had seen pass by. God, how he would make her squeal.

Hervé Milouins had worked for the de Bale family for nearly thirty years now. He had started, aged sixteen, as a trainee gamekeeper on the late Count's Loire estate. Milouins's father had worked for the Count after the war as chauffeur-cum-valet, and his grandfather had been woodsman on the estate from the 1920s to the 1940s.

Both men had died unexpectedly. Milouins's grandfather as a result of a rogue tree that had corkscrewed during woodland clearing, and Milouins's father in the process of saving the Count from an attempt on his life by elements of the OAS – France's illegal Secret Army Organization – whom the Count had alienated after the total withdrawal of his financial support following their botched assassination attempt on President de Gaulle in 1963.

Milouins's mother, Mireille, had continued the family tradition of service to the de Bales as the Countess's dressmaker and seamstress until her death from stomach cancer, aged sixty-nine, eight years before. His mother's privileged position in the de Bale household, and the fact of his father's personal sacrifice, had ensured that Milouins received special attention from the Count from an early age.

Following his military service, the Count had sent Milouins off to a dojo in Japan to perfect the art of unarmed combat. Milouins had become, in consequence, a red belt at both judo and karate and a black belt at tae kwon do, disciplines which he had kept up assiduously ever since. He had graduated to become the Count's bodyguard, aged just twenty-three, and, now that the Count was dead, he was fulfilling the same role for the Countess.

Over his many years of devoted service, Milouins had developed certain opinions about the Countess's adopted children, which did not necessarily tally with those of his mistress. He had even been party to the actual arrival of the children into the de Bale household. Firstly Rocha, who had been adopted as a teenager. Then Abiger and the rest of the rabble.

Milouins was privately convinced that the Countess had been wrong in farming the children out from such an early age into other people's hands. In this way, in his opinion, she had lost the children's affection, whilst securing the lesser asset of their undoubted respect. But he both sympathized with and understood the Countess's motivation. Her relationship with Madame Mastigou had to be kept secret at all costs, and this Milouins had ensured to the best of his ability over the years. It simply wouldn't have done for the Countess's private predilections ever to receive a public airing. Within the conservative – not to say reactionary – circles in which the Countess conducted the more visible aspects of her life, such a thing would have been tantamount to social suicide. Tolerance of a sort existed in those spheres – but it was a tolerance fuelled by the most exquisite discretion.

Milouins had decided very early on that the Count and Countess's eldest adopted son, Rocha de Bale – later to be known as Achor Bale – was a loose cannon verging on the psychopathic. It wasn't Milouins's place to comment on such things, but when Bale had been killed by Adam Sabir earlier that summer in the Camargue, Milouins had heaved a metaphorical sigh of relief that a potentially rogue element in the de Bale family – and one who had single-handedly condemned his mistress and her entourage to the attentions of the French police – was formally out of the picture.

The ensuing deaths of a further eight of Bale's siblings

in Mexico and France had been an unmitigated disaster. If Milouins had been a religious man, he might have suspected that God was trying to tell the Countess something, and that she was resolutely failing to listen. The only shaft of daylight had occurred when Milouins learned that Abiger de Bale had also managed to get himself killed somewhere in the Yucatan. Abiger, and his twin brother, Vaulderie, had been the banes of Milouins's life. Abiger, in particular, was permanently attempting to ingratiate himself with the Countess at the expense of anyone who happened in his way. Abiger's inheritance of all the Count's titles, following the death of Rocha, had simply made Milouins's position even more diplomatically complicated.

Privately, Milouins had always suspected that Abiger's heart had not been 100 per cent in the Corpus's work. It was clear that the man was far more interested in money and in the appurtenances of class than in any furtherance of the Corpus's aims. Milouins, himself of peasant stock, didn't have much time for class. The Countess and Madame Mastigou accepted him for what he was – a man of the people, with certain useful skills, who was, in consequence, accorded the status of a privileged servant. Such a quality of acknowledgement and accreditation satisfied Milouins, whose nature made it imperative that he work for somebody and be told what to do. But Abiger de Bale had always refused to play by the rules.

To Abiger, Milouins was his mother's footman, and would always be treated as such. Since his teens, Abiger had made it a point to humiliate Milouins whenever and wherever possible. There had been moments when the Countess had protested at Abiger's treatment of her manservant, but such moments had not fundamentally altered Abiger's behaviour.

So the prospect of Abiger's death in Mexico had delighted Milouins. Rudra de Bale, who would have been next in line to inherit the Countship and Marquisate, was a different prospect altogether. Rudra was manipulable. Insecure. Subdominant. A definite beta male. Whilst Abiger was an alpha of the first degree.

Abiger's sudden reappearance ten days before had at first disappointed Milouins, and then delighted him. The fact that he had caught Abiger breaking into the inner sanctum of the Countess's bedroom had been one of the highlights of Milouins's life. Surely the Countess would order Abiger killed? It was clear that the man had been up to no good. He'd admitted as much himself, when he had described how he had covered his tracks in Mexico and the US. In Milouins's opinion, innocent men didn't need to do such things. If he had really tried, but failed, to save his siblings from the cenote, surely he would have headed straight home to inform his mother?

Milouins didn't believe for one instant that Abiger had been chased the length and breadth of Mexico by a vengeful gang of *narcotraficantes*. No. Milouins was privately convinced that Abiger, imagining the rest of his siblings to be dead, had come back to France to kill the Countess and inherit her wealth. Why else would he have covered his tracks so fastidiously? Milouins had some vague notion of what the Countess was worth, and it was a considerable sum of money. More than enough to kill for.

Milouins still couldn't fathom, though, why he had not been able to find a weapon of any sort on Abiger's person. What had Abiger intended to do? Stifle her with a pillow? There were always marks and tell-tale signs after such a suffocation, surely. Was there anything in the bedroom, then, that he could have used and that would leave no clue? Milouins had ruminated on this for days. There was nothing. Nothing that would leave no tell-tale signs. What then? What had the man been intending to do? For he certainly hadn't been intending to conduct a simple tête-à-tête with his mother at three o'clock in the morning, as he so vehemently maintained. Anyone knowing the Countess even slightly would have realized that such a plan was doomed from the start. The Countess would simply have ordered Abiger out of her room and told him to approach her again at midday, when she formally emerged into public view.

And then, on top of that, the bastard had somehow managed to talk himself out once again from under the guillotine – at least vis-à-vis his remaining siblings – with his bullshit story about the Mexican gangsters and his heroic sacrifice on behalf of his family. Milouins had stood by the door, while Abiger had been concocting his story, convinced that the Countess and Madame Mastigou and the survivors from the cenote would see right through it, just as he did. But the Countess was an elderly lady now. And she had been badly hit by the death of her children. She didn't show this vulnerable side of her character to everybody, but Milouins knew that it was there.

So Abiger had inveigled himself back into everyone's

good graces, and was running the show once again. But Milouins wasn't fooled by him. Thank God, then, that the Countess had decided to take him off formal bodyguard duties and use him more proactively. This, Milouins felt, might afford him the very opportunity he needed to get the goods on the miscreant, Abiger.

The Countess, after all, was his responsibility and his alone. The Count had made that quite clear when he had called Milouins to his deathbed and delivered his final instructions. Milouins had sworn an oath to the Count that he would put the protection of the Countess ahead of anything in his life – marriage and a family of his own, for instance. That he would sacrifice his own future, if necessary, to protect her, and through her, the de Bale family name. One of the Count's final acts had been to ensure that a considerable sum of money be transferred to a private account in Switzerland in Milouins's name.

Milouins had appreciated this courtesy very much. The money had been more than enough for Milouins to buy himself a house in Port Grimaud, which he now rented out on a semi-permanent basis to a retired conductor. It would be to this house that Milouins would withdraw following the Countess's eventual death.

For Milouins sensed, now more than ever, that things were coming to a climax in the de Bale household, and that nothing that was any good lasted forever.

# 42

Milouins waved the taxi off. He turned to the man who had been waiting for him at the road junction. 'Are you sure this is the place?'

'Yes. My people have been watching it for three days now. The man called Sergei Alatyrtsev lives here.'

'Alone?'

'He has no family. He is a drunk. He draws a small pension. Enough for vodka, anyway. You've caught him just in time. Neighbours say that his liver has shrunk to the size of a golf ball. That when he limps past them they can smell the alcohol leaking through his skin. We have made sure he has not been able to emerge from the house for the past forty-eight hours, just as you asked. The man will be going crazy in there. He has no telephone. He has no means of communication with the outside world. He probably only had enough drink with him to last a day.'

'Will he talk to me?'

'By now he will talk to anyone who offers him a bottle.'

Milouins held out his hand.

The Ukrainian handed him a plastic bag with two

bottles inside.

'Will you stay and translate for me?'

'There is no need. This man speaks English.'

'My English is not strong.'

'But it is good enough. I understand you. This man speaks like me.'

'You do not wish to stay. That is the real truth, isn't it?'

The Ukrainian drew one hand heavily down his face as if he were scraping it clear of sweat. 'He is Russian. I am Ukrainian. Stalin starved my grandmother to death in the great famine of 1931. My grandfather was forced to eat human flesh to survive.' He gave a ragged sigh. 'What I am saying is that the Russians still have influence here. A lot of influence. And this man was once part of things. He might have friends left in high places. This way, what the eye does not see, the heart does not mourn.'

'Have you been paid?'

'Yes.'

'Then go. You are done here.'

Milouins watched the man hurry down the street. In many ways it was a good thing he was leaving. Milouins had no idea how the interview would go. How Alatyrtsev would respond to what he was about to lay on him. The Countess's orders had been specific. Milouins had very little latitude for error in the matter.

He stepped up and hammered on the door. 'Alatyrtsev. Open up. I have vodka for you.'

There was a long pause. So long, that Milouins was briefly tempted to hammer again. But he knew how slowly drunks moved. His own uncle had been an alcoholic. When Milouins was a young man he had been sent out by his father on many occasions to be his uncle's minder. His uncle had died, aged fifty. Not of cirrhosis of the liver. That was too specific. Milouins's uncle had died of everything.

There was the sound of shuffling feet. The feet came up to the door. There was another long pause.

'Vodka?'

'Vodka. Yes. I have two bottles – 50 per cent proof – for export only. I have the bag here. Let me in.'

Milouins half expected the man to say 'Who are you? Why have you not been allowing me out of my house?' But, as with his uncle, all normal forms of human interaction had been jettisoned long since.

The door opened a crack and a hand came out to take the bag.

Milouins threw open the door and stepped inside. The smell that assailed his nostrils made him want to gag. It was a mixture of urine, shit, sweat, cheap cigarettes, and the elusory sweetness of rotting meat. Milouins was grateful when the man turned back inside, leaving the door wide open.

Alatyrtsev made straight for the bottle Milouins was holding.

Milouins snatched it back at the last possible moment, only just avoiding touching Alatyrtsev's outstretched hand. 'We need something from you. For every question you answer correctly, I will allow you one drink.'

Alatyrtsev squinted at him. His expression turned cunning. 'We start with the drink.'

'No. We start with the question.'

Alatyrtsev stood swaying in the centre of the floor. With a violent jerk, he began scratching his arms.

Milouins flinched. He wondered for a moment whether Alatyrtsev might have mange, but then realized it was probably just a case of early onset DT's. Either way, the man reeked of death.

'What question?' Alatyrtsev sounded constipated. Urine trickled down his leg. His head had begun to shake. There was a ring of white scum around his mouth.

'Listen to me, Alatyrtsev. Thirty years ago you visited Moldova. The cave monastery at Orheiul Vechi. You were driving former Russian Deputy Minister of Defence Anatoly Karaev. You were his chauffeur. You stopped at a village called Cenucenca. Is this true?'

'A drink. I tell you.'

'No drink. You tell me first. Then a drink – 60 per cent proof, man. Imagine what it will taste like.'

Alatyrtsev's eyes were swimming in a bloodshot sea. He staggered across to an unmade cot in the corner of the room. He sat down and placed his head in his hands. Then he moaned.

The sound caused the hairs to rise on Milouins's neck and forearms. He cursed Alatyrtsev inwardly – how could any person calling himself a human being allow himself to fall so low? He coughed, in an effort to clear the protective phlegm from his throat. 'Karaev fell from the cliff. On the plateau. We have spoken to many people from the surrounding villages. His death coincided with the temporary disappearance of a boy. A boy who was later seen wearing Karaev's astrakhan coat. A boy who had been mysteriously injured. A boy whose father vanished under suspicious circumstances. We are interested in this boy. If you can tell us about him, I will not only give you these two bottles of vodka I have with me. But many bottles. As many bottles as you can drink for the rest of your life.'

Alatyrtsev's mouth fell open. 'For the rest of my life?'

'For however long it takes you to drink yourself to death.' Milouins smiled, but his eyes were frozen. He took a small cine camera out of his pocket. Placing the vodka bottles on the floor behind him, he pointed the camera at Alatyrtsev and began filming.

*Albescu, Moldova*
*20 November 2009*

# 43

Abi sat at a corner table of the Crusader Coffee Bar. The bar was situated in the central square of the town that, in effect, constituted Mihael Catalin's personal fiefdom. Around Abi, people were conducting their day-to-day affairs in what passed for normality. But there was something distinctly un-normal about the way they were going about their business. It was as if the people walking, shopping, and passing the time of day imagined that they were onstage somehow, and that everything they touched, or that surrounded them, doubled as part of a theatre set.

Abi was aware that people were watching him and his siblings with unconstrained stares. But that was hardly new. Travel anywhere with two women who looked like Nawal and Dakini, and you soon got used to stares. The fact that everyone who passed them had patriarchal crosses tattooed in the centre of their foreheads simply made the attention the Corpus was receiving a little more intrusive – sinister, even – than it might otherwise have been. Were these people really as stupid as they looked? It never ceased to amaze Abi how willing human beings were to behave like ruminants when faced with a so-called 'strong' leader.

Anyway, he couldn't talk. He was, to all intents and purposes, a strong leader himself. The only thing he lacked was a congregation. In recent months, his erstwhile followers appeared to be dying around him with painful regularity. Maybe he was doing something wrong? Or maybe – and here Abi allowed himself a secret smile – he really ought to branch out on his own? His idea of sneaking back to France to assassinate Madame, his mother, had been a truly excellent one. If it hadn't been for that bastard Milouins he would have succeeded. Anyway, there was always time. He was still technically in the United States – at least as far as the authorities were concerned. That bit of foresight would definitely stand him in good stead somewhere down the line. And as things were, he was rather enjoying himself. He liked suborning unsuspecting people. And he relished the power he was now exercising over Rudra and the girls. There was something invigorating in being able to order people around who would secretly like to kill you. It gave a little extra edge to an existence that would otherwise be deadening in its mundanity.

'That's her. That's the sister all right.' Abi jerked his chin towards a woman, dressed entirely in white, who was negotiating the heavy traffic fifty yards or so to his left.

'How can you be sure?'

'Because I have an up-to-date photograph of her here on my cell phone, and I'm looking at it as we speak. And because everyone who sees her crosses themselves as if they've just seen the Virgin Mary gliding by. She's the sister of the Second Coming, for pity's sake. These people have been trained to view her as some sort of guardian angel. Look at that man. He's just got down onto his knees. Have you ever seen anything like it?'

'How do you know all this, Abi?'

'Because Madame, our mother, has had a dozen investigators on her and her brother's back-trail, day in, day out, for the past fortnight. I give our mother that – when she decides to do something, she does it right. And her investment has paid off. I've just downloaded the latest report, thanks to the excellent free Wi-Fi offered by this place. At least Catalin is good for something.' Abi's eyes flicked over to Antanasia – she was talking intently to two women at the corner of the market square. His eyes drifted back to his cell phone. 'It seems that we've finally got what we were looking for. Milouins is even now in Odessa concluding certain financial and locational arrangements with an interested party. What he's just sent me should give us all the edge we need to persuade Catalin to work in our interests, as well as his own.'

'But Catalin hardly ever ventures out. How can anyone investigate him?'

'Catalin is a celebrity. A public figure. People who don't belong to his Church are only too happy to talk about him.'

'So why the interest in his sister all of a sudden?'

'Because she's the only way to get through to Catalin. The man is surrounded by a bodyguard of young men he calls his "Crusaders". They form an unbreachable wall around him. Catalin's no fool. He knows there's mystery in being elusive. This way, people fantasize about him.

Because, of course, they are never given the time to sum him up for what he really is.'

'And the sister is his weak point?'

'Exactly. She's not called Antanasia Catalin, by the way – she's called Antanasia Lupei. And he's Dracul Lupei. The Mihael Catalin bit is made up, as is so much else in this confidence trickster's story. He comes from a village called Cenucenca, in the east of the country. Antanasia was the local good-time girl, according to the reports we have. But she's mended her ways, thanks to her brother, and now she lives like a nun. Well, she doesn't walk like a nun, I'll say that much for her.'

'But if people know he's not who he says he is, why don't they vote with their feet?'

'Because they believe in him, Rudi, and true belief turns people blind. Plus, he's expedient. He's transformed himself, and them, into something other – something they're proud of. And no one wants to hark back to a past they find uncongenial. Plus, our friend has taken great pains to scrub away all lingering traces of his old self. But you can't scrub away people's memories. They stick to the wall like dried shit.' Abi stood up. He threw some money down on the table. 'Come on. Let's go.'

'What are we going to do with the sister? Kidnap her?'

'I hardly think so, Rudi. Not after the last fiasco. No. We need to talk to her. Nawal and Dakini, go and do your stuff. Rudi and I will manage the rest.'

# 44

It proved nearly impossible to corner Antanasia alone. People followed her wherever she went. She was known to everybody. And everybody wished to talk to her. It was clear that she was the day-to-day face of Mihael Catalin. His public relations persona. His woman-on-the-street. His earthly representative.

Nawal and Dakini split up and shadowed her every step. They knew their moment would come. It always did.

Abi and Rudra strolled around the town. They were watched wherever they went. The fact that they sported clean foreheads was enough, paradoxically, to mark them out from the crowd. From time to time someone would sidle up and talk to them.

'We can't understand you,' Abi would counter. 'We don't speak Romanian.'

Most would then try in broken English. 'Are you thinking of joining us? Is that why you are here? We welcome foreigners.'

Abi turned to Rudra. 'The sooner we are off these damned streets the better. I don't like the feeling here. When people want something too much, it infects the air around them like a virus. Personally, I don't think we should go anywhere near this man. He comes from a culture we don't understand. He will react in ways we can't anticipate. The Countess is too cut off from real life to understand this anymore.'

'Well, why don't you tell her so, Big Shot? You're always the one who knows so much. The all-seeing, all-knowing Abi.'

Abi turned to his brother. He raised his eyebrows. 'Do I detect a certain lingering resentment in your tone, Rudra? A sliver of disbelief?'

'Of course I disbelieve you. I was there, remember? Floating amongst the dead bodies. Do you think I'm stupid? You abandoned us in that cenote. Don't try to deny it. You might have pulled the wool over our mother's eyes, but you haven't pulled it over mine. I've come to terms, now, with what you did. I've had no choice. But I haven't forgiven you. When all this is over and done with I'm coming to get you, Abi. Then we'll see who is the best man out of the two of us.'

Abi forced himself to smile. 'Think what you will, Rudi. I've told you the truth. I really did warn the old man and the boy that you were down there. How else could I have known about them? But I see that I could repeat this until the maniac we are following brings Armageddon down on all our heads, and you still wouldn't believe me. So I simply won't bother.'

Rudra looked up. He opened his mouth to reply just as Abi's cell phone rang.

'Yes, Nawal? What is it?'

'We've got her.'

'Where are you?'

'I'm with her in a ladies' toilet three blocks south of the square. It's near a church with a golden dome. Dakini is standing in front of the door gesticulating to people that there's a flood in here. We can't keep this up for long. You'd better get here pronto.'

'We're on our way.' Abi checked out the skyline around him. 'Look. There's the onion dome. Let's go before Dakini starts a riot.'

Dakini wasn't standing in front of the WC block – she was lurking near the church.

'What's up?'

'They're still in there. I just got fed up trying to explain the flood to people who can only manage a sort of pidgin English. Nawal is leaning against the door so that anyone who tries it thinks it's locked. No one's gone anywhere near the place for the last couple of minutes anyway. We're lucky they didn't have one of those ubiquitous old Babushkas stationed at a table inside.'

'You stay out here. Keep watch. Act as though you're thinking of going inside the church.'

'Okay.'

Abi and Rudra hurried across to the service building. Both knew the thieves' motto that looking around oneself draws attention. Make it fast and make it confident – that way potential witnesses won't remember what they've seen.

Abi tapped on the door, said a couple of words to Nawal, and bundled inside.

Antanasia was standing near one of the empty cubicles. Nawal had her fighting baton out. She had taken up position a few feet away from Antanasia, as if both women suspected the other's hidden motivations.

'Any trouble?'

'None. She came in here alone. I waited for her to finish her business, and then detained her. She speaks English. No French though. They're not that civilized here.'

'Did you hit her?'

'Didn't need to.'

'Good. We don't want to alienate the clientele any more than necessary.'

Antanasia took a pace towards him. 'You are making a big mistake. My brother will be very angry. He has many people around him. You won't make it out of town if you are trying to kidnap me. You will be in prison within the hour. My brother will not pay.'

'We're not trying to kidnap you. What do you think we are? Siberian mafiosi? We simply need you to pass on a message for us.'

'A message?'

'We have heard that your brother is a difficult man to approach. We need to talk to him nonetheless. He'll find that it's as much in his interests as ours. You must call him and tell him that we need to see him privately. Without his Crusaders.'

'I won't do that.'

'Oh yes, you will. Look at this.' Abi held out his cell phone. 'Look at the video recording. Listen to what this man says. If you do as we ask, no one has to see this but us. If you play hard to get, we will release this clip to the Russians just before the Moldovan presidential elections next year. The gentleman concerned has agreed to testify in open court that your brother murdered his boss, the former Russian Deputy Minister of Defence, Anatoly Karaev, twenty-eight years ago, at Orheiul Vechi. We are holding our witness in a safe house to protect him from... shall we call it disharmony? When the Russians see this video clip, your brother's ambitions will be doomed. Him too. He'll be lucky if they only do a Viktor Yushchenko on him, and leave it at that. If he's truly the Second Coming, of course, he'll be able to piss the dioxins they dose him with out of his system, no problem. Otherwise he'll look like a salamander for the rest of his life. Is that a risk you're willing to take?'

Antanasia watched the tape. The noise of Alatyrtsev's voice was eerily amplified inside the white-tiled room.

'This is not true. My brother did not kill this man.'

'Bullshit. Neighbours say you even made a hand muff and matching jacket out of the guy's astrakhan coat. Do you remember doing that, maybe? Of course, Lupei probably found the coat abandoned on the hillside after the police and investigators had left. That must have been it. And then, walking home, he must have fallen and injured himself, necessitating a two-week stay at the Orheiul Vechi cave monastery. Did you know that Karaev was the old monk's brother, by the way?'

Antanasia snatched a hand up to her chest.

'Yes. That was why the ex-Minister was visiting the monastery. To pay a visit to his brother, and try to persuade him to come on down out of his hidey-hole and act like a normal human being for a change. Their mother was dying. Karaev wanted his brother to come back to Russia with him in time for the funeral. Let's face it, hermits are rarely at the ends of telephones.'

'I don't believe you.'

'Oh, you can believe me. It's all true. The old hermit saved your brother's life, at the cost of his own kith and kin. Privately, he seems to have thought that his brother was an evil bastard, and that he'd contributed to the Cold War. So when he realized what had happened out on the plateau, he persuaded the chauffeur not to give your brother away.'

'You can't prove that.'

'We don't need to. We've got the chauffeur's testimony about Karaev and the old monk. But then you suspected all this already, didn't you? We're just working from hearsay. But we'll let the Russians check it out. They're good at that. Especially when it comes to the unexplained deaths of their own people.' Abi flipped the cell phone back on itself. 'I'm sure they'll give good old Dracul a clean bill of health when the investigation is over. He can always have another crack at the Presidency later on. Oh, and one more thing while I'm about it. We believe your brother killed the old monk too. Repaid him for all his goodness and forbearance by offing him and taking his place at the hermitage. But we can't prove that either, of course. The monk has long since rotted into the ground. But certain people with your worst interests at heart are trying very hard to convince our investigators that Dracul went on to kill your father. That would be easier to follow up. We haven't found the body yet, but it'll only be a matter of time. It's lurking out there somewhere. Did I tell you we have five investigators working on it as we speak? They're scouring the hillside above Orheiul Vechi twenty-four hours by twenty-four. Your father disappeared on his donkey, apparently. I can't see old Dracul digging a hole just to bury a donkey in, can you? No. I can see that much by your face. He would have used an already existing space. And Orheiul Vechi is honeycombed with caves and potential sepulchres. What do you reckon? Think we're going to find them?'

Antanasia hugged herself. 'What do you want? Why are you doing this?'

'What do we want? That's simple. We want you to call your brother on this cell phone. Don't explain too much. Who knows who'll be listening? Just enough to ensure he doesn't call his minions down on us. Tell him you're coming with us. That we'll all be waiting for him a few miles outside his bailiwick. At... what's it called?' He turned to Rudra.

'The Virgin Mary's footprint.'

'Yes. That's it. The Virgin Mary's footprint. Near the Saharna Monastery. No one can creep up on us there. It's far too open and well used. And it's only a skip and a leap from Orheiul Vechi, in case Dracul spontaneously admits to your father's murder, and wants to lead us to the place of concealment himself. Do you think you can persuade him? We'd be very disappointed indeed if he let us down.'

'I think I can persuade him. In the circumstances.'

'That's my girl. I knew we could trust you to do the right thing. I mean, as the sister of the Second Coming – the sister of the founder of the Church of the Renascent Christ – what else could you do?'

# 45

'Hell of a waterfall. Must be all of 20 metres high.'

'What did you expect, Rudi? Niagara? Anyway, I'd have thought you'd have had quite enough of water for the time being.'

Rudra shook his head unbelievingly. He and Abi stepped through into the chapel that housed the glassed-in shrine to the Virgin Mary's footprint.

Rudra gazed at the shrine. 'Do you think it's real?'

Abi gave his brother a disbelieving grunt. 'Of course it's real. But it's also bullshit. Complete hokum. They call these things Petrosomatoglyphs. You find them all over Europe. Images of hands and feet were carved into the rock in megalithic times as an adjunct to the crowning of kings. The Catholic Church then hijacked them – as they hijacked and transformed all pagan images – and sucked the life out of them. This one was happened upon by a lucky monk. There's one in the Ukraine, too, at Pochayiv Lavra. Even the Welsh got into the act. They've arrogated the knees and breasts of the Virgin Mary to themselves at a place called Llanfair. That Lady really got around some. Though why she should visit Wales, or the Ukraine, or here, come to think of it, is quite beyond me. And what was the Mother of God doing anyway, stark naked, and kneeling on the ground with her bottom in the air? Can you answer me that one?'

'Don't you take anything seriously, Abi?'

Abi pointed through the open door of the shrine. 'Our friend. The one who's coming up the track to meet us. I take him seriously.'

Both men stepped out onto the footpath.

Dracul Lupei strode up the slope towards them. His long hair fell to his shoulders. It was parted in the centre. He had grown a small, neatly tended beard, mildly forked in the middle. He was wearing casual clothes, which didn't suit him, surmounted by a white tracksuit top with a hood. Publicity pictures always showed him dressed in flowing white robes, with a circular, embroidered collar, and an image of the Sacred Heart, encompassed by a crown of thorns, on his chest. As he approached Abi and Rudra, Lupei slipped the hood over his head. As the trio were entirely alone on the plateau, the movement seemed a little redundant.

'Are you people mad? Why have you called me here? To such a place? I will be recognized.'

Abi smiled. 'You know, I've been asking myself that question all morning. And I've got no answer for it. I've got another question for you, though. One that has been bothering me for years. The question is this. Why is Jesus Christ always shown wearing a beard? Why should that be, I wonder? I bet you've got the inside track on that one.'

Lupei stopped in front of the two men. He watched them for a moment, his head tilted to one side, and then he looked around himself. 'Where is my sister? You say that you haven't kidnapped her, and yet I see no sign of her.'

'Where are your men?'

'What men?'

'Your Crusaders?'

'I came alone, as requested. At the instigation of my sister.'

'I don't believe you.'

'I don't believe you either.'

Both men weighed each other up. 'Your sister is safe. Here.' Abi handed Lupei his cell phone. 'Dial this number. You can talk to her. We keep her with us until you and I have come to some sort of understanding. Then you can have her back with our compliments. We'll be partners by then, anyway. You can count on it.'

Lupei brushed away the cell phone. 'I don't need this. I control all modes of communication in and around Albescu personally. I have, of course, been monitoring all your calls. I have also seen the film clip you downloaded via my server at the Crusader Coffee Bar.'

'We assumed as much. We thought it would save time.'

Lupei threw his head back in mild surprise. 'It did. Tell me what you want from me? Not money, surely? That would be asinine.'

'No. We don't want money. On the contrary. We want to give it to you. Lots of it. We want to help you become President of Moldova.'

Lupei nodded his head slowly. 'So that is why you conducted the lengthy conversation with the woman you call the Countess in my coffee bar?'

'We thought it would speed negotiations up. Yes. Clear the air a little. Clarify our intentions.'

'What do you want for your money? Do you wish to control me? Is that it? To turn me into some sort of a gangster?'

'Just the opposite. We want you to remain entirely true to yourself. That's the deal. We assumed you would understand that much from overhearing the conversation I had with the Countess.'

'But you must want something more than this? Money rarely falls out of the sky like manna.'

'Well, you'd know something about manna, wouldn't you, Lupei?'

Lupei stared at Abi. It was clear that neither man would back down in front of the other.

Abi was the first to break the deadlock. 'All right. Let's agree to cut the bullshit. We know what you are. And thanks to your impressive monitoring of our communications – we expected no less, by the way – you know who we are. We hold Alatyrtsev. And twenty minutes ago I heard that our operatives had discovered two skeletons – one belonging to a donkey, one to a man – in a hidden cave up at Orheiul Vechi. I don't suppose you picked that up with your communications snooper? We're way too far outside your bailiwick here.' Abi raised his hands and turned, widdershins, in a circle. 'But with our help, all this can be your bailiwick too. In fact the whole fucking country can belong to you.

Then you can quietly rebury your father and his donkey, with our compliments, and have Alatyrtsev dispatched with an overdose of morphine. We'll even provide the morphine. And the syringe. Whether or not you use a spirit swab will be up to you.'

'This is all very witty. Very amusing.' Lupei wasn't smiling when he said the words. He threw off his hood and shook his hair out like a woman. The plateau was still markedly empty of tourists.

'Ah. A signal. Very neat.' Abi cast a sidelong glance at Lupei. 'Your Crusaders have done a great job sealing off the place, by the way. I suspect that the Virgin Mary is going to have a seriously bad foot day.'

Lupei surveyed the scenery without seeing it. 'How do you know the body is that of my father?'

'At this precise moment, it's only a guess. But we've just taken a sample of hair from your sister. What do you reckon it will show? But hell. Maybe you'll strike lucky. Maybe your father wasn't your father at all. Maybe someone else in the village impregnated your mother. That way the cosy relationship your neighbours tell us you've been having with your sister over the years will seem a little less – what shall we call it? – incestuous.'

Lupei fixed Abi with his eyes.

Abi clapped a hand to his mouth in an outrageously melodramatic gesture. 'But Jesus Christ. I completely forgot. It was the Holy Spirit who climbed down from the Pantecrator and fucked your mother, wasn't it? And not your father at all. Hey, Lupei. It's all a mix-up. A tragic misunderstanding. We're out of here. You're in the clear. You can have your sister back and everything.

Just get on with your life as if this didn't ever happen. We're sorry we bothered you.'

Lupei sniffed at the rapidly cooling air. His eyes were dead. 'I repeat my question. What exactly do you want from me?'

Abi's eyes hardened. 'It's simple. We know who is the mother of the real Second Coming. The one who has been predicted and pinpointed for the past 450 years – not dreamed up in the back room of a dirt farm in some one-horse town in the European equivalent of Outer Mongolia. We know exactly when he is due to be born. We also know that his mother is hiding out in a village somewhere in the north of Romania. We know who is with her. The Countess and I, representing the Corpus Maleficus, have a personal interest in these people. You need to have a similar interest. It is essential for all our plans that you kill this woman and her baby.'

'Why?'

'Do I really need to spell it out?'

Lupei made a sour face. 'No.'

'The Corpus don't have enough people to find her. And we don't know the country like you do. You have your Crusaders. They all speak Romanian. You can send them out looking for her without setting off alarm bells. Tell them she is the mother-to-be of a false prophet. Hell. Tell them she is the mother-to-be of the Third Antichrist. That should do the trick.' Abi could feel Rudra stiffening beside him, but he refused to turn round. 'Then kill her. You've killed before. It shouldn't be so hard. God alone knows you've got the motive.' Abi held Lupei's eyes with his. 'But listen. There are two men with her. An

280

American and a Frenchman. They are called Adam Sabir and Joris Calque. Part of the deal is that you leave these men to me.'

'What did they do to you?'

Abi hesitated. Then he shrugged. 'They caused my twin brother to be killed.'

'Ah. Revenge. That most exquisite of all callings. It humanizes one, doesn't it?' Lupei smiled. 'I, too, have known the elusive joys of revenge.'

'Are you trying to tell me something?'

'No. I simply want to know what is the sum of money we are talking about in relation to your request? I need proof that you are serious. I need to know that you are not just dilettantes playing around with fire. If so, the fire will consume you, I can assure you of that. How would this money be transferred to me, for instance? And would I have full control in how to spend it?'

'Full control. A private bank account. In Switzerland. In your name only. Fifty million euros.'

Lupei shook his head. 'That will not be enough. I will have people to bribe. Gangs to suborn. Wages to bankroll. If I am to become President of my country, small as it is, I need to seduce the opposition with money. I need to flood them with largesse. Either that, or I need to kill them. Such services do not come cheaply. If you wish to purchase the right to blackmail the future President of a nominally democratic European country – which I assume you do – you will need to pay considerably more than fifty million euros for the privilege. I will also need to construct a fallback position for myself and my sister in case things go badly wrong. The account, for instance, needs to be in both our names, so that my sister can act as my courier – my representative – should things not go entirely as planned. You understand my reasoning?'

Abi grinned. 'That's my boy. I can see that we have chosen exactly the right man for the job. But let's not say "blackmail". Let's say "influence", shall we? And would one hundred million euros be more acceptable?'

'Double that figure, and we have a deal.'

'Ouch.' Abi shrugged his shoulders. 'You drive a hard bargain, Lupei. I can see exactly why the moneylenders ran when your predecessor chased them from the Temple precincts 2,000 years ago. Fifty million down, then. And fifty million more when you can prove the death of the Gypsy woman, Yola Dufontaine, and her unborn child. The remaining hundred million when you hand me over Adam Sabir and Joris Calque alive.'

'And what else do you require for your money? Come on. I want to know what the catch is now. Before we begin our partnership.'

'Nothing. Absolutely nothing. Just be yourself, Lupei. The Corpus Maleficus have perfect confidence in you. To our way of thinking, you won't be able to resist stirring up a whole succession of hornet's nests once you've secured power. And we in the Corpus have always been in the business of stirring up hornet's nests. We are past masters at it. You will be our star pupil. Apart from the Gypsy girl and the two men, we are prepared to leave everything to your entire discretion. Agreed?'

Lupei's eyes were dancing. 'Agreed.'

Abi was pleasantly surprised. Privately, he had been convinced that Lupei would hold out for at least half a billion. Maybe the man was a cheapskate at heart? Either way, he, Abi, had fulfilled his part of the bargain.

Now, he would sit back and wait for Lupei to fulfil his.

# 46

―

'Did you kill him?'

Antanasia stood by the bed she shared with her brother. Her face was white. As the focus of the cult, only she, her brother and his Crusaders had the right to remain unadorned. The remainder of the adherents all had to be tattooed with the patriarchal cross.

'Who? Our father? You saw me kill him. You even helped me move his body.'

'No. You know I'm not talking about him. I'm talking about the monk. And this other man the Frenchman mentioned. Did you kill him too?'

'What's the difference? Surely it's a worse thing to kill one's father than to kill a perfect stranger? You approve of me killing the one, and yet, I can see by your face, you disapprove of me killing the other.'

'You killed our father to protect me.'

'I killed our father because I hated him. Protecting you was secondary.'

Antanasia dropped her eyes. 'But still.'

Lupei glared at his sister. 'But still.'

She glanced up. There was a terrible expectancy in her face. 'And the other men?'

'Why, otherwise, should I allow myself to be blackmailed by these filth?'

'Because you want their money.'

'Do you know how much money they are offering me?'

Antanasia shook her head so violently that her hair broke free from its barrette. 'It can never be enough.'

Lupei laughed. 'Oh yes, it can.' He hesitated, more aware of his sister's anguish than he cared to acknowledge. 'We have agreed on 200 million euros. A joint account. Held in Switzerland. With you and I as individual signatories with full fiscal control. If anything happens to me, Antanasia, you will be a very rich woman indeed.'

Antanasia caught her breath. 'This is impossible.'

Lupei shrugged. 'I don't think so.'

'But why? Who has such huge sums of money at their fingertips?'

Lupei made a dismissive motion with his hand. 'Not every country in the world is subject to the same endemic corruption we are.'

'And yet you encourage that corruption.'

'Only because it is in our best interests.'

'Your best interests.'

Lupei strode across the room until he stood directly in front of his sister. For a moment it seemed as if he was about to strike her. 'Don't you value the position I have given you? Don't you value the esteem in which you are held by our people?' He threw his arms into the air. 'All this is my doing. Everything we possess stems from decisions I have made. Don't tell me you regret giving up your old life, Antanasia? Did you enjoy being the plaything of any man our father chose to sell you to? Something he could offer to his friends like a bag of sweets?'

Antanasia could scarcely bring herself to speak. She had spent her lifetime being dominated, first by her father, then by her brother. Both had pimped her out to others. Both had abused her. Her only weapons had been the quality of her submission, and the single-minded love that she bore for Dracul, which had persisted in spite of all he had done – and witnessed done – to her. It was the sort of unconditional love more commonly found between a mother and her terminally errant son.

But there was something unholy and alienating about this new face her brother was showing her. Before the foreigners had arrived, she had been able to feign indifference to Dracul's methods. They were cruel, she had convinced herself, only to be kind. Her brother had benefited more people than he had disenfranchised. The town he had ordered his followers to build was a magnificent going concern – a beacon of light in a country doomed to poverty by its own recalcitrance. But now? What pact with the Devil was he signing? Why was he allowing himself to be so easily bribed? 'So what they told me was true? You did kill this Russian Minister?'

'I was twelve years old. The man struck me. Harder than any man had ever struck me before. I was bewildered. When I ran at him on the plateau I did not expect to kill him.'

'What did you expect then?'

Lupei said nothing. He canted his head upwards, effectively phasing out his sister, just as he would do to his audiences in the full flow of a homily. To any neutral onlooker it would seem as if Lupei had been called on to commune with a higher power from whom he hoped to derive strategies for dealing with the hoi polloi spread out in front of him.

Antanasia knew the trick of old and was no longer taken in by it. In recent years she had taken to calling it his 'miracle-worker's gaze'. 'And the monk? The old man who cared for you and healed you? The one whose place you took at the hermitage? The one who saved your life?'

Lupei hadn't struck his sister for a number of years. He was briefly tempted to raise his hand to her and secure her compliance that way. But the moment passed. She was a mature woman now, with a dignity all of her own. People looked up to her. Even Dracul had to admit that, although she still shared his bed, she was no longer the callow young woman he and his father had found so easy to quail and to mould to their wills. Perhaps he should lie to her, and lull her suspicions that way? But he had become so used to total obedience – to the instant acceptance of himself as immaculate and all-knowing – that he was no longer able to haunt contrivances.

For many years now, everyone he met had looked up to Dracul and approved his every word and deed. There was a component in his character that required unswerving obedience from everyone around him – and from Antanasia most of all. Whatever he did must be right by her. However gross his actions – however perverse his motivations – she, above all people, must accept him for what he was. And why was this? Dracul knew the answer only too well. The thought burnt through his guts like nitric acid. Like molten lead through cardboard.

Antanasia was all he had. Was all he would ever have. She was the only person who really knew him. The only one before whom he need wear no mask.

'Yes, I killed him. The old goat was dying anyway. I went to see him one night, while our father was having his way with you in his usual obnoxious manner. I ordered the monk to acknowledge me as his spiritual heir. To proclaim me as the Second Coming. Such a proclamation, coming from a man like him, would have strengthened my hand immeasurably. I would have achieved my ends far sooner than I in fact did. Instead, the old fool treated me to a deathbed diatribe. Tried to convince me that he had inferred who and what I was – and what I would become – by a sort of mystical osmosis. That he considered it his life's duty to convert me to the ways of righteousness – for one devil converted, according to him, was worth a hundred saints. So I converted him instead. Into a cadaver. I folded a potato sack across his face. He scarcely struggled. As I said, he was as good as dead anyway.'

Antanasia took a step backwards. 'But he called you a devil, Dracul. And you killed him for it. This is a terrible thing for you to acknowledge. What did he think you would become?'

'Me? Become?' Dracul laughed. 'There's no point listening to an old fool like that. He was out of his head.

Seeing visions. You remember what the place was like, don't you? The walls leached doom and gloom. Imagine living there for fifty years and scarcely talking to a soul. You'd be seeing devils too. I lived there for long enough myself. The cold ate into your bones like cancer and coloured everything you saw.'

'What did he see? What did he say you would become?' Antanasia had instinctively begun to edge further away from her brother.

Lupei shrugged. 'I suppose it will do no harm now. What does it matter what an old man said nearly thirty years ago?' He looked across at his sister – it was as if he was weighing up just how far he could test her – just how far she would be prepared to go in his service. 'He said I was setting myself up in opposition to God. That I was arrogating Christ's light to myself. That I would be like a dark mirror with no reflection to the people who would follow me. Those were his words. That was what he said.'

Antanasia shook her head. 'There was more than that, wasn't there? I know you, Dracul. I know when you are hiding things from me.'

Lupei permitted his gaze to drift across the bed and towards the window. The late November sun was edging below the horizon in a seething golden mass. Dracul seemed mesmerized by it. The sunset reflected off his face and turned it yellow, as if he had been afflicted with a case of jaundice 'Yes. You are right. There was one more thing.' He hesitated. 'Understand this. I had already suffocated him. The old man was clearly dead.'

'Tell me, Dracul.'

Dracul's mouth dropped open, like that of a child about to gag. 'So I withdrew the sack, satisfied that I had killed him. Then his eyes opened, and he drew in a terrible, ragged breath, like a man emerging from a near drowning.' Lupei screwed up his face. For a moment he resembled the artless young boy he had been before he had started his seemingly inexorable descent towards the void. 'He was old. Perhaps he took only shallow breaths? Yes. That must have been it. They say people who meditate only take one or two breaths a minute. And this monk was a meditator. I had seen him at it. Copied him, even.' Lupei looked disgusted – as if he had been let down in some way. Cheated of his expectations. 'Anyway, just as I was raising the sack above his head to kill him for the second time, he cried out "*Eloi. Eloi. Lama Sabachthani*". You remember? Exactly like Christ on the Cross. And then – well. It's absurd. He was dying. Who knows what was going through his head?'

'What else did he call out, Dracul?'

Lupei hesitated. His face seemed congested. Like a man with a fishbone hooked across his throat. 'He cried out "Antichrist! Antichrist! You are become Antichrist."'

*Brara, Maramureş, Romania*
*Friday, 5 February 2010*

# 47

This was the thirty-second village that Iuliu Andrassy, Crusader in the service of the Church of the Renascent Christ, had personally investigated. As one of Mihael Catalin's chosen apostles, Andrassy, like Antanasia, had been spared having his forehead tattooed with the patriarchal cross. This allowed him to blend in with the surrounding population, and, as an indigenous Romanian speaker – albeit one born in Moldova – to act, to all intents and purposes, as one of Romania's own.

Each village on Andrassy's list took a maximum of two days to cover. Each house had to be visited. Each isolated hamlet explored. Every householder quizzed. Already, thanks to near blizzard conditions, Andrassy had had to abandon his car on more than one occasion. On this particular morning he was sick to his heart at the thought of having to trudge through still more ankle-deep snow, on still more uncleared roads. If he didn't secure the offer of a bed for the night, he knew that he must, yet again, bunk down in the back of his wind-searched Simca and make the best of the three sleeping bags and the dubious paraffin heater that threatened to asphyxiate him if he didn't leave the windows cracked well open. Which was a clear case, he decided, of throwing the baby out with the bath water.

Most of the people Andrassy interviewed did not possess motor vehicles, but still travelled largely by foot – or, if they were better off, by horse and dogcart. Public transportation was non-existent. In the case of such isolated communities, local government did not feel the need to send in snowploughs after each individual snowfall. These people possessed shovels and brooms, did they not? And, anyway, spring would eventually come along and sort out their problems for them, so why hurry things? For centuries Romania's peasants had been self-sufficient enough to see to their own mess – let them continue, was the motto. Andrassy hoped, even if only briefly, to change this perception of government inertia and entropy.

Andrassy's cover was as a special representative working on behalf of an office created by Romania's President, Traian Basescu, tasked with conducting a survey of Moldovans with ethnic Romanian ancestry living illegally in Romania. If such people fulfilled certain criteria – having Romanian as their first language, for instance, and having at least one grandparent who had been born in Romania – the government would grant them Romanian, and in consequence, EU citizenship, together with all its concomitant rights, such as access to the wider EU, including France, Britain, and Germany, and to the lavish state perquisites allegedly accorded to EU citizens by those countries. They would benefit just as Romania's Saxons had benefited, twenty years earlier, when a newly reunified Germany had opened its borders to them. At least, that's what the heavily clipboarded Andrassy had been told to tell them.

Already more than 120,000 Moldovans had been vouchsafed Romanian citizenship in this way, he assured the villagers he visited – and President Basescu had promised that 800,000 more who were on the scheme's waiting list would have their applications expedited at the rate of 10,000 a month. Surely it made sense to register?

After an initial period of suspicion, Andrassy found that most people were only too happy to open up and pinpoint Moldovans living in their villages. When Andrassy concluded his general survey with the seemingly casual question 'No Gypsies living here, I suppose?' he nearly always got an answer. Gypsies would then be compared, unfavourably, to people who considered themselves ethnic Romanians, like the Moldovans and certain rogue Transnistrians, and Andrassy would be asked if there was not anything he, or representatives of the government like him, could do to rid the village of such unwanted pests?

'No. No.' He would exclaim. 'Our hands are tied in this matter. But tell me where they are living and I will note down their details on my chart for future reference. We are hearing bad things from France. They are ejecting Roma from the *bidonvilles* in their thousands and sending them back here. Pretty soon, your village will be flooded with refugees. Endlessly breeding refugees. We must all do what we can to protect you from such people. I will go and reason with these Gypsies. Please tell me again where I can find them.'

'Breeding. Yes. These Romani breed like rabbits. There is one down in our village even now who is pregnant. There will be more, I suspect. I doubt they believe in marriage. Or the sacraments. And they are thieves.'

'Do you mean they have stolen from you?'

'From us? No. Not from us. But we know, nevertheless, that they are thieves. All Gypsies are thieves, are they not? Blood is blood.'

In this way, Andrassy discovered the identity of all visibly pregnant women amongst the Gypsy population, without causing suspicion or alerting anyone to what he and the other Crusaders were about. A useful side effect of the fake survey was that the Church of the Renascent Christ would thus be able to obtain the names and addresses of the vast majority of Moldovans living illegally in rural northern Romania – something which would allow their leader, Mihael Catalin, to contact such people at a later date and promise them guaranteed EU citizenship, via Romania, were they, or, more importantly, their extended families in Moldova, to vote for him in the presidential elections to be held later that year.

Political leverage was therefore the main purpose of the survey – or so Andrassy had been told. The Gypsy/ Roma question he had been ordered to tack on at the end of every questionnaire was a voluntary adjunct, to be tossed in casually, almost as if one were passing the time of day. But whichever of the Crusaders isolated the particular woman Mihael Catalin was looking for would instantly find himself promoted to Senior Lieutenant. To Andrassy – who had been born a peasant, and whose entire life until the moment he had entered Catalin's service had consisted of a struggle to feed both himself and his family, the prospect of a status – any status – was akin to nirvana.

When he heard that there was a pregnant Gypsy woman, therefore, living down by the river in the lower part of Brara, and that her name was either Yula or Yola, Andrassy's pulse quickened. His orders were to pass all requisite details immediately onto his superior in the Crusader hierarchy. But Andrassy knew what would happen then. The man would steal the limelight for himself by transmitting the information to Coryphaeus Catalin personally.

No. Andrassy could not allow this to happen. He would conduct the investigation himself. If he isolated the particular woman his leader was looking for, he would persuade his wife to talk to Antanasia, the Coryphaeus's sister, and pass on the information through her – for Andrassy's wife, Georgetta, did much of the washing and ironing for the Catalin household, as well as participating in the house-cleaning rota, and therefore had privileged access to Antanasia, and, via her, to the Coryphaeus. In this way Andrassy would be able to garner all the available credit for himself.

Yes. He could see it now. Lieutenant Andrassy. Soldier – no, warrior, rather – in the service of Almighty God.

# 48

There were two people living near the abandoned Saxon house – a Roma man and his pregnant wife. Andrassy found it strange that there was not a larger group – in his experience Roma of all persuasions swarmed together like bees. But maybe these were outcasts? Gypsies were primitive beings, in Andrassy's mind. It was easy to assign to them any number of negative characteristics – particularly as Andrassy had never actually talked to one. He had simply inherited a hatred of the whole race with his mother's milk, and nothing he had heard since had persuaded him to either change his mind or tailor his prejudices in any way whatsoever.

When the cell phone his superiors had provided him with unexpectedly rang, Andrassy launched himself from his hiding place like a man who has just been stung on the calf by a fire ant. He held the cell phone away from his face as if he had been forced to retrieve it from a particularly pungent waste bin. The caller would almost certainly be his wife, speaking from one of the public telephones in Albescu, and reporting back to him on her meeting with Antanasia Catalin.

Andrassy belatedly remembered what he was meant

to be doing and ducked back down into his hiding place. He lowered his voice conspiratorially. 'Yes, Georgetta. What do you have to tell me?'

'Andrassy? Crusader Iuliu Andrassy? It is I. Mihael Catalin.'

Andrassy froze. He recognized Coryphaeus Catalin's voice immediately. For the past five years he had participated, in one way or another, at all of Catalin's public appearances. As well as developing a marked expertise at crowd control, Andrassy had also, by default, become deeply conversant with Catalin's worldview. He knew, for instance, that Moslems were agents of the Devil, that Protestants, Baptists, Evangelicals and Copts were antichristian, that Jews were the actual murderers of Christ, that Roman Catholics were followers of a 'perverted faith', and that Orthodox Christians were simply confused, and therefore potentially amenable to change and common sense given a raft of favourable circumstances and a little firm persuasion. He also knew that various parties from amongst the remaining Abrahamic idolaters were intent on sabotaging Mihael Catalin's universal acceptance as the Parousia, and that these parties must be rigorously expunged.

Andrassy had killed before – a few months previously, he and a few of his fellow Crusaders had cornered a Jehovah's Witness in a town about 15 kilometres south of Albescu. They had questioned the man in an abandoned warehouse and found that he intended to visit Albescu to report on conditions there, and to judge its suitability as a base for a proselytizing tour by the Watch Tower Society. Both the Jehovah's Witnesses and the Coryphaeus's COTRC held similar views about Armageddon – that only their followers would survive the Rapture. This man clearly felt that Albescu was in thrall to Satan and thus ripe for plundering.

At first the Crusaders had only meant to teach the Walkie-Talkie a lesson – but the beating had spiralled out of hand. It had been Andrassy himself who kicked in the man's head. As a young man he had perfected a party trick which involved the killing of a sheep with one backward-scything blow from the heel of his boot. The death blow came after a spirited Hopak dance, in which all the onlookers would be clapping Andrassy on, and shouting their encouragement of his ever more energetic kicks and stamps.

He had tried this same technique on the Jehovah's Witness as soon as it became clear that the man was too far gone to be dumped at the local hospital's emergency department. The other Crusaders, impressed by Andrassy's irrepressible sense of humour, had stood by their comrade, faking the millenarian's death as an automobile accident. Not one of them had cavilled at the contrivance, for all Crusaders were aware from the moment of their induction that killing in the service of their God was a very real possibility.

For the Bible, as Coryphaeus Catalin clearly explained to them, recounted many instances where God had given permission for his followers to kill – only *in extremis*, needless to say, and with the best possible of motives, but permission to kill nonetheless. The Great Flood of Noah, for example. And Abraham's war to rescue Lot. And what about Sodom and Gomorrah, Catalin would tell the haverers? Or the permission God gave to Satan to kill all Job's children and servants? Catalin cited one modern-day writer who had estimated that if one added up all the people who had been killed in the Bible exclusively in God's name, that figure would be close to two and a half million souls (not including the future killings discussed at length in Revelation, and relating to Armageddon).

Killing was perfectly acceptable, then, if the orders came directly from God. And who better to express God's will in this matter than His very own son?

As a result of this worldview – which might otherwise have been construed as clashing, in certain key ways, with the main thrust of Catalin's ministry – Catalin was forced to keep his Crusaders rigorously apart from the main body of his followers, both via the non-wearing of the forehead tattoo, and via the money and privileges he lavished upon them in recompense for the special duties they were occasionally called on to perform. Nobody else in the COTRC was allowed to know of these privileges, nor of the wider obligations the Crusaders might be required to discharge. Potential Crusader recruits were handpicked by other Crusaders, and interviewed, in the first instance, by Catalin himself. They then went through a series of tests – akin to rites of passage – in which they were progressively introduced to certain of their confraternity's more extreme methods of persuasive evangelizing.

Andrassy had passed through all these levels with flying colours. Until that moment his entire life had been consumed with the simple question of finding someone he could serve with a clear conscience and a dulled brain. And Coryphaeus Catalin was the perfect leader. It was he who thought things through. He who decided rights and wrongs. All Andrassy had to do was to follow and obey. He would have made the perfect concentration camp guard.

Dracul Lupei closed down Andrassy's file on the computer in front of him. 'Crusader Andrassy, I have a task for you.'

'Yes, Coryphaeus.'

'It is an important task. And one which entails the utmost secrecy.'

'I live to serve you, Coryphaeus. We all do.'

At the other end of the cell phone Lupei smiled. How easy it was for a strong man to exert power over lesser souls. Particularly when one had a pre-eminent status and unlimited sums of money at one's disposal. If only Antanasia were equally amenable.

Since his injudicious admission three months before that he had murdered both the old monk and the Russian VIP, Antanasia had refused to share his bed. At first Dracul had been tempted to use force to bring her to her senses, but had found himself constrained by the fact that Antanasia was now viewed as his main mouthpiece throughout Albescu and its surrounding area, and needed to be seen out and about. If he punished her as severely as he felt she deserved, questions might be asked.

Failing force, he next tried psychological pressure. But his sister remained adamant. She would serve him in public. She would evangelize for him. She would redouble her visible loyalty. But she would no longer sleep with him. Wouldn't let him touch her. The private side of their life together was over and done with.

Lupei tried gentler methods of persuasion. He swore to her that he had changed his ways. Reiterated to her that he had been a very young man indeed when he had committed the murders, and that he was no longer the same flawed person he had been before. That he was now responsible for the lives of thousands of people who believed in him and looked to him for leadership. A man with that measure of responsibility needed a soul mate, surely? One that he could trust absolutely. And who better than his sister, who had seen him through the horrors of their early life and into the triumphant uplands of his enlightened ministry?

'I am still your soul mate, Dracul. And I will always love you as my brother. But I realize now that what I let you and our father do to me was wrong. As the older of the two of us, I hold myself accountable for encouraging you, even if inadvertently, to consider that there were no moral barriers – no line to draw in the sand when you desired to get your way.'

Dracul shrugged. He had one final string to his bow. But he sensed, even then, that it was not made of maiden's hair, but rather of the hair of fallen women – that it would part, in other words, at the final testing, just like the maiden-hair hawser that held the ship of the Norse Prince Breachan away from the whirlpool of the Gulf of Corrievrechan. Only one virgin needed to have been untrue for the hawser to part, which it did, sending the prince and all his entourage down to Davy Jones's locker.

'All right then. I shall find myself another woman.'

Antanasia turned away from her brother. 'Please do.'

But both Antanasia and Dracul knew the impracticability of his claim. No other woman could match Antanasia in her brother's eyes. At night, after abusing her in the most bestial way, he would weep in her arms, and tell her his innermost dreams, knowing that, come morning, she would never reveal his secrets to others. Such certainty could not exist elsewhere. It was the ultimate sadomasochistic trip.

Normal women talked amongst themselves. Traded intimacies. Gossiped. Any woman chosen by the Coryphaeus would have enormous pressures placed on her. Her position could not, by its very nature, be explicit, for the Mihael Catalin his followers knew and venerated was renowned for his rigid adherence to sexual purity – it was one of his major selling points as a cult leader. He had made it a salient virtue to point to other cults whose leaders used and abused their followers. In his case, he would tell them, this had never been true.

None of his followers remotely suspected that he slept with his sister – it was beyond thinking of. And Antanasia, being of peasant stock, clearly understood what signs and signifiers to dispose of so that when it came to laundry time, the rota of women who cleaned the house would harbour no suspicions in their turn. The Mihael Catalin they knew never slept on the same sheets twice – each morning, after they had slept together, Antanasia would burn her brother's sheets in the Romanian Kujundzic tiled stove in her bedroom.

And if another woman did fulfil all the necessary criteria? What of his Antanasia then? What position would she still be able to hold? No realm could function with two queens, just as no kingdom could flourish with more than one king. Lupei had read his Machiavelli – he knew this for a fact.

Privately, Antanasia viewed the temporary withdrawal of her favours as a necessary leavening of her brother's absolute power over her. When he acknowledged his faults to her with an open heart – then, and only then, would she return to his bed. It pained her to have to admit it, but her brother was the only man in a lifetime of men who roused her on both a sexual and an emotional level. It was inconceivable to her that she should never again feel the urgency of his caresses, just as it was inconceivable to her that she could ever hope to find a similar satisfaction with another.

But Lupei, in his unwitnessed heart, had begun to formulate the view that if his sister had decided to shun him sexually, it must, by default, be because she desired another man more than she desired him. In Lupei's experience every act was total – there were no half measures. He was entirely incapable, therefore, of understanding the female mind. But the male mind he understood clearly enough.

'Do you like Gypsies, Crusader Andrassy?'

'I hate them, Coryphaeus.'

'Do you believe I am the Parousia?'

'Yes, Coryphaeus. With all my heart and soul.'

'This woman you are looking at – if she is indeed the Yola Dufontaine we are seeking – claims to be pregnant with the progeny of the Holy Spirit.'

'This is impossible, Coryphaeus, for you are that progeny. Everybody knows that. They say that the Metropolitan himself does not dare to acknowledge the truth as it would mean the destruction of the Orthodox Church and of his position at its head. But that he visits you privately and weeps at your feet like a child. Is this true, Coryphaeus?'

'It is true.'

'I am at your service, Coryphaeus. You are my master and teacher. Order, and I will obey.'

'Where are you at this exact moment?'

Andrassy's voice swelled with excitement. 'I am in the village of Brara. Opposite an abandoned Saxon house with a three-metre high carved wooden entranceway that the Gypsies have commandeered. You cannot mistake it, Coryphaeus, as the carving shows a dancing bear. The Gypsies are not living in the main house, however, but in the garden, like dogs. There are a number of tents, but only one seems to be in use at the moment. The house lies opposite the main bridge over the river that runs through the village. The houses nearby are all abandoned. Most people now live on the periphery of the village, near the fields. We are not overlooked in any way. People keep away from the Gypsies.'

'Have you told anyone else where you are?'

'No, Coryphaeus. I have not spoken to my Lieutenant for five days. He expects my report tomorrow. He has a list of the villages I am to visit, however.'

'Good. That is not a problem. I will contact him

myself and bring him up to date. No need for you to do so.'

'Of course, Coryphaeus. What is it you wish me to do, Coryphaeus?'

Lupei hesitated. He knew that he was about to recross the invisible demarcation line he had first broached with the triple murders of the Russian VIP, the old priest, and his father – the line that marked the threshold between accepted and expedient morality. Other, strictly collateral deaths, such as that of the Jehovah's Witness at Budopie and the rogue imam at Frabolul, didn't count. Individually ordered deaths, however, were a scar on your immortal soul, and needed to be answered for. Well, thought Dracul – I will answer for them right enough. But not to God. No. Never Him. I will answer for them to my real master, the Devil.

'I wish you to rid me of this woman, Crusader. I wish you to crush this interloper. Can you do this thing for me? Or shall I call in your comrades to take over from you?'

'There is thick snow here, Coryphaeus. No one can travel either in or out of the village by car. My comrades would be unable to reach me. But my own vehicle is parked back up near the main highway. I walked in, Coryphaeus. I am in the perfect position to walk out again when I have ascertained the woman's identity. You said "rid me of her", Coryphaeus. What did you mean, exactly?'

'I mean you to use your discretion in the matter. Then report directly to me. No one else must hear of this. If you please me in this thing you will be made Lieutenant.' There was a pause. 'After all, Crusader Andrassy, what is a mere Gypsy in the greater scheme of things?'

Andrassy grinned. His heart was soaring. 'What indeed, Coryphaeus?'

# 49

Lemma, Radu's wife, was close to nine months gone in her pregnancy. Two months or so ahead of Yola. Radu had worked it out on his fingers, and he now reckoned that Lemma had become pregnant that first night in May when he had taken her virginity. This made Radu very happy. It also pleased him that Lemma was to have her baby before Yola. This fact gave him a small edge over his cousin Alexi, who was nominally his senior in the Gypsy hierarchy that obtained in the Samois camp. Alexi had nearly left it too long with Yola. There was a five-year age gap between her and Lemma.

Not that he resented Alexi in any way. It certainly wasn't that. There were any number of crazy Gypsy men in camps scattered right across France, and Radu was as much given to the deliriums of excess as any other man. But in Radu's opinion, Alexi topped just about everyone he knew in sheer crackpot lunacy. How O Del could have chosen a maniac like that to father the Second Coming was a complete mystery to him.

As a child, Radu had been told that God acted in strange ways – perhaps this was one of them? What was it that his grandmother had always said? '*Te ala mangel*

*O Del, vi daži del puške ekh matora*' – 'If God chose, even a broomstick could fire bullets.' Radu loved Alexi like a brother, but he held no illusions about him. Still, if Damo and the forefather man from many centuries back said that Alexi and Yola were to be the parents of the Second Coming, who was he to cavil?

At around ten o'clock that morning – and well before the most recent snowfall – Sabir and Calque and Yola and Alexi, accompanied by Bera and Koiné and their parents, Flipo and Nuelle, had set off for the weekly market at nearby Oponici. Lemma was too advanced in her pregnancy to walk anywhere, so Radu had agreed to stay behind to send for help to the village midwife in the event that her waters broke prematurely. But nothing of that sort had occurred. Lemma had slept for most of the afternoon, and Radu had busied himself chopping wood for the evening fire.

At 4.30, Lemma emerged to make Radu a cup of green coffee. There had been a heavy snowfall at around two o'clock, and while he was waiting for his coffee, Radu walked a few hundred yards up the track to see what effect, if any, such a fall would have on the party's return. Maybe they would decide to stay over – in which case it would give him some time alone with Lemma. Although heavily pregnant, she was still not immune to a little gentle persuasion in the coupling department. It excited Radu to hold his wife's swollen belly in his hands while he dog-mated her. O Del had been very good to him, giving him an amenable wife such as Lemma.

Another of his cousins, Zoltan, had married a shrew who asked for money whenever her husband made sexual demands on her. This was because she had discovered that Zoltan had once gone with a prostitute. From that moment on, she told him, he would have to pay her just as he had paid the other woman. *Malos mengues!* That was a wife to be reckoned with. Still, Radu was grateful that O Del had allocated him the more submissive, tender-minded variety of female. Even Yola possessed a barbed tongue when she had a mind to it. Fortunately for him, Alexi was so crazy in his head that he rarely noticed when Yola was on the warpath, and simply steamed towards the cataract like a barge that has lost its rudder.

Radu cleared himself a place on a nearby wall, sat down, and lit a *papirosu*. It was pleasant out here, with the fresh snowfall all around. It made a man feel safe. Radu was grateful that the memories of what had happened to him three months before were nearly gone.

He finished his cigarette, dropped it into the slush made by his feet, and watched it sputter out. Then he strolled back towards the camp, happily speculating on what he might be able to persuade Lemma to allow him to do to her, once it became clear the others were not returning home. The great advantage of pregnancy was that there were no impure times of the month to prevent a man from gaining his satisfaction whenever the urge overcame him – if only his friends and his relations would let him be.

Radu stopped about eighty yards shy of the entrance to the camp and canted his head to one side. What was this? A man had sprung to his feet directly across the road from the tent he and Lemma shared. As Radu watched, the man frantically patted his jacket, fished out his cell phone, and then ducked back into hiding again.

Radu drifted across to the side of the road and concealed himself behind a wall. His throat was dry. His heart was pounding in his chest. He looked about himself for a weapon of some sort, but there was nothing. Before he had left on his weather inspection he had been chopping wood and had sunk the hatchet deep into a log to protect the blade from rusting. Now he didn't even possess so much as a penknife with which to defend himself.

Radu watched the place the man was hiding. Beyond the man, he could see Lemma bustling about the fire, preparing his coffee. So the bad man and his siblings had found him after all. During the course of the last three months, Radu had gradually relaxed his vigilance. The onset of winter was partially to blame, together with the fact that there was no way on earth in which the four people who had kidnapped him could investigate every village and every hamlet in northern Romania on the one-off chance of encountering a particular band of Gypsies. There were hundreds – no, thousands – of Roma in that part of the country. It was an impossible task.

Even Damo, and his friend, the Frenchman Calque, had begun to lower their guard. The occasional trip to the local bar had formed a part of this new *glasnost* – as well as today's communal trip to the market. And then again, the whole emphasis of everyone's thoughts had inevitably begun to turn away from the Corpus Maleficus and towards the two women's pregnancies, together with all the necessary preparations for two births in two consecutive months in a country which was not their own, and amongst a people who had no particular reason to care whether the babies lived or died. And now, on the instant, everything had changed.

Radu chanced another look from behind his wall. The man had not moved from his position. Was it the young leader, then, or the other, quieter man – the one with the limp? The man with the cell phone had moved too fast for Radu to be certain of his identity. But it was a fair bet that he would be in the process of calling for reinforcements from whoever he was speaking to on his telephone – that much was clear. Where there was one there would be the others, surely? All four of the creatures would then converge on Brara to exact their revenge.

Two hundred yards away from where Radu was hiding, Lemma ducked back inside the tent. As Radu watched, the man rose from his place of concealment, withdrew a clipboard from his briefcase, consulted something on the clipboard, and then crossed the road with a swiftness that made Radu's heart clench inside his chest. This time around, Radu got a clear view of the man's face. The man was entirely unknown to him.

Could he have been checking something? The electricity, maybe? Or a water pipe running to the river? Maybe that was why he was hunched down out of sight? Maybe the whole thing was totally innocent, and Radu was letting his anxieties get the better of him? What was that other expression his grandmother always used? A fly can't enter a mouth that's shut.

Radu dragged his hands down his face. No. He couldn't risk it. He had allowed himself to be lulled into a false sense of security once before, and he had been kidnapped as a result. He must not let such a thing happen again. This time he had Lemma and the baby to consider.

Taking advantage of the man's momentary lapse in concentration, Radu duck-walked behind the wall until he was directly opposite the gate to the yard. The man was now writing something on his clipboard. Radu scissored his legs over the wall and concealed himself in the lee of the three-metre-high entranceway. He risked a glance through the gate.

The man, possibly sensing a third presence, checked around himself in the way animals do when their instincts tell them they are being stalked by a predator. Radu flattened himself against the carved wooden frame of the entrance arch and cleared his mind of all thoughts, just as he did when stalking roe deer in the Samois woods. By turning himself into a blank, Radu hoped that the man would not intuit his presence.

From his new position Radu could just discern the sound of the tent flap being thrown back as Lemma re-emerged into the daylight. The scent of the green coffee beans she was roasting wafted towards him on the late afternoon breeze.

Lemma gasped.

In his mind's eye Radu could picture the shock on Lemma's face when she realized that a strange man was confronting her, and not the cherished young husband she was expecting back at any moment from his afternoon walk. Radu's soul stirred with an unbearable sense of foreboding. He gritted his teeth, but remained in place.

'Excuse me,' began the man, with a smile in his voice. 'But are you Yola Dufontaine? I have you down on my list as living here. I represent the commune, you see. And we are conducting a census.'

'A what?'

'A census. That's a listing of everybody living within the commune and its confines. This is a government order. I am responsible to the government for this locality.'

The man's voice was hesitant when it should have been filled with a bureaucrat's solid pomposity. The reiteration of the word 'government' was too emphatic. The smile in the voice had also disappeared. Radu shifted his position until he was able to see, albeit at an acute angle, through the entryway.

'Is your husband, Alexi Dufontaine, here with you, by any chance?' As he said these words, the man glanced around himself a second time. On this occasion, however, the look was not that of a prey animal, but of a predator. Of a man with power. Of someone who feels himself to be incontrovertibly, and unassailably, in the right. 'I will need the names of your other companions too. And their ages and places of birth. Perhaps your husband can provide me with these?'

'My husband is away. I am alone here. I do not know the names of my companions. You must come back another time. He will answer you then. He will speak for all of us.'

The man grinned. 'I see that you are making coffee. Is it just for you? When I came by earlier, there was a man here. If he is the head of your family, I must speak to him. It is hardly too much to ask.'

'He is away, I tell you. At the other end of the village. And without his presence, I am unable to tell you anything. You must come again when he is back. Come tomorrow. That would be better.'

Lemma was casting anxious glances about herself. She was talking loudly, in the clear hope that Radu would hear her and conceal himself before the official saw him. All Gypsies were adept at evading bureaucracy – it was an integral part of their DNA. Over the many centuries of their diaspora most had learned never to volunteer information unnecessarily – or if they were forced into a corner, to muddy the waters and lie. Officialdom fed at the trough of facts. Vary the facts, and the bureaucratic behemoth ground to a halt. This much should be obvious to anyone with half a brain, thought Radu. Even this asshole with his clipboard.

'But you are Yola Dufontaine, aren't you?'

'Of course I am. Who did you think I was?'

Radu's sense of foreboding increased. Lemma thought she was doing the right thing by pretending to be Yola – but Radu suspected a trap.

'I have you down on my list as expecting a baby. Your condition is clear even to me. When is the baby due?'

'Next month. Or maybe the month after.'

'Next month, eh?' Andrassy smiled. 'Or the month after? You are very big, Doamnă Dufontaine. I have a wife and children too. I have some experience in these matters. I would hazard your baby will arrive sooner than that.'

Lemma backed hesitantly towards the safety of her tent. 'I may not talk to you like this. It is not allowed. My husband will be very angry with me. You must go away. Come back and talk to him when he returns. He will give you all the information you seek.'

Andrassy took a step towards her. 'Here. Look.' He took a further step. He was glancing nervously to his right and left now, like a guilty dog. 'These are my official documents. These prove that I am a registered census taker. Can you read?'

Lemma, her eyes still fixed on Andrassy's, ducked back inside the tent. She began to fasten the front flap from the inside.

Radu exhaled in relief. Surely, now, the bastard would turn round and leave?

But as Radu watched, Andrassy dropped his clipboard, flashed a final look around the compound, and sprinted towards the tent.

# 50

Radu allowed himself no time to think. The distance between him and the tent was thirty yards. He covered it in four seconds. The man was already inside the tent when Radu reached the opened flap. Lemma was on the floor in front of him and the man was squatting over her, both hands encircling her neck.

Radu yelled and threw himself on the man's back. The man flung one arm behind him and struck Radu violently on the cheekbone with his elbow. Radu had never known such pain. He was thrown back against the interior of the tent. He had still not entirely recuperated from the bullet wounds he had sustained the previous November. Now he could feel his left eye closing. His right eye began to flutter in sympathy.

The man struck Lemma with his fist. Then he turned his full attention on Radu. Radu tried to push himself up from where he was caught between the groundsheet and the side of the tent. The man lashed backward with his heel and caught Radu high up on the thigh, deadening the entire leg.

Radu knew that he and Lemma were going to die. There was something primeval about this man. He moved like a cat. He struck without compunction. His only motive was to disable and incapacitate.

Radu raised both hands to ward off the blows that were raining down on him. He could no longer see out of his left eye. He almost wanted the man to kill him. That way he would not have to face the humiliation of knowing that he had been unable to protect the honour of his wife.

The man grabbed Radu by the collar and threw him down beside Lemma. Radu could feel himself swimming in and out of consciousness. The first scything blow with the man's elbow had done the damage. Radu could barely raise his arms to protect himself anymore.

Andrassy's punch had caught Lemma on the side of the head, throwing her violently to one side. Now she hunched up in a ball to protect her baby. She was scared that the man would kick her, and that the bag protecting her baby would burst, drowning him. She felt rather than saw Radu being thrown down beside her.

Lemma knew for a certainty that the man with the clipboard had killed her husband. Now that Radu was no longer there to protect her, he would turn his attention to her and her child. She had a sudden vision of the tent aflame, and the man walking away into the dusk. No one would ever know what had happened to them. There would be no burial. Her mother would never see her grandchild.

The man started on Radu again with his fists. Was Radu, then, still alive? Lemma wriggled away from the pair of them, her knees buffeting her swollen breasts. She kept her cooking implements in the far corner of the tent, behind the bed she and Radu shared. She stretched out her hand and reached for the string bag. The man came after her.

It was dark in the tent. Lemma grasped the handle of the first thing she could feel and swept around with it in an arc, until she was holding it straight ahead of her with both hands. It was the fish scaler she had inherited from her grandmother. The blade entered Andrassy's descending hand and immediately broke off. Andrassy screamed. Lemma struck at him again with the shattered haft.

Andrassy backed away and glared at her. She could feel the intensity of his gaze in the half-darkness of the tent. Lemma raised the broken scaler high above her head like a sacrificial celt. Radu lay in a heap behind Andrassy. He wasn't moving. For a moment Lemma was tempted to use the broken haft of the scaler to cut her own throat. Heaven alone knew what the man would do to her now Radu could no longer protect her.

'Put it down, or I shall kick you to death.'

Lemma shook her head.

'Look what you've done to me.' Andrassy pulled the broken blade of the scaler from his hand. As he did so he fixed Lemma with his eyes and howled.

Lemma could feel her bladder evacuating. Then she realized that it was her waters that had broken. The shock of the attack had brought on parturition. She moaned. 'Please leave me. My baby is going to come.'

Andrassy laughed. 'No, it isn't.' He flicked the blanket off the bed beside him, covering Lemma from head to toe, like a magician preparing for a conjuring trick. Then he threw his full weight across her.

Radu had regained consciousness sufficiently to hear both Lemma's plea and Andrassy's response to it. A vast sense of outrage suffused him. Lemma was carrying his first child. She was his wife. She looked to him for protection and comfort. And he had let her down.

Radu struggled to his knees. He swayed in place for a moment and then lurched forwards. He grabbed Andrassy around the throat and threw himself backwards, pulling Andrassy over with him, so that Andrassy lay on top of him, but with his back parallel to the ground. As he did so, Radu scissored Andrassy's body with his legs and held him as in a vice. Andrassy tried to free his arms from the nutcracker grip of Radu's legs, but he could obtain no leverage.

Lemma was struggling out from beneath the blanket.

'Kill him, Lemma. Kill him. He cannot move. I cannot hold him like this for long.'

Lemma began searching for the broken fish scaler in the half darkness.

'Quickly, Lemma. Quickly.'

Andrassy roared and thrashed. He threw himself first to one side and then the other. Each move was agony for Radu, but still he held on like the Old Man of the Sea had held on to Sinbad in the stories his grandmother had told him as a child. Slowly – inevitably – he felt one of Andrassy's arms beginning to come adrift. 'Quickly, Lemma. I am losing him'

Lemma had found the broken fish scaler. She held it against her chest. She was weeping uncontrollably.

'Strike him!'

Lemma shook her head.

'Lemma, strike him. I order you. I am your husband.' It was the only thing Radu could think of to say. It was clear that Lemma was frozen in place with fear.

Andrassy threw his head back, barely missing Radu's nose and mouth. He used Radu's loss of concentration to free one of his arms completely. Fortunately for Radu it was the one that Lemma had speared with the fish scaler – the hand lacked strength, and functioned like a sluggardly sort of fin.

Andrassy struck backwards with the arm. His damaged hand bounced off the top of Radu's skull. Andrassy shrieked in pain.

'He is getting free, Lemma. Please.'

Lemma leaned forward and poked Andrassy with the broken fish scaler. The shattered blade did not even pierce his flesh. Andrassy yelled and threw himself to one side, oversetting Radu and subtly altering the balance of power.

Radu could feel his legs weakening. He swung round on top of Andrassy and reached for the scaler. 'Quickly. Give it to me.'

Lemma handed him the scaler.

Radu pulled Andrassy's head back by the hair and plunged the shattered scaler into the area above his carotid artery, just as he would do to a deer before bleeding it. The fractured blade, however, was no longer fit for purpose. It pierced Andrassy's skin, but stopped just short of the carotid sheath.

Radu levered the blade back and forth while Andrassy bucked beneath him like a rodeo bull. Andrassy was moaning now – a sort of involuntary rictus, half human, half animal. It sounded like the echoes to the entrance to hell.

Then the moaning stopped.

Radu shook his head. The silence in the tent was deafening. 'What did you do, Lemma?'

Lemma eased herself backwards so that she was sitting on her heels. She held her bloodied hands up in front of her face and stared at them. 'I found the carving knife.'

# 51

Between them, they hauled and dragged Andrassy's carcass to the house. Lemma stopped every now and then to clutch at her stomach, but it was beyond Radu's power to spare her the discomfort. What they were doing was brutally necessary, and he did not have the strength to manage the job alone. Each time Lemma moaned, it cut his heart to the quick.

They settled Andrassy in a corner of the ruined entrance hall. Radu went through Andrassy's pockets and put the contents to one side. Then he covered Andrassy with stones, broken furniture, and pieces of fallen masonry – it wouldn't hide him forever, but it would fool the casual observer.

Radu kneeled down and sifted through Andrassy's things. 'Look. We're in luck. Car keys.' Radu held up the keys and stared at them. Then he lit a match and looked closer. 'It says Simca. And a number.' He pocketed Andrassy's wallet, cell phone, and a penknife, and covered the remaining articles with a brick.

'What is Simca?'

Lemma was sheet pale and her expression was strained. Her face seemed smaller to Radu, as if he were looking at her through the wrong end of a pair of binoculars. She had a livid bruise on one cheek, and there was dried blood by the side of her mouth. Radu cupped her face in one hand and rubbed the blood off with a moistened finger. 'Simca is a kind of car. They haven't made them for years. It will be easy enough to spot.'

'How so?'

'There is only one usable road out of here when there is snow. This man will have parked up near the highway – somewhere it is easy to get out again – and then walked on in. That is what I would have done in his place.'

'But I cannot walk, Radu. Back there. In the tent. My waters broke.'

'What? Why did you not tell me?'

'How could I? The man was trying to kill us. And then you needed my help dragging him. It would not have been right to burden you.'

Radu dropped his face into his hands. He took a few deep breaths and then looked up at his wife. He held out one hand and Lemma crept into the circle of his arms. 'I am sorry, Luludja. Sorry that I have brought you into this. Sorry that you have had to help me kill and bury this man.'

Lemma looked up. 'I am not sorry. You are my husband. I will follow you anywhere. I will do anything. You have only to ask me.'

Radu crushed her to him and kissed her many times on the forehead. 'We must collect all we can from the tent. Then we must walk as far as this man's car. We can manage it. Sometimes the waters break before labour, do they not? If there has been a shock. Or an emergency.

There may be much time before the baby comes.'

Lemma braved a laugh. 'Radu, are you now an expert in pregnancy? Where did you learn this art? Have you been married before and you are not telling me?'

Radu covered his eyes with his forearm, as a man will do who has been caught out cheating. He walked as far as the door of the house and looked out. 'I have watched. I have seen. I am the child of women too, you know.' He was pleased that Lemma was teasing him. Pleased that she had forgotten, even if only for a little while, about what had gone before. He needed to keep her focused on the issue at hand, and away from what was happening in her womb. 'But we have no time. Someone knows this man was here. They know what he was trying to do. They will send after him. When they find him, as they will eventually do, they will come after us. Maybe the police too. So we cannot think to cross borders.'

'What?'

'First we must go to the others. Warn them. Tell them of this.'

'But look at you. One eye is closed. You have bruises and blood all over your face. If anyone sees you, they will remember you. Later, it will be obvious to all that it was we who murdered this man.'

'I will cross that river when I come to it. Can you walk?'

Lemma's face changed. 'I can walk.'

Radu tried to smile, but his damaged eye gave him a grotesque appearance.

'Radu, you look like a gargoyle. I must see to your

eye. We can pack it with snow.'

'I tell you we have no time.' He led her by the hand back towards their tent. 'Dress yourself in layers of your own and Yola's clothes. As many as you can fit on. And take the heaviest shoes you have. Also clothes for the children. Then pack food into the rucksack. Anything you can think of that keeps. I shall fetch the sleeping bags and some extra clothes for the men.'

'The men have warm clothes already. The others too. I saw them leave this morning. You will not be able to carry everything, Radu. We should only take what is vital.'

Radu nodded. Lemma, like all Gypsy women, was easily the most practical of the two of them. 'Then we will take just the sleeping bags and the food.'

# 52

It was almost dark when they started up the road. The snow was falling more heavily now, and the village had a hushed, muffled appearance. Radu made sure they skirted the arc of light emanating from each house – there was no point in asking for trouble. No person in their right mind would venture outside in this weather, and a man and woman seen travelling together in such conditions would surely be remarked on.

When they reached the outskirts of the village Lemma had to sit down and rest.

'I will go on alone and fetch the car, Luludja. I will come back for you. You are too tired to continue.'

Lemma shook her head. 'No, Radu. You will never make it back. Look at the road. You will get lost in a drift. Then I will be here alone. We shall go on together.'

Radu supported her as they walked. With Lemma on one side, the rucksack on his back, and a triple-layered refuse sack full of sleeping bags over his left shoulder, Radu couldn't pretend that he was comfortable. His body ached where Andrassy had kicked and hit him, and his effective field of vision had narrowed down to about twenty feet. Being on the run wasn't a recipe for physical wellbeing, he decided. Or for happiness.

When the cell phone he had taken from Andrassy rang, Radu froze in place. He procrastinated for a moment, and then frantically divested himself of the paraphernalia he was carrying and speared the phone from his pocket.

Lemma snatched at his arm. 'Don't answer it, Radu.'

'Why not?'

'I don't think you should. If the phone is not answered, the person at the other end may think that the man is still busy killing us. Or burying us, maybe. It will give us more time.'

Radu gave Lemma a shocked look. 'Luludja, that is brilliant. I would have answered and given us away.'

'You do not use phones, Radu. We young women do.'

Radu sighed. He shook his head. He could just make out Lemma's face in the darkness through his one good eye. 'Lemma. I must tell you something.'

Lemma cocked her head at him. 'What is that?'

'I did a very wise thing indeed when I married you.'

Lemma pretended to be taken aback. 'You have only realized that now? After you have already paid my bride price? You are a terrible bargainer.'

'Yes. Only now. Before, I thought I had married a shrew. Like that woman of Zoltan's – Striga.'

Lemma's mouth fell open. 'A shrew?'

'Yes. I was convinced you would turn into a shrew, like Striga. I thought this happened to all women when they married.'

'But Striga makes Zoltan pay whenever he wants to close her eyes. Do I make you pay?'

'Not so far, Luludja. But there is always time.'

Lemma fell into his arms. He crushed her to him, and rocked her against him. 'I will protect you and our baby. You know that, don't you?'

'I know that.'

'I am sorry this is happening. You are cold and hurt and in pain.'

'It is nothing.'

'You are a queen.'

'You are a king.'

Radu pocketed the cell phone and hoisted the rucksack onto his back. He swung the sleeping bags over his free shoulder and took Lemma's hand. He felt stronger now – more able to cope with the situation they found themselves in. Only a woman's love could do this for a man. 'The contractions? How frequent are they?'

'They are slow. Many minutes between each.'

'Come then. I must get you to the car while we can still do this.'

'There is a car, Radu? You are sure of this?'

Radu's heart momentarily ceased beating in his chest. 'I am sure, Luludja. Men do not carry car keys with them that they do not need.'

# 53

They found the Simca parked in a lay-by about half a kilometre short of the main road. It was facing away from the village. Radu swept the snow off the roof and bonnet and then tried the driver's door. It was frozen shut. He tried all the other doors. The same.

'Lemma, look away.'

Radu unzipped his flies and began a jerky circuit of the car. He peed on all the locks and down the cracks of the doors, grimacing as he adjusted his urine stream to each fresh target. He could hear Lemma giggling behind him. He zipped up his trousers and bent down to scrub his hands with fresh snow.

'That was clever, Radu.'

'Mama always said that the dangling object she noticed when I was born would come in useful one day.'

'Maybe it will freeze off now?'

'Do you want to warm it up for me?'

Lemma covered her face with her hands.

Radu walked to the rear of the car and yanked open both back doors. He helped Lemma onto the seat and covered her in a triple layer of sleeping bags. 'You will get warm now. I will start the engine. You will see.'

'I know.'

Radu mouthed a silent prayer as he inserted the key into the ignition. 'O Del, if this engine starts, I will do anything you want me to do. O Del, if you protect Lemma and my baby, I will be faithful to you all my life.' And then, swiftly. 'O Del, I am sorry I just said that. I will be faithful to you whatever you decide. You may take everything. Lemma. Our baby. Me. I accept all you have in store for me. Thank you for protecting us so far. Thank you for your gifts. Thank you for your love. I am sorry for my past ungraciousness.'

'What are you doing, Radu? Your lips are moving. And you have a strange expression on your face.'

'I am praying to O Del that this car will start.' Radu twisted the key. The engine turned over a few times and then stopped. He tried again. Same thing. His mouth went dry. He could still taste the blood where Andrassy had hit him. 'There must be a choke around here somewhere. I am not familiar with these cars. If the battery dies on us, we will freeze to death.' By the time he realized what effect his words might have on Lemma, it was too late to repair the damage. He groped around beneath the dashboard, found a lever, and pulled it. Then he tried the engine again. It coughed into life. 'Ya! Ya! Ya! Listen, Luludja. Doesn't that sound sweet?' Radu waited until the mixture was exactly right, then he pushed the choke half in. The Simca settled down to a steady tick-over.

'Will it make it out through the snow?'

'No problem now. I checked in the back. There are snow chains for the front wheels in case we get into difficulties. And two sleeping bags. A paraffin heater, too, and a canister of fuel. Dried fruit. Honey. Blankets. This man came prepared. We will surely make Oponici at least. After that, who knows?'

'Why do you not put the snow chains on now?'

Radu shook his head. 'Because I am too cold, Luludja. And too tired. And we are in a hurry. It would take at least an hour to put the chains on with my frozen hands. And it would mean stopping the car again to do it. I cannot risk it.'

'You decide, Radu. I am warm here now. I am feeling much better already.'

'The snow hasn't compacted yet. The tyres will cut through the fresh snow as long as I don't over-rev the engine. I have done this sort of thing before.' Radu was not quite as sure of himself as he sounded – he was used to driving trucks, not sardine cans. But he knew how frightened Lemma must be, and how bravely she was covering it up. He would not make the same mistake again of adding to her fear with his rash comments. He forgot, sometimes, that she was only eighteen. Often, when he looked at her, she still seemed like a child to him.

He depressed the throttle as gently as he was able. The Simca spun a little, and then began to feel its way through the virgin snowfall and towards the main road.

*Le Domaine De Seyème, Cap*
*Camarat, France*
*Friday, 5 February 2010*

# 54

———

Abiger de Bale watched Madame, his mother, through the V-shape made by his partially opened knees. He was sprawled across one of the leather armchairs in her afternoon salon, his back against one arm of the chair, his legs thrown over the other, just as he imagined Boris Drubetskoy, his favourite character in Tolstoy's *War And Peace*, would have learned to sprawl on his ambition-fuelled flight to the top of the military tree.

Abiger knew that the Countess disapproved of sprawling. But in the past ten weeks or so, their relationship had undergone something of a sea change, insofar as the Countess no longer insisted that a third party be present at each of their daily meetings. The softening of her previously entrenched position had come as a welcome change to Abi, who had spent eight weeks out of the past ten glowering, first at Madame Mastigou, then at Milouins, both of whom were lamentably prone to formality when given free rein – in short, it was impossible to relax with either one or the other of them around. But with his mother alone, Abi was able to switch on the charm and get away with murder. Well. In a manner of speaking.

Once the deal with Mihael Catalin had been sealed, and his evangelical Crusader hounds loosed after Sabir and his Gang of Three, Abi had hurried home from Romania in the fond hope that Milouins might still be tied up babysitting the drunkard Alatyrtsev somewhere in the Ukraine, allowing Abi the necessary gap in the curtain in which to kill his mother and secure whatever remained of her fortune after comrade bloody Antichrist Catalin had got his grimy little mitts on it.

But it was not to be. Alatyrtsev had – unsurprisingly, given Milouins's neanderthal proclivities – succumbed to terminal alcoholism barely a day after making the confessional film Abi had shown to Catalin. The man had apparently drunk four straight bottles of 60 per cent proof Vodka on the trot, thrown up his arms, and died. So Milouins had arrived home ahead of him after all.

Abi had to laugh. He briefly wondered how Milouins had done it. But then he remembered reading a short story called *The Leathern Funnel* by Sir Arthur Conan Doyle, at the instigation of his father, the Count, when he was eight or nine years old. The story spoke of the trial and *tormenta de toca* – more euphemistically known as the putting to the 'Extraordinary Question' or water-boarding – of an eminent member of the Corpus Maleficus, Marie-Madeleine-Marguerite D'Aubray, Marquise de Brinvilliers, who had been accused of the murder by Tofana poisoning (a mixture of arsenic, lead, and belladonna, devised by the famous Italian poisoner, Giulia Tofana) of her father and two brothers, as a means of inheriting their estate.

The 'Ordinary Question', as Abi remembered it, consisted of eight pints of water being poured down the distended gullet of the victim, and the 'Extraordinary Question' to precisely double that figure. Abi grinned. One could always count on the Catholic Church to bureaucratize persecution – in fact they were very like the CIA in that regard. Give something a fancy name, and people soon forgot what it really consisted of. He privately decided that a paltry four bottles of vodka, in the case of Alatyrtsev, must have seemed like something of a rest cure to the man. What a splendid way to go, though.

Then another thought occurred to him. Maybe Milouins had opted to use the wooden horse and the distending rings to add a little extra spice to his undertaking? To squeeze every last piece of information out of Alatyrtsev? On balance, Abi decided, probably not. I mean, why? It would have smacked of unnecessary sadism, and might have left marks – not to mention the cost in extra time. But with a bastard like Milouins one never quite knew.

'Is your tame Antichrist really going to become President of Moldova, do you think? Or is he simply going to go on a gigantic beano with your 200 million euros and buy himself a television station?'

The Countess smoothed the immaculate mesh of her tweed skirt across her knee. 'My tame Antichrist, as you call him, is undoubtedly going to be elected President of Moldova come the spring – with the quality of funds he now has at his disposal, and in the poorest country in Europe, how can he possibly fail? And if he wants to buy himself a television station, I would consider it a very wise investment indeed. Look at our friend Silvio Berlusconi. Do you imagine for one moment that he would still be Prime Minister of Italy if he couldn't manipulate his own publicity via Mediaset's 90 per cent stake in all Italian national television broadcasts?'

'Don't tell me Berlusconi's a member of the Corpus Maleficus?'

The Countess laughed. 'Of course not. The man's a Freemason. Far too stable. People like him worship profit, not anarchy. We only ever recruit our members from the certifiably insane.'

The cell phone rattled in Abi's pocket. '*Mes excuses.*' He backed away to a corner of the room to inspect his cell-phone screen.

'Who is it?'

'Well, speak of the Devil. It's our tame Antichrist. He obviously has something of note to communicate to us. Maybe he has run out of money?'

The Countess made a downward movement with her arm. 'Switch him to the main line and put him on the loudspeaker.' She cupped one hand behind her ear, the better to hear.

Abi did as he was told. Catalin had not contacted them for nearly two months. It would be amusing to hear what he had to say. 'Monsieur Catalin.' He hesitated. 'Coryphaeus Catalin. I should tell you that the Countess and I are both present.'

'Good. Because I have news.'

'Please be discreet.'

'Of course.' Catalin gathered himself together. His

English was adequate but pedantic – his French poorer. Normally, he would have called on Antanasia to translate for him, as her mastery of English was good. But he could no longer afford to involve her in what he was about to say, thanks to her recent lamentable descent into sentimentality. 'The goal both of us have been seeking is within sight. It is held within the village of Brara. Opposite an abandoned Saxon house with a wooden entranceway with a dancing bear carved upon it. The house lies opposite the main bridge over the river that runs through the village. There are tents in the garden. The houses nearby are all abandoned.'

'And Brara is where?'

'In the Maramureş. You will find it on any map. The spelling is self-evident.'

'Are we talking about all four of the subjects previously discussed?'

'No. Merely the main one and her subsidiary. And this one is being dealt with now, even as we speak. I understood from our original conversation that you wished to finesse the other subjects of our joint endeavour yourself? I am sure these subjects will be close by. Maybe it would be a wise idea for you to come out to Brara yourself?'

Abi glanced at his mother. 'Yes. I think that would be in order. Are you sure the main subject will have been foreclosed?'

'I have ordered it done. Confirmation should come shortly. I will keep you informed.'

'Thank you, Coryphaeus. We appreciate your consideration in this matter.'

'And I will appreciate receiving the second tranche of our agreement. All is well here otherwise. I am looking forward to the opportunity to serve my country and cement its borders.'

'Cement its borders?'

'The illegal so-called Pridnestrovian Moldavian Republic, otherwise known as Transnistria, was stolen from us by the Russians in 1990. They are occupying it illegally. It will be my first task in office to rectify this situation.'

'To rectify how, exactly?'

'We shall, of course, invade.'

The Countess spoke for the first time. 'An excellent plan, Coryphaeus. Excellent. I shall make the move on our game board. Will you be using the nuclear-tipped Kh-55s we discussed some months ago in your initial attack? They are the bullet-shaped counters in red plastic in the third compartment from the right in your game box.'

'Yes, Countess. I shall be using the three Kh-55s you initially proposed. With Tiraspol hors-de-combat, I fairly believe that the game will be mine. I have made certain promises to the forces currently at my disposal vis-à-vis the 2012 endgame we discussed. I would not like to disappoint them.'

Abi was staring at his mother with a stupefied expression on his face. She raised her cupped hand from her ear and made a cutting motion with it. Abi realized that he was expected to wind up the conversation.

'I shall be in contact again, Coryphaeus, once I have returned to Romania. Let us hope that we can both put a line under our joint undertaking.'

'As you say.' Catalin broke the connection.

Abi turned towards the Countess. 'Nuclear warheads?'

'Merely nuclear tipped. Hardly earth-shattering. But enough for a satisfactory knock-on effect. One might call it the "initiation of a destructive spiral". Similar, in effect, to the undersea earthquake that triggers a tsunami. Disaffected elements from within the Ukraine have been offering such things on the open market for many years. I suggested to our mutual friend that he might like to dip his toe into the irradiated water. The Moldovan Army would not be capable of retaking Transnistria without such a weapon. The original Kh-55 has a 2,500-kilometre range when launched from a Tupolev bomber. The Ukraine was left with 1,612 of the things after the break-up of the Soviet Union, most of which needed to be scrapped. Who was going to miss three?'

'But 2,500 kilometres? From Moldova, that would be enough to target Moscow.'

'Exactly what I had in mind, Abiger. On a wind-stricken day out stalking, when aiming for the chest cavity, you target the head. After all, what is the Corpus Maleficus if it is not the absolute defender of chaos on earth?'

*Albescu, Moldova*
*Friday, 5 February 2010*

# 55

Antanasia stepped out from behind the screen that dominated one corner of her brother's study. Her face was white. She was holding one hand up to her neck.

Lupei tossed the cell phone onto his desk. 'What are you doing in here?'

Antanasia raised her head. 'I was trying to steal money. Since you have refused to reinstate my allowance, and since your Crusaders shadow me everywhere I go – ensuring that I cannot leave town or make my living in any normal way – stealing from you is my only option.'

'So you're not only a whore, you're a thief?'

Antanasia flushed crimson.

'A thief who couldn't help overhearing what I have just said on the telephone?'

Antanasia made as if she were covering her ears. 'I heard every word. It was disgusting. They are using you, Dracul. You will bring everyone down with you. There are times when I fear for your sanity.'

Lupei lunged at his sister.

Antanasia dodged him and struck out for the door.

Lupei dropped to one knee and scythed at her legs with his foot.

Antanasia vaulted over his shin. She grasped the edge of the door to steady herself, but the momentary hesitation was fatal.

Lupei grasped her by the back of the collar and cracked her head against the door frame.

Antanasia fell to her knees, coughing.

Lupei hauled her to her feet. Then he ran her towards their bedroom, the way SS concentration camp guards would run their victims towards the execution trench.

'No. No. You leave me alone.'

'I will not leave you alone.' He redoubled his hold on her. 'Who is it? Who have you been seeing these past three months?'

'I've been seeing nobody. How could I see somebody? Your men follow me everywhere.'

Lupei thrust open his bedroom door with one hand and steered the half-bedazed Antanasia towards the bed.

'Dracul. No. Don't do this.'

'What do think? That I'm going to rape you? You should be so lucky.'

He threw her down on the bed and began to lash one of her arms to the bedhead with his belt.

'What are you doing? Leave me alone.'

Dracul ripped off Antanasia's blouse and used it to secure her other arm.

Antanasia threw herself back and forth on the bed, but Lupei kept his knee firmly on the small of her back. 'Who is he? Tell me now.'

'There has been no one.'

'Then why have you not slept in my bed for three months?'

Antanasia forced herself to calm down. She understood her brother's moods. Knew how to handle him. The cracking of her head on the door frame had bewildered her, however, and she was not thinking as clearly as she might.

Dracul was rarely this violent towards her. In fact he had not beaten her for years. With a sinking heart she knew that the least she could hope to get away with in the present circumstances was a forcible sodomization – it had always been her brother's preferred sexual diversion. There was clearly something about her enforced submission to an act she cared little for which particularly excited him. He had learned the habit from their father, of course, alongside a number of other, less rarefied, predilections.

'I no longer sleep with you because I do not recognize you anymore. You are not my brother. You kill without compunction. You drag other people into your offences. I heard you on the telephone. Have you gone crazy? What do you think the Russians will do to us? Do you remember what they did in Georgia? This will be far worse. They will send in the Spetsnaz and they will wipe us out. You are insane.'

Lupei had finished tying her up. She was sprawled on the bed in front of him, her face thrust into the pillow, her back exposed.

He rummaged in the bedside cabinet and brought out a knife.

Antanasia threw her head to one side. 'Dracul. No.'

Lupei began to cut the remainder of her clothes off, until she lay, stark naked, in front of him. He threw the knife to one side. 'Are you mine?'

'Whose else am I?' Antanasia had begun to cry. She remembered her father, and his abuse of her. Remembered all the men she had been forced to entertain so that Adrian Lupei could afford his *rachiu*. Remembered all the bestial things he and Dracul had done to her over the years, and for which she had so fervently tried to forgive them. 'What are you going to do to me?'

'Give me the man's name. The man you gave yourself to. The man you prefer to me.'

'There has been no man, Dracul. No man that you don't know of, or that you didn't give me to yourself.'

Dracul walked across to the dresser. He opened a drawer, felt around for something, and then walked back towards the bed.

'What is that?'

'It is a knout. It's what the Cossacks use to punish their prisoners. The Tatars invented it. You see these multiple rawhide thongs? Usually they have lead weights or sharpened hooks attached to them. Then they are wetted with milk and dried in the sun to give them a good edge. When Peter the Great knouted his son to death, he had the knout changed every six lashes, because he feared that Alexci's blood would soften the leather and thereby lessen his pain.' Lupei made a face. 'This thing is an apology for a knout, in other words. It's the sort of thing you chastise children with. I am sorry to insult you with it.'

'Dracul, I have never willingly slept with any man except you. I love you. But I fear for you. You have lost all discretion. Power has gone to your head. You are beginning to enjoy tormenting people. But it is not too late. There is still time to stop.'

Dracul moved to the side of the bed. He picked up a remnant of his sister's clothing and tied it across his eyes, so that he was entirely unable to see.

'Why are you hiding your eyes? Why are you doing this?'

'Because I do not wish to see your shame.' Dracul swung the knout down onto Antanasia's back.

She screamed.

Then he began to strike her in earnest. Because of his blindness, half his blows missed their target, but the other half struck home. He knouted Antanasia across the entirety of her body – her back, her head, her buttocks, her legs. Nothing she said moved him. He was entirely deaf to her screams. It was as if he had detached himself from his own humanity and had become the engine of his sister's ruination. With each blow of the knout he would leap into the air, as if he were stepping on hot coals, or negotiating an asphalted road, in summer, in bare feet.

After fifty blows he desisted. He threw the blood-soaked knout across the room. His sister had not uttered a sound for some time.

Lupei strode towards the door, wresting the torn cloth from his eyes. He did not look backwards.

*Oponici, Romania*
*Friday, 5 February 2010*

# 56

Oponici was a mid-sized market town, with all that that entailed in terms of population density and problems of circulation. Whereas Brara was small and dispersed, Oponici was dense and concentrated. The roads, however, had been partially cleared thanks to the extra revenue brought in by the stallholders, so that the market traffic was flowing out of town at something resembling a smart walking pace.

Radu stopped the Simca on the very edge of town and turned round in his seat. 'You stay here, Luludja. I am going in by foot. You must keep your head down below the line of the seats, and you must not move for anything. Even if a policeman comes along, just cover yourself in the sleeping bags, and pretend to be asleep. You must promise me this, Luludja. I will be back shortly.'

'Don't leave me, Radu. I am frightened.'

'I have to leave you. There is no choice. I must find the others.'

Lemma had no strength to argue. The contractions were becoming more frequent. She knew she daren't leave the safety of the car.

'If I switch the engine off, will you be warm enough

under the sleeping bags? We need to conserve our fuel.'

'I am warm enough. I am sorry I was frightened. But please be quick. I do not want to have this baby alone.' There was the ghost of a tremor in Lemma's voice.

Radu steeled his heart. 'I shall come back here with Yola and the others. Soon you will have other women to look after you. This will be better for you.'

'Thank you, Radu.'

'I love you, Luludja. I love you more than anything.'

Lemma covered her eyes with her hand. Radu had never said these words to her before. She did not want the *mulos* – the spirits of the dead – to hear them and snatch them away from her.

Radu hurried through the empty streets and towards the market square. How had they reached this pass? His young wife in the back of a strange car, about to have a baby. He having killed a man.

He stopped dead.

In reality it was not he, but Lemma, who had killed the man. Radu felt an intense sense of pride that he possessed a wife capable of such an act. A wife capable of walking three kilometres through the driving snow when she was just a few hours off having a baby. Lemma might be only eighteen, but she was already a fine woman for a man to call his own.

Radu hesitated between the market square and the residential district, with its hostels and its guest houses. Maybe the party had not yet settled on a place for the night? Ah. That was it. They would still be drinking at the *crîşma*. That's what he would be doing on a market day, given half a chance. Lurking in the warmth of a good bar and hoping some drunken Gypsy would come in and show you the way to free lodgings.

He turned towards the marketplace and approached the windows of the town's main bar. This would be the place. He could smell it.

He peered in. The windows were steamed to the gunnels. Radu sidestepped to where he had noticed a thin stretch of cleared glass. He squinted through it with his one good eye.

Alexi was holding forth to a crowd of drinkers with much hand-waving and considerable hammering of the table. A pall of smoke hovered over him from the cigars and cigarettes of the men surrounding him. Radu mouthed a curse. He checked around for the others.

A door crashed open beside him, letting out a current of superheated air. Radu flattened himself against the wall. He didn't want anyone to see him. A beaten-up Gypsy was memorable to everybody. It would not be a good thing.

The man ignored him. He staggered towards a concrete building situated near the corner of the road. Radu realized that this was the public privy. He followed the man across to the privy and concealed himself on the side of the road opposite the street lights. When the man came out again, Radu slipped in behind him and hid himself in one of the cubicles. The place stank worse than a piggery. But Radu knew one thing for certain. When Alexi started drinking, he also started pissing. It was an inevitable equation. Like cholera after a flood. He had only to wait.

Three men came in, one after the other. None of them was Alexi. Radu thought of Lemma waiting in the car. But he didn't dare enter the *crîşma* himself. People would ask questions. Before he knew it, Alexi would make some expansive joke and draw attention to Radu's face. Later, the police would hear of it and link him and Lemma to the murder. It must not happen.

The door opened and a fourth man walked in. Radu peered round the cubicle door. It was the Frenchman. Calque.

Radu threw open the door.

'*Putain!*' Calque sidestepped and threw his arms up in the air. Then he squinted at Radu in the dim glow of the twenty five watt bulb. 'My God, man. I thought I was being mugged. What are you doing here? Whatever happened to your face?'

Radu took Calque's arm. 'They have found us, Captain. I killed the man they sent. He thought Lemma was Yola and tried to murder her. But she is well. Don't worry.' Radu couldn't bring himself to talk about the coming of the baby. In his culture, there were certain taboos. They were there for a purpose. It was considered possible to put one's mouth on a thing and bring down bad luck upon it. Such a thing as the having of a baby. It therefore went unmentioned. 'We have the man's car now. You must persuade everyone out of the *crîşma* and I will take you to where I have left it. I explain to you all on the way. This is very important. They will be after us soon. There is no time to lose.'

Calque flared his eyes. A closer look at Radu's face,

however, convinced him that Radu hadn't been drinking. He allowed Radu to hurry him back towards the inn. Five minutes later Calque emerged with the rest of the party.

# 57

---

'We cannot all fit into this one car. It is impossible.' Flipo, Radu's brother-in-law, was standing behind Radu's sister, Nuelle. Their children, Bera and Koiné, stood at their side. All were staring at the Simca. 'Even the six of you alone would be a tight fit in there. An impossible fit if you ask me.'

Yola had already climbed inside the car. She was whispering to Lemma. Lemma was nodding. Yola put her hand under the nest of sleeping bags. She withdrew it, sniffed her fingers, and then shook her head and smiled.

Sabir had a fair idea of what was going on. It wasn't the first time he had encountered the Romani taboo on talking about pregnancy before the event. He decided that Yola had been checking to see if Lemma might have an infection. But he had not the faintest idea how one could tell that much from sniffing one's hands. Still. He wasn't a woman, thank God. He could think of few worse things to happen to one than to be expecting a baby in a car in a white-out in a country that was not your own. 'What do you suggest we do, Flipo?'

'I have relatives in Hungary. The Corpus is not

looking for us. I will take my family there. It is never wise to stamp on the tail of a snake.'

'How will you get there?'

'I have a little money. We will travel by public transport. Our papers are in order. We are in the EU here. Hungary is in the EU too. It should not be so hard.'

Sabir felt in his pockets. He counted out some cash and handed it to Flipo. 'Will this help?'

'Yes. This is enough to get us through.' Flipo pocketed the money. He was not a man given to gushing. 'Nuelle. Say goodbye to your brother and your cousins. You too, children.'

'Where will you sleep tonight?'

'Alexi has already arranged that. He talked to a man called Stefan about it. He is a Chirpaci. A basket maker. He has a workshop in town. We will sleep there. Before this happened, you would have slept there too. There is a stove. It will be warm for the children.'

Flipo backed off and shepherded his children back towards the *crîşma*. Radu's sister hesitated for a moment. She stared through the misted windows of the car at Lemma and Yola. 'I have had two children. I should stay. Lemma will need me.'

Radu shook his head. 'Yola will look after Lemma. You have Bera and Koiné. They need you too. And we have no more room. Flipo is right.'

Nuelle nodded. But still she hovered by the car.

Radu ducked his head at her. 'You will be *Kirvi* – Flipo will be *Kirvo*. More I cannot say. I do not wish to bring down the evil eye.'

Nuelle kissed her brother – a rare thing for a Gypsy

woman to do in public. Then she brought his hand up to her forehead and laid it gently on her heart.

Calque watched her as she hurried down the street towards her husband and children. He sidled up to Sabir. 'What was that all about?'

Sabir lowered his voice. 'I don't speak Amari Čhib. But as far as I can tell, Nuelle did not want to leave Lemma. It is clear to everyone that Lemma is just about to have her baby, but no one will talk about it openly for fear of damaging the child's chances. Radu made an exception and told Nuelle that she will be godmother to the child, and Flipo godfather – I caught the words *Kirvo* and *Kirvi* amongst all the other stuff. As far as I know this is an uncommon thing to decide before the child is born – there is usually a formal ceremony after the birth. Radu is taking a terrible chance. If the *mulos* overhear him, they may take the child's soul before it is born as a punishment for his vainglory.'

'Sabir, do you believe all this stuff?'

Sabir shrugged. 'I believe the Corpus tried to kill Lemma tonight believing she was Yola. This much I got out of Radu. I believe that when the snow stops, this car and its number plate will be a death trap for us. I also believe that we need to find ourselves somewhere safe to lie up in before that happens. Somewhere Lemma can have her baby. And that every minute counts until then.'

Alexi helped Yola and Lemma out of the car. He had sobered up remarkably quickly given the circumstances. 'We need to take out the back seat. Then we can make a nest at floor level with the sleeping bags. Four people should fit in there easily. Lemma can lie on the floor.'

'Alexi, you're a genius. Never let anyone persuade you otherwise.' Sabir helped Radu lever out the unwanted seat, while Alexi and Calque busied themselves going through the boot. 'It might be tricky, though, when we cross the border.'

Radu shook his head. 'We cannot cross the border. The phone I took from the dead man rang over an hour ago. By now there will be people coming to see what has happened to him. They will find the body. We did not have time to hide it very well. Then they will tell the police maybe. This car will be known. If we turn up at any border with it, they will take us and we will be tried for murder.' Radu's face had taken on a haunted expression.

'Christ, man. You didn't answer the phone when it rang?'

'No. Lemma told me not to. She said it would buy us more time if they did not know exactly what had happened. They might think the man was still killing us.' Radu crossed himself.

Sabir nodded. 'That's a bright girl you've got there.' He checked up and down the street. The snow was settling again. 'What's our alternative to the border? You know this country, Radu. Where the heck can we go?'

'When I was shot, a man helped me. He is called Amoy. He is a Căldărari. This is a maker of copper pots and stills. He and his wife have many children. She is called Maja. She is a good woman. She will look after Lemma. These Căldărari are a large community. They will protect us.'

'But where are they?'

'In the south-west of the country.' Radu waved his hand in a vague southerly direction. 'Near the border crossing at Jimbolia. Not far from Timisoara.'

'That's a good ten hours' drive away. We are in the middle of a snowstorm, Radu. And there are only so many roads leading west. We'll never make it. The Corpus will be out looking for this car. The weather won't matter rat's piss to them.'

'No. Listen to me, Damo. You remember I told you about Driver Kol who drove me to the village? He is the cousin of Maja's cousin Palfi. Kol told me of a road that cuts right up through the Carpathian Mountains. It is closed in winter.'

'Great. You know why they close the roads over the Carpathians in winter, I suppose?'

'Kol says it's passable.'

'But this car will never make it, Radu. It must be thirty years old. It does not have snow tyres. It does not have four-wheel drive. It will be carrying six and a half passengers.'

Radu frowned. He did not like the baby being mentioned even in jest. 'There are chains in the back. Alexi and Calque are putting them on now. I believe we have some time before the man is found. We must drive hard. On the main roads. Until we get to the pass. It is our only chance.'

'Even if we make it to the road, it will be sealed off. There may even be patrols.'

'Yes. It will be sealed off. There will be barriers at either end. But Driver Kol says the army uses the pass for winter exercises. They keep the road clear for this reason. Sometimes the truckers secretly use it. If the army catches them the truckers pay off the soldiers with cigarettes. It saves them many long hours of driving. We cut through this way and we get Lemma to my friends. This is my plan. They will hide us. I know they will. Amoy is a good man. His wife, Maja, will be happy to see you and help with…' He trailed off. 'Things.'

Sabir knew when he was beaten. The car was Radu's. Lemma was Radu's. It was clear that the ball was no longer in his park. 'Alexi? Calque? Yola? What do you think?'

Yola emerged from the car where she had been making Lemma comfortable in the space vacated by the back seat. She glanced up at the sky. 'Damo, if we stay here any longer it will be spring. And you will be godfather twice over. Just think what that will cost you in presents, and the calling in of favours, and bribes for Alexi.' She glanced at the others. 'Alexi is drunk, Calque is exhausted, and Radu has been beaten up.' She pointed at Sabir. 'I elect you driver.'

*Le Domaine De Seyème, Cap*
*Camarat, France*
*Friday, 5 February 2010*

# 58

Abi left it until Rudra, Nawal and Dakini had finished their packing and were waiting down in the salon for the taxi to arrive. He entered Dakini's bedroom and filled another suitcase full of her clothes, leaving just enough room in the case for an overnight bag of his own. Then he went downstairs to join his siblings.

He cemented his plan on the way to Nice Airport. He had already used his false passport, in the name of Pierre Blanc, when booking the flights from Nice to Bucharest. For the internal Bucharest to Satu Mare flight he had given yet another name, for which he had no passport but merely a French identity card – but he was confident that that was all that would be required in an EU country. As leader of the party, Abi had access to all the tickets. It was an easy thing to make sure the others did not see what he had done – and an equally easy thing to explain away if they did. Vau had teased him for years about the compulsive complexity of his travel arrangements, and Abi had admitted many times, to any of his siblings who cared to listen, how much he enjoyed travelling under a multitude of different aliases – that way, he explained, if he ever decided to do something illegal on the spur of the moment, he had already protected his back.

But none of the others were going to see the tickets this time around. Abi was going to make damned sure about that.

On the final leg of the flight to Satu Mare he began putting his plan into action. He doubled up in his seat, as if suffering from intestinal cramps. 'Bloody airline food. I knew I should have had the beef like you people. They've probably given me salmonella with their fucking undercooked chicken.'

He made three trips to the lavatory during the final twenty minutes of the flight. At Satu Mare airport it was natural that he should make a further emergency trip, once the baggage was safely through. 'Look. Go and hire the car without me. I'll meet you outside. I'll be standing over there by that bloody great sign which says Ascovit, okay? Do you think you can do that?'

Rudra shrugged. He was used to Abi's moods. Dakini and Nawal swung their cases onto the luggage trolley. Abi dumped the suitcase with Dakini's purloined extra clothes on top.

'Sorry. But this is desperate. I've got to get myself some pills at the pharmacy. I need to rehydrate.'

'Seven Up is the best soft drink in terms of minerals. Get yourself some of that.'

'Great advice. Thanks, Nawal. You should have been a nurse.' Abi made a sour face at her and walked away, very slightly hunched, as if he was fighting off yet another diarrhoea attack. Thank God he was dealing with women like Nawal and Dakini. Ordinary women would have been fussing around him like mother hens by now. Nawal and

Dakini had never cared for him that much, anyway, so they were no doubt relishing his predicament – they probably wouldn't even bother to mourn him if he crapped his lungs out like Noiret, Piccoli, Tognazzi, and Mastroianni in his favourite movie, *La Grande Bouffe*. What was that motto Piccoli had quoted from the Bible? *Vanitas vanitatum omnia vanitas*. Or, to put it more succinctly, 'What's the fucking point?'

Once in the pharmacy, Abi checked his pockets for ticket stubs, passport, money, and credit cards. He had packed enough spare clothes to last him for the duration in the overnight case he had hidden inside the main suitcase. The rest he was wearing.

He watched, from a distance, as Rudra negotiated the car-hire desk. When he saw the three of them heading for the underground car park, he struck out for the Ascovit sign.

The weather had worsened, which came as a pleasant surprise. He had been counting on the snow, thanks to the long-range forecast he had checked back in France, but this was even better than he had expected. The roads around the airport had recently been cleared, true, but he was willing to bet that the snowploughs hadn't bothered with the B road that led from Livana to Negreşti Oaş and then on through to Sighetu Marmatiei. The one skirting the Ignis Mountains. The one with all the S bends.

The rental car pulled up beside him. Abi motioned Rudra out of the driving seat.

'But I thought you had the shits? What do you want to be driving for? You must be out of your head.'

'I'm wide awake and chock-full of pills. You guys might as well take it easy for a while. There's no way I'm going to be able to sit back and rest with what's happening in my stomach.'

Rudra raised an eyebrow. But he got out of the car and walked round to the back. Abi was a control freak. If he wanted to drive in a white-out, he was welcome.

Abi hurried round to the trunk. He rummaged in the suitcase containing Dakini's clothes, and brought out his overnight case.

'What are you doing now?'

'This is just in case I shit my pants again. I've got a spare change of clothes in here.'

'Ugghhh. Do you have to be quite so explicit?'

Abi tucked the overnight case in behind his legs.

'Are you really going to drive in all those clothes? This car is air-conditioned.'

'I'm freezing. I'll take them off when I warm up.'

'Suit yourself. There really must be something wrong with you if you feel cold dressed in a getup like that.'

Abi grinned and started the car. It was all going smoothly so far. It was such fun to out-think people – to really use one's head over a thing. He'd got out of the habit recently, roosting in luxury at his mother's house. It was good to be on the road again. Good to have some definite end in sight. This time around, Sabir and Calque wouldn't slip through his hands like they'd done in Mexico. He'd have his revenge for Vau's death.

And what about revenge for the others, he caught himself thinking? Oni and the rest? And now Rudra and the girls?

Well, he couldn't care less about them. Sabir could piss inside their corpses as far as he was concerned. But his twin brother? That was different. Vau was the only person on earth he had ever really given a damn about, and he wasn't about to allow his murderers to get off scot-free.

He forced his mind, with difficulty, back onto the issue at hand. It was hard to believe that Catalin had really found the Gypsy whore and dealt with her and her baby. But the man had seemed so certain. And the description he'd given of the village made sense. Maybe his tame Crusaders were good for something after all? But how come she'd been alone? What about her husband? If a woman was pregnant, people usually hung around to help, even if their help wasn't really needed. Husbands in particular. That was the way of things, apparently, in what passed for the real world. So for her to be alone didn't make sense.

Well. He'd work it all out when the time came. Before that he had other things on his mind.

It took the Corpus party twenty minutes to make the Livara turn-off – and as Abi had anticipated, the condition of the road began to deteriorate from there on in. But the car Rudra had hired was the rental agency's premium model, complete with winter tyres and four-wheel drive, so the road surface was a doddle apart from the black ice on the corners where the sun hadn't shone – but all you had to do when you saw the black ice was not to brake, and pray that the man veering towards you in the opposite lane did not brake either.

Abi reckoned that things would really start to get

interesting when they began their ascent towards the mountains. Not that the Negreşti Oaşroad was going to take them very high. Probably not more than 1,500 feet tops. But that was plenty high enough for what he had in mind.

*Albescu, Moldova*
*Friday, 5 February 2010*

# 59

Antanasia woke up to the sound of her brother weeping.

She was still lying on her stomach with her arms stretched out in front of her, but while she had been unconscious the torn clothes with which Dracul had originally bound her had been exchanged for handcuffs. The pain in her back, buttocks and legs was extraordinary. It was as if someone had run a steam iron across her body, only stopping, now and then, to allow the heat to radiate to its full effect.

She groaned, and forced her face deeper into the pillow. 'You've killed me, Dracul. I shall not survive this. I must not survive it.'

'You will. You will.' Dracul brought his tear-stained face close to hers. 'I treated your back with salve while you were unconscious. And I've injected you with a painkiller. Some morphine. It's powerful. Very powerful. Soon it will begin to take effect.'

Antanasia could indeed feel her pain diminishing. Her eyelids began to flutter. All the horrors she had undergone in her life seemed to wash across her like an outgoing tide. 'I want to die, Dracul. I can't go on living like this. You've ruined me.' She could feel her words meshing together, as if they were coated in molasses. 'Inject me more. I want to die.'

'You will not die. I won't let you. You are mine.'

Antanasia began to laugh. She had rarely laughed since her tenth birthday, which her father had celebrated by declaring that she was finally valuable enough to sell. The laugh turned into a cough, and then to a morphine-fuelled wheezing.

'How can you laugh? Look at you. Look at what you have made me do to you.'

Antanasia closed her eyes. She could feel her limbs being progressively deadened by the morphine. Why was it that it was always the men in her life who abused her? What was it about being a woman? Were all women treated like this? Did untold women walk the streets with dark horrors like hers tucked away in their hearts? Or had God chosen her as a sacrifice so that all other women might be allowed to walk free? The Eve sacrifice that her father had explained to her when first he had offered her body to his friends? Antanasia could feel her mind degenerating. She knew that she must speak soon, or she would be unable to voice her fears.

'Dracul, if you are truly the Second Coming, as you declare, perhaps you can cause a miracle to happen? Perhaps you can heal me? Perhaps you can cause to be blotted out everything that has happened to me in the past thirty years? If you can do this, I will truly believe you are a miracle worker.' She began to cough again, which forced her to open her eyes. As she stared ahead of her, the design on the wallpaper began to crawl up the wall as if it were alive. What did she have to lose anymore? Even physical reality was betraying her. 'There is an expression the French use. "Don't ever lower your arms – you might do it just before the miracle occurs."'

Dracul took Antanasia by the hair and held her face up to his own. She could see the dried tracks of tears upon his cheeks. His eyes were like dark wells within which monsters lurked. She wondered if her own eyes were equally besmirched.

'If you continue talking in this way, I shall be forced to strike you again.' He allowed Antanasia's head to fall back onto the bed.

Just before she lost consciousness Antanasia prayed to God that He would take her now, whilst she was still herself, and not merely the sum total of somebody else's pain.

*Sibiu, Romania*
*Saturday, 6 February 2010*

# 60

Sabir drove through the night. The way he figured it, the Simca must be known to someone, somewhere, and its number, in consequence, almost certainly flagged up. He also reckoned that, come morning, he and his companions would be that much more vulnerable to police checkpoints and random inspections, and that they clearly needed to have gone to ground by then.

Radu had assured him on numerous occasions that he and Lemma had buried the body of their attacker beneath a pile of bricks and rubble, but Sabir could only imagine the sheer panic that must have suffused them while they were doing it. He knew from bitter experience that murdering someone – even someone who deserved murdering – changed you in some way. Ingrained habits no longer counted. What you thought you had done and what you really did were two different animals entirely.

At around two in the morning it seemed as if Lemma's baby was finally about to make its appearance. Sabir pulled the car off the road and left the engine running, but it soon became clear that Lemma's increased contractions had been a false alarm.

As Radu could only see out of one eye, and as Alexi

was still recovering from his binge, Sabir agreed to let Calque take over the wheel for a couple of hours. It rapidly became apparent, however, that Driver Calque was having trouble negotiating the snowdrifts, so Sabir shunted across and retook the wheel. His teens and early maturity spent negotiating Western Massachusetts' often severe winter conditions had prepared Sabir well for February weather in central Romania.

Calque's driving, on the other hand, had clearly suffered as a result of his having been allocated a personal driver during his time as a senior officer in the French police force – the man drove in an oddly tentative fashion, given his normally decisive temperament, and had a marked tendency to brake at all the wrong moments and then grin stupidly, as though he really had intended for everybody to lurch forward in tandem as if on a rollercoaster.

They passed the old Saxon town of Sibiu at six in the morning, with the Carpathians, and their second highest peak, Negoiu – which they knew they must cross – clearly visible from the twenty-four-hour Romgaz service station they used for tanking up and buying provisions. There were few cars on the roads, and when they turned off through Avrig, in the foothills of the Făgăraş Mountains, and towards the Transfăgăraşan road itself, the traffic dropped to a trickle. If people wanted to travel by car between Wallachia and Transylvania, they were clearly using alternative routes.

'We're crazy doing this, Radu. We'll never make it across the pass in the dead of winter. Look at that sign. It says the DN7C peaks at more than 2,000 metres of altitude. Just imagine what it's going to be like up there. We've got to get Lemma to a doctor here and now.'

'But Driver Kol...'

'Fuck Driver Kol. You told me once that he drives a modern eighteen-wheeler truck. This car must be a least thirty years old, it has four indescribable wheels, and the snow chains have about rusted through. Plus we have your wife...' Sabir hesitated, mindful of Gypsy superstition. '... indisposed. Are you seriously telling me we should continue across a pass that, even in perfect weather, and at the absolute height of summer, probably forces any vehicle that crosses it to average less than thirty miles an hour? We're talking the Rockies here, Radu, not the fucking Berkshires.'

Yola put her hand on Sabir's arm. 'Listen to Radu, Damo. Please. It is no use shouting at him.'

Sabir stopped the car at the exit to the village of Cârţişoara. He looked up the valley towards the Transfăgărașan pass. 'Why should I listen to anybody? Take a look up there, all of you. Do you see what I see? The gates to that pass will be locked as tight as a tick's asshole. We'll have to turn back anyway. This is utterly pointless.'

'Please, Damo. Your language.'

Sabir shrugged. He was susceptible to Yola and she knew it. She had saved him from Achor Bale's clutches in that Camargue cesspit nine months ago, and she was able, in consequence, to cut herself a little slack with him whenever she chose to. Every man has his weakness, and Yola – his blood sister – was Sabir's. 'Okay, Radu. Spout.'

Radu was holding himself in with difficulty. The past fourteen hours hadn't been the easiest of his life, and he was still suffering from the aftermath of Andrassy's blow to his head. 'As I told you, Damo, the army keeps the pass open in the winter for its own purposes. I know for a fact that trucks sometimes use it too – if they can make it through unseen, or can find someone to bribe.'

'But not in an effing snowstorm.'

'No. No. Driver Kol said that the army has its very own snowploughs, which are kept permanently up near the pass. And this time of the morning all the Special Forces soldiers, the ones they call the Mountain Hunters – the Vanatori de Munte – will still be tucked up in their barracks down in the valley at Curtea de Argeş.'

'Unless they are finishing a night exercise.'

Radu shrugged philosophically. '*Na xanrrunde kaj či xal tut* – "don't scratch where you don't itch". Nobody will be looking for us up there, Damo.'

'You bet they won't. The army will probably find us and the car gently thawing out in some forgotten ravine come spring. It'll make one hell of a story. Think how happy the Corpus will be. All their broken eggs in one basket.'

'Please, Damo. The risk is ours.'

Sabir glanced at the four Gypsies crouching in the well made by the torn-out rear seat. Then he looked across at Calque. 'What do you think, *mon Capitaine*?'

Calque shrugged. 'I think we need to find out exactly what we're up against before we make a decision that we may regret later. As of now, we can still drive out of here. In an hour's time, with this volume of snow, it may be too late.'

'Well, how do you suggest we go about doing that?'

'Radu, did you say you still had the cell phone you took from the man who tried to kill you and Lemma?'

'Yes.' Radu dug into his pockets. 'Here it is. I never used it. I have his wallet, too, and a few other odds and ends.'

'I don't want those. Just give me the phone.'

Sabir grabbed his friend's arm. 'Calque, you can't be serious. You can't make a call with that. They could trace us back via the network.'

Calque shook his head impatiently. 'Radu, you said that the phone rang while you and Lemma were burying this man's body?'

'Yes.'

'Maybe whoever rang left a message?'

Radu shrugged. 'This is possible. I never thought to check.'

Sabir puffed out his cheeks. 'I must be losing it. That thought had never occurred to me either.'

Calque gave one of his 'cat-that-got-the-cream' smiles. 'None of us is thinking very clearly at the moment.' He fired up the cell phone, then fiddled with the buttons a little and held the phone up to his ear. He closed his eyes and listened. After a moment's hesitation he handed the phoned to Yola. 'The man is speaking Romanian. Can you understand him?'

Yola listened to the message. Then she played it again.

Calque took the phone back, switched it off, and replaced it in his pocket. 'So? Are we any further along?'

Yola nodded. 'It wasn't the Corpus that mistook

Lemma for me and tried to kill her. The man leaving the message calls himself Coryphaeus Catalin. In this message he is asking the owner of the phone, the man Radu killed – a man he calls Crusader Andrassy – to phone him back immediately and tell him if he has carried out his instructions to the letter.'

Sabir slapped the steering wheel with the flat of his hand. 'Catalin is the man I told Lamia about. The man I described to you all a few months ago. The man Nostradamus appears to be describing when he talks about the Third Antichrist.'

Calque's face was bereft of emotion. 'Well, it appears that the Corpus have contacted him, just as you feared, and have brought him round to their way of thinking – no doubt via the transfer of large sums of money. That much was inevitable from the moment they learned about his existence from Lamia.' Calque refused to look at Sabir when he said this. 'The dead man is clearly one of Catalin's infamous Crusaders. And where there is one, there will be more.'

'What do you mean?'

'I mean that this changes everything. We are much more vulnerable to a man with the reach of a Catalin, in his own territory, with an extensive network of religious fundamentalists at his command, than we were to four – albeit vengeful – members of the Corpus Maleficus. Radu is right. Our only hope, in the absence of a *deus ex machina*, is to keep clear of the main roads until we can find sanctuary somewhere. Radu tells us that he has some Romani friends who will take us in and look after Lemma – and later, Yola. The safety of the two women must be our priority. That is only just. But to reach this sanctuary, Radu tells us that we need to make for the south of the country. And our safest way to do that is to avoid the main roads and cut straight across the Carpathians. Anyone have any other suggestions?'

Silence greeted his words.

Sabir groaned and slipped the car into gear.

*Sighetu, Romania*
*Friday, 5 February 2010*

# 61

Abi glanced into the rear-view mirror. His two sisters were dozing. Dakini had her chin on her chest, with her mouth partly open, and Nawal was hunched against the side window, her head rocking in tempo with the car.

He looked at Rudra.

Rudra was watching him with busy eyes, like a man following the vagaries of a computer game. 'What are you hatching, Abi? I know that predatory look of yours.'

Abi gave a half-grin. 'Nothing, really. I was fantasizing about what I would do to Sabir when I finally got my hands on him.'

'Is that all?'

'Isn't that enough? Oh, and I was hatching a plan to burgle Fort Knox. And steal the British Crown Jewels. And I intend to raid the French Exchequer, too, when I have the time.'

'Don't you have enough money already?'

'Nobody has enough money.'

'Madame, our mother, has.'

Abi's grin transformed into a smirk. 'But that's hers, not ours, Rudi. Fingers off, little brother.'

Rudra laughed. 'You have a point.' He glanced back

at his sisters. 'What *are* our plans, by the way?'

'It's simple. We spend the night in Sighetu. Then, first thing tomorrow morning, we go to Brara. But we take it easy. We don't blunder in. We don't know what the situation is there. There could even be a police presence. This guy Catalin sounds confident, but he's only twenty years shy of the Communist era inside his head. My experience is that people like that have a certain mindset. They've been schooled to take no for an answer. If something costs a bit of extra effort, they simply won't do it. The bastard's even got his cell phone switched off.'

'So you don't think his people got the Dufontaine girl and her baby after all?'

'I should be stunned if they did. It would be way too neat. But we'll get a lead from them. Then we can go ahead and do the job ourselves. This Catalin person doesn't have the motivation we do.'

'Revenge, you mean?'

'Don't you want revenge, Rudi?'

'Sure. I want revenge. But with you I'm not so sure. You never cared for any of us. That much was clear, Abi, right from when we were little children. You seemed detached from the rest of us.'

'Oh, really? What about Vau?'

Rudra shrugged. 'Did you really give a damn about what happened to him? Be honest.'

Abi had half his attention on the road ahead. It was nearly time. But he didn't dare unlock his seat belt or the beeper would sound.

'Did you hear me, Abi?'

Abi gave an impatient nod. 'Yes, I gave a damn about Vau. I loved him. He was my twin brother.'

'But he was thick as two short planks. Christ, Abi, he was almost autistic.'

Abi felt like reaching across and cuffing Rudra on the side of the head, but he held himself in. Now was not the time. But it made what he was about to do considerably easier. 'Vau was marginal Asperger's. There's a world of difference between that and autism.'

'Marginal? That's a laugh.'

Abi turned to Rudra. 'Are you trying to bate me? If so, Rudi, I have to tell you that you're succeeding.'

'Bate you? Me? Now why should I do that? After all, it's not as if you left us all to die in a corpse-polluted sinkhole in deepest Mexico, is it?'

Abi blew out his cheeks. 'Christ.'

'Yeah, Christ. I told you I wouldn't forget it, and I haven't. I meant what I said when I promised you we'd have a reckoning at the end of all this.'

'And we've reached the end of all this, have we? Is that what you're trying to tell me?' Abi put a sneer in his voice. 'Well, I wouldn't call it the end. I'd call it pretty near the fucking beginning.'

'I'm not suggesting we hammer it out here and now.'

'Oh, really? That's big of you. When would you like to do it? Shall we set a date? December 21st 2012 sounds pretty neat to me. Let's agree to have it out then. On the day our little Maya friends have allocated for the Great Change. Is it a deal?'

'Sure.' Rudra held out his hand.

Abi wrenched the steering wheel to the left, slewing

the vehicle across the opposing lane. As he did so, he released the clasp of his seat belt.

Rudra was rocked violently to the right.

Abi threw the wheel in the opposite direction. As the car hit the nearside kerb he unlatched the driver's door and tumbled out of the car, clutching his overnight bag to his stomach. He went straight into a forward aikido roll, curled up like a parachutist, his chin tucked into his chest, his head protected by his arms. He had counted on the thick snow to deaden and slow his fall, and this proved to be the case. He rolled three times, then straightened his legs, converting his momentum into a lumbering run.

The car, meanwhile, continued on its original trajectory, its speed increasing with the angle of the gradient. It bumped across the verge and then careered down a steep meadow towards the gorge that Abi had been following with his eyes all the time he spoke to Rudra.

Would it be deep enough? If it wasn't, he knew that he would have to go down there and finish the job himself. But what was he worrying about? He would need to visit the car anyway to transfer Rudra from the passenger seat across to the driving one.

He had made damned sure of one thing, though. At no point in the proceedings had anyone witnessed four people together in the car. Three people had hired it, and three people had set out from the airport car park in it. Abi had made it very clear, too, when he had bought his sibling's plane tickets, that he was making the booking for a party of three. His own ticket had been bought on a separate day, and through a separate agency. And in a name that was not his own.

He squatted in the snow and brushed himself off, checking the road in both directions while he did it. It was empty as the overflow from hell. Which wasn't surprising, for he had made a point of waiting until he had seen no car for at least five minutes in either direction before making his move. If a car did come past, it was hardly likely that they would notice the fresh tracks leading off from what was, after all, only a minor road. At the rate the snow was cascading down, there would be no sign of anything at all in twenty minutes.

Abi rummaged in his bag and brought out a waterproof jacket and a pair of over-trousers. He put them on over his damp clothes. Leaving the bag behind him, he jogged to the edge of the gorge and peered over the side. The four-by-four was lying on its roof, parallel to a slow-running creek maybe thirty feet below him. Its wheels were still spinning. Its one remaining light cut a swathe down the line of the river.

Abi eased himself across the overhang and scrambled down the slope. He was aware of a visceral sense of excitement in the pit of his stomach. One part of him was tempted to stop and howl like a wolf in triumph.

He reached the car and looked inside. There was movement. 'It's all right. I'm here. I'll get you out.' He threw open the back door.

Nawal tumbled half out. She turned her face up to him. Her mouth was crushed, and part of her cheekbone had been pushed through one eye socket.

Abi freed the telescopic fighting baton from his sleeve.

He extended the baton, then bent at the waist and swung it as hard as he was able against her open wound – it was best to use the injuries that were available to him, and not create any fresh traumas that couldn't be explained away by the accident. He crouched down and peered through to where Dakini was lying. She'd clearly broken her neck. No extra prinking needed there.

He dragged Nawal's body completely out of the car, and eased the back door shut. Then he went round to the passenger side at the front.

Rudra was still alive. Just. This, too, he would enjoy.

Later, when it was all over, he unhooked Rudra's seat belt and dragged him across to the driver's seat. He attached the new belt and wiped his own prints off the steering wheel and gearshift. Then he rubbed Rudra's hands over anything a driver might have touched, making sure to get clear prints on the horn section and the rear-view mirror.

When he was done, he dragged Nawal's body into the passenger seat and attached her there. Both front air bags had deployed, and were now partially deflated, so he smeared Rudra's and Nawal's faces against the fabric. The side and torso airbags had also deployed, so he shunted all three of the corpses around a little to equalize things on that front.

'Fucking useless tat,' he muttered to himself.

It was clear that in any real accident the airbags wouldn't have kept anybody alive. The extent of Nawal's injuries had made her as good as dead anyway, and Rudra had been completely out of it when Abi gave him the *coup de grâce*, so there had been no fun there.

Abi decided that, on the whole, he could live with the disappointment, given the prevailing circumstances.

When he had tidied up to his satisfaction, he moved to the bank of the creek and rinsed his hands and the smeared fighting baton of all traces of blood. The snow was coming down even harder now. There would be no giveaway tracks come morning – just an easily explainable accident on a minor country road in post-blizzard conditions.

Abi scrambled back up the hill to his overnight bag. Inside he had a sheepskin balaclava, hand warmers, double gloves, chocolate bars, and water. He put on the balaclava, got the hand warmers fired up, and ate one of the chocolate bars. By his calculations, Sighetu was about three kilometres away across the hills. He had originally intended to go cross-country, but with the way the weather was shaping up, hardly anyone was out on the roads anyway, so why make life anymore difficult for himself than he needed to? Plus he would see any approaching headlights from miles away, and have ample time to hide.

He swung the bag over his shoulder and began to walk.

# 62

It was eight in the evening when Abi reached the outskirts of Sighetu. He straightaway began the search for a suitable vehicle to take him on to Brara. He had spent the past couple of hours working out exactly what he would say to Madame, his mother, when she got the news about the death, in a car accident, of three out of four of her remaining children, and he was happy with the upshot of his lucubrations.

His *coup de théâtre* on the airplane would come in handy there, for certain. He would explain to the Countess about his stomach – how he had been afflicted with diarrhoea, nausea, the works – and about his decision to stop over for the night at Satu Mare until things settled down again. His foresight about the extra suitcase, and the fact that none of the belongings found in the car would be his, would further back up his claim, which was that he had merely sent the rest of his siblings on to Brara to check up on things there, and they had agreed either to return for him, or to phone and tell him where to meet them, depending on the circumstances they found in situ. It was hardly his fault that Mihael Catalin had shut down his lines of communications and gone to ground, forcing the Corpus to undertake their own investigation of his claims.

During the course of his two-hour walk, Abi played out every possible eventuality in his head, including that of flight. He knew that Milouins and Madame Mastigou would be suspicious of him, but that Madame, his mother, given the quality of their recent relationship, might conceivably extend him the benefit of the doubt. What would he say when she questioned him as to his theories about the accident? That Rudi was a useless driver at the best of times, and that they had all been exhausted after their two delayed flights? That the snow conditions had been execrable and the airports all but closed down? That he had tried to persuade his siblings to put off their investigations until the morning, but that they had overruled him? Something to do with their resentment at what had happened in Mexico, no doubt. As he approached Sighetu, Abi had to consciously force himself to stop dwelling on the might-bes of the situation, and focus on the here-and-nows.

What he didn't need was a modern car with some complicated bloody alarm system that woke up half the town and drew everybody's attention to the stranger in their midst. Vau – or at least the Asperger's afflicted part of him – had been a genius at all that sort of technical mumbo jumbo, and Abi had been quite content to leave that side of things to him. But the five-year-old Romanian-built Dacia Logan he was now looking at wouldn't be beyond him. There were thousands of such vehicles in Romania, and he would have no problem at all in interchanging number plates. The cars were designed for crap roads too, with firm suspension and extra-high clearance. They had 50 per cent fewer parts than the Renault they were based on, and no fancy electronics. Perfect for the job.

The fifth one of his pass-keys worked on the lock. He checked around himself. At this time of the evening, and in these conditions, people were busy shutting down for the night, not winding up to go out on the town. Chances were, the theft of a car wouldn't be noticed until the morning, when he would be long gone and the car re-registered with different plates. Yes. He might as well go for it.

The same key that had worked for the door worked for the engine. Paradise. Why weren't all Western cars built like this? He gave the engine sufficient time to warm up, consciously winding himself down in the process – adjusting his breathing – moving from highly tense to merely alert.

The snow was still falling, but the roads were definitely passable. If things got worse, he would simply steal himself a four-by-four. Or a pick-up. *Saperlipopette!* He might even steal a snowplough. There was nothing – nothing at all – linking him to the three Western Europeans lying dead in the ravine. And he suspected that the local Sighetu police force wouldn't waste a great deal of their precious time and limited resources on an in-depth investigation into what was clearly just a tragic accident occasioned by the weather.

Abi felt a burgeoning sense of freedom. It really was true. He was the only one of his immediate family left alive. An unreluctant orphan. The last survivor of the

Devil's Dozen. He already held all the family's aristocratic titles. And now, when Madame, his mother, died – as she eventually would, with or without his help – he would be rich beyond the dreams of Croesus. And he was still in his twenties – limbs, brain and family jewels intact. Christ. He might even decide to get married and breed if the fancy took him. The world and all its goodies, Abi decided, were his oyster.

But first things first.

He still had to square the reckoning with Calque and Sabir. Once that was done, his triumph would be complete.

*Albescu, Romania*
*Saturday, 6 February 2010*

# 63

Dracul Lupei let it be known around town that his sister had been stricken with the typhoid. He blamed it on the Transnistrians himself. People from that part of the world came to Albescu all the time looking for salvation, and his sister had been in the habit of interviewing most of them on arrival to see what they could contribute to the communal interest. Such people tended to bring stuff in with them – diseases and suchlike. In the future, he – Mihael Catalin, the Renascent Christ, the Chosen Harbinger of Revelation – would enforce a strict period of quarantine for all foreigners. Not all drinking water was as safe as that provided by his own purification plant. Yes. He would place this at the very top of his agenda.

Privately, Lupei ordered his Crusaders to guard the house and not let anyone in – even the cleaning women. And that included Iuliu Andrassy's wife, Georgetta. Typhoid was dreadfully contagious, and Coryphaeus Catalin, given who he was, would nurse his sister himself and thus protect the rest of the community from danger. Perhaps he could even contrive another miracle?

He had informed Georgetta that her husband was on

a secret mission for him, infiltrating the Evangelicals, and would thus not be home for a number of weeks – and that, because he was working undercover, he would inevitably be out of telephone contact during that period. Georgetta was a peasant and therefore gullible as hell, except when it came to money. She didn't question the Coryphaeus's story – everything he said and did was all right by her. She was merely worried that he would have no one to do his washing and to clean his house while he nursed his sister back to health. She would have time on her hands without her husband around. Surely he would like her to look after him?

No. The Coryphaeus wouldn't. He would manage alone. Abnegation was good for the soul, and had not the Lord Jesus Himself been forced to spend forty days and forty nights in the wilderness during the period of trial immediately following His baptism? The Coryphaeus would therefore dedicate himself to fasting and to the mortification of the flesh while he tended to his sister's welfare. What had Cimarosa said in his Requiem? *Juste judex ultionis, donum fac remissionis, ante diem rationis* – 'Just judge of vengeance, grant me remission before the final day of reckoning'.

Privately, Lupei had tried to contact Andrassy on a number of occasions during the twelve hours following his original phone call, but he had eventually given up in disgust. Instead he had called Andrassy's superior officer in the Crusaders, Lieutenant Markovich, and told him to pull all his subordinates off what they were doing and converge on Brara to see what was going on. Then he had lost interest.

What really interested him was Antanasia. He would enter her bedroom and stare at her for hours on end as she lay, unmoving, on the bed. Recently, as well as dosing her up on morphine, he had tried switching her to Rohypnol when the pain became too great for her to bear. He liked the Rohypnol effect. One time he had even made love to her from behind, while she was still unconscious, the mush from her unhealed wounds spreading like jelly beneath his thrusting body. The orgasm he had achieved in this way had been the most significant of his entire life. It had made him feel like God Himself.

Having Antanasia entirely in his power gave Lupei an extraordinary sense of potency. There was no thought in his mind that she might die. He was sufficiently convinced of his own pre-eminence to no longer doubt his capacity to influence nature to his own advantage. If he did not wish her to die, she would not do so. If he wished to kill her, he would. If he chose to mark her body, this was his prerogative. He had taken her from his father, and she was his to do with as he would. Every path was acceptable, just so long as it reflected his will.

Recently, he had become even more convinced of the truth of his asseveration that the world would end on 21 December 2012. The Mayans, who had originally earmarked the date as the end of the Long Count Calendar and the Cycle of Nine Hells, and then – based on the quality of response of the world community, as the beginning of the era known as the Great Change – simply did not know what they were talking about. They were good at calendars, but useless as eschatologists.

As a race, the Mayans were largely passive. Content to let things happen to them rather than to trigger events themselves. Look at what had occurred under the Spanish. Total bloody capitulation.

He, on the other hand, was a doer. A catalyst. A changer of history. If he said something would happen, it would. This was not vainglory on his part – merely the simple acceptance of an established fact.

As future President of Moldova, he would order the launch of all three of his Kh-55s at midnight on 20 December 2012 – one aimed at Tiraspol, one at Kiev, and one, for good measure, at Moscow. Frankly, he didn't expect the Moscow one to make it through the Russian Federation's missile shield, but by that stage it wouldn't matter anymore. The die would have been cast and the gamble taken. Russia would respond to the destruction of its 14th Army outpost in Transnistria in the only way it knew how – with force. And Lupei had always hated the Ukrainians, so destroying a virtually unguarded Kiev would be an unforeseen bonus. Nobody would imagine Moldova, the poorest country in Europe, to have access to nuclear weapons. So Russia would strike at Romania, thereby involving the rest of the EU and NATO. The whole thing would be immensely satisfying. With luck it would spiral out of control and wipe out the whole seething lot of them.

Lupei still found it almost inconceivable that his followers had not clicked that the cross they had had tattooed across their foreheads constituted the 'mark of the beast'. Did none of them read their Bibles? Did none of them know that it was idolatrous to worship graven images? And that 'graven', in the strictest biblical sense, merely meant the 'engraving of an image onto a surface'? Wasn't skin a surface, then? Hadn't they read Revelation, Chapter 14, Verses 9 to 11?

> And the third angel followed them, saying with a loud voice, If any man worship the beast and his image, and receive *his* mark in his forehead or in his hand, The same shall drink of the wine of the wrath of God, which is poured out without mixture into the cup of his indignation; and he shall be tormented with fire and brimstone in the presence of the holy angels, and in the presence of the Lamb: And the smoke of their torment ascendeth up for ever and ever: and they have no rest day nor night, who worship the beast and his image, and whosoever receiveth the mark of his name.

Lupei knew that his followers had doomed themselves from the moment they agreed to the forehead tattoo. This tattoo had become a passion with his people – they clearly felt that by permanently marking their flesh they would curry favour with him, and, via him, with God. Instead, they were simply marking themselves out as victims for the 'fire next time'.

The thought pleased Lupei immeasurably, and further reinforced his view that people were swine to be led wherever their herdsman – and that herdsman was he – chose to lead them. And like swine, they had no earthly clue that the butcher awaited them. They were content to linger at the trough and await their swill, in the blind belief that they were part of an everlasting charity programme designed to allow them to live without thinking.

Well, he would show them. Those who had the most faith in him would suffer most. And chief amongst these was his sister, Antanasia. Named after a saint who was beheaded by the Emperor Diocletian because she didn't have sense enough to sway with the wind, Antanasia's absurd goodness in the face of all the evils that had befallen her during her life made her a worthy successor to her namesake. Lupei would only be able to consider himself totally evil, and thus worthy of the Devil's trust, if he was able to destroy or undermine all that was totally good.

His sister had betrayed him. With whom, he did not know. But he would find out. He had the time. And the inclination. And what was that thing his father had always said to justify his abominations? Ah. He remembered now. The sweetest crime of all is to outrage those who love you the most.

*Transfăgărașan Pass, Romania*
*Saturday, 6 February 2010*

# 64

'This is it, then. Abandon hope all ye who enter here.'

Sabir watched as Radu and Alexi struggled with the lock of the massive snow-gates that barred the entrance to the Transfăgărașan Pass. Just as he was on the verge of advising them to give up on it and climb back inside the car, Radu stepped triumphantly backwards, dragging the right-hand part of the gate with him.

After Alexi had secured his own section of the gate, he gave a mock bow, sweeping his hand across his chest as if he were flourishing a musketeer's hat. 'You see, Damo? Gypsy know-how. We can get in and out of anywhere. Houdini was a Gypsy, did you know that?'

'Bullshit, Alexi. He was Italian-American.'

Alexi screwed up his face. 'Well he should have been a Gypsy.'

Calque – bundled up in as many clothes as he could find, and looking disturbingly like the Michelin Man – was standing beside Sabir smoking a cigarette. At every exhalation, his breath fluttered the descending snowflakes, clearing an eerie track around his face. 'Actually, Harry Houdini was born Erik Weisz, in Budapest, Hungary, and his father was a rabbi. So you are both wrong. And do you know where that expression you just used comes from, Sabir? The one about "abandoning hope"?'

Sabir was giving himself a fireman's warm. 'No. I don't.'

'It's from Dante's *Inferno*. The context is particularly apposite to the situation we find ourselves in.'

'Really?'

'Yes. Do you want me to recite it?'

'Calque, you will recite it to me whether I want you to or not.'

Calque flicked his cigarette away. He brushed vainly at the snowflakes which had settled in the pleats of his jacket. 'My translation, of course.'

'Of course.'

'The original Italian goes:

*Per me si va ne la città dolente,*
*Per me si va ne l'etterno dolore,*
*Per me si va tra la Perduta Gente...*
*Lasciate ogne speranza, voi ch'intrate.*

'Which I would loosely translate as,

Through me you pass into the city of woe,
Through me you pass into eternal pain,
Through me you enter the highway of lost souls...
Abandon hope, all ye who enter here.'

Calque frowned at the ground. 'Actually, I seem to have missed a bit out somewhere. But that's about the gist of it.'

'For Christ's sake, Calque. You really are the gloomiest bastard I've ever met.'

Calque grinned. It pleased him immeasurably that Sabir was feeling confident enough to start ribbing him again. He decided to push the envelope a little further – it was the only way he would know for certain if Sabir had truly emerged from his three-month post-Lamia depression.

'So the point I am trying to make is that you were guilty of a Freudian slip, Sabir, when you used this expression so freely. You thought you were being amusing, but it secretly shows that – at least as far as your unconscious mind goes – you are actually in a Dante-esque state verging on total despair. The truth will always out to those in the know.'

Sabir struck himself on the forehead with the flat of his hand. 'Zounds, Calque! Where did you learn all those big words? And are you sure you still want me to drive? If I'm in total despair, as you suggest, I might decide to end it all on the spur of the moment, and take you guys along with me for the big sleep.'

Calque ignored the implied insult. He breathed a metaphorical sigh of relief. 'That's a risk that I'm prepared to take. You've seen my driving. And the others are clearly in no condition.'

Sabir shook himself like a dog. He was half aware that Calque was testing him. But whereas the day before he might have cavilled, now, following the mistaken attempt on Lemma's life, and the consequent threat that that implied for the rest of them, he felt it was no longer appropriate to dwell purely on himself and his own feelings.

He had undoubtedly fallen prey to morbid self-analysis over the past few months. It was high time to shake himself out of it. All Sabir's life he had felt most comfortable when succouring others. Now that Yola and her baby had clearly become Mihael Catalin's main target, it behoved him, as her formal blood brother, to place her and her child's safety before his. It would be a liberation of sorts.

'Well, come on then. Stop standing there gabbing. The snow won't wait for us. The sooner we get to the top, the sooner we can start down the other side. You'd better pray that the chains don't part on your "highway of lost holes".'

Calque began a slow handclap. 'Very funny, Sabir. One can tell you are a writer. You have such a way with words.'

As if it had been hearkening to Sabir, the road instantly became much harder to negotiate. It was obvious that the army had been through and cleared at some point during the previous day, as old snow was bunched up at the side of the road in ten-foot piles – but that night's snowfall had ensured that a six-inch layer of fresh snow had more than made up for the shortfall. On a number of occasions, all three of the male passengers had to get out of the car to push, while Sabir kept the Simca in low gear and tried to get the chains to ground without spinning.

As they crawled up a particularly steep incline near the top of the pass, the car lost all forward momentum and began to slide uncontrollably backwards with everyone still inside.

'Don't brake! For God's sake don't brake, Sabir!'

Sabir did his best to guide the Simca backwards, bouncing the chassis off the banked snow at the side of the road in an effort to slow its vertiginous descent. Fifteen or so seconds into the slide, however, it became clear that the car was reversing out of control.

Sabir glanced into the rear-view mirror. He could see a corner looming up, 300 metres below them. He realized that if he couldn't stop the car dead in its tracks before then, he would be faced with a catch-22 situation of either steering backwards into a tree, or risk spinning over the side of the canyon towards certain death.

Radu threw himself across Lemma in a vain effort to protect her from the imminent collision. Alexi twisted in place so that his back was facing the rear of the car, and then pulled Yola in between his legs, so that his body would protect her and the baby from the full force of the impact.

Sabir touched the brakes three times in an effort to slow their slide, but each time the car lurched nearer to the gorge. In desperation, he threw the wheel in the opposite direction to the bank, ensuring that the tail of the car slewed across the road and pitched into the heaped snow at the side of the road, flipping the vehicle around on its axis until it faced forwards again.

Once he had got the vehicle facing downhill and no longer slip-sliding backwards, he touched the throttle and steered directly for the same bank he had just struck with the tail of the car. This time the Simca angled head first into the compacted snow and ground to a stop. Calque was thrown forward against his seat belt, while

Sabir managed to brace himself against the steering wheel. The four passengers in the open well behind him slammed into the back of his seat.

The Simca settled deeper into the bank and conked out.

Sabir sat, his hands at precisely ten to two on the steering wheel, and stared at the unfenced corner twenty yards below him. He didn't want to guess how steep the fall-away was, but it surely numbered in the hundreds of feet. If he had allowed the car to angle out across the corner, the Simca would have behaved like a matchbox full of lead shot – everybody inside would have been stirred around as if by an invisible ladle, eventually to be dashed to pieces on the rocks below. Silence had never felt so sweet.

One thing, though, was abundantly clear. The car was no longer in any fit state to take them to the top of the pass.

Sabir looked behind him. 'Is everybody all right?'

'Yes. We were able to brace ourselves. Everybody is okay.'

Sabir looked at Calque.

Calque was holding his nose.

'Are you hurt?'

Calque nodded. 'That's the second time this year that I've broken my nose in a car accident. First as a passenger with Macron. Now with you, Sabir. Next time, I drive.'

'Stop twitching. Let me have a look at it.' Sabir flicked on the courtesy light. It threw out a thin shaft of luminescence – hardly enough to illuminate its own surround. 'I don't think it's broken again. It's just bleeding. You've got a bad gash on the bridge. Hold this against it.' Sabir handed Calque his handkerchief.

'What are we going to do now?'

Sabir shook his head. He leaned forwards and tried the engine. On the second turnover, it fired. 'Bravo, Simca. It's probably not going to take us anywhere, given what's just happened to the chassis, but at least we'll have a little heat.'

'Sabir?'

Sabir checked that the headlights and all the vanity lights were switched off. Then he turned to his companions. 'Calque, you and Radu had better stay with the women as you're both injured. Alexi and I will strike out for the top of the pass. There's bound to be a hut of some sort up there. If we do find one, we'll break in and try to get a fire lit. Then we'll rig up some sort of sled device for Lemma. When we've got the place warmed up, we'll come back down and get you. We've got two thirds of a tank of gas. The engine should tick over until we get back. While we're away you can gather together all the things you think we are going to need. That way we won't waste any time on the journey back. We'll have to bundle Lemma up and get her under cover as soon as possible.' He hesitated, looking at Yola. 'Have we still got some time?'

'A little. Yes.'

'Great. That's great news.'

'What if you don't find a hut?'

Sabir glanced away. 'That's not a problem. We'll build an ice palace over the car – the same sort of emergency ice palace they taught me to build on the Hardangar Plateau in Norway when I went Nordic skiing. We've got the bank. We've got the snow. We're already halfway there. We'll seal the car off like an igloo, with a chimney to let out the foul air. It'll be ten or fifteen degrees warmer in here than outside. That way at least we'll survive the rest of today and tonight without freezing. Plus we've got a paraffin heater for when the engine gives out. Radu says that the army comes through here on a regular basis. We've got food. We've got water. We'll simply hunker down under cover and wait for them. They can't possibly miss the car – it's blocking half the road.'

Calque peered at Sabir over the top of his bloodstained handkerchief.

Sabir refused to meet his eye.

*Brara, Maramureş, Romania*
*Saturday, 6 February 2010*

# 65

Crusader Lieutenant Cosmin Markovich, aged forty-four, colour of hair brown with threads of grey, marginally overweight, residual arthritis in his left hand from half a lifetime spent as a steel worker, was proud of his position as one of Coryphaeus Catalin's top echelon commanders.

Markovich's life had seemed somehow incomplete until his wife, Florenta, had learned, through a girlfriend, of the Coryphaeus's existence. He had disapproved at first when Florenta had suggested they attend one of Catalin's Sunday prayer meetings, and had resented the waste of fuel. But Florenta was nothing if not persuasive, and she and her husband had come to an eventual accommodation which had involved a lot of giggling and numerous visits to the bedroom.

Later, after the prayer meeting, both had admitted to each other how impressed they had been with the Coryphaeus's single-minded approach to religion. They had moved, two months later, lock, stock, and barrel, to Catalin's model town of Albescu, where Markovich immediately found work in one of the Coryphaeus's factories. It hadn't taken long for Markovich to be marked out as a potential Crusader – and since that time, five years before, the sky had seemed the limit.

As a Crusader – and with all the privileges that ensued as a result of his abrupt elevation from the hoi polloi – Markovich had developed a relish for power and for the better things in life which had totally eluded him for his first forty years. From a poverty-stricken youth he had now graduated to a respected middle age, in which he held both rank and, he believed, the esteem of the majority of junior Crusaders under his command. Florenta, too, seemed happier, now that they could afford the children that, before, he had been forced to refuse her.

All in all, then, Cosmin Markovich felt that he owed Mihael Catalin all the good things in his life – and his loyalty was, in consequence, unswerving. The three-bar patriarchal cross tattooed on his wife's forehead had afforded him a few confused moments, it was true, but he now realized that it had merely constituted a necessary test of his and Florenta's steadfastness, and, as such, an upwardly mobile rite of passage towards the inner echelons of the Church of the Renascent Christ.

Now Markovich stood outside the Saxon house in Brara – which his subordinate, Iuliu Andrassy, had marked out as belonging to the apostate, Yola Dufontaine – and tried to work out from the blood markings left in the snow and inside one of the tents exactly what had occurred. Markovich knew that Andrassy had been the proud possessor of a thirty-year-old Simca motor car. What had happened to that vehicle? And what had happened to Andrassy himself? Had he killed the Gypsy woman and then panicked? Or had the Gypsies killed him and then stolen his car? It was hardly likely that a proto-fascist like Andrassy would have developed a sudden soft spot for his victim and eloped with her. Georgetta Andrassy was not what you would call a handsome woman, it was true, but she kept a sparkling home, and her cooking was second to none. The fact that she was built like a brick shithouse was neither here nor there.

Markovich bit his lip. He knew that he must very soon complete his written report to Coryphaeus Catalin. He also knew that he needed to provide his leader with something concrete in the report or else his stock would drop vertiginously. The three Crusaders he had managed to pull in from the surrounding district had clomped pretty much everywhere in the village asking their questions, but to no real effect. There had been fresh snowfall in the past few hours, and this had complicated matters further.

At this time of the year, as Markovich knew very well from memories of his own extended family, the local people hibernated. And such people weren't much interested in the problems of the Roma at the best of times. Come early spring, half the village would have been standing here musing on the situation, and adding their ten *bani*-worth to the communal pot – but in the dead of winter they kept to their homes, not even bothering to eavesdrop on the strangers through the frosted windows of their hermetically sealed houses.

This thing with Andrassy and the pregnant Gypsy woman, though – the one they had all been asked to search for – was clearly important, or the Coryphaeus would not have dragged Markovich away from his duties to investigate it. So what was he to tell the Coryphaeus? Cosmin Markovich was at a complete loss. Never in his life had he been faced with such a thought-provoking conundrum.

And this man – this jumped-up European aristocrat named de Bale whom the Coryphaeus had sicced on him with no warning at all – he wasn't helping much either. The man made Markovich uneasy. He was so overwhelmingly confident – so certain of his right to instant obedience, that it hit Markovich's top note. When Markovich had questioned his presence on the scene in an early leg-lifting bid to establish dominance, de Bale had simply told him to call his leader. That all would be explained to him then and there. And when Markovich did as he was told and called up the Coryphaeus on the dedicated Crusader line, the Coryphaeus had seemed almost irritated to hear from him.

'Yes, of course I told the Count de Bale all that had happened. He is to be afforded every courtesy by you and your men. And you are to follow his orders to the letter. He and his family are major contributors to our Church and I have no wish to antagonize them. At least not at this early stage in the proceedings. Finding the woman and neutralizing her is part of an extended agreement we have with him – if this is carried out effectively, funds will be forthcoming. Funds that this Church desperately needs if it is to continue its work of enlightened evangelization. Eggs need to be broken in order to make an omelette, Crusader.'

'Yes, Coryphaeus.'

'Now listen to me carefully, Markovich. I don't want you to bother me again. My sister is very ill. I am required to look after her and heal her. All my energies are focused towards this aim. De Bale will be the one to tell you what to do about the Gypsy and her companions. Obey him in everything. Treat him as you would treat me. Use the connections we have inside the Romanian police to locate Andrassy's car and to trace where he went after he left Brara. Next time you feel the need to communicate with me, use e-mail. Only phone me in emergencies. Otherwise, wait for me to telephone you. Is that understood, Markovich? E-mail only. Written reports. That's the way to go.'

'Yes, Coryphaeus.'

'Excellent. I'm relieved that I can count on you. Your wife will receive a side of Aberdeen Angus beef from my butcher at the earliest convenience.'

The connection was cut and Markovich was back on his own again. Or at least, not exactly on his own, but with this Frenchman from out of nowhere – and who seemed to have so much clout with the Renascent Christ – peering over his shoulder. What was he to do?

Well it was obvious, wasn't it? Even to an idiot. Obey.

# 66

Abiger de Bale watched Markovich from the very spot that Andrassy had used to spy on Lemma all those hours earlier. He was trying to work out in his head whether Markovich would be worth the bloody trouble or not. Whether it would be better to dump him and his bevy of spotty, blank-faced young assistants, or use them as cannon fodder.

On the whole he decided it would be wiser to keep them on board. They all possessed firearms – and, presumably, knew how to use them. And any scruples they may have had about killing in the cause of their faith had clearly been corrupted long ago. Lupei/Catalin, on the other hand, was manifestly not only corrupt but also barking mad, and therefore not to be trusted with anything beyond the securing of the Moldovan Presidency from the equally corrupt camarilla of crooks he was up against. Any real challenge – the murder of a Gypsy woman and her unborn child, for instance – was clearly beyond him.

The prospect of letting a man like that loose with a trio of nuclear-tipped Kh-55s when the Russians were camping just across the border in Transnistria was ludicrous. According to the Countess, the Corpus saw themselves as 'the absolute defenders of chaos on earth'. Well, chaos was all very well in its place – but if, after dealing with Sabir and his cabal, Abi wanted to retire from the fray and enjoy the late Madame, his mother's, money at his leisure, a nuclear war in central Europe was the very last thing he needed.

Abi stared down at his feet. He had made the dreaded phone call to the Countess two hours before, using as his pretext that the Romanian police had contacted him about the tragedy that had befallen his family because his was the only number – apart from that of his two dead sisters – on Rudra's airport-purchased pay-as-you-go cell phone. All lies, of course – but the world revolved around lies, and he revolved with it.

His mother's response had been predictable – eerie, but predictable. Nothing, but nothing, must be allowed to get in the way of the Corpus's big moment. Not even the tragic deaths of three out of four of her remaining adopted children.

Abi decided that his mother was as mad in her way as Catalin. Neither of them would be dangerous in the normal run of things, but when you factored in money, ambition and hubris on the part of the Countess, with power, vainglory, and a seriously loose hinge on the part of Catalin, you created a hazardous catalyst – somewhat along the lines of heating a mixture of tetrachlorobenzene and methyl alcohol over an open flame and praying it wouldn't explode.

And now the power that Catalin already possessed was set to increase exponentially with the injection of the Countess's millions. Giving him another 150 million euros, on top of the 50-million-euro down payment he had already received for simply signing along the dotted line, struck Abi as adding insult to injury.

He shrugged and glanced back across the road. First things first. This was the exact spot he would have chosen for himself had he wished to overlook the Gypsy camp without being seen, so it seemed the obvious place for him to start his investigation. The snow had covered up all the tracks, true, but Abi soon found the used butt of a cigarette jammed into a crack in the stone. Then, when he scrabbled in the snow, he discovered an empty crumpled pack of Moldovan Temp cigarettes which exactly matched the used butt, and which hadn't yet had time to deteriorate into pulp.

He stood up and strode towards the wooden entranceway Sabir and the others had been using. There were two tents in the orchard. Gypsies lived in tents by preference, and not in houses – and the house was a wreck anyway. Abi stopped dead in his tracks.

But Sabir and Calque weren't Gypsies. They wouldn't choose to live in a tent if they could possibly avoid it. They would find themselves a roof and four walls.

Abi switched direction and headed for the house. He was beginning to work out what might have happened in his head.

It soon became clear where Sabir and Calque had been living. Three connecting rooms at the back of the ruined house were still habitable. One had been transformed into a bathroom, complete with zinc bathtub, basin, and slop bucket, and the other two rooms had been converted into more or less useable bedrooms. Abi decided then and there that he would never, ever, go on the run. What a comedown for Sabir compared to his bijou little home in Massachusetts. Abi still regretted not burning the place to the ground while he had the chance.

He rifled through what remained of the two men's possessions without finding anything of note. But one thing did interest him – there were scarcely any clothes left. But he had seen clothes, surely? He walked back to the door. Yes. They'd been bundled up and then abandoned, as if someone had changed their minds at the very last moment and thrown them to one side. That was significant in itself. If the tents were equally bereft, much would be answered.

Abi started through the ruined front of the building. Then he stopped. There was a pile of rubble and broken furniture near the shattered entranceway. He stood and looked at it.

'Markovich!'

'Yes, Sir?'

'Was it snowing yesterday. When Andrassy was here?'

'Please speak slower, Sir. My English is not good.'

'Snow.' Abi made sprinkling motions with his hands. 'Did it snow when Andrassy was here?'

'Yes, Sir.'

'Has it been snowing since?'

'Yes, Sir. Many times.'

'Look over there. At that pile of junk.'

'Yes, Sir. I'm looking.'

'You see the drifted snow next to it? The moving snow?'

'I do. Yes, Sir.'

'That's taken weeks to build up, hasn't it?'

'Probably, Sir, yes. The wind does this sometimes.'

'But there's no drift on the pile. Just a light covering of fresh snow. Is that likely given the recent conditions?'

Markovich shrugged his shoulders. He didn't really understand what the Frenchman was going on about, but he thought it best to humour him.

'Start digging, Markovich. I think we've just found your missing colleague.'

*Transfăgărașan Pass, Romania*
*Saturday, 6 February 2010*

# 67

The wind chill outside the Simca had to be felt to be believed. Sabir and Alexi stared at each other like two golfers unexpectedly caught beneath an isolated tree in an electrical storm. Both men ducked their heads and began to ascend along the serpentine tracks left by the runaway car.

Sabir was the first to unravel his scarf and tie it over his ears and across his mouth, leaving only a small gap to see through. Alexi soon followed suit. He looked like a wild man with a toothache.

They trudged round the first corner, hunched forward like a pair of geriatrics. Ahead of them the road snaked onwards and upwards.

'Half an hour,' Sabir shouted. 'That's tops. Lemma won't be able to survive more than half an hour out in this wind, even if we bundle her up and carry her. If we find nothing by then we come on down again and build the ice palace. Agreed?'

'Agreed.'

Privately, Sabir thought the whole expedition a waste of time. They'd freeze their bollocks off trudging uphill, and then they'd freeze their arses off coming back down again. Who in their right minds would build a hut all the way up here? In the summer, people had their cars. In the winter, they kept away from the place. The whole thing was futile. Lemma would probably have had her baby and celebrated its first birthday by the time they got back down again.

He checked his watch. Twenty minutes into their walk. It felt like two hours. He could feel his nose and ears beginning to liquefy.

'I'm going to jog, Alexi. Do you think you can jog?'

Alexi nodded.

Sabir broke into a ragged trot. He could feel the numbness creeping from his toes back to his heels. Both men were emitting great plumes of steam.

Sabir gritted his teeth. Three more corners, he told himself. I am going to jog round three more corners. Then I'm going to sprint back to the Simca and get warm again. Calque and Radu can build the bloody ice palace while Alexi and I unfreeze ourselves.

Sabir stopped in his tracks. Ice palace? A fucking ice palace? What were they going to build the fucking ice palace with? They didn't possess a shovel.

He thought back to what they had found in the trunk of the car. Sleeping bags. paraffin heater. Fuel. Spare food. Yes, all that. But no shovel. He'd been so pleased with his brainwave about the ice palace that he'd completely forgotten that everyone carried an emergency fold-up shovel when going on a two-week hut-to-hut Nordic ski tour. You couldn't build an ice palace or dig yourself a snow grave without one. That, and extra ski tips in case of mishaps.

But no shovel, no ice palace.

Bloody fool.

Alexi stood close to him and pointed down at his watch. His eyes were red-rimmed. Ice was forming in his hair where it wasn't covered by the scarf. Even his eyelashes were frosting up.

Sabir shook his head and motioned him onwards. He spread out both hands, indicating another ten minutes. Then he put up a tentative thumb.

Alexi hesitated. Then he nodded. Both men were feeling the strain. They were well above the 5,000-foot mark now, and the storm was increasing. The snow was coming at them, not from above, as before, but straight on, in curtains. And it was getting harder to breathe. It was as though the storm was eating up the oxygen and leaving only a vacuum behind it.

Sabir started to jog again, but he soon slowed down. His feet were beginning to hurt. He looked across at Alexi and saw that his friend was suffering too. Alexi had been hitting the bottle of late, and this was telling on his fitness. As Sabir watched, Alexi yanked the scarf away from his face and fought for breath. Sabir realized that if they didn't find shelter soon, he'd have a crisis on his hands.

'You go back, Alexi. I'm going to carry on for a bit. You'll be down again in twenty minutes. Then you can warm up in the car.'

'No, Damo. We go on.'

Sabir hesitated. It wouldn't do to waste time arguing. The pair of them only had so much energy to mete out. And when it was gone, it was gone.

He continued up the hill. Alexi followed him.

'Try and keep in my footsteps, Alexi. That way you won't fall behind. Just keep your head down and concentrate on each step. Don't look up. Don't look back.'

Three more corners, Sabir said to himself. We'll round three more corners. Then we'll go back and try to get the car moving again. Maybe we can freewheel down the col?

He shook his head, as though he were thinking out loud before an audience. No. There are too many flat areas between the *lacets* and the zigzag bends, he told himself. We'd never be able to push the car through the snow. We'd simply exhaust ourselves and die. How dumb it had been to agree to move in the space of two hours from being normal, comfortable human beings, futures intact, to facing death by unwanted refrigeration. Truly, thought Sabir, we choose our own fates in this world.

He looked up. At first the lake didn't seem like a lake. Merely a flatter expanse of colour in a kingdom of white. A field, maybe, or a meadow, that had been protected from the normal process of drifting by the peaks surrounding it. Then Sabir realized what the peaks were. They were the actual summits of the mountains they had been moving towards for such an endless time.

He saw dark water at one end of the lake, where the freezing process hadn't taken hold. Maybe there was an inlet there? A run-off? Perhaps that kept it clear.

Alexi slapped him on the arm.

Sabir turned his whole body round to face Alexi. It

was as if all his separate joints and ligaments no longer functioned, and his torso had become one rigid entity. Hardening. Fossilizing.

'Look.' Alexi pointed to the far end of the lake. 'A house.'

The lodge was draped in snow – there must have been ten feet of it on the roof, and more on the outhouse and veranda. Snow had piled in layers onto older snow until the whole edifice had begun to look like an over-decorated blancmange. Streamers of ice were hanging off the eaves and gables, and the wooden picket fence that surrounded the property resembled a wave, frozen in the very act of breaking.

'That's it. That's what we need.'

Both men broke into a shambling run.

Alexi even started to laugh.

*Bistriţa, Romania*
*Saturday, 6 February 2010*

# 68

Markovich snapped the cell phone shut. 'This car of Andrassy's...'

'The Simca. Yes.'

Abi was staring out of the window. One of Markovich's men was driving the Crusaders' ten-year-old Lada Niva Diesel. Abi was in the passenger seat, with Markovich directly behind him. The two remaining Crusaders had stayed behind in Brara to deal with Andrassy's corpse.

It wouldn't do to involve the Romanian police at this stage of the proceedings, thought Abi, so he had ordered the Crusaders to dig a grave inside the ruined house, seal it, and then pile junk on top of it. It was highly doubtful that anyone would bother to renovate the house in the foreseeable future. The grave might lie undisturbed for years. Just like the thousands of graves secretly dug throughout Romania during the Ceausescu era. What did it say in Ecclesiastes? 'Men come and go, but earth abides.' Abi's mouth jerked in the suggestion of a smile.

'It was seen eight hours ago at a garage near Sibiu.'

'Why are we only hearing about this now?'

Markovich made a face. 'We did not think it was important to find the car. Of course, I asked our contact in the Romanian police to put out an initial theft report. But I didn't think that anything would come of it. I thought the pregnant Gypsy woman had probably run away and Andrassy had followed her.'

'Run away? A pregnant woman run away?'

Markovich swallowed. 'I expected to hear from Andrassy at any moment. I didn't expect him to be dead. Do you think the woman killed him?'

Abi gave a snort. 'No. I think the damned fool allowed himself to be bushwhacked – probably by the husband. It is the sort of lesson one learns only once during the course of a lifetime.' Abi spread the map out on his knee. 'Now tell me, Markovich. Where is this place called Sibiu?'

Markovich leaned across the seat. 'Here.' He stabbed at the map.

'Why would they be making for there, do you think?'

Markovich shrugged.

'What are these mountains shown on the map? Here. Just below Sibiu.'

'Those are the Carpathians.'

Abi allowed the breath to flutter out from between his lips. He turned to the driver. 'You. Do you speak English?'

'Yes. I was a guide before.'

'Then guide me. How many people were living at this camp Andrassy invaded?'

The man glanced tentatively into the rear-view mirror. Markovich nodded.

'The villagers were not sure when we asked them. They thought seven or eight.'

'Describe them to me.'

'The villagers?'

'No, the Gypsies, you fool.'

'Well, there were two pregnant women...'

'Two, you say?'

'Yes. One old crone I talked to said that there were definitely two. One about to pop, and the other one a little farther back down the line. Two months to go. Maybe three. Then there were two children.'

'There were children?'

'Yes. Young children. A boy and a girl.'

Abi closed his eyes. 'All Gypsies?'

'No. Two foreigners as well. Non-Romanian speakers. Both men. The rest were Gypsies. But not native Romanian either. They had accents.'

'How many women altogether?'

'Three. At least as far as they remembered.'

'So we're talking about the two pregnant women and the mother of the children?'

'Yes. I suppose so.'

'And the men?'

'Well, I'm not sure. The crone said they came and went.'

'But the two pregnant women had husbands with them?'

'Oh yes.'

Abi looked down at the map. So Radu had survived being shot by the girls after all? Which meant that he'd somehow managed to join up with Calque, Sabir, and the two Gypsies – the carrier of the so-called Second Coming and her husband – after someone, probably the Gypsy with the dead horse, had patched him up again. Abi inclined his head in grudging respect. So the bastard had known the name of the village all along. Well. It figured. He should have skinned the two children in front of him and had done with it. That's what came of being sentimental. He wouldn't make that mistake again.

But there was one thing he knew for certain. Radu must have been scared shitless when he finally came back to his senses. Petrified that his four kidnappers would head straight back to Samois and revenge themselves on the children now that they'd lost him. Or work on his wife, maybe. Get to him that way. So it made perfect sense that he would call his wife, the two kids, and their parents over to join him. That would explain the number of people at the camp. The whole thing was logical when looked at in that light. Because Radu would be unlikely to involve complete strangers in something he knew could mean life or death.

So maybe it was Radu's wife who was the second pregnant woman? Yes, Abi remembered Radu pleading with the four of them to let him go back to Samois and tell his pregnant wife that they were taking him along with them to Romania. What had he said? Abi riffled through his mind as if it were a filing cabinet. 'But I must say goodbye to my wife or she will worry. We married earlier this summer. She is pregnant. It will be difficult for her.' That had been it. Abi worked it out on his fingers. Yes. Had to be her. He knew for a certainty that Yola Dufontaine wasn't ready to spawn yet, because he and his mother had gone over the tape recording of Lamia's final telephone call concerning her with a toothcomb. He had names. Ages. Everything. He just about knew the colour of her underwear.

He dropped his hands onto his lap. So Radu's wife had been the one about to give birth? That changed things. Because Radu, as the Corpus had found out to their cost, was nothing if not quick-witted. Finding that Gypsy pot-smith – the one whose horse Abi had killed – and persuading him to smuggle him across the border on the spur of the moment was hardly the work of a moron.

Abi ran his finger back down the map and towards the border area where the four of them had originally lost sight of Radu.

The pot-smith drove a cart. So it was hardly likely that he lived far from the border. Probably went across every day.

Abi drew a pretend line from Sibiu to the border crossing. It went plum through the centre of the Carpathians.

'Andrassy's Simca. Was it roadworthy?'

'Oh yes. He slept in it sometimes. When he couldn't find a place to stay overnight. Just as we do in this. He had sleeping bags. Food. A paraffin stove. It's impossible to function in this weather without chains or winter tyres – Andrassy would have had snow chains at least. He wasn't high up in the command structure. So his car was old. But it functioned.'

'Are all these roads that cross the Carpathians open?'

'All of them. Except this one.' Markovich pointed to the Transfăgărașan Pass. 'This is shut in the winter. It is impossible to cross it. So you can discount it. The Simca will travel by the main roads like everybody else.'

'Why should we discount it? They know very well that we will be looking for them. It is a simple thing to place a watcher on each of the three open roads I see marked here. They would know that too. A vintage Simca is an easy car to recognize.'

'But it would be madness to attempt to cross the pass in winter.'

'There would be no police there. No one to register number plates. No danger of being overseen.'

'But the army. They would stop you.'

'The army?'

Markovich looked a little sick. 'I mean the Romanian Special Forces – the Vanatori de Munte. Everybody knows that they use the mountains for winter exercises. Their base is at Curtea de Argeş.'

'You mean the army keep the pass open all through the year?'

'Well…' Markovich swallowed. 'Yes. I suppose so. I have heard that truck drivers use it sometimes. To save time. When the weather is not as bad as it is now. That they bribe the soldiers to let them through.'

Abi closed the map. 'Take me there.'

*Albescu, Moldova*
*Saturday, 6 February 2010*

# 69

Antanasia Lupei lay on her belly, her arms stretched out in front of her, her legs in the shape of a V behind her. They, too, had been shackled.

She had been jerking awake at odd times recently, with no clear idea of where she was. Once she had woken to find her brother lying on top of her, thrusting at her with his hips like a dog. For a while she had thought herself back at her father's house again, with her father still alive, and her brother snatching a moment with her, as he sometimes did, when her father's back was turned – pushing her up against the bedroom wall, perhaps, or spread-eagling her over the kitchen table while their father was haranguing the neighbours in one of his drunken rages. But physically she had felt nothing of what Dracul was doing to her. No inkling of penetration. No sense of outrage. No pain. All was numb. It was as if a ghost was mating her.

Curiously, her lips and head had seemed numbed, too – almost as if they had been injected with novocaine. She wondered if Dracul was drugging her, and then realized that of course he was. She would not have been able to tolerate his weight on her wounds if that had not been the case.

Later, when she woke again, she craned her head round in an effort to ascertain the true state of her back, but she was unable to free her neck from the pillow. It was then that she discovered that Dracul had strapped her to the bed with a fretwork of leather thongs. If she forced her eyes to the right – to the very extremity of her capacity to see – she could just make out the smudge of one of the straps against the light.

'If you don't tell me the name of the man you have been seeing – the man you have been preferring to me – I shall turn you around and knout you on your front.'

Antanasia closed her eyes. So he had been there all the time, watching her. Had he finally lost his mind? The pragmatic peasant in her had long ago decided that there was a danger that this would happen. It was abnormal for a man with a temperament as extreme as Dracul's to live in an environment where nobody dared gainsay him. Where people assured him that he was God. That everything he did was perfect and just. If you subjected a man ridden with unacknowledged guilt as Dracul was – to such adulation, you risked creating a monster. Antanasia found herself desperately wishing to see her brother's face. To judge for herself how far he had ventured down the irrecoverable path to madness. But he had made it impossible for her to look at him. Impossible for her to meet his eyes. Impossible for her to confront him face on.

She drifted back into a half-sleep. During the course of the past fifteen years – the years roughly paralleling Dracul's success as a cult leader – Antanasia had begun a process of self-education through reading. There was satellite television, too, at the house, and Antanasia had endeavoured to teach herself the rudiments of history by watching foreign documentaries. Thanks to such documentaries she now knew that Dracul's hero, Joseph Stalin, had turned from a revolutionary luminary into a tyrannical despot as a result of just such an unsettling equation as her brother was now experiencing. That Molotov and Kaganovich had convinced their leader, in 1932, that all that he did was just. That the hundreds of thousands of kulaks he had killed as a result of his state-fomented famines in the Ukraine were necessary casualties on the road to successful collectivization.

'I will make soap out of them,' Stalin had declared jubilantly.

Antanasia had had occasion to speak to many Ukrainians during the course of her duties as the visible face of her brother's ministry, for Albescu was a bare 50 kilometres from the Ukrainian border. As a result of these encounters she had heard numerous stories of the great famine of 1931 to 1933. Now, for reasons that escaped her, these stories were forcing their way back into her head – but filled out, coloured, and heightened, as if the opiates her brother was dosing her with were making them real.

One story, in particular, had begun to haunt Antanasia's semi-lucid hours. An eighty-five-year-old woman – the traditionally headscarved grandmother of one of Dracul's Crusaders – had motioned her aside one day. The old woman had pointed out a bread shop – one of many in Albescu.

It had been an everyday scene. An orderly queue

of customers had begun to form outside the shop. Soon people were being served – thanking the baker, carrying off their purchases, passing titbits down to their children. It was a picture that was being repeated on tens of thousands of similar streets around the world.

'So, Babushka? What do you wish to tell me?'

The old lady had looked up at her, her eyes moist with remembrance. 'I grew up just one hundred kilometres east of here. Near Sharhorod in the Vinnyts'ka Oblast. In what was then called the Russian Ukraine.' She crossed herself. 'It might as well have been ten thousand kilometres away from what you are seeing now.'

'What happened, Mother? Why did you call me away? What is it that I am seeing?'

'In 1933, when I was nine years old, Stalin sealed up the borders of our country so that no one could either enter or leave. From that moment on, forty thousand people from our part of the Ukraine were forced to queue up every day in the hope of receiving bread. Most of those queuing were women, just like the ones you see in front of you here. Queuing in the hope of feeding themselves and their families. But that is the only similarity between then and now. There is no other.' The old woman had begun to cry.

'It is all right, Babushka. Do not tell me this if it grieves you to do so.'

The old woman had raised her tear-stained eyes. 'I must tell you this, my princess. Otherwise you will not understand. Not understand why I and my daughter and my son-in-law have given up everything we had to come over here and live with you. As part of the Coryphaeus's community.'

Antanasia had felt a cold chill of unease ripple across her body. Like the stroke of the first zephyr that betokens a storm. She had taken the old lady's hand. 'Tell me then, Mother. I am listening.'

'On this day that I am describing to you I was sent by my father to guard my mother's place in the queue as she was too weak anymore to guard it for herself. My mother, you see, would not have tolerated my father doing what she considered woman's work. She was still proud. A Ukrainian woman through and through. I stood in the queue for many, many hours, while my mother rested nearby in the road, unable to catch her breath. Finally, in order for those left in the queue to continue standing upright, each woman took hold of the belt of the woman in front of her. If we had not done this we would have fallen to the ground through sheer exhaustion. This waiting continued throughout the day. The pregnant and the maimed and the elderly were given no priority, my princess – they too had to stand in line and wait, or, if they were too weak, to fall by the wayside with no hope of bread. Comrade Stalin, you see, had brought us all to exactly the same condition. As my father would have said, "he had equalized us all".The Babushka shook her head. Her lips began to tremble – stark, spasmodic movements, as if she were trying to finish a sentence, but could no longer do so.

'Finally, after hours of silence, broken only by the spasms of coughing and the shuffling of feet, one of the women began to wail. This sound acted like a virus. Soon, all the women were wailing. The wailing was so loud, and it endured for so long, that it was as if the endless line of women had transformed itself into a single, tortured animal, fit only for the slaughterhouse. An animal inexplicably capable of understanding what lay in store for it. An animal suffering the torments of elemental dread.'

Antanasia snatched a hand to her cheek. 'But how did you survive, Babushka?'

The old woman sighed. 'There were bands of men at this time of which I am speaking. Party activists mostly. Committed Communists. They infested the countryside, spying on us from the watchtowers Comrade Stalin had had built to make sure the farmers did his bidding. Their primary task was to maintain quotas. Comrade Stalin had caused certain fields to be set aside as testing grounds for yields, you see. These fields were heavily fertilized. Then the grain they yielded was measured and recorded. The kulaks, without the benefits of pesticides and fertilizer, were then expected to match these yields. To pay to the state four fifths of the value of such yields before they were allowed to feed their families. But these yields were an impossibility, my princess. So we starved. The bands of men then came and humiliated the famished peasants. Treated them like dogs. Pissed on their remaining food. Raped their women. Forced the men to fight each other and to bark at each other like dogs for their entertainment. And they were always looking for children they could steal.'

'To steal?'

'Yes. To violate for their further amusement, and then to sell for eating.'

Antanasia dropped her hand to her throat.

'They stole me. My father was weak. But he ran after them. Begged them to let me go. To take him instead.'

'What did they do, Babushka?'

'They had their way with me. They made my father watch. Then they killed him and jointed him like a pig. Later they sold the quarters to our neighbour in return for a cask of pickles.'

Antanasia shook her head. She couldn't take her eyes off the old woman's face. 'And you?'

'They liked me. One of the men in particular. I reminded him of his daughter back in Georgia. So they kept me with them to toy with. This is how I survived the next five years. Later, when the Germans came, we women knew just what to expect. There was no difference.' The old woman half turned away.

'Babushka, why are you telling me this?'

The old woman smiled. She covered Antanasia's hand with her own. 'Because I have seen your eyes, my princess. And I recognize what I see in them.'

'What? What do you see in my eyes? Tell me.'

The old woman's face closed down. 'See? Nothing. They are just eyes. They are like mine. And the eyes of all the godforsaken women who have gone before me.' She hesitated, as if she were dissatisfied with her summing-up. With the way she had concluded her story. She raised her head almost angrily. 'What can eyes ever do? Later, during the Great Terror of 1938, these eyes of mine saw the shooting of 300 people in one night. My Georgian "father" was the main executioner. He used the same Nagant pistol he had killed my father with. Two men would hold the person to be executed by the arms, as you would hold a pheasant by the wings. This is designed to force the neck to stretch out. My "father" then shot the prisoners at the base of their skull. Another of my "fathers" would finish those who were not entirely dead with a shot to the temple. Then the bodies would be laid in pits that had been blown into the frozen ground by dynamite. They called this killing "the black raven flying".'

The old woman shrugged – a thousand years of suffering was encapsulated in her movement.

'This is what I wanted to say to you, my princess. Those eyes of yours. Those eyes now filled with tears. They are like my father's eyes. And my mother's eyes. They are like the eyes of the black raven that flew over us that night and carried away in its beak the souls of the dead and the dying.'

*Transfăgărașan Pass, Romania*
*Saturday, 6 February 2010*

# 70

Alexi levered back the shutter with a snow shovel he had liberated from one of the sheds. He smashed the window pane and reached in for the catch. When the window was open he gesticulated for Sabir to enter the lodge ahead of him, while he checked nervously around as if he expected a posse of Keystone Kops-style policemen to come pelting out at him from some hiding place he had overlooked during his reconnoitre.

'Don't worry, Alexi. We're probably the only sentient beings in a radius of twenty square miles from here. Even Father Christmas and his forty elves would have stayed at home on a night like this. I can't speak for the reindeer, of course.'

Sabir see-sawed his legs through the gap in the window and dropped heavily down into the hallway. The interior of the lodge was as gloomy as a morgue. The shutters were sealed for the winter, and dustsheets covered the furniture, giving a spectral appearance.

Alexi slithered through behind him.

'Look,' said Sabir. 'A paraffin lamp. They were obviously expecting company.'

'Are you serious? They were expecting us?'

Sabir smacked Alexi's forehead with his hand.

'Oh. I see. You were making fun.' Alexi lit the lamp, adjusting the metal reflector at the back so that a thin shaft of light cut through the gloom ahead of them. 'What is this place, Damo?'

'A hunting lodge, probably. At least, judging by the number of deer antlers and bear heads they have scattered about these walls. Shine a light on that photograph, will you?'

Alexi tilted the paraffin lamp so that its light shone upwards.

'Yep. Just as I thought. That guy in the middle – the guy with the fur hat and the silly earflaps and the rifle, surrounded by all the sycophants – that's Nicolae Ceausescu. You know. The former Communist President the Romanians took out and shot during the 1989 revolution. This masterpiece of Soviet baronial style must have belonged to him. Maybe they're keeping it on as a museum of hunting trophies?'

Alexi looked blank.

Sabir shook his head and started down the corridor. It never did to underestimate Alexi's total lack of knowledge about anything that did not directly concern him. If you'd asked him who the French President was he'd probably have told you de Gaulle.

'Come on, Alexi. Tear yourself away from the historical tour. We've taken far too much time already. What we need to do is to find a stove and light it. Then get back to the others. This storm is not going to let up anytime soon. We need to get them all up here and safely tucked away before darkness falls.'

The two men worked their way through the house until they found a snug room at the back with pitch pine panelling and a wood-burning stove. Dried logs and kindling were piled high in an indented bay behind it.

'Incredible. There's enough fuel in here to outlast a siege.' Sabir was tempted to say that the whole thing was starting to feel like Goldilocks and the three bears, but then thought better of it. There was no point in painting the Devil on the wall. And how would one go about explaining Goldilocks to Alexi?

'You light the stove, Alexi. And for Pete's sake make sure the chimney doesn't go up when you do it. We don't want to arrive back here to a burnt-out shell. Then we'll seal the room up. It'll be as warm as toast by the time we bring Lemma up here. I'm going to see if I can hunt out something we can drag her up on.'

Sabir passed through into the kitchen. As he did so, he checked out a couple of the cupboards. Tinned goods galore. The place was clearly in regular use for part of the winter season. As a ski lodge, maybe? Or perhaps they still hunted here in November and December?

He followed his nose down to the cellar. If they kept skis, that was where they would keep them.

He almost stumbled over the two antique wooden sledges with steel runners that someone had tipped up against a wall. Both were of a size used to transport dead game – deer carcasses, maybe – back to camp in winter conditions. He aimed the paraffin lamp at the wall. Yes. Two leather ski harnesses hung there. But how was he going to get the sledges out? True, there was an outside entrance to the cellar through which they would normally have been collected, but this time of the year it would be blocked by about ten feet of snow.

Sabir manhandled both sledges up the cellar steps and upended them near the door. They fit through the gap with about an inch to spare on each side. Maybe his luck really was turning? He went back down the cellar steps and checked out the back rooms.

Skis. Both Nordic and downhill. Boots. Sticks. Goggles. Sabir felt the same excitement in the pit of his stomach as a gambler who suspects he is on an elusive winning roll.

He had already started gathering up a double-armful of the skis when the thought struck him. How many of the party would actually be able to use them? Calque? Hardly. Radu? Forget it. And Alexi?

He edged up the cellar steps. 'Alexi? Are you up there?'

'Yes, Damo. I am waiting for you. The fire is lit. I have sealed the room. I have even brought a mattress down from upstairs for Lemma to lie on. There is everything here we can possibly want. We could stay for weeks. Hell. We could even bring up both the kids here until they are teenagers. Come spring, we could pitch a tent outside. Have ourselves a little fresh air.'

'Have you thought about now? About water? Stuff like that?'

'Can't we drink snow?'

Sabir mused a little. Then he shrugged. 'With the wood-burner running? Yes. You're right. I suppose we can. As long as it's not yellow, of course. But tell me something, Alexi. Can you ski?'

'Ski? What do you think I am? A member of the jet set?'

Sabir sighed. Crazy to have even thought about it. He decided that Alexi was at one and the same time the most predictable and the most unpredictable man he had ever met. Being friends with him was like being trapped in a whirlpool wearing only vintage-style rubber waders.

'Find me some rope, will you? Then tie these two sledges together. One behind the other. When you've done that, climb back through the window and see if you can clear an entrance around the front door. Are you okay with that?'

'I will do it. Just for you, Damo, I will do it.'

Sabir clattered back down the cellar steps, fished the better of the two harnesses off the wall, and then went to look for some boots. If Alexi couldn't ski, he damned well couldn't sledge either. And Sabir didn't relish teaching him the delicate art of steering and braking with his boot tips in a white-out.

The third pair of leather boots he unearthed more or less fitted him. He checked the catches on the Nordic skis, meshed the skis and the boots together, then worked his heels up and down a few times. Not perfect, but they would do. He helped himself to the longest pair of ski sticks he could find and clumped back upstairs. He was trying hard not to think of what would happen if they were caught inside the house by an itinerant caretaker or a passing army patrol. Deportation would probably be the least of their worries. Breaking and entering. Aggravated theft. Vandalism. Given the time and the inclination, Calque could probably rustle up the names of a whole further raft of crimes they were committing.

On the way back to the hall Sabir passed a conspicuously locked room. He hesitated for a moment, tempted to go on. But curiosity got the better of him. Alexi wouldn't have finished clearing away the snow yet. And until that was done, they didn't have a hope of getting both sledges out the front door.

Sabir checked around the lintel and under the floor mat just in case someone had left the key there. No luck. He touched the wood. Not as thick as all that. Well, in for a penny in for a pound, as the Brits would have it.

He took a few steps back and rammed the door with his shoulder. Something gave. He tried a second time. More give. On his third run the door burst open. Sabir went back and collected the paraffin lamp that Alexi had left by the front door. Then he looked inside.

Banks of hunting rifles and shotguns. Cartons of ammunition. And a double-rack stacked with bottles of wine and Kvint brandy.

'Hey, man. Look at that.' Alexi was standing open-mouthed behind him. Quick as a flash he fished a penknife out from under his coat and carved the capsule off one of the brandy bottles.

'Alexi. This isn't the moment.'

'If this isn't the moment, Damo, I don't know what is. *Salud, y força al canut.*' Alexi upended the bottle and took a long slug. 'Ha!' He made a face, considered the bottle for a few moments more, then took a second slug – the expression on his face was that worn by the first ever explorer of a virgin continent. 'You know what, Damo? I piss on the Corpus. I piss on the Antichrist. I piss on the police. I piss on the Church. Hell. I piss on anyone who doesn't agree with me. *Na le tjiri kher te ličhares e pori la sapnjaki; punrranges si te ličhares lako šero.*' He upended the bottle for a third time, then he corked it with an emphatic gesture, and slipped it into his pocket.

'Okay, Alexi. Translate.'

Alexi grinned. 'It's simple. My grandfather taught it to me when I was a child. It means "You don't need your boots to crush a serpent's tail, when you can crush its fucking head with your bare feet."'

# 71

Lemma was suffering contractions every two minutes. She had recently passed some pink-tinged mucus which Yola had hidden from the men. Now Yola placed her hand beneath the covers. Lemma's uterus felt as hard as iron. That, twinned with the rushes, told her that the moment was near. She'd been present at plenty of births in her time. This one was no different. It was only the location that presented something of a problem.

Sabir hammered on the passenger door.

Calque nodded and made a hushing motion with his hands. He backed out from his position on the front seat and closed the door swiftly behind him to conserve the heat inside the car. 'Well?'

'Good news. We have a place. A hunting lodge. Twenty minutes or so up the road. There's a fire going. Food in the scullery. Everything we need.'

'Tell me you're not joking?'

'I'm not joking.'

Calque shook his head. 'Lemma is just about to have her baby, Sabir. Yola's not saying anything, but you can cut the tension back there with a knife. Radu looks green. You'd think he was the one that was pregnant.'

'We can't let her have the baby here.'

'What do you mean? What choice do we have?'

Sabir hesitated. 'Well, I'm no expert at these things. But at some point the engine in this Simca is going to stall. Or overheat. Or simply run out of gas. Then we'll have a real crisis on our hands. It strikes me that to subject a baby to a white-out, pitch darkness, and minus fifteen degrees of wind-chill straight after its birth is not a recipe for a long life. The baby will be better off inside its mother during the journey to the lodge.'

Calque glanced uncertainly down at the roped-together sledges.

'Listen, man. I can do most of the heavy pulling using my Nordic skis. We've even got the right sort of harness. I got Alexi down here without breaking his neck, so I can sure as heck get you all back up again.'

Calque didn't look convinced.

'I come from Massachusetts, Calque. I've skied in the Berkshires since I was three years old. And getting back up a slope is simpler than coming down. Take it from me. You just need more muscle. So you three guys can push at the back while I pull the sledge from the front and steer the thing. Yola can ride with Lemma and hold her hand. Or whatever you hold when a baby's coming.'

Calque gave a grudging nod. The true extent of the cold, after the relative warmth inside the Simca, had shaken him to the core. 'All right, Sabir. As usual, you make it all sound eminently reasonable. But you be the one to explain all this to Yola, okay? I've already got a damaged nose. I don't want to lose a few teeth into the bargain.'

Sabir nodded. He ducked inside the car. Calque could see him gesticulating with his hands through the windows.

'What's it like up there at the lodge, Alexi? Is Sabir exaggerating the comforts? To hear him, you'd think it was the Ritz-Carlton.'

Alexi was jumping up and down to improve his circulation. He felt around in his jacket without interfering with his rhythm and came up with the bottle of Kvint. 'It's as good as this tastes.' He tossed the bottle to Calque.

Calque caught the bottle in one hand, uncorked it, and took a swig. '*Foutaise de montalbique!* But that's good.'

'There's more where that came from. Wine too.'

'Wine? What sort of wine? Don't tell me it's Eastern European?'

'Calque, for crying out loud. Stop boozing and come and give us a hand with Lemma.'

Calque tossed the bottle back to Alexi.

Between them, the four men eased Lemma from the floor of the Simca to outside. Yola side-stepped out of the far door, making sure not to bump her swollen stomach. She bundled the sleeping bags together and constructed a nest on the back of the first sledge. The men settled Lemma onto the sledge and tucked her in. She was whistling and snorting by now, her face bright red against the snow.

Yola hesitated for a moment. She cast a wistful look back at the car and then shook her head like an overweight woman refusing a bar of chocolate. She climbed onto the sledge beside Lemma. 'You can leave the second sledge behind. I need to stay close to my cousin.'

Sabir bent down and cut the second sledge free. He upended it against the snow wall, and tucked away the rope end. Then he slammed the car door. 'We'll leave the Simca running in case we need to get back here in a hurry.'

'But what if the fuel runs out?'

'Radu, there's a fucking palace up there waiting for us. This Simca is never going to go anywhere again. When the army sees it, and finds it's out of gas, they'll know someone is up here. Then they'll come and get us.' He eased himself into the harness. He wasn't feeling quite as confident as he made out. 'Are you all ready?'

There was a muffled reply from the semi-darkness beyond the trail of sledges.

'Okay. As Jimmy Durante used to say – at least according to my father's version of events – "let's went".'

# 72

Lemma gave birth to her baby ten minutes into the traverse. The first any of the men knew about it was a loud shriek, followed by silence.

Babir stopped dead in his tracks. He could feel the short hairs rising on his arms and neck beneath the thick layers of his clothing.

Radu threw up his hands and rushed forwards. 'What has happened? What has happened? Why did Lemma scream?'

Yola's head appeared from beneath the nest of sleeping bags. The falling snow settled around her hair like a coronet. 'Your wife is eighteen years old, Radu. Young women such as her don't need long labours. You are the father of a daughter.' She gave a tired grin. 'Now please stop waving your arms around and get us up to the lodge. We need to tie off the umbilical cord and make sure the placenta has emerged in one piece.'

Radu stood for a moment as if frozen to the spot. 'The placenta?'

Alexi rolled up a snowball and threw it at him. The snowball struck Radu straight between the eyes. 'Wake up, Papi. Now it's your turn to push.'

Radu hardly seemed to notice the snowball. He shook himself like a man roused out of a deep sleep, and hurried back to his place behind the sledge. This time the men really threw their hearts into the work. Radu was desperate to see his child, but he knew that Yola would never forgive him if he stopped the sledge again to satisfy his curiosity about his daughter.

'I'm going to call her Lenis,' he shouted. 'After my grandmother. It means soft-voiced. Because she came into the world without a sound.'

At that exact moment they heard the traditional baby's bellow.

Alexi shook his head. 'Just listen to that. Soft-voiced, my arse.'

'You could always call her Stentora,' shouted Calque.

'Stentora? Stentora? What sort of a name is that?' said Radu.

'A very loud one,' said Calque.

# 73

———

Abi stood near the snow-gates and watched as Markovich checked the locks.

'Any tampering?'

'No. These are still locked.'

Abi shook his head. 'I don't believe it. Let me look.' He kicked the Lada Niva's door shut behind him and strode over to the gates. He took the lock in both his hands and examined both it and its chain as a jeweller might inspect a damaged string of pearls. 'What's this then?'

Markovich craned over him. 'I don't see anything.'

'These scratches. And look down here. Below the gate. Ruts.' Abi scooped back the snow like a dog marking its shitting place. 'Can't you see, man? The snow has barely had time to cover them back up. A vehicle has definitely been through here within the past few hours.' Abi ducked under the gates and walked a few yards towards a tree that overhung a corner of the road. 'Yes. Look at this. Where the tree has protected the road. More tyre marks. The fresh snow hasn't covered them yet. Did you say Andrassy had snow chains?'

'I'm almost certain.'

'Well this looks like snow chains.'

'But it could be the army. Or the police. Or anyone.' Markovich looked terminally uncomfortable. 'Mr de Bale… Count de Bale… I think we are on a wild goose chase here.'

'Why not phone your boss again and see what he has to say about it?'

Markovich ducked his head. He looked disgusted. He hadn't eaten for ten hours, and he missed his wife. She'd probably be cooking dumplings and meatballs. Plus he had a case of Czech beer which he had won in a recent game of skat. He could almost taste how the beer and the meatballs would melt together in his mouth. Then he would upend his wife and get her giggling, before having sex with her in their favourite position – her on top and facing away from him with her hands on his knees. Sublime.

'The Coryphaeus has told me not to telephone him anymore. Not to bother him.' Markovich couldn't keep the peevishness out of his voice.

'Oh, really? And did he not tell you to obey my orders before he downed tools?'

Markovich sighed. 'Yes. He did.'

Abi strode back to the barrier. He took his picklocks out of his pocket and worked the lock back and forth until it snapped open. 'You see? It's not rocket science. A child could figure this out in five minutes.' He threw the gates open. 'It's my bet they'll never make it to the top of the pass in that load of crap they are driving. Hand me one of those pistols. We three have work to do.'

# 74

'Someone needs to keep guard from one of the upper rooms.'

'Keep guard? Keep guard for what?'

Alexi was toasting the newborn baby in a second bottle of Kvint brandy. Radu had joined him. Even Calque had cracked open a bottle of 2007 Romanian Cramele Rotenberg he had found in the cellar and was to be heard loudly proclaiming that it was not unlike a home-grown St Emilion he particularly favoured – not unlike it at all.

Alexi, for his part, was clearly getting into his stride. Drink always made him voluble – too much drink made him vainglorious. 'Who is going to turn up here in the middle of the night, Damo? A bus-load of tourists perhaps? Or maybe some pilgrims to Voronet who have lost their way in the white-out? The only visitor we're likely to get is a wolf, attracted by the smell of Yola's cooking. And I can't see him knocking on the door and asking to be let in.' Alexi struck Radu on the shoulder, inordinately pleased with the image he had conjured up for himself. 'No, Damo, if you feel the urge to go upstairs and stand guard over us like John Wayne, please be my guest. Me and Radu are going to get good and drunk. Maybe Captain Calque will get drunk too?' Alexi grinned broadly. 'Hey! Mr Policeman! Are you going to water the baby's head with us?'

Calque, who was already on his third large glass of Merlot Captura, nodded sagely, as if he had just been asked to encapsulate the essence of Schopenhauer's determinism in one easy-to-remember sentence.

The birth of the baby had had a strange effect on them all – Calque more than anyone. Sabir could see that his friend was in no mood to take responsibility for anything more that night. Nature, it seemed, had triumphed – for the time being at least – over rationalism. The men were celebrating both the birth of a baby and their own deliverance from evil – the urge was clearly an antediluvian one, shared by a thousand generations of scattergood forefathers. Sabir wondered why he was unable similarly to let go. Then, all of a sudden, he knew.

He shrugged, forcing the unwanted image of Lamia back out of his mind. Normality. Routine. Action. That's what he needed. The shrug was his way of pretending that the steamroller that had flattened his life was made of cardboard, not steel.

They'd already settled Lemma and Lenis – Radu having drawn the line at the name Stentora despite Calque's impassioned pleas – into the snugly heated parlour, and fastened the front door from the inside so that the lodge was sealed tight. Sabir, for his part, had located the main fuse box and tried the master electrical switch, but nothing had happened. It seemed that, in the depths of winter anyway, the entire grid for that part of the mountains was switched off.

After cleaning Lemma and the baby and making them as comfortable as possible, Yola had gone off to fire up a second wood-burning stove in one of the unoccupied rooms. This one had a convenient flat top with a couple of removable cooking grids. Now she was busy heating up the contents of some of the cans she had found, and melting snow in a never-ending stream on the second hob. She had also uncovered some old potatoes and a few desiccated apples in a forgotten vegetable tray – she was mixing these with some tinned pork and white beans to make a stew.

In other words everyone had decided on their respective roles bar Sabir.

Sabir understood himself well enough by now to know that he was incapable of winding swiftly down after the exertions of the last few hours. And drink alone had never punched his ticket. He clearly needed to find some other form of displacement activity.

He walked down the corridor and chose himself an exceptionally ugly Romanian-made Dragunov 'Tigr' hunting rifle from amongst the ordnance held in the armoury. The chain that ran through the trigger guards was attached to the walls with a set of four simple screws. It took him two minutes to unscrew them with his Swiss Army knife.

He scratched around and pocketed a box of 7.62mm 'Russians' that he intended to chamber later. After a moment's hesitation he isolated three shotguns and two cartons of Brenneke-style shotgun slugs that were probably intended for the dispatch of large game that had not been killed outright by a visiting hunting party's rifles. He leaned the shotguns up against the door next to the room they'd allocated for the nursery. Then he went upstairs.

He found the ideal observation spot in the central bedroom on the third floor of the house. With the shutters open he had a double-view across part of the lake and down the valley to the first blind corner. Nothing approaching the lodge from either the front or the sides could hope to get by unseen – and the back of the lodge was protected by the lake. The storm had gentled a little in the past half-hour, and now the moon's reflection on the recently settled snow lit up the surroundings like a sports arena prior to shutdown.

Sabir grunted and hurried back downstairs. He ducked inside the armoury. Yes. There it was. An IOR 10x56 hunting scope. Pointless attaching it to his rifle – without zeroing in and matching to the rifle it was as good as useless. But he could use it in lieu of binoculars.

Alexi poked his head out of the room in which Yola was doing her cooking. Behind him, Sabir could hear the sound of raised voices and laughter.

'Come on, Damo. Don't be a killjoy. Come and have a drink with us. Supper's going to be ready soon. You need to wet your whistle first.'

Sabir clambered back upstairs as if he hadn't heard. If they'd all conveniently forgotten about Crusader Andrassy, Mihael Catalin, and the failed attack on Radu and Lemma, he hadn't.

# 75

Abi squinted through the Lada's windscreen. Markovich was in the back seat and his subordinate, Trakhtenberger, was driving. 'What's that? Up ahead. Covered in snow.'

Trakhtenberger stopped the car. So far, the Lada Niva's four-wheel drive had made short work of the slope leading up to the pass. The snow might be fresh, but it hadn't yet started to drift.

'It's a car.'

'Switch off the headlights.' Abi tried to wind down his window, but nothing happened. 'Open your window, man.'

Trakhtenberger tried his window. Same thing. 'We need to silicone-spray them. They stick sometimes when it's really cold. I was meaning to see to this before we started out, but I forgot.'

Abi cursed all amateurs and their amateurishness under his breath. 'Switch off the engine.'

Trakhtenberger made a face. But he did as he was told.

'Can you hear it? The engine of that car is still running. Is that Andrassy's Simca?'

Markovich sucked at his teeth. 'I think so. From the

little I saw through the snow it seemed the same colour. But why is it pointing downhill? According to your theory they should have been heading up the valley.'

'It's obvious that they've had an accident. Probably slid down the slope and spun round. And now the idiots can't see us because of the snow piled up over their windscreen.' Abi threw open the Lada's door. 'Take your pistols. Then get out and cover me.'

Markovich leaned forwards and touched Abi on the shoulder. 'We can't shoot anybody up here. It would be madness. The army comes through all the time.'

Abi shrugged Markovich's hand away. 'Who is talking about shooting? This is the perfect spot for a car accident.' He tapped the place on his sleeve where he concealed his fighting baton. 'We take them and we beat them to a pulp. But we leave them half-alive. Then we shove them back in the car and tip them over the edge of the cliff. It works. I've done it before. Quite recently, actually. By the time the car finally settles, the bodies inside have passed through the equivalent of a cement mixer. No clues. Nothing. Just minced-beef patty. That must be a thousand-foot drop over there.'

Markovich swallowed. For all his seniority in the Crusader hierarchy, he had never killed a man before. Neither, it seemed, had Trakhtenberger, whose hands were shaking where they held the steering wheel.

Abi rolled his eyes. 'You both stay tucked up in here then. I'll do the deed. Just don't get any clever ideas about bolting with the car, or I'll hunt you both down just like I've done with them, and to hell with who your master is. Do you understand me?'

Both men nodded. They seemed relieved to be off the hook.

Abi ducked out of the car. Fifty yards separated him from the Simca. He could hear the breathy mutter of the exhaust through the declining sough of the wind. He began to regret the loss of his brothers and sisters. At least with them you knew where you were. They had all been killers. Every last one of them. They'd have had Sabir's car surrounded before Abi had even mouthed the order.

Keeping his back to the cliff face, Abi side-stepped towards the car. He cocked the semi-automatic when he was twenty yards short of his target. There was no earthly chance of anyone hearing the double-click of the slide over the noise of the engine. And if they hadn't caught the flash of the Lada's headlights through the windscreen five minutes before, it meant that they were probably dozing anyway. This would be a piece of cake.

When he got close to the car he ducked down and manoeuvred himself alongside the passenger door. He grasped the handle and gave it a light tug. If it didn't give, or was locked, he had decided to fire through both front windows, making sure that the spent bullet exited through the far window and didn't fall into the Simca. That would be enough to give him access. He could clean up the glass later.

The door gave.

Abi threw it open and faced into the car, straight-arming the pistol ahead of him with both hands extended.

Nobody in there.

He threw open the back door.

The back seat had been taken out.

He reached across and switched on the interior light. There was blood and fluid on the floor of the rear seatwell.

Abi bent forwards for a closer look. No. This wasn't arterial blood. Nor was it the quality of blood you saw from a flesh wound. Abi had considerable experience of both. This blood was mixed with mucus.

So Radu's wife was either on the verge of having her baby or had already had it? An unfortunate thing to have to do in a snowstorm. But why had she – and the others in her party – abandoned a warm car for the freezing cold outside?

Because they had found somewhere better to make for, that's why.

Abi walked out into the centre of the road. Sledge marks. Clear as day. He turned round and glanced back towards the car. An abandoned sledge was upended against the snow wall, its guide rope cut. So where had that bastard Sabir found two sledges? A sledge shop?

He switched off the Simca's engine and shut all the doors. It wouldn't do to have an empty tank when the car finally hit the valley bottom. A fire would answer all their prayers.

He motioned to Markovich to come up and join him.

Markovich looked relieved when he realized that no one was inside the Simca.

'Look there. Sledge marks. And here. Look at the cut rope. They obviously found they didn't need two sledges to make a caravan.'

Markovich nodded. It was clear that he didn't

understand quite where Abi was going with his observation.

'Are there any houses up here?'

'Houses?'

'Ski lodges, then? Hunting lodges? Army barracks?'

'There's a private hunting lodge. At least I think so. It used to belong to the President. It's up near the lake somewhere.'

'How far is the lake?'

'How should I know?'

'How indeed?' Abi motioned to Trakhtenberger to bring up the car. 'They'll be up there. You can count on it. Snug as rats. Are you a good terrier, Markovich?'

'I'm sorry?'

'Are you good at unearthing rats?'

Markovich shook his head. He no longer cared what the Frenchman thought of him. This whole situation had turned into a nightmare, and he wanted out of it. But the Frenchman had a pistol. The man scared him witless. Markovich glanced at Trakhtenberger. Trakhtenberger looked scared too.

Markovich climbed into the back of the Lada and hunched forwards over his knees. He thought about his wife. The meatballs and dumplings she had doubtless cooked for supper would be cold by now, and his wife would be dozing in front of the television. He laid his head on the seatback in front of him and wished he was at home.

'Drive, Trakhtenberger, drive. Take us to General Secretary Ceausescu's private hunting lodge.'

# 76

Yola brought Sabir a plateful of stew and a glass of red wine. 'They're all drunk down there. It's getting very rowdy.'

'Celebrating the baby?'

'Celebrating the baby.'

'One can't begrudge them, I suppose. How is Lemma?'

Yola smiled. 'She is sleeping. Despite all the noise. One sometimes forgets how young she is.' Her expression darkened. 'It has been a bad time for her. She has been forced to carry many of the weights that were meant for me and my baby. The attack. The kidnap of Radu. Being taken away from her home. I feel bad about this.'

'It's hardly your fault.'

'I know this. It does not stop me feeling bad.'

Sabir walked to the window.

'Why are you looking? Nobody will find us up here.'

Sabir glanced back at her. 'Do you really believe that?'

'Yes.'

'I don't.' He brought the telescopic lens up to his eye and checked out the valley. 'The Corpus want you dead, Yola. Both you and your baby. They've more than proved that already. And now they've brought Catalin into the equation, things can only get worse. And it's all my fault. Because I flagged you up to them with my big mouth.'

'What are you going to do with that rifle? Shoot them? Or will you eat them with your big mouth?' She was smiling.

Sabir didn't respond. 'I'll shoot them if necessary. If I see them before they see me, that is.'

Yola hitched her shoulder at the door. 'You're angry about the others, aren't you? You think this celebration is premature? That they should be watching, not drinking?'

'I'm watching.'

She shook her head. 'You haven't eaten your stew.'

'Leave it with me. I'll finish it later.'

She cocked her head to one side. 'You are thinking of the woman, aren't you? The one you lost?'

'I think about her all the time.'

'There are other women, you know. All you need are eyes to see. *O džukel kaj piravel arakhel kokalo.*'

Sabir groaned. 'Alexi does that to me all the time, Yola. It's very irritating. What does it mean?'

Yola pretended to write on her palm. 'It means "a dog that is prepared to wander will always find a bone".' She clamped the hand unexpectedly to her stomach and gave a grimace. 'I'm sorry. He surprises me, sometimes, when I am least expecting it.'

Sabir raised an eyebrow. 'He? Did I hear right? Have you just acknowledged you are actually expecting a baby?'

'You know that well enough.' Yola rolled her head

sheepishly. 'Recently, he seems to be kicking me all the time.'

'May I feel?'

She shook her head. 'No. You shouldn't touch me. I may pollute you.'

Sabir threw up his hands in mock surrender. 'Yola. Sometimes I think I'm beginning to understand you and your people. That I'm slowly getting my head around this concept of *romanipen*. And then you blindside me again.'

'Damo, listen. Even mentioning what is going on with me is bad. I should not have done it. Even words can pollute.'

'Yeah. Yeah. Dumb of me.'

She moved up beside him. She hesitated for a moment and then reached down and took his hand. Gently, she laid it on her stomach.

He grinned. 'Yes. I can feel him all right. No wonder he made you jump.'

She stepped back and crossed herself. Then she spat on the floor. The she inserted her thumb between the index and middle finger of her right hand.

'I recognize that movement. It's the *mano fico*, isn't it? To ward off the evil eye?'

Yola nodded. 'Things move slowly in our culture, Damo. Many things broke down as a result of the Ghermani war – the one your people call the Second World War. But our dead are still linked in dreams to the living. That is the *cacipen*. To change too fast would be to insult the dead. They would forsake us. Then we would be lost. If one is not part of a community of both the dead and the living, one is nothing.'

'I am part of no community.'

'You are part of our community. You are my brother.'

'Your brother is dead. The Corpus killed him.'

'But you have taken his place, Damo. This is as it should be. When my brother shared his blood with you, you became a part of him. And so a part of me. That is why I let you touch me just now. Because you are my brother. I would have killed a *gadje* before letting him touch me.'

'But you did not kill me.'

'No.'

'Because I am your brother?'

'Yes.'

'And because I am no longer a *gadje*.'

'Oh no. You will always be a *gadje*.' She smiled at the shock on his face. 'But you are our *gadje*.'

Sabir smiled back. 'Yola. I am fortunate to have a sister such as you. Did I ever tell you that?'

# 77

'Cut the lights before you hit every corner.'

'But it is dangerous. We will tip over the cliff edge.'

'Do what I say, Trakhtenberger.'

'When may I put the lights back on again?'

'When we have ascertained that there is no lodge, and no lake, round each corner.'

Trakhtenberger was tempted to glance back at his commander, but the Frenchman beside him was holding the pistol on his lap, and Trakhtenberger had always felt uncomfortable around pistols.

He cut the lights, coasted round the next corner, and switched them back on again. He prayed that there would be no lake. No lodge. And very definitely no people. That the ones they were pursuing so relentlessly had found some other way down the mountain – an unseen track, for instance – and that this would be the end of it. He had liked Andrassy. The man had been a joker. Always game for a laugh. But when Andrassy had killed the Jehovah's Witness with his boot, Trakhtenberger had been tempted to give up being a Crusader and return to his village. It had been made clear to him, however, and in no uncertain terms, that this was not an option open to him.

'You have this man's blood on your head as clearly as we have. He was an apostate. The killing is righteous. The Coryphaeus has pardoned us and forgiven us the sin of it already.'

Trakhtenberger didn't want to be involved in any more killings, pardoned or otherwise. He wasn't a religious man. The Coryphaeus was impressive, yes. But Trakhtenberger didn't believe for a moment that he was the Second Coming. But one ate well in Albescu, and earned good money. And one's wife was happy. And happy wives kept their husbands satisfied.

Before he had come to Albescu, Trakhtenberger would have done anything – sacrificed anything – to get away from working in the fields. It was hot in the summer, and cold in the winter. And the few times when it was just right, you were too exhausted to enjoy it. No, it was far better to attach yourself to someone with the power to make decisions on your behalf. Someone who would see to it that you were well fed and well provided for. In return for deference, of course. And obedience. That was the deal. And he had been happy to take it.

But not with someone like this Frenchman. This felt like attaching oneself to a runaway train.

'Stop the car.'

Trakhtenberger pulled up.

'Cut the engine.'

Trakhtenberger cut the engine.

'Turn the key so that the steering wheel does not lock. Then let the car coast back round the corner. Don't pump the brakes, though. I don't want any light to show.'

Trakhtenberger did as he was told. His heart was pounding in his chest. Maybe the Frenchman had seen the lake? He, on the other hand, had seen nothing. Even now he was still having difficulty adjusting his eyes to the moonlight. The snow around them was almost luminous. At any other time Trakhtenberger would have admired the scene. Now it resembled purgatory.

'Both of you. Follow me.'

Trakhtenberger exited the car and followed Markovich and the Frenchman round the corner. He saw the lake almost immediately. How had he not seen it before? And there, on the far bank, was the lodge, dominating the landscape like a gigantic Christmas cake, with the moon as its solitary candle.

The place looked uninhabited. No lights anywhere. Trakhtenberger shivered. The sooner they were in the car again and heading back the way they'd come, the better.

# 78

Sabir had seen the brief shaft of light reflecting off a low cloud. At first he had squinted and shaken his head. When he set the telescopic sight to his eye, however, he caught further movement at the edge of the road.

He cracked open the French windows and eased himself out onto the balcony. He didn't want any glass between himself and what he was looking at. No sudden flash of the moon. No giveaway glint of light.

He cleared away the snow and rested the telescopic sight on the wooden crossbeam of the balcony, shading it with his hand. Now he was outside again, he could feel the cold eating through his clothes.

What had he seen on the corner? It was as if he had caught a dynamic backward movement of some sort. A deer, perhaps. Maybe that was it?

He sucked in his breath just as if he were about to discharge a rifle. The telescopic sight settled, giving him a fairer perspective. He let his breath out smoothly, as one would when blowing on freshly lit kindling down a piece of copper tubing.

First one figure came round the corner. Then another. There was a short pause. Then a third figure followed.

Sabir watched them for a moment, in case it was the Romanian army on night exercise. But nothing followed them. No tanks. No armoured personnel carriers. No grunts carrying machine guns.

Sabir had gone through this scenario a thousand times in his head. He had spent three hours up here alone in the room. He had ironed out every wrinkle. Weighed up every possibility. There was only one way to play it.

He backed in through the French windows and sealed them behind him. Then he seized the Dragunov and hurried downstairs. He had five minutes tops until they reached the exterior of the lodge.

The place was silent as the grave. Everyone was asleep.

Sabir woke Calque first.

Calque opened his eyes wide. He seemed to have trouble focusing.

'They are here. Three of them. Don't say anything. I have prepared for this. Do exactly as I say.'

Sabir padded across the room and woke the other men. 'You must come out into the hall. Quickly.'

Radu and Alexi were having difficulty standing upright, let alone engaging in any forward momentum.

Sabir bundled the empty bottles and dirty plates inside the sleeping bags while the three men were attempting to pull themselves together. He dumped everything he'd collected behind a sofa in the corner of the room.

'Alexi. Calque. Take a shotgun each. Not you Radu. I need you to go in and lie beside Lemma. Act as if you have been sleeping near her. Watching over her. As if there have only ever been the two of you here. We will be waiting elsewhere in the house. Do you understand

478

what I am saying?'

Radu shook his head. He was deeply, unmanageably, drunk.

'Listen, man. If Lemma is still asleep, do not wake her under any circumstances. Go and lie beside her exactly where Yola has been sleeping. But you must send Yola out here to us. Quietly. They will be here in less than three minutes. When they enter your room, act surprised to see them. As if they have caught you napping. Play up your drunkenness. Get them to lower their guard. Do anything you can think of. Then we will come for you. Do you understand that?'

Calque pushed past Radu and into Lemma's room. He was cursing steadily under his breath.

Yola was stirring. She had heard the whispering.

Calque knelt down beside her. 'Listen. They are here. Three of them. Coming up the valley road on foot. No. Don't wake Lemma.' He helped Yola to her feet. 'Sabir says the rest of us must hide. And it's far too late in the day to argue with him. They would have caught us with our pants down if he hadn't been watching. We have at the most three minutes until they reach the house.' He shook his head in rueful acknowledgment of his own irresponsibility. 'Radu and Lemma must stay in here alone. They must act as if there has only ever been the two of them in the lodge. Ever since they stole Andrassy's car and left the village. It is our only chance.' He grasped Yola's arm and led her out into the hall.

Sabir steered Radu past them and into the room. He pointed beyond Lemma's sleeping form. 'Get into the sleeping bag,' he whispered. 'Pretend you are asleep. Let them be the ones to wake you. If Lemma tries to talk, stop her.'

Radu climbed into the sleeping bag. His eyes were wild.

'Do you trust me, Radu?'

Radu mouthed something, but his words were indistinct.

'Good. I reckon you must be sobering up. That was almost audible.' He backed away. 'Remember what I said. You are both sleeping. Let them wake you. It is better that Lemma is truly surprised. It will help, too, that you are still as drunk as a lord.'

Sabir hurried into the corridor. Yola was shaking Alexi. Alexi's head was rattling around on his shoulders like a Punch and Judy puppet.

'Yola, leave him alone. He'll sober up quickly enough. I need you for something else.' He took her arm. 'When we go into the storeroom, I want you to take the third shotgun. You know how to use one?'

She shook her head.

'It doesn't matter. Just point it at their stomachs and flare your eyes. Men are scared shitless when women wave guns about, because they suspect they don't know what they're doing. Rest the shotgun on your hip if you're really going to fire it, or it'll blow you back out through the wall.' He ushered Calque, Alexi, and Yola ahead of him. 'This way. Behind the open door. So that if they check the place out you'll have a moment's grace to get the drop on them.'

'Where are you going to be?'

'Across the hall from Lemma. In the bathroom. There's

a shower stall over the bathtub. I'm going to be behind the curtain. I'm going to leave that door wide open too. That way they'll be less likely to check it out. Plus I'll be able to hear what's going on. You three only come out if you hear my voice. Have you got that? Otherwise you keep *shtum*.'

Calque nodded. He was by far the least drunk of the three men. At fifty-five years old he was well past the self-abuse stage in his life, and knew how to pace himself when drinking alcohol. Which Radu and Alexi didn't. 'Are you sure Radu is up to this? He drank a raft and a half of brandy. Enough to fell a horse, if you ask me.'

'He won't need to act, then, will he?'

Calque made a face. 'Aren't you taking one heck of a risk, Sabir?'

Sabir backed away. 'Only one way to find out.'

# 79

Abi stood in front of the lodge. He pointed down at the ground. Then he beckoned Markovich forward so that he could whisper into his ear. 'See. More sledge marks.' He kicked at the snow. 'This has all been stamped down. They're in here all right.'

'But how are we going to go in after them? They will have locked the door.'

Abi sighed. 'We'll go in through the back. Locks this age are not a problem to me.'

'Maybe they have guns?'

'Where from? They left their camp on the double and in the middle of the night. They've been on the run ever since. Do you think they had time to stop at a gun shop and weapon-up? Hey. That's a thought. Maybe they'll still have the kitchen knife they skewered your buddy Andrassy with?' Abi mimicked the face of a frightened cat. 'Christ. What'll we do? We only have pistols.'

He frogmarched Markovich and Trakhtenberger to the rear of the lodge. He scanned the ground in front of him. 'Good. No one's been in or out through here yet.'

He took off his gloves and set to work, with Markovich aiming the flashlight over his shoulder. He had the lock unpicked in two minutes.

'Listen. Don't hang together when we go inside. You, Trakhtenberger, can take the left. Your boss can take the right. I'll be checking ahead. You can forget about behind us. These people are total amateurs. Charmed fucking amateurs, but still amateurs. But keep quiet from now on in. Empty houses eat sound and spit it back at you again when you least expect it.'

Trakhtenberger looked ill. Markovich – in what may have been a final bid to regain the high ground – was copying the expression and body posture he had seen Russian Spetsnaz soldiers use in a recent documentary about the Chechnya crisis.

Abi was tempted to burst out laughing. Instead, he started up the corridor, the pistol held loosely ahead of him in one hand. No movie fakery for him. He had killed before and he would kill again – and killing, he knew, was a matter of will, not style. He could feel the anticipation burning in his gut. It was what he lived for. The two idiots behind him could go hang. He suspected they would be as much use in a crisis as Tweedledum and Tweedledee.

The doors along the main corridor were all open save one. Abi eased each door a little wider open with his hand as he passed by, and flashed a light through into the interior. Then he continued on his way. Sitting room. Dining room. Storeroom. Bathroom. He stopped outside the single remaining shut door.

He pointed to Trakhtenberger. Then pointed to the ground. Then back to Trakhtenberger. 'You stay here,' he mouthed. He made a circular movement with his forefinger. 'Keep watch.'

Trakhtenberger nodded. He was more than happy to stand guard out in the corridor. 'What the eye doesn't see the heart doesn't grieve over' had pretty much summed up his philosophy of life from the age of about three onwards.

Abi tested the door handle. It gave. He threw open the door and bundled through, with Markovich keeping station close behind him. Abi was holding his flashlight tight to the barrel of his pistol.

He saw Lemma immediately. It was clear she was still asleep. Something was moving near her, though. Abi raised his pistol/flashlight combination. He instantly recognized the Gypsy they had kidnapped at Samois – the one who had given the girls the slip back at the border. He was briefly tempted to shoot him outright, but held fire because he still needed information. There would be plenty of time to take his revenge later. This time around he would flay the bastard alive and use his skin for sailcloth.

'You. Up on your feet.'

Radu lurched upright. He began to rock like a man whose shoes are glued to the ground. Lemma was stirring in her bed. The baby began to cry.

'What is wrong with you, man? You must have been expecting us. Stop weaving. You look as if you are about to piss yourself.'

Radu weaved a little more. He wasn't pretending. He had drunk the best part of a bottle and a half of brandy.

'Are you drunk or something?' Abi stepped forwards. He sniffed Radu's breath. 'Jesus Christ.' He turned round and shone his flashlight directly onto Lemma's face. 'Do something to stop that brat crying. Give it your tit, woman. Or I'll beat its brains out against the wall over there.'

White-faced, Lemma pressed the baby to her breast. She looked helplessly at Radu. Her expression echoed exactly what she felt in her heart. She knew her husband's every mood. Knew when he was out of his head with drink and when he was still in control. A single glance told her that he would be of no possible use to her in the crisis they now faced.

'Where are the others?'

'The others?' Radu squinted at Abi. Abi aimed the flashlight square between Radu's eyes. Radu threw his hand up in self-defence. 'What others?'

'Spare yourself a lot of grief and answer my question. What others do you think? Sabir. The policeman. Your pregnant girlfriend and her husband. Those others.'

Radu was weaving again. It was as if he was lurching in and out of the drunken state with each alternate breath. 'They are back in Oponici. They have been visiting the market. Lemma and I did not have time to warn them.' With each fraction of a sentence, Radu rocked some more. He sounded like a robot. 'They must still be there. It is a three-day market. People come from all around. They bring horses. Chickens. Ducks...'

'Shut up, you drunken fool.' Abi rapped the side of Radu's head with his pistol. Not enough to disable him, but hard enough to gain his attention 'You. Gypsy. Listen to what I am saying. You stay exactly where you are. Do you get that? You don't move one foot from here. Markovich, you stay and cover him. If he moves, blow his balls off.'

Abi began a brisk tour of the room. He aimed his flashlight at everything. Checked over every surface. Squatted under every table. 'Where did you both eat? You must have eaten? I can see no plates or leftovers here.'

Radu ran his hands down the numb expanse of his face. A thin trickle of blood had started from the corner of his eye. 'I didn't want to upset Lemma with the smell. So I cooked in another room. Down the corridor.' He was slurring badly, as though the increased oxygen he had been gulping in was magnifying the effect of the brandy. 'There is another wood heater. With a hob. I found tins in the storeroom. I made pork stew.'

'How many doors back down the corridor is this other room? The one with the hob?'

'This side. Second door.' Radu bent down and began to throw up. Long, uncontrollable spasms that made him grip his stomach as if his guts would follow the stream of vomit out onto the floor. If he hadn't convinced Abi of his drunkenness before, he had convinced him now.

'What a fucking loser.' Abi stood with the pistol held down at his side. 'Markovich, stay with them. If the baby cries anymore, shoot that. This idiot is not worth wasting a bullet on.' Abi hitched his chin at Radu. 'Did you hear what I said, Pikey? There is going to be no more sparing of children on my watch. I'm going outside to check on your story. When I get back you'd better have something specific to tell me. Like exact details of where I can find Sabir and Calque and the expectant parents – not just some vague crap about a duck market. Otherwise your wife is going to wish she had suffered a miscarriage back there in the car. We've been here before, remember?'

Abi strode into the corridor. He waved his pistol at Trakhtenberger. 'Anything moving out here?'

'Nothing, boss. It's quiet as the grave.' Trakhtenberger swallowed. He didn't like pistols being waved at him. Neither did he enjoy standing in a pitch-dark corridor being ordered around by a mad Frenchman whom he had clearly heard talking about killing babies. Trakhtenberger liked babies. He and his wife had had three of them. He was beginning to get a very bad feeling indeed. And he desperately wanted to pee.

'Come with me. I don't trust that drunken arsehole of a Gypsy further than I can throw him. We need to sift through this place with a toothcomb.'

He started up the corridor, the beam from his flashlight carving a disorderly arc in front of him.

Trakhtenberger hesitated for a fraction of a second. But what else could he do? It wasn't as if he could run outside and hail a passing taxicab.

He hurried up the corridor after Abi.

# 80

Sabir was faced with a dilemma. The last thing he had expected was for the three men to split up so quickly. The fact that Abiger de Bale was running the show didn't bode well either. When they had last met, three months before, in Mexico, de Bale had ordered Calque to be hoisted up to the roof, strappado-style, as a direct prelude to a particularly unpleasant form of torture which involved scissors and boiling water. If the *narcotraficantes* hadn't opened fire a few moments later – giving Sabir the opportunity to take Calque's entire bodyweight onto his shoulders – Calque would have been crippled for life. That was the quality of the man they were facing.

De Bale and his cohort skirted the bathroom where Sabir was hiding. Sabir had heard every word de Bale had said to Radu. He knew the two men were on their way to check out the second sitting room. He also knew that the third man was back in the main salon covering Radu and Lemma. Should he wait for them to congregate together again? More importantly, was there anything in the second sitting room that could give away their numbers? Maybe he should try to get the dropdown on de Bale now, and to hell with the consequences? Not leave things to chance?

Each second he failed to act increased the danger they were facing. He had heard Radu being sick. Knew he couldn't count on any real support from that quarter. Alexi would be in a similar condition if the empty bottles he had cleared away in his rush to disguise their presence were anything to go by. If only those two bloody fools had been able to curtail their celebratory urges for the span of one night. If only the people who owned the lodge hadn't left their bloody cellar stacked with booze. If only wishes were horses.

At least Calque and Yola were compos mentis. Calque, he knew, could shoot, but Yola had probably never heard of a safety catch, let alone a double-trigger. She'd point the shotgun, pull the first thing that came to hand, and nothing would happen. She'd be better off throwing the thing at her assailants and then legging it.

Sabir's mind seethed with possibilities. Should he wait for the two to enter the second sitting room and then hurry across into Lemma's room and try to bushwhack her assailant? Or should he wait for them to come back down the corridor? Catch them in a nutcracker action between him and Calque? But what about the man watching Radu and Lemma?

Abi had a flashlight. He would search the room and find the extra sleeping bags behind the sofa. He'd be out in two minutes, on the run. In anything like a fair fight, Sabir knew that he and his companions wouldn't stand a chance.

Fuck... Fuck. Fuck. Fuck. Fuck.

Sabir took off his shoes and laid them beside the bathtub. He waited until he heard Abi and his companion enter the second sitting room. Then he padded across into Lemma's room.

A man he did not recognize was holding a gun on Radu and Lemma, his face livid in the light thrown by the paraffin lamp near Lemma's bed.

Sabir raised his rifle and pointed it directly at the man's head. He dropped his right hand from the stock and held it to his lips. Then he made a falling motion, pointing at the pistol in the man's hand. He was moving forward all the time on his stockinged feet, just like he'd seen it done in the movies.

'Disarm him, Radu. Then gag him. Do you understand me?' He contrived a hoarse whisper, which he hoped wouldn't carry out into the hall.

He waited until Radu had secured the man's pistol before heading back into the corridor. He half expected to see de Bale running towards him with the same 'berserker' look his crazy elder brother had given him the previous summer. He edged back into the bathroom and slipped on his shoes. Then he waited.

The door to the second sitting room burst open. There was the sound of running feet.

Sabir edged the Dragunov around the door and fired blind.

The running stopped. There was the sound of a thud.

'Don't move. Stay right where you are. You are surrounded.'

Sabir waited for the inevitable string of return shots. Nothing happened. Then he heard Calque's voice.

'It's okay, Sabir. You can come out. We have him.'

Sabir emerged from the bathroom doorway. He was holding the Dragunov straight out in front of him as if he intended to bayonet a dummy as part of some training exercise.

One man was lying on the floor. Another was pressed against the wall. Yola had hold of the flashlight. It was shaking.

'Christ. I didn't hit one of them, did I?'

Abi twisted his head from where he had been forced against the wall by Calque and the barrel of his shotgun. 'Two sledges, not one. I should have guessed. Why would the Gypsy have collected two sledges and then abandoned one? What a fool.' He shook his head. 'Well, that was a nice little ambush you contrived there, Monsieur Sabir. Classic, I'd say. Diversion upfront. Main attack from behind. Shame about my friend here. Did you actually mean to kill him? Or was it just a freak shot? I couldn't help noticing that you weren't any too keen to put yourself in harm's way. Let your friends take the strain, eh? But don't feel guilty about shooting an innocent man. All great generals do it.'

Sabir stepped across to the dead man. He glanced down. Trakhtenberger's head looked as if someone had tried to ram a hole through it with the sharp end of a crowbar. He forced back an overwhelming urge to gag. 'I wish it had been you. I really do.' He lifted the rifle and aimed it directly at Abi's face.

Calque took a step towards him, one hand upraised. 'Sabir. You can't do this. Lower the rifle.'

Sabir ignored him. 'On the ground, de Bale. Now. I've

just killed one man. So it's no big stretch…'

Abi dropped to his knees. 'Sure. I'll lie down, Sabir. Don't get your knickers in a twist. I've been needing a break. It's been a long hard day at the coalface.'

Calque gently eased the barrel of Sabir's rifle to one side, so that it was not aiming directly at Abi.

Sabir made a disgusted face and began to back away. 'Calque, you and Yola tie him up. I don't want to touch the sonofabitch. And make sure to check him and the dead man for car keys. I saw the reflected lights of a vehicle earlier. They'll have parked it back round the corner somewhere. But it won't be far. It took them under a minute to return on foot from wherever they left it. Alexi, you stand over him with the dead man's pistol while they do it. If he moves, let him have it.'

Alexi made a big to-do about re-cocking the semi-automatic. Each of his movements took up double the airspace they would normally have needed. 'You see, Damo? I've remembered the lesson you gave me after that time I had a chance at this cocksucker's brother. I botched it, remember? When I forgot to lock and load the pistol. I won't miss this time.' He prodded Abi with his foot. 'Hey, man. You see these gold teeth? Your brother gave me these.'

Abi craned his neck round. 'Rocha gave you some gold teeth? You've got to be kidding. He was tight as a duck's arse.'

'No, I mean he smashed in my teeth and then…'

Sabir turned and looked back. 'Alexi?'

'Yes, Damo?'

'Shut up.'

# 81

They locked de Bale and Markovich in the cellar. The dead body of Trakhtenberger they left in the hall where it had fallen. There was no time anymore for sentiment.

'Leave the shotguns and the rifles behind. They'll weigh us down. We'll take these pistols instead. But we need to make sure that all our prints are wiped off the long guns. The rest of the household stuff doesn't matter.'

'But the two down there will eventually get out. They'll shop us to the authorities.'

'They'll get out. Yes. But we'll be long gone by then. And they won't have any transport, remember? And they certainly won't shop us to the authorities. Catalin won't want to start a paper trail that leads straight back to him. Not in a presidential election year.'

Calque stared down at Trakhtenberger's body. 'I hate leaving that bastard de Bale behind us. I wish you'd killed him instead of this man.'

'So do I. But what alternative do we have? I noticed you weren't any too keen on the idea of my shooting him when I threatened him with the rifle earlier. If you've changed your mind in the interim I can always hurry back down to the cellar and execute him. A single shot to the back of the neck is *de rigueur*, I gather. But then I'd have to kill the other man too. It would be absurd leaving witnesses, wouldn't it? The upside would be that it would stand as my very first hat-trick as a hit man.'

'That's not funny, Sabir.'

'You don't say? Hey. Don't tell me. You were a policeman in a former life? Maybe you want to turn me in yourself after what I did to this man?' Sabir could scarcely bring himself to look down at Trakhtenberger. His guilt about the man was making him angry. 'I've been directly or indirectly responsible for the deaths of three people in the past year, Calque. How do you think I feel about it?' Sabir held up both hands. 'You can handcuff me now if you want. I'll go quietly.'

'That's exactly what you said to me last summer, Sabir. When I asked you to hand over Achor Bale's pistol. My answer is the same now as it was then.'

'And what's that?'

'Don't be absurd. It was either them or us. I have no problem at all with anything you have said or done in the interim, Sabir. You may be something of a loose cannon, but your recent vigilance – when all I could think of to do was to take a drink – has just saved all our lives. And I, for one, am not going to forget it.' He sighed. 'I suspect, though, that the man down there in the cellar is going to cause us more problems before he's finished.'

'We could always lobotomize him from a distance. Alexi's wonderfully good with knives, I hear.'

Calque laughed. 'Sabir, in his present condition, Alexi couldn't hit a seagull on a barn door.'

# 82

—

They found the Lada Niva parked fifty yards below the final bend before the lake. The engine was still warm. Sabir got into the car and turned the key in the ignition. The motor caught straight away and settled into a steady diesel rattle. Sabir checked the gauges. The gas tank was almost full. He slapped the steering wheel with both hands and offered up a fervid prayer of thanks.

He knew that he didn't dare risk the car off-road. The slope down to the front of the lodge hadn't been cleared for months. He stopped 50 metres short of the entrance and flashed his lights.

Radu and Alexi were definitely soberer than they had been half an hour before, but they were still rocky on their legs. Sabir hurried down to help them carry Lemma and her baby across to the car. Given the sheen of sweat on the two men's faces, he reckoned they needed complete rehydration and approximately ten hours of uninterrupted sleep before they would be of use to either man or beast. If this happened every time a baby was born, God alone knew what their livers would look like in fifteen years' time.

'Are you sure you know where this camp is, Radu?

The one that gave you shelter when you were wounded.'

'I know exactly.'

'And you think we'll be safe there?'

'I know we'll be safe there.' Radu was still having trouble getting his mouth to coordinate with his brain. 'It's a big community. Amoy is a senior man amongst the Căldărari elders. I told his wife, Maja, about Lemma and our baby. Maja has had many babies. Maja is a good woman. She saved my life, you know? She will look after Yola and her baby when the time comes. Trust me in this.'

'Right. Take this map and see if you can plot us out a route. You can read a map, can't you?'

Radu shrugged.

'Because if you can't, you must describe all you know about the place to Calque, and he will work it out for you.'

'I can read a map. I am not an illiterate, like Alexi.'

Alexi pretended to cuff his cousin, but his heart wasn't in it. To Alexi, the term 'illiterate' was a compliment – it described someone who had not wasted the better part of their lives learning *payo* nonsense they would neither need nor use.

'I suggest the rest of you settle back and get some sleep. All of you.' Sabir eased the Lada across the crest of the Făgărașan Pass and down towards the valley below. 'But before you do, look over there, everyone. Do you see what I see?'

'See? What do you see?' Alexi was staring nervously out of the window.

'Daylight, Alexi. I see daylight.'

# 83

Early on during the fracas in the hall, when it had become clear that he was surrounded and had no back-up left, Abi had made effective use of the darkness by secretly palming his penknife. He had fancied that he might be able to reach across and slit Sabir's throat when the bastard was least expecting it. But the opportunity hadn't arisen.

Although the ex-policeman – Claque or Catafalque or whatever his name was – had clearly received training in how to deal with potentially dangerous men, he didn't know diddly-squat about conducting body searches in the dark. He had overlooked not only the penknife in Abi's hand, but also his picklocks and the fighting baton concealed up his sleeve. It was almost as if the man desired him to escape.

Abi turned that thought over in his head for a moment and then discarded it. Wishful thinking. The guy just wasn't that bright.

Abi eased the penknife open behind his back and began to saw at the clothesline the policeman had bound his hands with. Markovich was sitting opposite him in the darkened cellar. Abi could just make out the

Crusader's face in the burgeoning dawn that was even now pinking the cellar's frosted windows. He made very sure indeed that Markovich did not see his movements.

'How many men have you got under your direct command, Markovich?'

There was a moment's silence while Markovich decided whether or not to answer.

'Cat got your tongue, Markovich? Have you forgotten the orders you were given by your boss, the New Messiah?'

Markovich grunted. 'I was thinking about Trakhtenberger.'

'Well, don't. He's worm meat. Think about my question instead.'

There was another pause. Markovich almost spat out the answer. 'Twenty. Maybe thirty. It depends.'

'Depends on what?'

Markovich sat up straighter. 'Where they are detailed. What my orders are concerning them. Their responsibilities at home. At the present moment I have five Crusaders guarding the Coryphaeus's house back in Moldova, and a further ten or so out here on the road in Romania, registering Moldovan voters for the coming elections.'

'Why does the Coryphaeus need his house guarding?'

Markovich seemed surprised at the question. 'Well, he doesn't. Not most of the time, anyway. But it goes in phases. Sometimes he will call on us. Usually when he wants to be undisturbed for a specific period of time. He refuses to be disturbed at the moment, for instance. This happens sometimes. He goes into seclusion with his sister. This time he has told the people that his sister has the typhoid. But I do not think this is true. They are probably meditating. The guards are there to keep well-wishers away. It can go on like this for days.'

'The meditating?'

'Yes. Antanasia Catalin is a very holy woman. The Coryphaeus thinks highly of her. They meditate together.'

Abi bit back a cynical snort. Well. Meditation was one way of putting it. 'So those are the only Crusaders actually back in Moldova, then? The rest of the gang are out here cold-calling?' Abi's hands were now free. He continued to hold them behind his back.

'I suppose so. Yes. That is the case. But what are you getting at? I should have thought our main problem was not how many men I have under my immediate command, but how to get out of this stinking place. The Coryphaeus is going to be very angry with me. I have failed him.'

'Don't worry about getting out, Markovich. I have a plan. And I'll even see you right with the Coryphaeus. But answer my question first.'

Markovich was slightly mollified by Abi's tone. 'Well, there are always the reserves. Men who work full time, but who can be called on as Crusaders in an emergency.'

'But at the moment there are only five armed Crusaders in Albescu?'

'I told you that. Yes. But why are you asking me all these questions?'

'Just to pass the time. I am fascinated by your Coryphaeus. As you know, we support him whole-heartedly in what he is aiming to do. To the extent even of funding his presidential campaign. That is why I am interested in the vote-gathering aspect of his work.'

'You are funding him?'

'Yes. With a considerable sum of money. That is why he trusts me. That is why he put me in charge of you. Our people have made commitments. I'm sure he has told you all this.' Abi decided that a little subtle flattery wouldn't go amiss. 'And we intend to honour these commitments despite this recent fiasco.'

Markovich nodded his head as if he had been fully cognizant of the situation from the outset. 'It is bad what happened to Trakhtenberger. He had a wife and three children.'

'We will make sure she has a pension.'

'Really?'

'Yes, really. Trakhtenberger died in the line of duty. His widow deserves to be compensated. His children will be well cared for. You have my word on that.' Abi was grateful that Markovich was not as yet able to make out his features in the rapidly receding gloom. His capacity for playacting was hardly up there with Jean Gabin. 'The Coryphaeus has a splendid house, I presume?'

'No. No. It is very humble. Nothing splendid about it. The Coryphaeus lives just like you and I.'

'I'm very glad to hear it. Is the church attached to his house, by any chance?'

'No. The house overlooks the church, but it is not attached. The house has its very own driveway, you know. Have you not seen it?'

'No. I have not had that privilege. The Coryphaeus

and I met elsewhere. But I shall doubtless visit him at some point in the future. I look forward to it very much.' Abi could scarcely contain his glee. 'I am glad you have the house well guarded, though. But five men does not seem like enough to safeguard such a vulnerable edifice.'

'I agree with you. I agree with you completely. I have often said as much to the Coryphaeus. Two men on and two men off. It is simply not enough.'

'So you've arranged it like that? But what about the fifth man?'

'Ah. That was my idea. I am very pleased about that. I have earmarked this man to use his discretion. To check up on the house when the men guarding it are least expecting it. Even the Coryphaeus does not know about him. This way the guards will always stay on the alert.'

'A wise move. A wise move indeed.' Abi stood up and shucked off his bonds. In one fluid movement he picked up the snow shovel he had marked out earlier and swung it at Markovich's head.

Markovich had a split second in which to either cry out or throw himself to one side. He opted for the cry.

Abi's blow took him full on the temple. Markovich's head smashed back against the wall. He curled up into a ball and began to howl.

Abi belted him on the knee.

Markovich lurched forward, shrieking.

Abi stepped across and rammed the edge of the shovel down on Markovich's neck – it was the same movement a man would use when cutting turves. The blow severed Markovich's spinal cord.

Abi squinted down at his handiwork. Then he wiped

his prints off the handle of the shovel and replaced it neatly in the rack.

He moved to the door and took out his picklocks. The thought of the policeman's cursory body-search still amused him. Abi suspected that he could have got away with a sub-machine gun concealed up his right trouser leg if he'd felt so inclined. Maybe the guy had been drinking, too? Nothing these amateurs did would surprise him anymore. Sabir, on the other hand, bore watching. The man had the luck of the Devil.

He opened the door. Listened. Then relaxed.

He hefted Markovich over his shoulder and carried him upstairs. He dumped him down beside Trakhtenberger, cut his hands, and disposed of the rope. Then returned to the cellar and collected the discarded Nordic skis, boots, and ski poles that Sabir had been using earlier.

On his way back upstairs he glanced at the shotguns and the Dragunov rifle that Sabir and his cohorts had left behind. He shook his head dolefully. No. There was no future in any of those. Not for a man on foot. He helped himself to a parka jacket, some gloves, and a ridiculous fur hat with earflaps that was hanging behind the storeroom door.

He hesitated for a moment on his way out of the lodge.

Grunting, he dumped the skis, boots, sticks and clothing outside the front door, and went back inside.

He hurried through into the room in which Lemma had been sleeping. He bundled up the used bedlinen and the sleeping bags in a pile on the floor. He slit the sleeping bags open with his penknife, then surrounded the heap of stuffing with wood from the log pile. Then he raked the embers out from inside the wood-burner and spread them across the stuffing, criss-crossing the whole with kindling. His improvised pyramid was smoking in a most satisfactory manner by the time he left the room.

He went into the rear sitting room and did the same with the sleeping bags in there. He soon had a second fire going. He added some eviscerated sofa cushions to the blaze for good measure.

He returned to the hall, switched his shoes for the Nordic ski boots, then threw his used footgear back inside the lodge. He left the front door ajar. There was nothing like an open doorway to create a draught.

He attached the Nordic skis to his leather boot-tips and tested their spring and flexibility. When he was satisfied with the setup, he put on the coat, hat and gloves, and forged down the valley in the direction he had arrived. It was downhill all the way.

Abi reckoned that it shouldn't take him more than three or four hours of ski time to reach the main gates. He would steal himself a car in Cărţişoara and take it from there.

Behind him, the fire began to rage out of control.

*Albescu, Moldova*
*Sunday, 7 February 2010*

# 84

Abi watched the two Crusaders from his hidden position high up beneath the triple bells on Albescu's church tower. It was just as Markovich had indicated. The two guards were taking turn and turn about the Coryphaeus's house, which the church tower clearly overlooked. They seemed bored. And cold. There was much foot-stamping and hand-slapping, and the men's muttering carried clearly up to him on the frozen night air.

Two hours into their tour of duty, the third Crusader – the one who was meant to be on a roving spy commission – turned up. All three men huddled together and shared the thermos of coffee the third Crusader had brought.

Surprise visit, my arse, thought Abi.

The visiting Crusader added a hefty dash of something alcoholic to the men's mugs from his stainless steel hip-flask. The volume of sound rose. The men were clearly settling in for a good grumble.

Abi hastened down through the empty church. It was now or never. The Crusaders would be looking at a minimum two further hours of guard duty before they could hope to be relieved. They would be making the most of their illegal break.

Looping well beyond the men's sight line, Abi hurried round to the temporarily unguarded rear of the house. The place had not been designed to keep people out. It had been designed to make a statement about the importance of the person occupying it in relation to those living around him.

Abi vaulted over the rear fence and made straight for the back door. Even if the Crusaders broke up their coffee klatch that instant and returned to their posts, he would still have a minimum of sixty seconds' leeway to crack the door.

He checked the lock and smiled. Bog-standard Russian design. Primitive mechanism. A wooden bar and twin supports would have been more effective.

He heard the crunch of the returning Crusader's boots just as he triggered the mechanism. He darted inside the door and eased it shut behind him. He counted to sixty. Nothing. He was inside.

He took off his boots and tied them around his neck. What a bloody fool he'd been not to carry his old shoes down from the lodge with him. These boots were all very well in the snow, but their leather Nordic tips and Vibram soles didn't make for noiseless walking on parquet flooring. He cursed himself for not having taken the time to whittle away the excess leather with his penknife while he was waiting in the church.

He eased his fighting baton from the sheath inside his sleeve and silently extended it. He could hear a raised voice from upstairs. A man's voice. Haranguing somebody. There was a peevish quality to it that he recognized. Lupei.

507

Was he talking to his sister? Or was there somebody else in the house? Maybe his sister really did have typhoid? Abi had to find out.

He started up the polished wooden steps. No danger of pressure pads here. Or of hidden cameras. The floor and walls were bare of all covering. Abi made a face. One could hardly call the house welcoming.

He reached the landing and stopped again. The same voice was droning on. Was it a recording? No. This was a live human being speaking. But it seemed to Abi as if Lupei either had a static audience, or was simply talking to himself. Maybe he was rehearsing one of his sermons in front of the mirror?

Abi moved closer to the door. He listened for any rustling, coughing, or nose-blowing that would indicate more than one person in the room. An audience, maybe. Anyone.

There was utter silence.

He frowned and cracked open the door.

Lupei was standing in the centre of the room. He was staring down at the bed. He had a whip in one hand.

The woman on the bed was clearly unconscious. The sheets on which she lay were soaked through with blood. She was naked. Lupei had attached her to the bed with a series of leather straps so that, at first glance, his victim appeared to be covered by the shadow of prison bars.

As Abi watched, Lupei began whipping the woman on her front and chest, using a steady, almost leisurely, action of the wrist. Some of the blows landed close to the woman's face. Others struck her across the stomach, breasts and upper thighs. It was clear that

Lupei was beating her to some sort of design. His entire concentration was focused on the woman in front of him, and on where next to place his lash.

Abi strode up to Lupei and struck him behind each knee with his fighting baton.

Lupei pitched to the ground and began to retch.

Abi kicked away the whip.

Ignoring Lupei completely, he gazed down at the woman on the bed. It was Antanasia, Lupei's sister. There was no possible way, however, that the amount of blood visible on the bed sheets could have come from the front of Antanasia's body, which was clearly exposed to Abi's eye, and as yet largely unmarked. The blood had to have come from her back, which was entirely concealed from him in her present position.

It was also clear that Antanasia was still unconscious. Lupei had been beating an unconscious woman to death.

Abi bent down and struck Lupei across the front of both thighs – this, he knew, would effectively cripple the man, and prevent him using his legs to escape. Abi put some real power into the blows, and found that he enjoyed doing it. He was angry about the woman and what Lupei had done to her. It was a novel experience for him.

Lupei curled himself into a ball and began to keen.

'Shut up, or I'll belt you in the teeth.'

Lupei bit off his cries and stared up at Abi.

'I've come to arrange the transfer of the 150 million euros my mother still owes you. The only difference from what we originally agreed and now, is that the transfer is going directly into my account. You will speak to my mother personally, and give her the new account details. If you cooperate with me, I'll let you live. If you play for time, I'll cripple you. If you clam up, I'll kill you.'

Lupei began to weep – deep, racking sobs, which shook his body as if he were suffering from exposure.

Abi took a step backwards. He didn't know exactly what he had expected to find when he made the decision to break into Lupei's house, but this wasn't it.

'I need to punish her. She has betrayed me. She deserves to carry the mark of the Devil.'

Abi rolled his eyes and glanced back at the bed. 'Is your sister tranquillized?'

'She betrayed me.' Tears were streaming down Lupei's face. Snot was running out of his nose. His mouth was like a child's mouth. Wailing. Unconcerned with its appearance.

'How long have the two of you been in here, man?'

'She needs to be punished. She deserves to be punished. Will you punish her for me?' Lupei floundered across the floor towards the knout, dragging his useless legs behind him. He reminded Abi of the beggars one sometimes sees in the Maghreb, propelling themselves around on wheeled platforms, faking amputeeism. 'Here. You must strike her with this. It is the only suitable tool to use on the Coryphaeus's sister. I have explained this to her. And that Peter the Great used a similar one on his son, who also betrayed him. He changed knouts every six stripes, so that his son's blood wouldn't soften the rawhide and lessen his pain. You must do the same. I have more knouts in the drawer over there. Go on. You will enjoy it. Beat her to death.

Then I will do whatever you want me to. Sign over whatever you want me to sign.'

Abi stepped closer to Lupei. He cocked his head to one side like a dog listening for his master's footsteps, and stared at the man beneath him. The Third Antichrist? What a joke. He put his foot on the knout and shunted it away from Lupei's hand.

'You must do this for me. You shall have all my money. Every last cent. I am a rich man.'

Abi shook his head. The man was clearly mad. 'Don't you remember who I am, Lupei?'

Lupei shrugged. 'I don't care who you are. Who you are doesn't interest me in the slightest.' He tried to rise, but his legs wouldn't answer him.

Abi struck him on the right shoulder with the tip of his baton. He wanted to hurt Lupei. Wanted to snap him out of the fantasy land he was inhabiting. 'You're not whipping anybody. That part of your life is over.'

He strode across the room and began unsnapping the leather straps that bound Antanasia to the bed. When he'd freed her from the straps, he attempted to ease her up into a sitting position, but her back was stuck to the sheets. Abi glanced at Antanasia's face. She was clearly unconscious. Way beyond feeling any pain.

Abi ripped the sheets from her back in one fluid movement, wincing as he did so. He felt a sudden, uncomfortable connection to this woman – as though it was completely natural that she should look to him, a near-total stranger, for succour. He remembered his first sight of her in Albescu. The way she walked. His joke to Rudra that she looked like no nun he had ever seen.

He turned Antanasia over onto her front and gently inspected her back with his fingertips. 'For pity's sake, Lupei, how long has this been going on?'

Antanasia's back was a suppurating mass of weeping flesh. The knout had bitten deeply – at times almost to the bone. It was clear that the main damage had been done some time before, and that her wounds were badly infected.

'Beat her! Beat her!' Lupei screamed. He began scrabbling across the floor like a hermit crab, his eyes fixed on the knout.

Abi uttered an incoherent roar. He strode across to where he had kicked the knout and picked it up. His first blow took Lupei on the side of the head, near his right eye. Lupei screamed. He began to froth at the mouth as if he were having an attack of epilepsy.

It was at this point that Abi lost all control. He began to thrash Lupei with the knout – blow after blow after blow. Lupei did his best to avoid the lash, but his legs and right arm were no longer functioning, and he was only able to propel himself in ever-diminishing circles, like water exiting from a plughole.

At one point, Abi kicked Lupei over onto his side and began to work on his back. He had no real intention of killing the man – he needed him far too much for that – but merely of punishing him. Exacting an impartial revenge on him for what he had visited on his sister. But Abi's bloodlust, never far beneath the surface, now flared out of control.

Abi thrashed Lupei solidly for ten minutes, until the sweat was standing out on his face and neck, and his shirt, beneath his stolen parka jacket, was wringing wet. He thrashed Lupei until the man was so far beyond death that he no longer resembled a human being.

He stopped once, halfway through the scourging, and gazed over towards the bed, where he fancied he had caught the flash of a partially opened eye. But Antanasia was curled up on her side, just where he had left her, her face the colour of calcite.

When the job was done Abi tossed the blood-soaked knout across the room and flicked the blood off his hands like a surgeon ridding himself of excess bactericide. Then he stared down at Lupei's body, as if he was surprised at what he saw. He struck himself between the eyes with the flat of his hand, leaving the bloody imprint of a palm on the centre of his forehead.

'There, Monsieur de Bale. Now you've really gone and shit your pot full. You've just beaten 150 million euros to death.'

Abi stared numbly down at his victim. He hadn't lost control like that since he was sixteen years old, and taking revenge on a school bully who had been targeting his brother. He'd cornered the boy down an alley, meaning only to mark him. In the end he'd smashed his hands, knees, and feet with a hockey stick. When he realized the boy had recognized him, he'd finished the job by beating in the back of the boy's head. Then he'd dropped his trousers and reattached the hockey stick to his leg with two luggage straps, so that the shaft fitted snugly inside his boot, and the head looped over his belt and underneath his shirt. When he was certain it didn't show, he'd limped out of the alley as though he'd wrenched his knee. Later, he'd burnt the wooden hockey stick. It had been Indian style. With a clubbed head. Best mulberry. He'd never found another one like it.

Abi turned and gazed speculatively towards the bed. No. Maybe everything wasn't lost quite yet. He would still need a fall-back position in case the next part of his master plan didn't work to order. Maybe Lupei's sister was it?

Antanasia was stirring fitfully. Abi watched her, caught midway between fascination and horror. He remembered interrogating her. How beautiful he had thought her. How extraordinarily self-possessed. It was rare for any woman to make an impression on Abi beyond the fleetingly sexual. But Antanasia had done so, to the extent that Abi – acting quite out of character – had even formed a halfway concrete plan of contriving to see her again.

One part of him now wondered whether his furtive return to Albescu hadn't partly been on account of her? He found himself struggling to understand how the pair of them had contrived to migrate from the women's section of Albescu's public conveniences to here? What ridiculous confection of fate had thrown them together in Lupei's bedroom, with a dead man lying on the floor between them, and Antanasia beaten half to death on the bed?

Abi tore his eyes away from Antanasia and strode out of the room. He cast around the house until he identified Lupei's study. He went inside and began going through Lupei's papers, searching for bank statements. He knew

Lupei kept a Swiss bank account in his and his sister's name – he, and Madame, his mother, had helped set it up through her own bank in Lugano. But just knowing about the account wasn't enough. He needed the dedicated bank code and account number, otherwise he might as well go home and take up knitting.

He found a locked file beneath Lupei's desk. He prised the lock open with his penknife. Yes. Here were the bank statements. The account held 49,830,000 euros. Abi punched the air. So Lupei hadn't had time to take delivery of his weapons of mass destruction after all? Maybe the bastard had had them on advance order, payable in full only when he became President? One couldn't put anything past a man who would happily beat his sister to death over a series of days, keeping her alive on painkillers and tranquillizers in the interim. At least when Abi had killed his sisters, he had done it cleanly and without excessive gloating – except in the case involving the attempted drownings in the cenote, but that had been unprecedented. A true one-off. The exception, he felt, that proved the rule.

What a fool Madame, his mother, had been to think she could control a matter like Lupei. There she was, one of the richest women in the world, and instead of relishing what she had, all she could think of to do with her moolah was to arm a maniac with the seeds of her – and her own society's – destruction. It beggared belief. She didn't deserve the money.

From the very beginning Abi had never seen the point of the Corpus Maleficus – as far as he was concerned all it had ever been was an excuse to have a good time, paid for in full by somebody else. The remainder of his family, however, had approached the thing with an earnestness verging on the deranged. It was that which had killed them in the end. Well, hadn't some joker once opined that 'you are always killed by what you love'? Or was that the name of a song? It almost made you weep.

As well as the bank statements and account details there were two passports at the bottom of the locked file. Lupei's and Antanasia's. Abi pocketed Antanasia's and chucked Lupei's into the wastepaper basket. He wouldn't be needing that anymore.

He flicked open his cell phone and dialled Madame, his mother's, number. It was a calculated risk, this splitting of his eggs into two baskets. If it all turned out badly it could cost him a fortune. But what better alibi? And as far as the authorities were concerned, he was still in America anyway.

'I have good news, Madame. Catalin has fulfilled his part of the bargain. His Crusaders have killed both the Gypsy girl and her husband. With their help I then found Sabir and the policeman as they were attempting to make off over the Carpathians. In tomorrow's newspaper you will read of a disastrous fire at one of Nicolae Ceausescu's old hunting lodges, up near the Făgăraşan Pass. Two bodies in it. Burned beyond recognition.'

There was a long silence at the other end of the line, which Abi chose not to fill.

'You are suggesting we send him the residue of his money then?'

'I think he has earned it, Madame. The man is clearly a psychopath of the very first order. I think we can assume he will use it well.'

The Countess sighed. It was as though a great weight was lifting itself from about her shoulders. 'Abiger, I am very proud of you. I do not say this lightly.'

Abi made a face into the phone. Thank God, he thought to himself, that the damned thing isn't set up to transmit images. 'I have only done my duty as a member of the Corpus, Madame. And as your son. And as the proud inheritor of Monsieur, my father's, titles and appurtenances.'

'Nevertheless.'

Abi bowed his head. 'Nevertheless.' He was tempted to burst out laughing, but managed to control himself. Talk about rampant archaism. Here he was, twenty-five years old, and forced to talk like a dowager duchess at an *ancien régime* tea party.

'Will you be returning home now? I shall need you to liaise with Catalin for me, as you have first-hand knowledge of the man's character.'

'In a week or so's time, Madame, if that's all right? I have a few things to clear up here first. But I am at your entire service should you find my absence in any way inconvenient.'

'Ah. By clearing up, do you mean your brothers and sisters?'

'Yes, Madame. One of us needs to attend the funeral. It seems the least we can do.'

'Yes. Yes. I suppose so. Well. Wish them my best on their journey to wherever it is they are going. The whole thing is a tragedy, of course. Our entire adopted family wiped out in less than a year. But they did their duty, every last one of them, and I am very proud. I am gratified, too, that you, at least, are left to carry on your father's work. It would have been a catastrophe if no one was left to give honour to his titles.'

Abi rolled his eyes. 'A catastrophe. Yes.'

You callous old bitch, he thought to himself. Apart from Oni, you never really gave a damn about any of us. Even me, your technical favourite. If one of Lupei's nuclear-tipped Kh-55s broke through the ceiling and landed on my head at this exact moment, you would probably slam the phone down and begin a game of backgammon with Madame Mastigou.

'I shall certainly care for the old traditions, Madame, just as Monsieur, my father, would have wished. You can count on that.'

'I know I can, Abiger. In fact I am certain of it.'

*Bogdamic Camp, Romania*
*Early Monday Morning,*
*8 February 2010*

# 8 5

It took Adam Sabir's party the better part of a day and a night to reach Amoy's camp. A few hundred yards short of the entrance, Radu indicated to Sabir that he should halt the vehicle.

'I'll get out here and walk in. I need to talk to Amoy and Maja privately before we enter. They don't like strangers here. But the camp will recognize me. The local people around here hate the Roma, and would burn them out if they could. But there are too many of us. It makes our people cautious, however.' He hesitated. 'Damo. Do you have a gift I could offer Amoy?'

'A gift?'

'He is a very poor man. He lost his horse because of me. It would make it easier for him and Maja to be able to offer us hospitality without embarrassment if I give them some money as a gift. They have children to feed. Amoy earns very little. It would be customary for me to take something to them as a token of gratitude for looking after me that time when I was injured. They will not suspect it came from you.'

Sabir felt in his pockets. 'I have our reserve – 900 euros.'

'No. Not that much. They will think we have robbed

a bank. Give me 200. But it is a risk. I must give the gift without qualification. If Amoy refuses to help us the money will be lost.'

'That's a risk I, for one, am prepared to take.'

'Good, Damo. Good. You are half Gypsy already.'

Alexi leaned across the seat and slapped Sabir on the shoulder, his eyes glittering at the sight of the money. 'You see, Damo? Radu agrees with me about you turning into a Gypsy. Maybe we find you a wife in the camp, eh? Radu, you look out. If you see an ugly one, or a double-widow, or someone who is ill, or barren, or who has the tongue of a viper, tell their father that Damo is available. He is rich, and he is available. And I, Alexi Dufontaine, volunteer to act as middleman.' He grinned, showing his new gold teeth. 'Damo, if you want, you can advance me my commission now. That way you get better service in the long run.'

Sabir shoved the remaining euros as far back in his pocket as he was able. One never knew quite to what extent Alexi was joking when he veered off on one of his inevitable tangents.

Radu hurried towards the camp. Lights were being switched on as people got up. Fires were being lit. Preparations were being made for breakfast.

Sabir turned to Calque. 'Do you think de Bale has managed to inveigle himself out of that cellar yet?'

Calque smiled. 'I'm sure he has.'

'What do you mean "you're sure he has"?'

'Mean? Well, it's simple. I bungled my search of him on purpose. It was dark. We were under pressure.'

Sabir stared at him. 'I don't quite understand you,

Calque. What are you getting at? Please enlighten me.'

Calque sighed. 'I should have thought it was obvious, Sabir. I made sure that whatever de Bale brought in with him was still on him when I tied him up. Picklocks. Knives. What have you. Even that telescopic fighting thing he waved under my nose out in Mexico that time. The one he keeps hidden in a sling up his sleeve.'

Sabir stiffened. 'What species of brain maggot made you do that? He might have come straight out after us again. The man's as crazy as a sackful of cats. I left a fucking long rifle in there.'

Calque puffed his cheeks impatiently. 'Come straight after us travelling on what? A pair of skis? We were always going to be long gone before he and his pal managed to break out of the cellar.'

Sabir forced himself down a notch. 'Okay. Yes. I see your point.'

'This way we can rely on him and his colleague covering up all traces of the man you inadvertently killed. De Bale doesn't want the police involving themselves any more than we do. And anyway, I have a suspicion that the good Count may be busy working to his very own agenda.'

'What makes you think that? Do you know something I don't?'

'Just call it my policeman's instinct. I've never quite believed in this particular de Bale as a Corpus zealot. Any 666 signs behind his eyes refer to pounds, euros and dollars, if you ask me, and not to the Beast. Added to which he seems to get a particular kick out of exercising power. And in order to exercise power you need a good reason. A good excuse. And what better excuse is there,

Sabir, than saving the world from the Devil? Hey? Answer me that one.'

Sabir shook his head. Sometimes Calque meandered down side-roads of his very own invention. Sabir saw no earthly reason why he should follow along behind and make a goddamned fool of himself.

Radu returned after fifteen minutes. He tapped on the Lada's side window. Sabir wound it down.

'It is good. They are letting us in. Maja has found us two caravans belonging to her relatives. People who have gone to Rome for the Pope's Easter Mass.'

'The Easter Mass?'

'Yes. It is the best time in the year to steal. People are always looking up into the air. To make the most of the opportunities, though, one must arrive a few weeks early. That way you catch out all the foreign pilgrims before they have had time to settle in.'

Sabir rolled his eyes. 'Oh yes. I ought to have guessed.'

Radu shrugged. 'These people are happy to rent us their caravans while they are gone. We leave them more money if we stay for a long time.'

'Maybe they leave Damo their unmarriageable daughters too?'

Radu pretended to give Alexi a cuff with the back of his hand. 'Okay, Damo? You fine with this?'

'I'm fine.' Sabir glanced uncertainly at Calque. 'You really think Yola will be safe here? Having her baby, I mean?'

Calque glanced at the lights of the camp. From a distance it looked as if the entire US Mediterranean fleet were laid out below them. 'Safe as houses.'

*Albescu, Moldova*
*Early Monday Morning,*
*8 February 2010*

# 86

Abi spent some considerable time ministering to Antanasia's wounds. But there was little he could achieve without penicillin. Lupei's array of tranquillizers, saline drips, and painkillers, however, was a wonder to behold.

Abi dosed Antanasia with more Rohypnol, and then wrapped her body in disinfected gauze. He had made a rather lame attempt to clean the deepest wounds on her back, but eventually gave up and left them for later. It was clear that there would be more suturing to do, including the reopening and abrading of old wounds once the infections had died down. But that was for the future.

Abi knew that he was safe inside the Coryphaeus's house for the time being. Markovich had explained to him about Lupei's odd habits. It would surprise nobody in town if Antanasia's brother didn't emerge for days, especially if they accepted his bullshit excuse that he was treating his sister for infectious typhoid. But Abi also knew that he needed to sneak Antanasia away well before dawn if he was to have any chance at all of getting out of there without alerting the Crusaders. Each hour he spent in the house after that added exponentially to the likelihood of getting caught with his pants down. God alone knew what private arrangements Lupei had entered into. Maybe Little Red Riding Hood herself came in with a basket of food for him at breakfast time? I mean, a man would need to keep his strength up for all that whipping.

Abi determined to wait until well after the next change of guard, trusting that Markovich's roving Crusader would repeat his trick with the thermos about two hours into the new men's shift. Fortunately, the windows of the house gave clear views in every direction. He would wait until he saw the three men clustering together again before ferrying Antanasia out to his stolen car.

In the meantime he continued with his ransacking of the house. As well as Antanasia's passport and the Lugano bank details, he discovered a roll of 20,000 euros in clean notes taped under the central drawer of a breakfront desk. Tacked up beside the roll of notes was a well-oiled Czech-made 9mm CZ 75 pistol. Abi wasn't one hundred per cent happy with the 75. He would have preferred the ambidextrous CZ 85, being a left-handed shooter – but beggars couldn't be choosers. At the very least it felt good to be in possession of a pistol once again – and one with a first-rate reputation for reliability. There was nothing on this earth more likely to plaster egg all over your face than firing at somebody and nothing happening. Either that, or what had happened to him a couple of years before with a Savage, when two bullets had come out at once, neatly skewering his intended victim in either shoulder rather than plumb through the heart, which is where Abi had originally aimed.

Vau had finished the man off for him, and then both of them had stared at the Savage in disbelief and burst out laughing.

Ah, happy days.

At the thought of Vau, Abi allowed his mind to drift back to Sabir and Calque.

Yes. Those two would keep. He could afford to place his revenge for Vau on the slow burner. He had other fish to fry first.

# 87

Abi stole the German-registered Mercedes Geist Phantom motorhome just short of the Hungarian border post at Valea Lui Mihai. He had watched it come through the checkpoint, and had then tailed it for 40 kilometres, until its owners stopped for a coffee break.

He had threatened the husband and wife with the CZ, forced them to drink Rohypnol, and then driven them off the road in his stolen car, where any passer-by would assume from their postures that they'd stopped off for a kip. With the dosage he had given them, they would be out for a good twelve hours, with little or no memory of what had happened to them when they woke up. Ample time for him to recross the border lower down at Oradea, with a trumped-up story of having received a panic stricken phone call from his family back home.

The chances of the border guards querying Frenchman Pierre Blanc driving a German registered vehicle were infinitesimal. Hungary and Romania were both in the EU – they'd probably wave him straight on through. And who would ever suspect a man in a luxury motorhome of wrongdoing anyway?

Just as a precaution, though, Abi concealed the still

heavily tranquillized Antanasia in the storage space beneath the single permanent bed. If one of the border guards discovered her there, he'd knock him out and make a run for it – steal himself another car further downstream and disappear into the ether. It was a gamble worth taking. Life was valueless unless you put it on the line.

Once safely across the border, Abi drove west, through Austria, Switzerland and down into France, stopping only briefly to snatch a nap, freshen Antanasia's dressings, or change her drip. He had been able to buy some amoxicillin over the counter in a Hungarian pharmacy, as well as more suture needles and gut, and he was therefore able to work on Antanasia on a number of occasions during the journey, stitching and cleaning where appropriate. But still he kept her tranquillized. Abi had tried to persuade himself that he was doing this for Antanasia's own sake, and to spare her terrible pain, but there was more to it than that, and he knew it. He needed time to think.

The motorhome, for its part, proved to be stupendously well-equipped – the German couple driving it had clearly been intent on a lengthy tour throughout Eastern Europe, and had laid in their favourite stores accordingly. There were jars of knackwurst and sauerkraut and pickled gherkins – a homemade potato salad and red-cabbage-and-apple compote in the fridge. Two salamis and a Westphalian ham hanging behind the counter. A case of best Alsatian wine. Shrink-wrapped loaves of vollkornbrot and pumpernickel. The interior of the vehicle looked and smelled like a delicatessen.

Abi even found a wardrobe stuffed full of female clothes for when Antanasia finally recovered and was needed for bank duty. It never occurred to Abi for one moment that Antanasia might object to what he had in mind. He had saved her life, hadn't he? Neutralized her maniac of a brother. Naturally she would be grateful.

Just in case the Germans were better connected than he thought, Abi unscrewed the French plates from the first suitable car he found and disposed of the German ones down a storm drain. There was no way he would be overstepping the speed limit in the white elephant he was driving in any event. The chances of being stopped by the police and having his papers checked were scarcely worth bothering about. Driving the Geist was like wearing an invisibility cloak in a girls' dormitory.

He made the outskirts of St Tropez on his third full day of driving thanks to copious quantities of 'special edition' Red Bull he had bought in Austria, where the drink was rumoured to contain cocaine.

Just outside Madame, his mother's, estate – at a lay-by near La Croix Valmer – Abi settled down for the extended sleep he knew he still needed. He made up the double bed in the Geist, and then, after a moment's hesitation, transferred Antanasia from her own bed to his.

Then, pulling the dead weight of her onto his free arm, he tucked the eyeshade down across his face and fell into a profound sleep.

# 88

—

Abi awoke to his alarm clock at a little after ten o'clock that night. Antanasia, too, stirred in her sleep.

Abi stripped back the bed sheets and inspected her dressings. The amoxicillin had done its job well and her open wounds were no longer, for the most part, putrid. Some of the lighter lacerations were already scabbing over, and the deeper ones were blooming a healthy red where he had stitched them and put in drains. One or two of the principal wounds had proved so extensive, however, that Abi was still only surface dressing and irrigating them – it would be another few days at least before he could risk an effective running suture. But things weren't as bad as he had once feared. There would be no need for emergency hospitalization and the concomitant loss of control over Antanasia that that would entail. Not to mention the explanations. Any civilized hospital would instantly bring the police down on his head on such clear evidence of abuse.

In the case of the worst wounds – some of which had been almost circular due to the particular formation of the knout – Abi had pared away a percentage of the proud skin, effectively converting the circular wound into an elliptical one. In this way he figured he would be able to stitch the edges of the wound together with some degree of cosmetic verisimilitude once the wound was completely infection-free. Antanasia's back would never look as it had before, that much was for certain – but it would certainly look better than it would have done had she been forced to endure even a few more hours of her brother's tender care.

The top part of her shoulders, measuring roughly from her shoulder blades to her neck, and incorporating her upper and lower arms – which had been drawn away from her body by the ropes with which she had been bound – were relatively unscathed, as Lupei appeared to have focused the greater part of his attention on her back, buttocks, and upper legs. This meant that, at the very least, Antanasia would be able to wear a reasonably low-cut dress without anybody noticing the full extent of her scarification. Why this should matter so much to Abi was a profound mystery to him. He even caught himself working on Antanasia's suturing strategically, as if he were approaching a particularly challenging jigsaw puzzle.

Abi owed his excellent training in advanced first aid to Madame, his mother. The Countess had sent all her children on a series of extended combat injury and casualty drill courses while they were still in their teens. In this way she hoped that the lessons they learned would stay with them for life. And she had been right. Abi had attended a number of FPOS and first aid refresher courses in the interim, but the fundamentals had always been there, with each course acting as a deepening of already existing skills. At each course he attended, Abi found that he was head and shoulders above most of the other attendees from the outset. This had left him with two precious gifts – a cool head in a medical emergency, and an almost complete lack of squeamishness when it came to the functions of the human body.

Once he was satisfied with her wound dressings, Abi sat Antanasia on the lavatory, just as he had done numerous times before during the trip, relying on the fact that she was tranquillized, and thus half unconscious and unlikely to object to the implied intimacy. Then he fed and watered her, checked her bandages again, and gave her a little more of the tranquillizer. He was switching brands on a regular basis now, so that she would not become dependent on one more than another. The longer she stayed out of pain, he reasoned, the swifter her eventual recovery would be.

When she was safely back asleep, Abi drove the Geist to within 400 yards of the front gates to his mother's house. It was just before midnight. Perfect timing.

Leaving the CZ and his fighting baton back in the vehicle, Abi hurried the remaining distance to the house and hammered on the front door.

Milouins answered, just as Abi had known that he would. Abi had been counting on the near racing certainty that the Countess and Madame Mastigou would already have retired to bed, and that the premises would therefore be clear of servants – apart from the ubiquitous and ever-faithful Hervé Milouins, of course. This was the way things always were in the Countess's household. Nothing ever changed. Earth abides.

'Ah. The Prodigal Son returneth. We weren't expecting you back for another three days. I hope you weren't counting on being borne in triumph through the adoring throng? It's well after midnight. Everyone is asleep.'

'What a splendid welcome, Milouins. It's so good to be back in the family home again.' Abi manufactured a grin to take the sting out of his words. He could feel a knot building in his stomach. 'Things went better than I thought. I dumped my stolen car back in St Tropez and walked in along the beach. No one will ever connect the two.'

Abi noticed Milouins glancing down at his new shoes. He felt a minor surge of triumph. Before entering the property he'd painstakingly scuffed them through the dirt and sand by the side of the road to add verisimilitude to his story, for he knew just how beady Milouins was when it came to protecting the Countess's privacy. He avoided the man's eyes when they returned to his face. Pointless confronting him when there was no necessity.

'It's far too late to disturb the Countess.'

'Milouins, I don't want to disturb the Countess. I just want to sleep. I've been travelling non-stop for what seems like weeks. I don't even want food. Just my bed.' Abi was counting on the fact that Milouins knew that he was *persona grata* with the Countess at the moment, and that as her manservant he would clearly be exceeding his duties by turning away her favourite – no, let's face it, only son – in the middle of the night.

'You'd better come in then. But keep the noise down. We don't want to wake up the whole household.'

'The two lovebirds, you mean?' Abi felt that it wouldn't

do to step too much out of character. He also wanted Milouins to confirm that no one else was in the house.

Milouins made a disgusted face.

'Am I going to set off anymore alarms if I go upstairs?'

'Yes. And there are cameras. And a few other things too. So I suggest you sleep down here. In the study. Where no one gives a shit what you get up to.'

Abi shrugged. Secretly, he was delighted at the way things were turning out. Being in the lower part of the house suited his plans to a T. 'I suppose I'm to be allowed a blanket? And a bottle of water, perhaps?'

'I'll bring them to you.'

'Thanks, Milouins. You're a brick.'

Milouins left without answering. Abi could hear his *basso-profundo* grumbling echoing off the hallway panelling.

When he was certain he was alone, Abi made straight for the study. He threw three of the sofa cushions onto the floor, and plumped up one of the armchair cushions for his head.

Milouins appeared in the doorway and tossed him the blanket and a two-litre bottle of Evian water, rolled together into a sausage shape.

Abi caught the package against his chest. By the time he looked up again, Milouins had left. He could hear the man's heavy tread going up the stairs.

Abi lay down on his ersatz bed and tucked the blanket around himself. He placed the water within easy reach. A little more sleep wouldn't do him any harm.

He set the alarm on his watch so that it would vibrate, not ring, in ninety minutes' time.

# 89

Abi awoke out of a profound sleep. He had been dreaming of Antanasia. He had been trying to save her from falling into a deep crevasse that opened out below her onto a sheer cliff face, just like the one he had climbed up to get out of the cenote. He was hanging out over the edge of the cliff, with his feet jammed into crannies behind him for support, holding Antanasia's hands with his. He could clearly see what lay below her. The drop seemed endless. Like a highway of death. Antanasia was looking up at him, perfectly confident in her manner, no panic on her face at all – almost as if she were looking through him and at some place far beyond.

In his dream, Abi was desperate to pull her up, but he could not. He had used up all his strength. When he was no longer able to hold her, she smiled at him, a look of ineffable beauty on her face, while her fingers gradually slipped through his. The memory of that smile stayed with Abi as his watch alarm woke him up.

The nightmare unsettled him badly. He never had nightmares. He was not a nightmare type. It angered him that he should have one now, just when he needed a clear head. What was it about this woman that affected him so? Was it because she was the first person in his life he had looked after for any length of time? Or was it the fascination mixed with disgust that he felt whenever he thought about her relationship with Lupei?

Abi gave an angry snort. How could someone as upright as Antanasia bring herself to conduct an affair with her own brother? How was it possible? And yet a hidden part of Abi sensed, with the small degree of balance of which he was capable, that with a man like Dracul Lupei, anything was possible. The bastard had been a force of nature. Definitely not the type to take no for an answer. Defy him, and he would cut you down, just as he'd been doing to Antanasia when Abi had stumbled in on them. Peter the Great and his son? Lupei had clearly been suffering from *folie de grandeur*. Abi found that he derived an intense satisfaction from having killed him.

He allowed that positive thought to perambulate through his brain. How did it feel to be the saviour of Europe? Because that was what he was. If Lupei had lived, the man would have brought Armageddon down on all their heads. A nuclear war on European soil would have killed countless more people than Hitler, Napoleon, and even Stalin and Mao Zedong had contrived between them. Lupei would have made a worthy Antichrist cut from the same egomaniacal cloth as the others.

But he, Abiger de Bale, had put a damper on him. And all because he wanted to enjoy the fruits and luxuries of a wealth far beyond the rather too modest dreams of Croesus – a wealth that was even now hovering at his fingertips. One could construe such an act as the final triumph of capitalism over anarchy, thought Abi. The simple fact of feeding one's belly and getting one's end away, set against marching off to yet another pointless and destructive war in a litany of pointless and destructive wars. No contest. The money won out every time.

Abi got up and padded out into the hall, all thoughts of Antanasia and her final smile driven from his head. He stood for a long time, his nerves attuning themselves to the noises inside the house. He glanced up the stairs. He wouldn't be venturing up there. Chances were that Milouins hadn't been bullshitting when he claimed that he had engineered some fresh traps after the travesty of Abi's previous midnight visit.

Abi grinned and headed down towards the cellar. He had noticed the propane 'pigs' on his last trip through. Each gas tank was designed to hold 1,000 gallons of liquid propane – enough to heat and service a house the size of the Domaine de Seyème and then some. Propane tanks were intrinsically safe. But the fuel itself was intrinsically unstable. Natural gas was a far better bet in most cases, but the Domaine de Seyème was so far off the beaten track that it wasn't eligible for the town supply. Added to which, the Countess insisted on the house being completely independent. No unexpected winter outages for her. It was for this reason that she kept a large portable generator in the room next to the propane tanks for emergency use during power cuts, together with a 500-litre diesel tank, one further room across, to service it. More grist to the mill.

Abi crouched down and began to set up the ancient three-bar electric heater he had retrieved from an adjacent storeroom. He plugged it into the wall socket and switched it on. He nodded inanely and pretended to warm his hands at the glow.

When the heater was working at full whack, he switched on both of the propane tank bleeder valves. This wouldn't be enough to cause an actual explosion, but once the gas from the bleeder valves took fire, the relief valves would automatically be triggered, causing an escape of gas from the top of the tank. This escape was designed to lower the pressure inside the tank, and so avoid an explosion.

But with the three-bar heater still on, and with the bleeder valves already burning, this gas, too, would eventually ignite. The regular blasts of flame from the relief valves would then reflect back off the roof of the cellar, heating up the tanks to such an extent that they would eventually blow, creating a fireball that would move through the opened cellar rooms until they encountered the diesel tank used to feed the generator. Then all hell would break loose.

Abi estimated that the whole thing should take about three long minutes from start to finish, once the bleeder valves had ignited. Just enough time for Milouins to stumble downstairs from his bedroom and throw open the main cellar door to create a convenient updraft.

Abi hurried back up the steps, shutting the cellar door behind him. He padded into the study, soaked the blanket in water, tossed the empty Evian bottle into the wastepaper basket, and replaced the used cushions back onto the sofa. Pointless leaving unanswered questions for the investigators.

He opened the sash window and eased himself out, then snapped the window back into place. He flicked the sash shut with the blade of his penknife. Placing the dampened blanket over his head like a shawl, he sprinted for a nearby stand of trees. Behind him he could hear the house alarm begin to sound. Well. That would certainly wake Milouins up if the smell of gas hadn't.

He was almost to the second stand of trees when the first concussion hit. He was thrown forwards as if he had been ejected out of a fast-moving train. Abi rolled over and over, the wet blanket entangling itself in his flailing limbs. He curled up beneath the blanket and waited, his hands clamped to his ears.

The second explosion was far larger than the first.

Once the shockwave had passed over him, Abi got up and began running again. The diesel tank hadn't gone up yet. That was still to come. He wanted to be a very long way off indeed for that one.

He was 800 metres from the house when the final explosion was triggered. An immense fireball rose 150 feet into the sky, and a wall of heat bloomed out towards him like the thermal radiation from an atomic blast.

Abi ran on. He didn't need to look behind him. Nothing human would be able to withstand such a detonation. The countryside was lit up like day in front of him.

He veered towards the road, still holding the steaming blanket over his head. When he reached the Geist he glanced instinctively into the back to see if Antanasia had been awoken by the explosion.

She was fast asleep. The dose he had given her would be good for five or six hours yet.

Abi slipped the Mercedes into forward shift and headed off in the direction of Cavalaire and Le Lavandou.

# 90

Abi had owned the house in Mallorca for a number of years now. It was situated on the north-west part of the island, near the small hamlet of Lluch Alcari.

The *finca* itself was located down a long stony track, about halfway between the village of Deia and the turn-off to Lluch. The land through which the track travelled did not belong to Abi, but the fisherman's stone house was his and his alone, together with the six terraces below it, and the fifty-foot palm tree that towered nearly as high as the *finca*'s third storey.

There was an unobstructed 180-degree view of the Mediterranean in front of the house, which spanned, on the left, as far as the Punta de Deia, and, on the right, to Es Canyaret and the bay of Sa Muleta. Abi had put in a heated swimming pool the previous year, and he intended to use this pool as part of his master plan for bringing Antanasia back to the sort of physical condition he would require of her before she could accompany him to Lugano to access her and her brother's numbered account.

Abi now regretted his fool idea of getting Madame, his mother, to transfer the remainder of the funds she owed across to Lupei. But at the time he had taken the decision he had not been entirely sure that his plan to kill her would work out – and the near-certainty of getting his hands on a minimum of 200 million euros, had been a whole lot better than getting his paws on nothing. At least now the 200 million would be outside the estate for tax purposes, so every cloud had a silver lining.

The killing had turned out very well, given the circumstances. Abi had received the news about the Countess's tragic death in a gas explosion via his US cell phone. There had been three fatalities, apparently. The Countess. Her companion, Madame Mastigou. And her manservant, Hervé Milouins. Burned to a cinder. Nothing left but ashes.

Abi had been briefly tempted to say that it couldn't have happened to nicer people, but he had prudently held his tongue. He had promised his mother's lawyers that he would fly over from Boston and meet with them within the month – but in Brussels, not Paris. When they had cavilled at this, he had read them the riot act in a most satisfactory manner – he still had business of his own to conduct in America, he claimed, and was not at anyone's beck and call. Madame, his mother, was dead. There was nothing left of her to bury. Not even a forlorn scrap. Her property holdings and business empire were in good order and under excellent management, and he was her sole remaining heir under Napoleonic law. Where was the hurry? They could busy themselves with probate in the interim, and whatever else lawyers got up to in order to justify their exorbitant fees. He imagined the French State would want its pound of flesh from him too, so they could start negotiating on that straight away.

There followed a period which, in retrospect, was the most puzzling in Abi's life. Antanasia knew nothing of his past, and he chose not to enlighten her. He was merely the son of the person with whom her brother had had certain financial dealings, and who had happened upon her, in the nick of time, and saved her from an agonizing death. Thanks to being beaten to within an inch of her life, and to the endless succession of tranquillizers and painkillers with which her brother, and later Abi, had dosed her with, Antanasia had no real idea of what had actually occurred back at the house in Albescu, nor did she remember much of what had gone before. So Abi simply made it up.

According to his version of the story, he had entered the house meaning to talk to Lupei, and had heard strange noises emanating from upstairs – imprecations, followed by the screams of a woman. He had then stumbled in on her and Lupei.

Seeing him, Lupei had rushed into his study. He had come out brandishing a pistol. Abi had been forced to strike him with the first thing that came to hand, which had been the heavy ivory handle of the knout, which resembled, in size, a knobkerrie or a shillelagh. The blow had been a lucky one for Abi, but an unfortunate one for Lupei, because it had killed him on the spot.

Abi had then carried Antanasia out of the house under cover of darkness, because he knew that otherwise the Moldovan authorities would arraign her for her brother's murder, and he wished, at all costs, to prevent such an injustice from happening. He had therefore obtained false identity papers for her, but these were scarcely good enough to fool bona fide customs officials. But they were, however, plenty good enough to fool the mayor of the local town near which they now resided.

Abi had therefore arranged for himself and Antanasia to go through a civil marriage ceremony in Soller Town Hall – when she was physically up to it, of course. He fully acknowledged that this would be a marriage of convenience – he was not remotely suggesting that Antanasia consider herself his wife in more than name only. But only in this way would he be able to protect her from the Moldovan authorities and afford her an entirely new identity.

She would become a French citizen and a countess to boot, with all that that entailed in terms of privileges and appurtenances. It was the least he could do in the circumstances, given the dreadful sequence of events that had led up to their flight, and for which he felt partly responsible. If he hadn't encouraged Madame, his mother, to grubstake her brother, the man's latent megalomania might have been limited to the town of Albescu and its environs. The virtually unlimited sums provided by the Countess had clearly gone to the man's head, however, culminating in his insane attack on his sister.

That was Abi's story, anyway, and he was content with it. It appeared to answer all Antanasia's questions, and it placed him in a good light.

Abi, however, forbore to mention that marriage to Antanasia would also give him equal rights to the money in her and her brother's account, all details of which he had erased from the Albescu house – but there was no point in muddying the waters unnecessarily. Antanasia knew nothing yet of the transfer of the funds, and it was correct that this should remain so until well after the wedding. Abi could then explain to her exactly what had occurred, and how the money, by rights, belonged to him anyway, following the unfortunate death of the Countess in a gas explosion. But that he was more than happy to share the money with her if she so desired.

He suspected that the saintly Antanasia would simply sign the money over to him pronto, so grateful did she appear for the role he had played in her rescue.

At first Antanasia had refused to take anything from Abi – far less his title. But Abi slowly began to wear her down, aided by the fact that Antanasia was now totally alone in the world, and bereft of family, friends, position, and country. Abi had not been named after Abiger, golden-tongued Prince of Hades, for nothing. He benefited, too, from the distinct advantage of having saved Antanasia's life.

When first Antanasia had seen the state of her back in a mirror in the master bedroom, she had wept uncontrollable tears, as much for the sins of her brother as for her own dilaceration. Later, she had asked Abi who it was that had treated her back and sutured her wounds. Abi had played down his role just enough to persuade Antanasia to dig a little deeper. When she eventually prised out from him all that he had done, and the lengths to which he had gone to protect her from the endemically corrupt Moldovan authorities, she somewhat inevitably began to feel even more grateful towards her saviour.

Abi, for his part, was gradually coming to realize quite to what an extent Antanasia had embedded herself beneath his skin. He dreamed of her nearly every night now. When he massaged her back with salve, and treated the wounds on her neck and breasts, he received a sexual charge beyond anything he had ever known before. Antanasia was forty-one years old. He was twenty-five. Normal men of his age concentrated their attention on callow young girls with perfect figures and the urge both to please – and to be pleased – at any cost. Such females bored him. They came in cartons, like cigarettes, and provided him with little or no pleasure beyond the purely mechanical.

But there was something about Antanasia that had moved him from the first. Was it her goodness, perhaps, so very different from his own inherent murk? Or her emotional maturity, so far beyond his own that it wasn't even worth trying to compare the two? Either way, she was the first entirely selfless person that he had ever known. When she touched his arm, or allowed him to support her in the swimming exercises he had designed in order to flex the healing flesh on her back and prevent it contracting, it felt as if he was being touched by the hand of God. The feeling both exalted and irritated him. It was a paradox – and Abi hated paradoxes.

Later, when Antanasia urged him to tell her about himself, Abi experienced not the remotest problem in muddying his back trail. Virtually everyone who knew anything about him was now dead. And Sabir and Calque – those two poisonous smutches in an otherwise immaculate world – soon would be, once Abi had married, and then bedded, Antanasia, sorted out his finances, and brought his life back under some measure of control. For Abi was more and more convinced that he'd called it right in Romania when he'd told Markovich that Sabir and Calque's self-styled Holy-Mother-of-God party would doubtless be making their way across the Carpathians and back to the very spot where Radu had been looked after following his botched shooting by the girls. Because the bastard certainly hadn't healed himself, had he? Someone had harboured him and fed him and seen to his wounds.

This had seemed logical to Abi at the time, and he saw no reason to change his opinion now. When the moment came, all he would need to do would be to post himself near the border crossing that he, Rudra and the girls had first used on entering Romania, and wait for the copper-pot maker to come clomping back across from Serbia in his horse and cart – if the fool had managed to find himself a second horse by now, that is, and recovered sufficiently from the shock of tangling with Abi's freakish sisters.

Apart from lying through his teeth about what he'd done with Radu, the pot man had also blurted out to them that he crossed the border at the same time, and at the same spot, every day. Why should the man change his routine now? What was he? William Randolph Hearst? John Paul Getty? In Abi's experience, impoverished peasants tended to function more through habit and expedience than through anything remotely resembling free will. There was little reason to hurry, therefore. Added to that, Yola Dufontaine was late-stage pregnant. And late-stage pregnant women didn't travel if they could possibly avoid it. The entire Sabir-led party would therefore be hiding at the pot maker's camp – it was a ninety-nine per cent certainty. Abi could feel the sweet bubble of revenge stirring in his stomach.

In the meanwhile, and in order to win Antanasia for himself, Abi was quite happy to extemporize a pretend life in which he, Abi, was the hero, and the Countess, his mother, the villainess. He was gradually coming to realize, though, that the healthier Antanasia was becoming, the less he could count on her taking everything he said at face value. She was beginning to ask questions.

Like many consummate liars, Abi found himself gradually embroidering the stories he was foisting on Antanasia and then immediately forgetting quite how far off-message his fantasy had already carried him. Abi had always been an adept at thinking on his feet, but Antanasia's persistent questions were beginning to make even his toes curl.

First off, she began to question him about his initial blackmailing of her brother. Then she began having strange visions about her knouting, in which she claimed to have opened her eyes and seen Abi murdering her brother. Beating him to death. But not remotely in the way he had initially described to her. Less than a day after that little revelation, she claimed to remember having lurched awake in the Mercedes campervan at some point during their trip, and seeing a scintillating bright light, accompanied by a rolling noise and a pervasive smell of burning. Abi, who had not told her yet how his mother had died, felt himself turning green.

First he assured her that her so-called 'recovered memories' were simply morphine hallucinations. That it was inevitable she should be having nightmares, given what she had endured and the amount of junk that had passed through her body, and that dream logic dictated that he should feature as the butt of her anxieties as he was the most obvious person for her unconscious mind to grab hold of. There was not the remotest foundation to any of her imaginings – she must believe all that he had told her. It was the gospel truth.

Secondly he told her that he was falling in love with her, and desired to marry her for herself, and not simply in order to give her a name and an identity. Like many men, Abi believed that women were easily blindsided when it came to their emotions – tell them you loved them, and they would happily dwell on that fact to the exclusion of virtually all else.

Antanasia had stared at him intently after his unexpected revelation, and then vouchsafed that if she were ever to consider marrying him, she would need to know just a little more about his background, and the origins of his great wealth.

Slowly, painstakingly, she began to tease out of him what the Countess, his mother, and the society of which she had been the head, were about. She also began to focus her attention on the single-mindedness with which he was aiming to run to ground the group of individuals he had been searching for in Romania, and for which he had enlisted her brother's help.

The one-on-one nature of Antanasia and Abi's relationship – the almost hermetic vacuum in which they were forced to live – made it more and more difficult for Abi to elude Antanasia's questions. Reluctantly he began to avoid her company, pleading pressure of work relating to his mother's estate. His greatest fear was that his mask might slip after so many years spent succumbing to his own basest desires, and that Antanasia would suddenly recognize the glaring similarities between him and her brother. This he could not allow, as her approval of him still meant the gaining of a large fortune which, given the amount of inheritance tax the French authorities were threatening to deprive him of, was becoming an increasingly significant part of his game plan.

Abi decided, therefore, that he would need to bring forward his showdown with Sabir and Calque, and leave Antanasia to her own devices for a while. If she sat in the villa alone and unable to travel, and with only her own thoughts for company, it might force her to come to terms with the fact that she had nobody and nothing left in her life bar Abi. That he was her lifeline and her saviour and the only means by which she could re-enter the human merry-go-round.

When she broached the subject of the money she knew her brother kept in a joint account in Switzerland, Abi almost pissed himself.

'Yes. Yes. I've been meaning to tell you. My mother did make the final payment on account to your brother. But, strictly speaking, it was made following his death. The money should still, by rights, form part of her estate, and therefore come to me. I'm sure you would not wish to benefit in any way from such a clear abrogation of natural justice? Nor would you wish for the French tax authorities to extort their pound of flesh when the money can perfectly well stay put in Switzerland with only the minutest of tinkerings.'

Antanasia shook her head. 'The money is yours, Abiger. It is blood money, and I don't want it. I shall sign it over to you without any need for you to marry me, or to give me your name. I ask only one thing in return.'

Abi gave a sick smile.

'I wish to travel with you back to Romania when you go there to take revenge on the men who killed your brother.'

# 91

'What are you doing?'

'What does it look like I'm doing?' Abi could feel the anger simmering away inside him. He wrapped the assault rifle in a blanket and stowed it underneath the bunk bed at the rear of the Mercedes motorhome. He felt like a Viking berserker readying himself to rush at the enemy.

'And what is that?'

'It's a Kevlar KM2 interceptor vest. The sort the US military use.'

'A vest?'

'I call it my Wolf Pelt. It's to protect me from bullets. You wear it underneath your normal clothes. It will stop anything short of a rifle round.'

'And you keep such things at your house as a matter of course?'

'It's how I live my life. I love weapons. I love the smell of them. The weight of them. What they can do.'

'You're serious about this, then? You're going to carry these weapons through four border crossings?'

'Did you ever think I wasn't? Three of the men I am going up against have pistols. I know this for a fact.

Do you want me to get killed?'

Antanasia hugged her arms around her body. 'Abiger, why are you doing this? You have everything you want in this world. You are a good man.'

'I am not a good man. You say I have everything I want in this world. You're wrong. When I said I love you, I meant it. But I know I can't have you. I'm not a fool. You don't know the half of what I've done. If you did, you'd run down that track screaming. So if I can't have you, I'll have the next best thing. I'll have my revenge. Apart from you, my twin brother is the only person I have ever loved in this world – the only person who never betrayed me. Some people would call him stupid. Backward even. But he was a part of me.' Abi tore open his shirt. 'You see this scar? That's where we were fused together at birth. Him and me. We shared a kidney. The doctors threw it out. One kidney is enough for anybody, they told the Carmelite nuns, as they accepted the sacrificial offering of Vau and me from our mother. Whoever the bitch was.'

Antanasia took a step towards him.

'Stay away from me.'

'Why?'

'Because I can't allow myself to touch you anymore. Because any normal woman would have stepped away from me, and not towards me, when I told them that. You get under my skin, Antanasia. I can't handle it.'

Antanasia nodded.

Abi raised his head in surprise. 'You know, don't you? You understand?'

She nodded again.

'I've spent my entire life taking what I want, whenever I want it. I've decided that you're going to be the exception that proves my rule.'

Antanasia lowered her head. 'Every man I've ever known has taken what he wanted from me without my permission. Why should you be any different?'

'That's the reason I can't touch you anymore.' The words caught in Abi's throat. 'It's the only thing I can offer you that's of any value. Call it my love gift to you.' Abi gave a snort – it came out as a half-choke, half-laugh. It was the sort of sound a man might make who was fighting unexpected tears. He rammed the bunk bed onto its housing and attached the locks with an unnecessary show of force. 'Do you still want to accompany me to Romania? Think before you speak.'

'Yes.'

'On your own head be it, then.'

*Bogdamic Camp, Romania*
*Saturday, 28 February 2010*

# 92

---

Yola sat watching Sabir across the fire. 'You're hiding something from me. I've known it for months now. Whenever you look at me your eyes slide away from my face like a guilty child's.'

It was the first time the two of them had been alone for weeks. There was a funeral at the camp, and all the men were off drinking, while the women were biding in with the corpse. Calque, for once, had agreed to join the men, with the vague notion of learning more about Romani customs for a book he intended to write when things got safely back to normal. Lemma was asleep in one of the caravans with her baby. Sabir, still in vigilant mode since the crisis at Ceausescu's hunting lodge, had stayed behind, and had been duly surprised when Yola had appeared out of nowhere and sat across from him, easing her legs beneath her swollen belly.

'They're getting drunk again, I suppose?'

'Don't be so hard on us, Damo. It's our habit. It's our way of involving the dead for one final time in our lives. Of losing ourselves in them. Then they are gone. Forgotten.'

Sabir shifted uncomfortably. 'I'd like to be forgotten.'

'We could not forget you.'

He laughed. 'Not unless I died.'

'I would not forget you then, either.'

Sabir lowered his eyes. 'I appreciate that. Sometimes I say foolish things I don't mean. It's best to ignore me.'

'Are you still mourning Lamia?'

Sabir spread his hands in a gesture of helplessness. 'No. I know she betrayed me. I know she intended to kill you out there in that quarry. Losing her has forced me to go back over our relationship and rethink the whole thing. I'm slowly beginning to understand what happened to us both. The tragedy of it.'

'She did love you, though. She gave her life for you in the end.'

'I know that too. That's what makes the whole thing so bloody unconscionable.'

'I'm sorry. I do not understand.'

'So bloody unfair. So bloody dishonest.'

Yola raised her head. 'You will find another woman, Damo.'

'Where? Under a toadstool? Will I trip over her on the beach? Or maybe she'll parachute out of a plane and I'll see her fluttering down over my head like a butterfly?'

Yola shifted position. 'The baby is kicking. Do you want to touch him again?'

'If anyone sees me touch you like that I'll be drummed out of the camp. They'll probably chase me into Serbia and pin me up on a wanted board.' Despite his protestations, Sabir got up and walked round to Yola's side of the fire. He sat down and allowed her to place his hand on her belly.

'There. Can you feel that?'

'He's like a cat in a postal sack.'

Yola laughed. Then her face lengthened and all laughter left it. 'Tell me, Damo.'

Sabir snatched his hand away. He hunched forwards over his knees. 'That was a stitch-up.'

'A stitch-up?'

'What you just did. When one person tricks another into doing something they don't want to do.'

'Didn't you want to touch my baby?'

'You know very well what I mean.'

Yola sighed. 'So are you going to tell me?'

Sabir looked away from her. 'I've got no choice. The thing's been eating at me for months now. If I don't spit it out I'll choke on it.'

Yola closed her eyes.

Sabir took in a deep breath. 'I don't think your baby is the Parousia, Yola. I think I called it wrong. I think I've blown everything from the beginning and I'm only now beginning to understand just what damage I've done to everybody.'

Yola sat silently for a while, her eyes still shut. 'Is this why you carry that pistol tucked into the back of your trousers, beneath your shirt?'

'That's to shoot myself with. If my mother can kill herself, why can't I? She didn't know she was a shaman, and I know I'm a fake one. Where's the difference?'

Yola turned and stared at him – a no-nonsense stare that ate up the words he had just spoken and spat them out again where they belonged. 'Tell me the quatrain, Damo. It is the only one of Nostradamus's verses that you kept from us. We all trust you so much that I didn't realize that you had done this until Alexi asked me how you actually knew our baby was special – was the Chosen One. Then it came to me. You had told us of all the verses bar this one. You had held this one back.'

'Your baby *is* special.'

'But not the Parousia.'

'No. I no longer think so.' Sabir kicked at the fire embers with the toe of his boot. 'I'm sorry. I began to suspect this some months ago, but I didn't have the nerve to tell you. I didn't want to let you and everybody else down.' He laughed. 'So I talked myself back into believing it. It's what people do when they're scared to face the truth about themselves. When they're in mourning for something that never existed in the first place.'

Yola laid a hand on his arm. 'Listen to me, Damo. I am happy that my baby is to be a normal person. I prefer it this way. The other has been weighing on me. Particularly concerning Alexi. You know him. Almost better than anybody. He is not capable of keeping his feelings in check. One day he will blurt everything out to someone, and there will be a crisis. He will end up killing some innocent person. Or being killed.'

'And you love him?'

'He is mine. I am content with that. He is a good man. Mad. But good.' She burst out laughing. 'If O Del were to take him away from me, the hole Alexi left behind him would be so big that I would fall into it and drown. If Alexi ever grows up, he will be a mighty man.'

Sabir shook his head. 'I never thought you'd take it

this way. I thought you'd both turn on me. Reject me as your brother.'

'One cannot reject a brother. It is impossible.' Yola touched Sabir lightly on the side of the head with the back of her hand – it was something she would have done to no other man. 'Don't tell me the details of the verse now, Damo. I was wrong to ask it of you. Wrong to, as you call it, "stitch you up". Gather everybody together and tell us tomorrow. By that time I will have prepared them. It will not come as such a shock.'

'You are a wonderful woman, Yola.'

'I'm an ordinary woman, Damo. Married to an ordinary man. And expecting an ordinary child. I am content with that.'

*

Sabir stood with his hands in his pockets, staring at his friends. Radu and Alexi were suffering from major hangovers – Calque merely looked a little pale. Lemma was nursing her baby beneath her shawl, and Yola was sitting next to her, watching.

'Well, where to begin?' It was the single most stupid thing Sabir could think of to say, but still he said it. He felt like yelling and tearing his hair out and running round in circles like a child having a tantrum.

Calque eased himself into a more comfortable position. 'Why not just give us the quatrain? It's something you should have done months ago, Sabir. In Mexico. Instead of carrying it around with you like a sackful of dirty washing. Then maybe...' Calque brought himself up short. He knew just how far he could push Sabir. And where Lamia was concerned, he wasn't on the firmest ground.

'Thank you, Calque. I can always rely on you to tell it like it really is.'

Alexi and Radu seemed disconnected from the current conversation. Sabir was beginning to wonder when was the last time he hadn't actually seen them drunk. The enforced idleness at the camp was having a very bad effect on them. No wonder Gypsy men had an average life expectancy of fifty years.

'Very well then. It goes like this. And much good may it do all of you:

*Le Guion paranaistra l'apara,*
*Gitane gumaternée guisandrie:*
*Mira Bronzino – Mater Christi Samana,*
*Elleuper, effronteux, effondrerie.'*

'For God's sake, Sabir. It's in double Dutch, not French.' Calque squinted at his friend. 'I thought I knew my own language. But this is something else.'

'Yes. It does seem a little elusive at first glance. But it's in Old French all right. You'll find nearly all the words in Frédéric Godefroy's *Lexique de L'Ancien Français*. Paris and Leipzig 1901. Published by Bonnard and Salmon. I know because I checked.'

'Enlighten us then, Oh Great One.'

Sabir groaned. 'Well, that's the problem. It's open to interpretation.'

'And you interpreted it one way? And now you've

decided maybe you were wrong, and you ought to have interpreted it another?'

'Something along those lines.'

Alexi gave a snort, stood up, stretched himself, and ambled away, clutching his stomach.

'Your audience is abandoning you, Sabir. You'd better get on with it before you lose everybody.'

Sabir sighed. 'This whole thing is giving me a bad feeling. I should never have embarked on interpreting this alone. To misquote Shakespeare, as you'll no doubt tell me, I've been a very fool.'

'Your reading, Sabir.'

Sabir closed his eyes. One could almost hear his photographic memory latching into gear. 'First line. *Le Guion paranaistra l'apara* means "the Guide through-births the revealed one". Which I take to mean that the Guide recognizes the Parousia. *Aparable* is Old French for clear or brilliant. Something which is decided by right. To *paranaître* is to bring to birth, in the sense of to make appear – to *faire paraître* – to make visible. Nostradamus uses the word *Guion* or *Guyon* a great many times in the course of his 942 quatrains – and it always means a leader, a guide, or a chief.'

Calque caught Yola's eye and hunched his shoulders. Because they knew him so well, it was clear to both Calque and Yola that Sabir was hurrying through his reading on purpose – to disguise some awkward fact that did not suit him. It was not the first time they had witnessed this sort of behaviour from him.

'But you're our Guide, Sabir.' Calque slowed down his delivery on purpose. He even deepened his voice a little to add more gravitas to the point he was trying to make. 'You're the one Nostradamus is talking about.'

Sabir gave him an old-fashioned look.

'No. I mean that. You have been guiding us from the very beginning. It was you who recognized the quatrains. You who found the crystal skull. Both Ixtab and the Halach Uinic recognized you as a shaman/guide in Mexico. They saw you as one of Los Aluxes – the spiritual guardians left behind by the gods to protect the holy places of the earth from desecration, and then to prepare what remained of the world for a better future. So *you* should be the father of the Parousia, according to the verse. Not its protector. Not its through-birther, whatever that may be. I should have thought that much was clear. You have been purposefully misreading this line.'

'Fuck off, Calque. I'm not in the humour for this.'

'Damo.' Yola was watching him intently. 'Translate the rest.'

Sabir closed his eyes and returned to the memory place inside his head. '*Gitane guiternée guisandrie:* "A female Gypsy, tortured, cheated." The word *guiterne* implies a stringed or fretted instrument of some sort – a whip, possibly, or a scourge. Maybe the sort of whip that was used to chastise Christ on the way to Calvary? But I've probably misread that too.' He gave a long sigh, as of one forced to do something profoundly against his inclinations. 'Next we have *Mira Bronzino – Mater Christi Samana*. That's an easier one. It's Latin. It means "the Mother of Christ is a Samana – look at Bronzino". There's an extra addition to this, however – the word Samana itself implies an ascetic. A teacher. The

Gautama Buddha, for instance, was a Samana. Its strict meaning is "one who strives" – a good person. Saintly, even. Someone who follows the Buddha's "middle way" between hedonism and austerity. Not a complete ascetic, in other words. Someone who has known the pleasures of the flesh and not rejected them outright. A sort of Mary Magdalene figure.'

Sabir was getting into the swing of things. His gaze was on fire. 'In the Pistis Sophia, the greatest of all Gnostic writings, Jesus is asked sixty-four questions. Thirty-nine of these come from the Magdalene, who is described thus: "Mary, thou blessed one, whom I will perfect in all the mysteries of those of the height, discourse in openness, thou, whose heart is raised to the kingdom of heaven more than all thy brethren." This is the woman whom Jesus cured of the seven demons. The woman who may have been Jesus's wife. The greatest portrait of her is by Agnolo Bronzino – the man mentioned in the verse. Here. I have a copy of it with me. Look at it while I describe it to you.'

Calque took the postcard Sabir was holding out to him. He went over to sit beside Yola. They looked at the postcard together.

'Bronzino was an exact contemporary of Nostradamus's – born one month before him, near Florence. The portrait you are looking at is Bronzino's pietà. Painted in 1530, when Nostradamus was twenty-seven years old and Bronzino was twenty-eight. It's in the Uffizi. In it, the Magdalene holds her left breast in one hand, and the upper right thigh of the dead Jesus in the other. She is a mature woman – poised and beautiful. This is no snippet of a girl.

Plus it is she who is the focus of the light. Not the mother of Jesus. Not the face of Jesus. In no other pietà is Christ held in this fashion – at the most, his mother holds his hand. The portrait is unbearably intimate. To hold him like that implies that this woman knew Jesus – knew him carnally. And that she is not afraid to acknowledge this fact in front of his mother. It is not how any normal woman would hold a stranger. Nor even a mother her son. A woman only holds her breast like that if her heart is being torn out of her chest. And if you look closer, you will see that the shawl she is clutching to herself is in the form of a baby. She is cradling a metaphorical baby, therefore, and also the dead father of that baby. It's so obvious that I can't understand why nobody has seen it before. The entire portrait is configured in the form of a triangle. These three are bound together. Mother, son, wife. Tell me you can see it?'

'We see it.' Calque's eyes were fixed onto the postcard. He shook his head and handed it to Yola so she could look more closely.

'When I first met her, Yola construed the female orgasm as "having one's eyes taken out". This woman is climaxing with her eyes wide open. It's categorical.' Sabir was beginning to look uncomfortable. Like a man who suddenly realizes that he has given away far more than he intended.

'You're going too far, Sabir. Are you trying to tell me that in this picture, painted nearly five hundred years ago, we see the woman who is to be the Mother of the Parousia in the very process of impregnation?'

'Of spiritual impregnation, yes. The true impregnation

only comes later, after she has passed through the fire. After she has rid herself of the seven demons – or seven devils, what have you – spoken of in Luke 8:2 and Mark 16:9.'

'You've done your homework, I see.'

'I've tried, Calque. I've really tried.' Sabir placed one hand over his eyes as if he wished to pray.

Calque recognized the movement as a sign of concentration – but also of attempted abnegation. He realized that Sabir was hovering, yet again, at the very end of his tether.

'Finally we have *Elleuper, effronteux, effondrerie.* More Old French. "Tricked, impudent, demolition." The last word can also mean a "turn up for the books" – a "surprise". Something that happens on the "spur of the moment". This is someone who has had a bad deal in their life. Someone whom others have abused. *Effronteux* can also mean "outraged".'

'In the form of a rape?'

'No. It doesn't have that meaning.'

'So. Let me get this straight. A clear reading of the quatrain, taking into account the suggestions contained within it, and the sheer sound of it – what you call euphonic translation in your book, Sabir – would give us:

The Guide is the father of the Parousia
Look at Bronzino – the Mother of Christ is a Gypsy,
Tortured, cheated, of the bloodline of the Samanas
Outraged, tricked, on the spur of the moment.'

'Yes. Something like that. Something along those lines.'

'And this is the quatrain you decided meant that Yola was to be the mother of the Parousia?'

'Yes. What's so strange about that? Achor Bale had outraged and nearly killed her down by the river. He'd even threatened to sever her fallopian tubes so she could never have a child. I saved her. If I'm this Guide person, as you aver, then one could argue that by saving her I gave her life – I allowed her to be reborn. She is a Samana. And also someone of the "middle way" – Yola is no ascetic, if she'll forgive me talking about her in the third person. She has no sisters. She is of the right age, at the right time, and in the right place. She is pregnant. What do you find wrong with all that?'

'What do *you* find wrong with it? You're the one who has convoked us all here. You must have some idea of why you are doing this? Why you've changed your mind?'

Yola stood up. 'It's not me.' She handed the postcard back to Calque. 'I know that now for certain. I'm not tortured and cheated like the woman in the verse. And Alexi is not the Guide. He has never guided anyone anywhere. And I didn't get pregnant on the spur of the moment. Alexi and I planned my kidnapping. He took me to Corsica. I even planned where he would pluck out my eyes.'

Sabir sat with his head in his hands.

'You are to be the father of the Parousia, Damo. Just in time for the Great Change of 2012 that the Mayans foretell. And like your shaman-hood, you simply cannot accept it. This is your greatest weakness. As Calque says, you refuse to see what is beneath your eyes.'

Sabir looked up. His face was livid and despairing. 'So who is to be the mother? Lamia? Maybe she came from Gypsy stock before her adoption and we didn't fucking know it? Maybe she decided to try and kill you to protect her own baby – a baby that neither of us, incidentally, knew that she was carrying? Either way it seems I've rather missed my chance there, haven't I? Because she's dead.' Sabir stood up to go.

'Sabir. Leave the gun.'

Sabir met Yola's eyes, his gaze softening. 'Don't worry, *luludji*. I'm not going to kill myself quite yet.'

# 93

Abi parked the motorhome in a lay-by on the far side of the highway, a few hundred metres shy of the Serbian side of the Romanian border. He'd tried to persuade Antanasia to make her base in a nearby hotel, from where he promised to collect her when the whole thing was over. Antanasia refused, just as Abi had known that she would.

It wasn't the best of spots, but Abi figured that the Mercedes Geist would blend in with all the container lorries and their resting drivers – many of whom were busy entertaining prostitutes in their hastily converted cabs – and the banks of taxis waiting to be summoned by shoppers overwhelmed with purchases from the very same market the copper-pot maker had no doubt been attending before he clip-clopped back across the border and saved Radu's life a few months before. It was better than the open road, anyway.

Over the course of the next twenty-four hours there were long periods when neither of them spoke a word to the other. Such lacunae, however, were interspersed with sudden periods of intense questioning by Antanasia.

'Tell me about the Parousia, Abiger. Tell me about that.'

Abi faked an intense concentration on the road ahead – he had no place to hide, and he knew it. 'I thought you understood all about that. I thought your brother was the Parousia. That's what he told everybody, wasn't it? That's what the long hair and the beard and the flowing clothes were all about, wasn't it? Tricking people into believing he was the Second Coming?'

Antanasia stared silently at Abi from the passenger seat. The motorhome was so wide that four people could have squeezed into the gap between the front seats. The distance loomed between them like a no-man's-land.

'Okay. That was unfair of me.' Abi shot a glance at her from over his right shoulder. 'Jesus. I don't what it is that you do to me. Now you've even got me apologizing to you.'

Antanasia lowered her eyes. She knew not to confront Abi when he was angry – she'd had more than enough of that sort of training from her father and brother.

Abi spat out his words. 'The murderer Sabir blurted the truth out to my sister, Lamia, when he was ginch-struck and thought that he was in love with her. My older brother, Rocha, told us the same thing a few months before. That one of Nostradamus's fifty-eight lost quatrains – quatrains that only Sabir has access to – tells when and where and via who the Second Coming will be born.'

'But this is incredible.' Antanasia decided that she would try and change Abi's mood. She wasn't scared of him – but anger of any sort unsettled her.

'Incredible, yes, but apposite, given the belief many have that 21 December 2012 is going to mark a Great

Change in the human tide. A change for the worse or the better, depending on how we play it. Madame, my mother, and the rest of the Corpus Maleficus were determined to make sure that it was the worst. Your brother was a major part of their plan.'

'And you?'

'I don't care either way. The world can go to hell as far as I am concerned.'

'As long as you get what you want out of it?'

'That's pretty much the long and the short of it.'

They were both silent for some time.

'Has the Parousia already been born?'

Abi shrugged. 'Not to my knowledge. He's still a bun in Yola Dufontaine's oven as far as I can make out. The last sight I caught of her – which was, admittedly, in a pitch-dark hunting lodge in the middle of the Carpathian Mountains – I'd say he's due within the month.'

'Are you going to kill him too?'

'No. I have no interest whatsoever in promulgating my mother's idiocies. I'm after Sabir and Calque. And there's a Gypsy called Radu I wouldn't mind offing too. But him I can take or leave.'

Antanasia shook her head. 'How does Sabir know that Yola is to be the mother of the Parousia?'

'Search me. But I think it has something to do with the female line of Gypsies who have been guarding the verses since the sixteenth century – Nostradamus left the legacy to them via his daughter, Madeleine. The theory seems to be that one of this line of women – of childbearing age around the time of the Great Change – will be the mother. Yola seems to be the obvious candidate. Plus she's pregnant. Plus she's a Samana.'

'A Samana?'

'That's the family who protected the verses. The Samanas. I know this for a fact because my brother Rocha killed Yola Dufontaine's brother, and he was called Babel Samana.'

'But I am a Samana, Abiger. The Samanas are Romani. My mother was a Romani Gypsy. She was called Zina Samana. She was murdered when I was still a child. For being a witch.'

Abi stared at Antanasia. His eyes flicked across her face and body without fixing anywhere. His face was a mask. 'Are you pregnant? Is that it? Is that what you're trying to tell me?'

Antanasia raised a hand to her throat. 'Of course not.'

'Are you sure your brother didn't rape you while you were unconscious? That would be the final irony. The fucking Third Antichrist fathering the Second Coming through his own sister. Even the Bible can't outdo that one.'

Antanasia remained silent for a very long time. 'He did rape me, yes. But not in a way I could get pregnant, if you understand my meaning. Before that time, I had not had sex with him for three months.' She covered her face with both hands so that Abi could no longer see her. 'I did not want to say this to you. To anyone. I am ashamed.'

Abi gripped the steering wheel as if he was about to rip it from its housing. 'I'm glad I beat the bastard to death with his own whip. I'm glad I made him suffer. My only regret is that I should have taken longer over it. Far longer.'

Antanasia dropped her hands. 'So you didn't kill him the way you told me? By accident? When he was threatening you with a pistol?'

'No. That was a lie too. In fact pretty much everything I've ever told you has been a lie. I keep on telling you this and you refuse to believe me. Maybe you think everything's one great big lie?' Abi gave a shrug. 'Maybe you're right, at that.' Antanasia's admission had broken something in Abi. Shattered some invisible barrier that had prevented him from telling her about his true self. 'Let me lay it on the line for you then. Your brother tried to bribe me to finish whipping you to death after I'd as good as incapacitated him. You've got to hand it to the man – if there's such as thing as evil, he was evil as all hell. And he carried it with him all the way to the countdown.' Abi's expression turned bitter. 'Something he said must have got to me. Some particular thing. Or maybe it was the sight of you lying there, strapped to his bed? I'd seen you once before, you know.'

'Of course. When your sisters kidnapped me.'

'No. Before that. Walking in town. In Albescu. Dressed all in white. Talking to people. One man even fell to his knees in front of you. People came up and kissed your hand. Just like the fucking Virgin Mary.' Abi's face turned ugly. It was as though he was disgusted with himself. Nauseated by his true feelings. 'I don't know what it was, but the sight of you moved something in me. I didn't dare acknowledge it at the time. I'm not the sort of man such things happen to.' He paused. For a moment it seemed as if he wouldn't go on. Then he drew a long, ragged breath. 'You could call it a sense of recognition. I don't know. I don't think in those sorts of ways. Anyway, when it came to a choice between you and your brother, you won hands down. If I'd known what I know now about him I'd have roasted the bastard in his own stove and transformed him into a block of lard.'

Antanasia lowered her head. Heavy tears fell from her one visible eye. She brushed lamely at her blouse as if she wished to extinguish all sign of their appearance. 'Dracul was not a good man. Neither was my father. My mother was not a good woman either, although she never abused anybody beyond lashing out at us on occasion with her hairbrush. When people claimed she had conducted a Black Mass – a *Slujbă Neagră* – at a willow grove near the town of Călaraşi, I did not believe them. She was not a witch – she was a healer. What the local people saw as witchcraft was probably just Romani medicine-making. But they killed her for it. And the loss of her sent my father mad. That's when he started his abuse of me. The lending and selling of me to his friends. And being forced to witness this abuse drove Dracul mad in his turn. Everything is connected in this life, you see. Evil stems from evil.' Antanasia raised her head. 'This is why you must not go through with what you are intending to do, Abiger.'

'Too late.'

'What if I were to tell you that, as well as transferring the money out of our Lugano account, I would also give myself to you? You say you want me. You can have me. To marry or not, as you wish. But in return for this I would ask you to turn back from what you are intending. To live decently. Without harming people anymore.'

The groan seemed wrenched from the tormented interior of Abi's soul. 'I've told you, Antanasia. It's too late.'

# 94

Abi saw Amoy crossing the Serbian–Romanian border late afternoon on the second day. Grinning, he scuttled back into the main body of the stationary motorhome. He peered at Amoy through the convenient gauze curtains that the original German owners had installed throughout the vehicle for privacy's sake. Antanasia, who had sat patiently with Abi throughout all the hours of waiting, was fast asleep in the passenger seat.

Earlier, Abi had watched Antanasia sleeping. He had been tempted to stretch across and touch her. To take her in his arms. To carry her back to the double bed in the rear of the Mercedes. Might not a lifetime of enforced submission to the desires of men be habit-forming? Abi had no idea why he felt so protective of her, therefore. Why he didn't do to her what he would have done to any other woman in similar circumstances. It was a genuine mystery to him.

Once he caught sight of Amoy, however, all that was forgotten. The real game was on again. There would be ample time for the other later.

Amoy was clip-clopping along the far side of the hundred-metre feeder lane separating Abi's motorhome from his horse and cart. He looked at least ninety per cent asleep. Maybe this new horse he'd procured for himself knew the way back home on his own? thought Abi. Maybe I did the bastard a genuine favour shooting the other one?

Abi gave Amoy a ten-minute head start and then eased the Mercedes into a U-turn and followed after, keeping his speed down to around five miles an hour. After twenty minutes he saw Amoy turn into a Romani campsite and lose himself amongst the caravans there. The campsite was considerably larger than Abi had imagined. There was no way he would be able to get a just perspective on it without being seen, so a recce was out of the question. The ground was as flat as a pancake in every direction.

Cursing, Abi drove the motorhome down a track near the camp and parked 50 metres above a fast-flowing river. He put out an arm and shook Antanasia awake. 'I need to sleep now. I'm going in tonight. The whole thing's perfect. I couldn't have designed it better myself. I can do what I have to do and be across the Serbian border in ten minutes. An hour after that we'll be over in Hungary and the trail will be dead as a fish. Then we can head across Austria and into Switzerland. Will you wake me up in three hours?'

Antanasia stared at him, her eyes still drooping with sleep. 'Just like that. You're going in just like that. What if they are not there?'

'They'll be there.'

'What makes you so sure?'

'I can smell them. Plus I've just followed the idiot pot

maker home. He's the one who smuggled Radu across the frontier last autumn. I'm willing to bet that he picked him up again straight after we'd gone, and treated his wounds. I'm pleased now that I shot his bloody horse. My mistake was not to burn his cart as well. My imbecile sisters must have overlooked Radu when they conducted their search of the cart. He was probably rammed in there all the time, in some hidden compartment. These Gypsies have smuggling in their blood. Why do you think they live so near the border? Heck, you're one of them, aren't you? Or so you claim.'

Abi threw himself down on the single cot, leaving the double bed for Antanasia, as was his wont. After a bit, she laid herself down too. Words were superfluous. She felt as if she were frozen in time.

In her heart Antanasia didn't know exactly what she was waiting for – but she knew that whatever it was, she must see it right through to the end. Of all the men she had known in her life, Abi had come the closest to treating her kindly and with humanity. True, he wanted something of her. But he had saved her life and healed her back. And he hadn't abused her – at least not yet – although she both knew and recognized those moments when he had been tempted.

He was angry with her now, though, and liable to say things he didn't mean, so she knew that she must tread carefully. She also realized that the thought of him entering the camp and either killing or being killed made her feel intolerably lonely. Why were all the men she was close to warped in some way? Flawed? Were all men like this? Was it God's pattern for them?

Antanasia curled herself up on the bed and thought through the main events of her life. Had she truly called all the miseries that had assailed her down on herself? Did she really suffer from the curse of Eve, as both her father and her brother had insisted? Or maybe she had inherited bad blood from her mother, and was cursed that way?

On a number of occasions, and particularly after her mother had first bolted and then come sidling back home a few weeks later, her father had forced both mother and daughter to listen to him reading God's words to Eve from Genesis 3:16.

'Pay attention, the pair of you. These are the words God used to Eve directly after cursing the Serpent. I'm not making this up. It is written here in the Holy Bible. Listen, I tell you!' His eyes had flashed cold fire at them. Even now, Antanasia could feel the memory of her fear of him eating into her stomach. '"Unto the woman he said, I will greatly multiply thy sorrow and thy conception; in sorrow thou shalt bring forth children; and thy desire *shall be* to thy husband, and he shall rule over thee." There. What do you think of that?'

Next he would read out the section in which God curses Adam on account of Eve, and condemns him to till the earth via thorns and thistles. '"Cursed is the ground for thy sake; in sorrow shall thou eat of it all the days of thy life. BECAUSE THOU HAST HEARKENED UNTO THE VOICE OF THY WIFE!" You see?' he would shout. 'It is because of you women that I sweat in the fields and lose my crops. That the locusts come, and the corn blight, and the rye ergot.'

'You've switched the words around,' said Zina. 'I've read the Bible too.' This, as Antanasia knew, was not quite true – her mother never read anything. 'The words don't come in that order. You've done it to suit yourself, you bastard.'

Then Adrian Lupei would raise his hand to both of them, until he had satisfied himself that they were sufficiently chastened and would obey him in everything. If Dracul tried to intervene, as he sometimes did when this form of behaviour first began, he would be beaten too. Harder than the women, because he was a boy, and he should be able to take it.

Despite all this, Antanasia's mother never lost her resilience or her sense of humour. 'He is a small man, your father,' Zina would tell her daughter. 'A tiny man. If I didn't have both of you to worry about, I would leave him forever.'

'No, Mama. Don't leave us. Never leave us.'

Now Antanasia wished that her mother had not listened to her pleas. That she had saved herself. That she had run away once and for all and never come back.

For her death had destroyed everything that was good in her children's world, allowing evil to slip, alongside her unquiet spirit, in through the back door.

# 95

Amoy saw the Mercedes motorhome almost immediately. He had noticed it first the day before, but parked in a marginally different spot. It was an outrageous piece of German engineering. But Amoy would have liked one anyway.

With a vehicle like that a man could go anywhere. Could take his family anywhere. Odd, though, that its owners would spend two days in succession at the border crossing. Maybe their papers weren't in order? Maybe they had some deal going with the border officers, and were celebrating with whores and champagne? Although anyone who used the border whores must have a screw loose in their heads – they were drug-ridden and diseased, the whole lot of them, and in the pockets of the police. Amoy thanked God that he had a strong wife who produced many children for him, and who kept him more than exercised in that department, as well as off the streets.

He looked wistfully at the Geist, then continued on his way. Later, from far away, he saw the motorhome do a U-turn and start along the road behind him. He looked forward to taking a closer look at it as it came past him.

But the motorhome did not come past him.

Amoy turned round on his seat. The motorhome was keeping pace with him, but about a kilometre back. The countryside was so flat that the Geist was clearly visible, like an oversized dung beetle, against the skyline. Why would anyone drive a powerful motorhome like that at a mere ten kilometres an hour? Amoy felt the cold edge of fear flush along the surface of his skin.

Amoy tied the reins to the seat beside him. The horse knew his way home. He had passed this way nearly a hundred times in the past few months. He knew his oats were awaiting him.

Swallowing compulsively to try and overcome the sudden dryness in his mouth, Amoy dropped down from the cart and eased himself into the scrub at the side of the road.

Crouching, he made a circuit of a few hundred metres in the rough form of a crescent, then squatted down in a stand of reeds and watched the motorhome approach.

The driver was the young leader who had shot his horse last November. There was a woman sleeping beside him. But this was not one of the women who had accompanied the leader and his companion in the initial expedition in which they had shot Radu – the sorts of women a man would have paid good money to have nothing whatsoever to do with. This was a beautiful woman, with lustrous hair and a pale face.

He'd seen enough. He cut back over the scrubland until he caught up with his horse and cart again. He flattened himself across the seat to make believe he had been sleeping all the time, and leaving his horse to find its own way home.

When he approached the final turning into the camp, Amoy sat up and stretched, making a big deal out of straightening the jacket and trousers of his crumpled black suit. He wasn't much of an actor, but he sensed his piece of theatre would suffice, as the motorhome was still a good half-kilometre behind him, and virtually lost in the burgeoning dusk.

Interesting, too, that the young leader hadn't thought to put on his sidelights.

## 96

Abi licked the envelope and secured it. 'Here. Keep this safe.'

'What is it?'

'It's in case something happens to me. You can read it then.'

'Is something going to happen to you?'

'No. It never has before. I don't see why it should now.' Abi checked his camouflage face-paint in the mirror. 'I'm prepared. They're not. This AK-47 is my favourite weapon. It fires at a rate of 600 rounds a minute. You tape an extra banana magazine upside down to the other one, like this. That way you don't have to feel in your pockets if it comes to a firefight. When you run out of ammo you simply upend the magazine, slot it into place, and you're back in action again. I've got four more magazines in this pouch on my hip. I could hold off a small army. The men I'm going up against only have pistols.'

'And you've got your Wolf Pelt.' Antanasia's voice quavered a little as she spoke the words.

'Yes. I've got my Wolf Pelt. My magic formula against bullets.'

'Please don't do this, Abiger.'

'We've been over this a hundred times now. I can't change. I won't change. But one thing I'll promise you. When this is over, I'll never kill another man. If you'll still have me after this, we'll marry and you'll be my countess. In a few years' time you'll forget this ever happened. You'll come to realize how deeply unimportant it is in the general scheme of things.'

For a moment it looked as if Abi would reach forward and kiss her. Antanasia stood waiting. She would let him, she decided. Maybe kissing her for the first time would change something in him? But Abi let the moment slip by. He was too wound up in the prospect of action to care anymore about women. That would come afterwards. Antanasia sensed that much.

Abi would come back to the motorhome. They would drive away. He would be wound up after the killings. When he thought it was safe he would stop the vehicle and try to make love to her. Antanasia knew that she could not support this. It would mark a return to everything she despised about her past life. A return to the old ways, where her value to a man was nothing beyond the desire she elicited from him and the convenience she represented in the slaking of those desires.

Never again would she allow a man to take her without her permission. Never again would she allow herself to be used as a plaything. Not after what Dracul and her father had done to her. Not after that.

Antanasia watched Abi cutting through the scrub in the direction of the camp. She watched him all the way until he was out of sight.

Then she sat down and wrote her own letter.

# 97

***

Abi stood behind a tree and watched the camp. He made a face. It was ten o'clock in the evening. Surely even Pikeys didn't go to bed so early? And yet the camp was bare of people. Could they have sensed he was coming? Impossible.

It had to be a wedding then. Or a funeral. Something of that sort. Maybe they'd all traipsed out the front gate while he'd been asleep? With the benefit of hindsight maybe he should have kept watch. But how did anyone anticipate something like this? The place was like a cemetery. And he'd needed the sleep. It never did to go into combat with staring eyes and a muzzy head. And Benzedrine was for wusses.

Abi padded towards the camp, his weapon at port arms. He'd hold up the first person he saw and elicit information from them. Everyone here would know about the foreigners. And they'd be so surprised to see a fully armed man in camouflage gear they'd probably shit themselves. They'd reckon he was Romanian military, maybe, or police special operations – counter-terrorism, say, or customs ops. That should be enough to start a most satisfying riot. Surprise and chaos. That's what was needed. Then he'd have everything on his side. And who would be the last to leave? Why pregnant women and those nursing babies. And their protectors, needless to say.

Abi stood in the centre of the camp and stared around himself. It was uncanny. Not a soul around. Not even an old crone. Could it possibly be a trap?

He ducked into the nearest caravan and checked it out. No one. Nothing. He felt the top of the cooker. Stone cold. So it had to be a wedding. The whole darned lot of them had hunkered off while he'd been asleep. What a fucking joke.

He stepped out of the caravan.

Amoy, surrounded by approximately fifty men from the camp, stood opposite him. About 30 metres away. Well inside the 300-metre range of the AK-47.

As Abi watched, the men filtered around him in a loose circle. Most of them carried pitchforks, staves, or machetes. One or two had pistols. One had an old Lee-Enfield .303 rifle. Probably pre-Great War.

He would be the first to go, thought Abi. You could count on that.

He felt like laughing out loud.

'Any of you guys speak French?' Silence. 'English, maybe? I'm going to assume some of you speak English, then.' Abi made sure the caravan he'd just inspected was tight against his back. It was a permanent structure – or at least as permanent as something like that could be, in that its wheels were off and it was set on a solid bed of bricks. This meant that nobody could shoot his legs out through the gap underneath. 'There are a lot of you. True. But I have this.' Abi tapped the AK-47. 'And I'm prepared to use it. You people basically don't stand a chance. But I don't want to kill you. I want the two foreigners you have with you in the camp. If I get them I'll leave the rest of you to go about your business. Nobody needs to be any the wiser.'

Abi could sense that something was about to happen. There was a smell in the air. He recognized it as the smell of fear. The fear that men exude when they know that some of them are about to die.

Abi had never had any intention of waiting for their answer. He began running and firing at the same time. The man with the Lee-Enfield was the first to fall, alongside two men who were foolish enough to be standing near him.

Abi made for the thinnest part of the line. He felt a pistol round snap into his vest and another graze his neck.

He cut down the men in front of him, smashed one man in the face with the stock of his weapon, then switched magazines at full sprint. As he was switching he caught sight of Sabir running parallel to him, surrounded by a group of men. Abi instantly knew that it was Sabir who had taken the two shots at him.

He was just about to turn and bring the AK-47 to bear when he heard Sabir's voice rising over the surrounding clamour. 'He's wearing a Kevlar vest. Go for his head or his legs. If you hit his body it won't hurt him.' A second voice translated what Sabir had said into Čerhari Romani.

Abi heard the shotgun go off behind him. He caught

the full force of the blast on the back of his legs – lower buttocks and upper thigh. He pitched forwards onto his knees. Almost instantly he lurched up again and continued running. He needed to get out of there pronto. If the second shotgun barrel took him in the head he was done for.

He upended the AK-47 over his shoulder and fired behind himself as he ran. He could see the far edge of the camp now. He needed to get clear before anyone else got a lucky shot in. He could feel the blood cascading down the back of his legs. If the pikeys got hold of him now that he'd dry-gulched a few of them, they'd gut and joint him and feed him to their pigs.

The fresh magazine gave out and Abi threw both it and its taped twin away. He'd taped and loaded them wearing gloves, and he was wearing gloves now. There'd be nothing to identify him left in the camp. Nothing to DNA him with. His face was painted in thick stripes. He was wearing full camouflage. If they didn't physically get their hands on him he was still home free. Antanasia could see to his wounds. She owed him that much.

He cut through the trees. The pikeys were keeping their distance now after finding out what he could do with the AK. Abi slowed and checked around himself. He was on the opposite side of the camp to the Mercedes. Well. He would simply have to work his way back round again.

He thrust one of his four remaining magazines into the weapon. He reached back and felt his legs. Dripping. Numb. But they'd hold him up for a while still. Fuck that man with the shotgun. There'd be cloth and filth and all sorts of junk in the pellet holes. Probably give him the mother of all infections.

He stopped by a tree and picked off two of the men following him. Trust Sabir to hide himself in the crowd.

Abi spat the foul taste out of his mouth.

He was half tempted to rush back towards the camp again. Catch them out that way. Take another dozen or so with him.

But his legs. How long would they carry him?

Best to cut around towards the Mercedes. But wide. Amoy and Sabir would have the entire camp out looking for him. So he'd work well to the side. Come back in from the far bank of the river.

No one had a clue who Antanasia was yet. They wouldn't bother her if they found the Mercedes. She was just a happy camper bivouacking for the night.

Abi broke open a morphine auto-injector and injected his worst-affected leg through his combat trousers. He knew the morphine would mess up his respiratory rate, but the pain was becoming crippling, and he needed to do something about it fast. All the initial numbness had worn off now, and it felt like the back of his legs had been napalmed. Savaged by fire ants.

He checked behind him once more and struck out diametrically away from the Mercedes. An hour. Give me an hour, he said to himself, and I'll make it back home.

# 98

Antanasia listened to the gunfire at the camp. It was far worse than she had anticipated. She knew nothing whatsoever about firearms, but she thought she could make out the lighter pop of small arms fire, followed by the heavier, hammering sound of Abi's AK-47.

So Abi had come up against some opposition? Compared to the snap of the pistol shots, the AK-47 sounded like something conjured up in hell. The sound a tank makes when compared to a two-horsepower Citroen. She felt desperately sorry for whoever was on the receiving end of such a barrage.

Antanasia laid her letter down beside Abi's. It was a pointless act because she sensed that he wouldn't be coming back. But maybe someone would read it and understand.

She stepped out of the caravan.

The evening was soft for the time of the year. But the river would be bitterly cold.

She glanced towards the camp. Gunfire flashes reflected off the low clouds like lightning.

Antanasia walked to the top of the slope leading down towards the river. She could just make out the dark of the water against the lighter smudge of the bank. The river was twenty feet across. She could tell by the suck and swell of the rip that it was deep. Still charged with melted snow from the mountains.

She lay down on the slope, her arms held across her chest. She could feel her mind emptying itself of all that had gone before. She felt an unutterable sense of peace.

She allowed herself to roll down the slope, counting on the speed she picked up to launch her far out into the main part of the stream. But at the last moment her direction skewed, and she found herself rolling to one side and up a small bank. She stood up, a half-smile on her face.

Slowly, painstakingly, she walked back up the slope. This time she lay herself down at the far edge to allow for the slant of the incline and the shape of her body.

She took a deep breath and let herself go.

She rolled down, again at an angle. But on this occasion she had judged it right. Her body struck the water at running speed and she was sucked under.

She closed her eyes and welcomed the numbness.

# 99

Sabir had broken away from his companions early on in the firefight. He had seen Abi take the buckshot in his legs – had seen him drop to his knees and then lurch forward again. He thought he'd hit him twice with shots from his pistol, but one round had clearly been taken by the Kevlar vest, and the other? Well, who knew where it had ended up? But it hadn't incapacitated the bastard, that much was for sure.

Sabir decided to concentrate on his search for the Mercedes, because hunting a camouflaged man in the dark was an utter waste of time. Amoy had described the vehicle to him in rigorous detail. The deal was that Amoy and his family could take it, come what may. The thing was probably stolen anyway, so what harm was there in a bit of plunder? Sabir had also guaranteed a lump sum to any man's family from the camp who was killed or injured during the course of the firefight. He had a suspicion, given Abi's accuracy with that burp-gun of his, that he might have to declare bankruptcy and sell his house in Stockbridge come sunup.

But the Mercedes, and the woman inside it, was the key. The others could go off in hot pursuit of the maniac, but Sabir sensed that Abi would eventually come back to the woman and to the vehicle that, between them, would as good as guarantee his escape.

Sabir had lost sight of Calque early on in the firefight. The ex-policeman had fastened on to one of the pistols and seemed determined to have it out personally with Abi, whom he still blamed for setting him up for torture in Mexico, and whose brother he held responsible for the murder of his assistant, Paul Macron, the previous year. Sabir had tried to dissuade Calque from participating all through the initial negotiations they'd had with Amoy.

'Why don't you hand your weapon over to a younger man? Alexi, say?'

But Calque had given him a withering look and refused to contemplate not being involved.

Sabir now found himself fretting about his friend. He'd been unfair to Calque over the past few months. Cutting him out of the loop in so many ways. He regretted that now. Calque was the only real friend he had left. Alexi was all very well, but the man was an anarchist and a flibbertigibbet – a delight in so many ways, but impossible to count on. And Radu was wound up in his family and his culture and took things far too seriously. But Calque? Calque was his. In fact Calque was pretty much all he had.

Sabir came upon the river on his left-hand side. He flicked on his torch for a split second to confirm that he was walking along a dirt track, then flicked it off again. Pointless turning himself into more of a target than he already was. When his eyes had readjusted themselves to the darkness he focused all his attention on the paler line of the path against the darker line of the sedge, working also to keep the susurration of the river always on his offside. It was then that he heard the splash.

Sabir hesitated for a moment, and then struck down the bank. Could Abi have circled round, got on the far side of the river, and be crossing back? Maybe the bastard had seen the flash of his torch? But then he would have fired in his direction. Whatever burp gun he was carrying had clearly been set to full automatic, given the unholy racket it made when fired. Close up, the sound was enough to loosen your sphincter and almost cause you to piss yourself.

Sabir waded through the reeds at the side of the river bank. Something white swelled out of the water in front of him and slid underneath again.

Without thinking, Sabir dived in. Whether he was remembering back to last summer, and the time Achor Bale had tossed Yola into the river like a sack of rotting potatoes, or whether his thoughts had returned to his mother, and the distorted shape of her body beneath the overflowing bathwater in which she had chosen to slit her wrists, he knew not. He only knew that the white shape was human. That the person in the river needed him. Perhaps he was someone from the camp? Someone injured by gunfire, who had wandered away from the main battleground, lost themselves, and fallen in?

Sabir rose high on the river swell and forced himself under, his arms outstretched. His pistol had long gone, and when he felt the numbing cold of the water he knew that he would not last long either. He could feel his heart hesitate, then redouble its pounding after the initial shock of his dive.

His hands grasped material. He realized that he was travelling at the same rate as the person he was holding.

Sabir kicked wildly for the side of the bank nearest the track. He was holding the person in his arms now, tight against his chest.

He snatched at a handful of reeds with his one free hand, and almost lost his grip when the body, encircled by his arm, was brought up short against the current.

He swallowed half a pint of river water as he fought against the current to win the body. Finally, knowing that he was losing purchase, he grabbed the person by the scruff of their shirt and dragged them behind him as he eased himself out, arse first, like a reversing spider.

Once on dry land, he threw the person face downwards onto the bank. He now realized, for the very first time, that he was dealing with a woman. He checked the woman's airway with his finger, and then pressed down onto her back with both hands. After three full-strength compressions, she brought up a lungful of water and began to cough.

Sabir was seizing up fast. The woman, he knew, would be in a far worse state. If he waited even a few minutes more, he would be as good as inanimate. Of no use to anybody.

He picked the woman up, threw her across his shoulders, and began to run. He reached the track and continued upstream in the direction he had been going when he first heard the splash.

The breath was coming out of him in groans. He

stopped for a second, redistributed the woman's weight around his neck, and resumed running.

Ahead of him he saw something pale against the night sky. He slowed down and squinted. It was the silver Mercedes.

Sabir grunted and stumbled towards it. He felt for the door with one hand and threw it open. He eased the woman inside.

He switched on the lights and got his first real look at her. Her face was deathly pale, her hair plastered to her brow. She seemed familiar to him in some way that he couldn't define.

He glanced up. A shower. There was a shower stall. Hot water maybe.

He stripped off the woman's wet clothes, followed by his own. He would be of no earthly use to her if he cramped up. Already his hands were turning into claws with the cold.

He lifted her against his chest and carried her bodily towards the shower.

'Please God let it be hot,' he mumbled to himself.

He switched on the faucet and waited. Steam oozed out of the shower bracket.

Sabir tested the water and backed the woman in ahead of him, supporting her entire bodyweight in his arms, her head across his shoulder. The feel of the hot water on his head and back transformed everything. Soon he was shaking uncontrollably – but a sizable part of that was laughter. They would be all right. They would both be all right.

It was then that he felt the striations on the woman's

back. He turned her round. Her back, buttocks and upper legs were a mass of partially healed wounds. This woman had been beaten within the past few weeks – and beaten badly. Sabir froze for a moment, his arms stretched out in front of him, bearing the entirety of the woman's weight.

Sabir stood her under the shower until the hot water gave out. Then he rubbed her down with towels he found in the next-door cupboard. When they were both dry he eased her towards the double bed, threw back the duvet, and got in with her. She was shaking again.

He pulled her towards him and covered them both with as many blankets as he could reach.

She was still shivering, but she was coming to. He could feel her coming alive in his arms.

Crazily, uncomprehendingly, he could feel himself hardening against her.

The woman turned towards him, her eyes wide open.

It was the woman from the Bronzino painting. The same mouth. The same eyes. The same auburn hair.

Antanasia regarded Sabir quizzically, as if becoming aware of his presence for the very first time. To Sabir, her eyes were wells in which a man could drown himself. Antanasia put one hand down below the sheets and held him, surprised at her own temerity.

Sabir bent forwards and kissed her. There was no sense to it. No logic. Only instinct. He was lost in her. Entirely lost.

Antanasia responded to Sabir's kiss in a way that she had never responded to any man before him. It was a total giving of herself. A total surrender. No man – any man – could possibly misconstrue it.

Sabir held her as if she were a part of him. He breathed her in. Every part of their bodies touched, as if they were one being, locked together.

When Sabir entered her Antanasia cried out. Her eyes were fixed on his. They seemed to be looking directly into his soul.

Antanasia watched him arching over her. She held him gently by the small of his back, guiding him, steadying him. For the very first time in her life she was accepting a man voluntarily – allowing him to make love to her with total release. Total impunity. Not holding anything back.

As Sabir increased the rhythm of his movements, Antanasia felt all the evils of the world leach from her. She felt revived – revivified – as if, only now, could she honour the true meaning of her name, which suggested 'one who was reborn'. An 'immortal'. Antanasia felt immortal in this man's arms.

When Sabir climaxed inside her Antanasia felt seven successive waves of ecstasy suffuse her, each one longer and deeper than the last. She held him inside her, pushing against him, moaning, her eyes wide with shock and longing. During the final luxuriant wave, Antanasia held Sabir close to her breast, as one would hold a child.

Finally, she closed her eyes. What had happened? How had she come to this from the river? Who was this man she had taken inside her with such overwhelming determination? With such overpowering love?

The door to the Mercedes burst open and Abi stood in the entranceway. He was leaching blood, his eyes hooded, his pupils thin as pinpricks thanks to the three injections of morphine he had dosed himself with on the journey home.

He was hallucinating. Clearly, he was hallucinating. Because all he could see was Sabir and Antanasia, together in bed.

Abi burst out laughing. He shook his head, like a horse tormented by botflies. His nose, cheeks, and eyebrows were numb. He could no longer feel any part of his body. It was as if his mind and his physical being were entirely disconnected.

'No,' he said. 'This is not what I am seeing. This is not possibly what I am seeing.'

He raised the AK-47 and brought it to bear on the couple in front of him.

'This is impossible.' He dropped the barrel for a second. 'This is sheerly impossible.'

Calque stepped up behind Abi and shot him in the head. He couldn't reach the top of Abi's skull, so he could only fire into the base of it, just above the nape of his neck. The pistol was a .22. Hardly more powerful than a cap gun. But close to, it was devastating.

Abi dropped to his knees, the AK-47 swinging round in sympathy with the movement of his body. His eyes turned up in his head.

The bullet was still lodged inside his skull. No sign of it externally. Hardly any sign that he had been shot at all.

Abi fell onto his back. The AK-47 caught on a cupboard door and hung, transfixed, in space.

Calque took a step forwards.

'My God,' he said.

# EPILOGUE

*Silbury Hill, Avebury, Wiltshire*
*6.35 a.m.*
*21 December 2012*

'How are you feeling, Sabir?' Calque cast a sidelong glance at his friend. He was used to Sabir's moods by now – the man had been lurching from the mercurial to the exuberant for the past few weeks, with the mercurial winning by a short head. It was as if he were preparing for something – some test, perhaps – of whose ultimate parameters he was still ignorant.

'How do you think I'm feeling, Calque? I'm camping out in a rental car, in England, in a fucking rainstorm, in the certain knowledge that, in precisely half an hour's time, the Halach Uinic expects me to slog up a 130-foot-high man-made hill and magic up a rabbit.'

'A rabbit?'

'Yes. A rabbit. You know. With big ears. The sort magicians pull out of a hat and the audience goes "aaahhhh"?'

'I'm sorry, Sabir. You are making no sense whatsoever. What is this thing about rabbits?'

Sabir bent forwards and touched the rim of the steering wheel with his forehead. Slowly, steadily, he began to knock his head against the vulcanized rubber. 'So that he doesn't have to drop his trousers in front of a worldwide television audience of half a billion people, Calque, with scrambled egg plastered all over his face.'

Calque rolled his eyes. Why had he asked the question? Would he never learn? Sabir was a delightful companion for the most part, but when he felt under pressure he was apt to swerve off the main road and go cross-country. 'A sublime use of mixed metaphor, Sabir. You have surpassed even your own towering standards. That was positively Ciceronian.' Calque cleared his throat. 'You misunderstood me. What I meant was, how are you feeling about Antanasia and Alexandreina's involvement in the ceremony of the thirteen skulls?'

'Oh. That.' Sabir flopped back against the seat. Whenever he thought of his wife and two-year-old daughter, whom they had nicknamed Sanda, Sabir felt the onset of what the writer G. K. Chesterton construed as 'absurd good news'. He thanked God every day for the gift of them. When Antanasia put her head on his shoulder and snuggled close to him at night, with the sound of the Mediterranean leaching through the open windows of their bedroom in Mallorca, and with their child sleeping contentedly in the next room, Sabir knew that his life had reached the summit of happiness – things could never get any better than this. 'I'm feeling pretty good about it, actually. This is the right thing to do. I'm even starting to think that writing that damned fool book wasn't the unmitigated disaster I thought it had been. *The Second Coming* indeed. *Nostradamus, the Night Serpent, and the Mayan Great Change*. Why didn't you warn me, man? It was the dumbest idea I've ever had. Before that, only the Romani knew about Sanda. After publication, with all the brouhaha about Nostradamus's connections with the Maya that accompanied it, she belonged to everybody. I clearly underestimated the public's relish for conspiracy theories.'

'Your publishers certainly didn't.'

'Well, there is that, I suppose. At least I made somebody happy. But I can't imagine what I was thinking of. The words vainglory and rodomontade spring to mind.'

Calque lit a cigarette and let the smoke bleed out of the partially cracked window. 'Sabir. There are moments, and this is one of them, when I genuinely fear for your sanity.'

Sabir had the grace to smile. 'You mean I win on the swings and I win on the roundabouts?'

'Something like that. And if we're on to metaphors, you also have a marked tendency to shut the stable door after the horse has bolted.'

Sabir screwed up his face like a child who has just had his ear swiped. Then he checked his watch and glanced out of the window. 'Look, Calque. We've still got a few minutes before the ceremony. Run all that stuff by me again, will you?'

'What stuff?'

'The stuff about the plane of the elliptic and the precession of the equinoxes. I might need it if the crystal skulls keep shtum.'

Calque sighed. 'It's the plane of the ecliptic, Sabir, not the elliptic. Please let's start how we mean to go on.' He closed his eyes. At times like this he wished that he was back with the police force, apprehending felons. He took a final drag on his cigarette and dropped it through the half-open car window. 'At this very moment, somewhere high above our heads, the sun is conjuncting the Milky Way and the plane of the ecliptic for the first time in 25,800 years. This is considered a significant event, Sabir, both to the Maya and to ourselves. Such a wobble always precedes a great change – whether spiritual, geological or transformational, nobody rightly knows. Whether humanity is swept away in the process is clearly a moot point – and something that we may discover today via the thirteen crystal skulls. Rabbits permitting, of course.'

Sabir grinned. He faked a gravel-throated movie voiceover. 'And while heaven, with its 400 billion stars, is grinding into gear above us, and Father Sun is kissing the cosmic womb good morning, earthlings patiently wait, a million trillion light years from the action, and discuss rabbits.'

Calque cleared his throat. 'Precisely.'

Thanks to the worldwide success of Sabir's book, tens of thousands of people were gathering at the foot of Silbury Hill in the pre-dawn murk. Most had staked out their spots near one or other of the great video screens, but others were camping at the foot of the slope in the hope, clearly, of sensing at least something of what was happening on the summit. Torches, headlamps, and candles in all manner of holders shone out from all sides, illuminating the landscape in every direction. TV cameras and news crews were on standby. People had pitched wind breaks, two-man tents, and hazel bowers covered in plastic sheeting in a vain effort to protect themselves from the weather. It was hard to work out if dawn was actually on the way, or if the orange glow surrounding everything was not merely the residual lustre from ten thousand artificial lights.

Calque squinted through the streaming windscreen. 'Maybe we should move.'

'Maybe we should.'

Calque threw his side of the car open and stepped out into the rain. 'Pah. This English rain.'

'It rains in France too.'

'Yes. But that is French rain. English rain is as thin and sour as English beer. French rain is sweet. You are half French, Sabir. You ought to know that without my having to explain it to you.'

The two men shouldered their way through the crowd to the very base of Silbury Hill. The pair of them blended in perfectly. Calque had pulled an anorak hood up over his head and partially across his eyes – thanks to the rain, this did not seem remotely out of place. Sabir, who had categorically refused the Halach Uinic's offer of a shamanic robe for the ceremony of the thirteen skulls, looked like any other gloomy, nondescript man in his mid to late thirties, intent on seeing for himself what the newspapers insisted on calling 'The Scoop of the Millennia', or, in the case of one notorious tabloid's headline the previous day, 'The Maya Take A Flya'.

Silbury Hill had been cordoned off so that the slopes leading to its summit were entirely clear of people. Ingress, too, had been safeguarded via a manned ropewalk along which the Halach Uinic and his priests would proceed with the thirteen crystal skulls, which would then be placed on plinths, with the exact distance stipulated by the codex separating each skull. The skulls would be positioned facing outwards, not inwards, with twelve of the skulls representing the twelve points of the original version of the compass rose favoured by the ancient Romans and the Chinese – the formulation known as the Rose of the Winds, or the Windrose. This was in turn based on the twelve signs of the Zodiac, each positioned at 30° of the circle. The thirteenth skull would be located directly in the centre of the ring made up of the twelve other skulls.

The women's party, led by Ixtab, would then approach from the direction of Avebury on the far side of the hill, the theory being that Alexandreina was to be placed on a cushion beneath the plinth holding the thirteenth skull, directly between her mother and father, who would be symbolically meeting over her, as if in a handfasting.

Sometimes, when contemplating the miracle of his wife and child, Sabir found it hard to believe that he owed everything he possessed in this world to that piece of filth, Abiger de Bale. It had been de Bale who had saved Antanasia from her brother. De Bale who had treated her wounds when she was at risk of dying from them. De Bale who had transported her all the way to the camp at Bogdamic. De Bale who had killed the Third Antichrist and destroyed the Corpus Maleficus. De Bale who had made them both rich. It was even de Bale who had provided them with their home – the home in which Sabir had hatched his disastrous plan to write the book that would finally resuscitate his reputation. Maybe that was de Bale's ultimate revenge? Give a man what he most wanted in life and he was sure to wreck it. God acted in strange ways indeed.

When he and Calque had finally opened the letter de Bale had written before his assault on the camp at Bogdamic, it was to find that, in the unlikely event of his death, he had left his entire estate, free of any encumbrance whatsoever, to Antanasia.

*It is hard to admit in life that you may have been wrong. But even harder to rectify the damage whilst keeping yourself intact. I may be wrong now in going out and seeking revenge. But it is my nature. I cannot change at this late date. I am like the scorpion in the Sufi story that stings the frog who is carrying him across the river even though it means certain death for them both. I have a fountain of hate in me which I have found it impossible to plug. It is like the scar on my stomach. I wish that it were not there to remind me of my brother, but it is. This hate has lived with me for twenty-five years. It has become me. It is a part of my character, like the sting to the scorpion. I must drain it to the very dregs.*

*I love you, Antanasia. I never thought that I could say this to anyone, but to you the declaration is surprisingly easy. This is the one and only love letter that I shall ever write. I know, too, that you can never be mine in anything other than a partial way. I would damage you. Despoil you. Take you to hell with me. If I am killed this evening,*

*accept Madame, my mother's, blood money as my*
*parting gift to you. Do with it what you will. Give*
*it to the pikeys, if it makes you feel better. Start*
*a foundation. Build a fucking library. I won't be*
*around to care. I did one good thing in my life and*
*that was to save you from your brother. How odd*
*that I should choose to point to only that after a*
*lifetime of justified obloquy.*

*Signed and sealed on this, the 28th February*
*2010, by Abiger Delaigue Fortunatus de Bale,*
*Comte D'Hyères and Pair de France, Marquis de*
*Seyème and Chevalier de Sallefranquit-Bedeau,*
*lapsed member of the Corpus Maleficus and failed*
*defender of chaos on earth.*

The day after Abi's death, Amoy, Radu and Alexi
transported his body high into the Carpathian
Mountains. Leaving their car, they hauled the corpse,
which was still in an advanced stage of rigor mortis,
towards the burned-out shell of the hunting lodge.

Finally, when they were within ten minutes' walking
distance of the lodge, they sat Abi in a hidden cleft
in the rocks and forced his hand around another of
the pistols – a .38 this time – that they had liberated
from the Coryphaeus's Crusaders. Alexi – a self-styled
expert on firearms ever since he had botched his shot
at Abi's elder brother the previous summer due to a
misunderstanding about the principles of lock and load
– raised Abi's hand and angled the ensuing shot down
into the corpse's head, so that the exit route of the
bullet would disguise the entry route of the .22 Calque

had fired into the back of Abi's skull.

'I've just killed a dead man,' he declared. Then he threw up behind a nearby bush.

'This is good,' Amoy said. 'The police will think this cunt puked his guts up before shooting himself.'

Joris Calque had faked a letter for them back at the camp, exactly mimicking Abi's writing from the note left in the Mercedes. In the letter Abi admitted culpability for the murder of Mihael Catalin, and exonerated Catalin's sister, Antanasia, of all responsibility in the matter of her brother's death. In Calque's forgery, the fictional Abiger de Bale also admitted to the murder of the two men in the lodge, and confessed that it was he who had burned the place down in order to cover up the evidence of his crimes. He now bitterly regretted his actions, and found that he could not live with the guilt of what he had done. He had been out of his head with grief over his siblings' death in a car accident, and blamed Catalin and his men for the ensuing tragedy. This is why he had returned to the scene of his crime to do away with himself.

'Isn't that going a bit far?' said Sabir.

'You can never go too far when bullshitting the police,' said Calque. 'Take it from me. I'm an expert.'

The forged letter was then placed in Abi's original passport, which Amoy tucked inside the cadaver's top pocket so that there could be no possibility of an identification error, however inept or unwilling the investigating authorities proved to be.

Calque summed up the matter by opining that such a plan would not have held up in France, or Britain, or Germany, or indeed most of the other 188 Interpol countries. But in Romania – a country which had no real interest in either Abi or any of his victims, all of whom happened to be Moldovan – Calque suspected that obvious answers to obvious questions would be welcomed, and that the resources of Interpol might not, in the final resort, be called upon. Why waste valuable police time on a murderous bunch of foreigners who only killed amongst themselves? He trusted that Abi's suicide would complete the vicious circle in the minds of the authorities, and end the matter once and for all.

Whilst this was happening, Sabir drove with Antanasia to Lugano to arrange for pensions to be paid to the families of all those killed or wounded by de Bale during his attack on the camp. The pensions were to be drawn from the money held in her brother's account, to which she had joint access. The process proved to be a simple one. The money was legally Antanasia's already, as, due to the way the thing had been set up, one account holder automatically inherited on the death of the other. This time around, though, Antanasia changed the number and identity of the account, and ensured that the new joint account was in her and Sabir's names only.

In the months that followed, Sabir used his power of attorney to set up a charitable foundation, just as de Bale had cynically suggested, with Calque as the managing trustee and drafter of the document of establishment, alongside Yola, Radu, Alexi, and the mandatory French state representatives, whose grasping fingers never missed their slice of pie. Calque took to the necessary bureaucracy like a duck to water, glorying in every irritating detail of how to ensure that the bulk of the funds available be allocated for what the document of establishment stipulated – namely for the benefit of Romani people of whatever background, whatever doctrine, and whatever origin, so long as at least one parent qualified as Gypsy or Rom.

Without Calque's presence the foundation would have reverted to bedlam in very short order indeed. With him at the helm it steered the equivalent of a shaky path along a lee shore. But children were educated (when their parents wanted them to be), women were protected (to the extent that they chose to be), and traditional Romani culture was honoured (even in its absence).

Calque had learned enough from his time spent with Yola, Alexi, Radu, Lemma and the others to know that Gypsies did not relish *gadje* ways or *gadje* patronage or *gadje* interference in their affairs. So he limited himself to running the accounts and managing the basic structure, and he allowed Yola and the others to do the rest. And when they didn't feel like it, or went AWOL, or refused to turn up because of a wedding or a funeral or the celebration of a baptism, he smiled broadly at anyone within range and told his secretary to close the office and take a holiday. He would do the same.

As godfather to Alexandreina Sabir, Calque had numerous other duties to perform anyway, most of which involved long lunches that stretched on into the early evening at Son Reus, or walking trips across the Mallorcan Serras in which he took turn and turnabout with Sabir in carrying Sanda piggyback or in her baby sling.

It pleased Sabir that Calque had come into his own in the past two years. Calque's relationship with his own daughter had long ago foundered on the rocks of his non-relationship with the girl's mother, so Sanda became a surrogate granddaughter whom Calque could spoil, and dandle, and not feel threatened by, except when she bit him, which was often. Sanda even contrived to sink her teeth into him when he was walking her in her sling. Calque construed these unannounced attacks as signs of affection, refusing to believe that Sanda was frustrated that he did not possess milk-bearing breasts like her mother. Sabir watched the pair of them jockeying for domination with the weary air of one who has already seen it all, and expects to see it again very soon.

When Sabir reached the top of Silbury Hill, he turned at the sound of the horn. Ixtab and her party of women were approaching the Halach Uinic through the churning mud on the hillside. The first echoes of pre-dawn were in the sky. He watched as Ixtab motioned to Antanasia and Alexandreina to precede her across the cordon sanitaire and approach the place of the skulls.

Sabir felt as if he were seeing his wife for the very first time. He felt an overwhelming sense of familiarity with her, as if she was linked to him in some visceral, relational way that he couldn't quite fathom. It was the same feeling he had sometimes experienced when watching his mother, at a distance and unaware of him – an almost quizzical feeling, as of some secret connection, some mystery, that he was unable to access.

As he watched her, Antanasia glanced up at him,

and he recognized in her eyes the same sudden shock of recognition that he had experienced.

From the moment their eyes met, the two of them were linked. Sabir, for his part, felt unable to concentrate on anything else. He could hear Calque prattling on beside him, but he could not make out his words. The feelings he was receiving inside his head, however, were clear and to the point. He needed to place himself beside this woman – this both familiar and unfamiliar woman, who was at the same time recognizably his wife, but also more than his wife. He needed to feel her aura – to link her aura to his. He noticed, too, that Antanasia was graduating towards him, as if she felt a similar compulsion towards unity.

Ixtab was watching them both. Her heart was hammering in her chest. Never in her life had she encountered such an immediate conjunction of souls. She could almost hear the sound of it in front of her. As she watched, Sabir reached down and swung his daughter onto his shoulders. It was an instinctual move, but to her it seemed in some way shocking – almost a *lèse-majesté* – whilst being, paradoxically, liberating also.

At the same moment, each parent took the other's hand, as if the action were in some way preordained. Neither said a word. Ixtab could feel the energy emanating from the two figures cresting, like a wave, in front of her. She glanced at the Halach Uinic. His eyes were wide open as if in shock. She nodded at him. He nodded back. Both felt an ineffable sadness, as though at the loss of a loved one.

Antanasia and Sabir took their places naturally at the

centre of the tump, each still holding the other's hand. Around them, the Chilans swiftly set up the crystal skulls on their plinths. The thirteenth crystal skull, which had been kept scrupulously apart from the others, was only brought up when all else was in order.

The two camera crews took their prearranged positions on the periphery of the tump, facing to the south-east and to the north-east respectively, so that their sight lines would not overlap. Then Yola and Alexi Dufontaine appeared at the head of the track with their son, Valah. Ixtab, without knowing why she was doing it, coaxed Valah from his father's arms. When Yola made as if to stop her, Ixtab shook her head, and made a calming motion with her hand. She stopped outside the cordon sanitaire and swung Valah across it. She had no idea why she was doing what she was doing, but the impetus was overwhelming.

Valah, nine months older than Alexandreina, instantly recognized his regular playmate and ran towards her, shouting.

Ixtab moved to stand beside Yola and Alexi.

'Why did you put him in there? He is not the Parousia.'

'There is something. I don't know what it is. But I had to. It was as if someone was calling for him. Alexandreina herself, perhaps. Please be patient.'

The thirteenth skull had been placed on its plinth in the centre of the Windrose. The moment Alexandreina saw Valah running towards her, she took a few hesitant steps towards him, a broad smile on her face, as if she had been expecting him. Antanasia made as if to move towards her daughter, but Sabir stayed her hand. The two of them took a step backwards.

Valah, still running, snatched Alexandreina's hand in his and swung her round him in a circle, just as they would do at Son Reus when playing together in the garden. Alexandreina lost her footing and the pair of them tumbled to the ground, giggling. They seemed oblivious to everything else that was happening on the hilltop. The Chilans, who had just finished arranging the skulls, hurried back across the cordon sanitaire, casting nervous glances over their shoulders, and leaving only Antanasia, Sabir and the two children inside the circle.

The children, now covered in mud, approached the circle of the skulls, hand in hand and laughing. Valah pointed to the central skull. He appeared to recognize it. Alexandreina broke away from him, a mischievous grin on her face. She toddled up behind the skull and encircled it protectively with her arms. Valah, squealing with delight, ran towards her. He grabbed both her and the skull in his arms. Momentarily – subliminally – the skull seemed to throb in response to the children's touch.

Then there was silence.

Antanasia squeezed Sabir's hand. They stood together a little way back from the children, at the periphery of the circle of skulls. Antanasia snatched a glance towards Yola, who was standing next to Alexi near the rope barrier, looking anxious. Antanasia raised her hand and beckoned Yola and Alexi towards her with a smile.

Yola hesitated. Antanasia redoubled her invitation.

Yola stepped across the cordon sanitaire, leading Alexi by the hand. He needed little encouragement. His eyes were alight with joy at the sight of the two children playing.

Linking hands, the four parents approached their children. There was no thought involved anymore – no contrivance. Their faces seemed younger. Bereft of knowledge. Cleansed.

Each knelt down, encircling Valah and Alexandreina, who were still clutching the crystal skull and laughing riotously, in a protective net.

As they cemented the circle of their hands, the dawn broke through the clouds and lit up the surface of the hill.

Sabir could feel the energy flowing through him and into Valah and Alexandreina – then strengthening, and flowing through Antanasia, Yola and Alexi, and back into him again. It produced a feeling of such ecstasy, such supreme wellbeing, that it seemed to Sabir as if everything was right with the world. Everything harmonious. That no more questions needed to be asked.

He found himself falling to the ground in submission, his hands still gripping those of his companions. He wondered if the others were doing the same, because he could no longer see with his eyes – all his energies were concentrated internally, on the overwhelming feelings surging through his mind and body.

He could feel a force above him now. He felt part of the force – connected with it. He felt part of the hill beneath him. Part of the air about him. Part of the sky above him. He could no longer differentiate sound and sensation. No longer differentiate his body from the child's body or the woman's body or the man's body beside him. He was the hill. The air. The sky. He was the sun beating on his back. The rain kissing his skin.

He was the children in front of him, and the people beside him. He could feel himself surging into the air, carrying his own child and the mother of his child with him, each holding one of his hands.

Slowly he began to see again. Dead children. Dead women. Dead men. Thousands of them. Millions of them. Moving beside him, ever upwards.

He opened his arms and the woman and child moved into him, as if he was both contained and containing. One and many.

From everywhere around him, people were moving towards the skull. Some hesitantly, some at a run. Ixtab, the Halach Uinic, and the Maya Chilans all joined the burgeoning circle. No one jostled, no one pushed. The circle simply extended itself, ever outwards, until it spanned the entire acreage of the hillside and beyond like a lilting sea of corn.

All lay down. All clasped hands. The cameras were abandoned where they had fallen.

Sabir's voice rose high above the silence.

He was the Guide. He knew this now. Knew this for certain.

Slowly, but in a notably steady tone, and from somewhere far back in his memory, he began declaiming Rumi's *Ode*.

What can be done, O believers, as I no longer recognize myself?
I'm neither a Christian nor a Jew, a Magian or a Moslem.

I'm neither of the East nor West; of land or sea;
I don't belong to nature; nor to the stars in the sky.

I'm not of the earth, or water, or air, or fire;
I'm neither of Heaven, nor the dust from this carpet.

I'm not from India, China, Bulgaria or Saqsin;
Nor from the kingdom of Iraq, or Khorasan.

I'm not from this world, or the next, from Paradise or Hell;
I'm not of Adam's seed, or Eve's, from Eden or Rizwan.

My place is placeless, my traces traceless;
I'm neither body nor soul, as I belong to the soul of my Beloved.

I have no need of duality, as I have seen two worlds as One.
The One I seek; the One I know, the One I see, the One I call

He is the first and the last, the outward and the inward,
I know no other than He – there is only Him.

Love's cup intoxicates me as both worlds slip from my hands.
My only business now is drinking and merrymaking.

If once in my life I shared a moment without You,
From that moment on I would repent of my own life.

If once in this world I earned a moment with You,
I'd trample both worlds in a triumphal dance.

O Shams of Tabriz, I'm so drunk with this world
That only stories of carousal and revelry can now pass my lips.

# ACKNOWLEDGEMENTS

I'm very grateful indeed to all those people who have helped me during this trilogy's (*The Nostradamus Prophecies*, *The Mayan Codex*, *The Third Antichrist*) five-year voyage from conception to parturition (Author's Note: even an elephant manages hump to birth in 22 months, whilst the world's longest pregnancy of up to 38 months belongs to the southern European alpine salamander, but only if the animal lives at an altitude of between 1,400 and 1,700 metres – it can have triplets, though, which is comforting). But that's all by the by, and typical of this author's butterfly mind, which he chooses to conceal beneath a comparatist's veneer.

Firstly, I'd like to thank my agent, Oliver Munson, of Blake Friedmann, who has acted, first as midwife, and then as occasional obstetrician during the entire gestation period – his callipers never slipped. Also my outstanding editor, Laura Palmer, who has been a total joy to work with, particularly on this final book of the trilogy, which she took under her wing and incubated (I can't shake my gravidity kick at this late stage – there are three pregnancies in this book alone). I'd also like to thank my copy-editor, Shelagh Boyd, who has followed me through at least seven books without a single termination – quite a feat. And Madame Raton Laveur, aka Michèle O'Connell (raccoon parturiency: 65 days), who read and commented and encouraged during the entire course of writing this book – I still remember her mimicking of Parisian actress Arletty's drawled 'Atmosphère!' (from Marcel Carné's sublime *Hôtel du Nord*) at a particularly crucial time in the book's genesis.

Finally, my beautiful wife, Claudia, who has patiently endured my mewling, puking and caterwauling through any number of books. I love you.

# The Secret Meaning of Names in *The Nostradamus Trilogy*

**Abiger (de Bale):** Abiger is the grand Duke of Hades. He is often pictured as a handsome, armoured knight, carrying a lance, a standard, or a sceptre. He has sixty of the 'infernal regions' at his command. He is a demon of the 'superior order', renowned for his knowledge of war and of how to conduct it. He is able to foretell the future, and is a master at retaining the loyalty of his men.

**Acan:** Acan is the Mayan god of wine – or rather its Mayan counterpart, balché, which is made from fermented honey mixed with the bark of the balché tree.

**Achor (Bale):** The inverted form of **Rocha**. Akar-Bale is also an extinct Andaman Island language, continuing the secret language/ communication theme that runs throughout all three books.

**Adam (Sabir):** Adam was the first man to be created by God. He is the ancestor of all men – the primal man – the universe's primordial being. His name derives from the Kabbalah, in the form of Adam Kadmon, which in turn derives from the Judaic concept of the archetypal man. Each human being is believed to reflect this archetypal form, as in Leonardo da Vinci's drawing of Vitruvian Man. Adam Kadmon is also, metaphorically, the 'body of God'. See **Sabir**

**Adrian (Lupei):** Adrian originally means 'from Hadria', as in the Roman Caesar Hadrian, but its alternative meaning is 'dark'. Lupei means a 'wolf'. Thus 'dark wolf', which I felt described the man well.

**Agaberte:** Agaberte was the daughter of the Scandinavian God Vagnoste. She was an enchantress with remarkable magical powers, able to transform herself into a wrinkled old crone or into a tall, vibrant woman capable of reaching up and touching the sky. She could overturn mountains, rip up trees, and dry up rivers at will.

**Ahriman:** Ahriman was the Zoroastrian personification of pure evil, capable of fomenting lies against the Holy Spirit.

**Alastor (de Bale):** Alastor was a superior demon and chief executioner of Hades. In generic terms his name means an evil, avenging spirit. The name was also used by Zeus when he chose to take the form of an avenger of evil deeds, particularly relating to the family. Later, the term came to mean a 'scoundrel', or one who 'falsely possesses another'.

**Alatyrtsev (Sergei):** The surname Alatyrtsev comes from the Old Russian term *alatyrets*, meaning 'abusive', 'confused' or 'uncertain'. Sergei means a 'servant' in Russian. Both meanings relate to Alatyrtsev's character.

**Aldinach (de Bale):** Aldinach was an Egyptian demon who often chose to disguise himself as a woman. He could cause earthquakes, hailstorms and tempests, and had a particular predilection for sinking ships. I use this hermaphroditic quality in the book.

**Alexandreina:** Alexandreina (nickname Sandu) is of Romanian origin, and means 'defender of

mankind' or 'protector of men' – it is the female form of the name Alexander.

**Alexi (Dufontaine):** Alexi stems from the Greek, and means 'defender'. Dufontaine means 'of the fountain' or 'from the source'. Alexi may be a fool, but he is a stout-hearted fool.

**Amauri (de Bale):** From the French, meaning 'name of a count'. I used this to imply de Bale's noble background.

**Amoy:** The name is originally Jamaican, and means 'beautiful goddess', but I took the name from Amoy sauce, which derives from Amoy Island in south-eastern China, and describes a particular dialect spoken in Fukien province. I liked the idea that Amoy's mother named her son after a favourite sauce.

**Andrassy (Iuliu):** Andrassy means a 'man' or a 'warrior'. The name Iuliu is of Romanian origin and means 'youthful' or 'soft-haired' – it stems from the Roman name Julius, meaning 'downy-haired' or 'easily manipulable due to innocence', which is the case with Andrassy.

**Antanasia (Lupei):** Antanasia is the Romanian variation of the Russian Anastasia, and means 'resurrection' or the 'breaker of chains'. Alternatively 'one who will be reborn' or who is 'immortal'. Antanasia's surname,

Lupei, is from the Romanian word *lup*, which means 'wolf'.

**Asson (de Bale):** An Asson is a sacred voodoo rattle used by the Houngans (priests) and Mambos (priestesses) of Vodoun. It is generally made from a gourd and decorated with beads and snake bones. The Asson represents the Chief Loa, Damballah, and the sound it makes mimics the Damballah's serpent language. It is used in the Loas ritual, and serves as a symbol of authority, in the sense that it implies the formal ordination of the bearer.

**Athame (de Bale):** An Athame is a sacred sword or dagger used by witches and priestesses. It has a black handle, and the double-edged blade is generally inscribed with symbols. It is one of a number of magical tools used in traditional witchcraft, and may refer to the Key of Solomon, a famous Grimoire (magic book) dating back to the Middle Ages. The Athame is also an energy intensifier. The name derives, in its corrupt form, from the late Latin *artavus*, meaning a 'quill knife'.

**Babel (Samana):** Babel comes from the Hebrew word *balal*, meaning to 'jumble'. It was the name of a biblical tower whose builders intended it to reach heaven. It can also mean a confused gathering or a concatenation of sounds – a cacophony even. The name derives from a time when all humans were deemed to speak the same language, and implies multi-ethnicity. The surname, **Samana**, is similarly oriented, in the sense of being a Creole language, used on southern plantations, and later, post-1820, in the Dominican Republic.

**Badu:** Badu depicts the dominant personality in a relationship – one who is powerful and strong. In its African form, it can also imply the 'tenth' (in a numerous family, say).

**Bale:** Bale stems from the word Baal, or Ba'al, and means 'master' or 'lord'. The name also has links with Ba'al Zebûb or Beelzebub, which was deemed in certain Christian writings to refer to Satan himself. Baal was generally ranked as the king of hell, however, with sixty-six legions at his command (see **Abiger**). He was Satan's lieutenant, if you will. The Lord of the Flies.

**Bazena:** Bazena can mean one who is 'ill' or 'not in harmony' with herself. It is a variation of the Polish name, Bozena, which implies 'happiness' or to be 'blessed by God'. The change in spelling is crucial here.

**Bera:** Bera means a 'gift'. It can also mean 'one who is clean'. In its Germanic/Icelandic form it can also mean a 'bear'.

**Berith (de Bale):** *Berith* is the Hebrew word for 'covenant' – in Babylonian, the word means 'fetter' or 'bond'. Berith is one of the Grand Dukes of Hell. He is alleged, according to various demonological sources, to be able to turn all metals into gold. He is a notorious liar, and can never be trusted. He sports red clothing, rides a red horse, and wears a golden crown – he can only be summoned by means of a magical silver ring. He has twenty-six legions of demons under his command. He only speaks the truth when prophesying. There are some who link him with Nostradamus's 'red man'. His name was taken from Baal Berith (see **Bale**), a form of Baal worship familiar in Beirut (Berith).

**Bouboul:** Babul or Bouboul is an ancient Hindi term for 'father', usually, but not exclusively, used by daughters, particularly when they are in the process of leaving their father's house for that of their husband. It may derive from the Persian *bulbu'*, meaning a nightingale.

**Calque (Joris):** Calque is the seventeenth-century Old French word for to 'trace' or to 'copy'. The word can also imply a loan translation, in terms of an expression transferred from one language into another and then translated (e.g. skyscraper: *gratte-ciel*: *Wolkenkratzer*). Calque's Christian name, Joris – a Flemish variation on George – means an 'earth worker', a 'farmer', or a 'husbandman', i.e. one who builds from the bottom upwards. I felt that both names described Calque's character.

**Catalin (Mihael):** Catalin means 'pure' or 'chaste' and Mihael means the 'one who is like God'. The names were quite consciously taken on by **Dracul Lupei** to imply immaculacy.

**Dadul (Gavriloff):** Dadul means to do something 'ridiculous', 'crazy' or 'legendary'. Also someone who is quick with their hands.

**Dakini (de Bale):** Dakini stems from the Tibetan, and means 'she who traverses the sky' or 'she who moves in space' – a sky dancer or sky walker. The word generally implies a witch or a female demon who appears to a magician during certain rituals, often related to the dead. The Dakini is frequently shown as a young, naked, dancing figure, holding a skull cup filled with menstrual blood (the elixir of life) and a curved knife. She wears a garland of human skulls, and holds a trident staff against her shoulder. Her hair is wild and hangs down her back, and her face is contorted into a wrathful expression. She is prone to dancing on corpses to show her mastery over ego and ignorance.

**Dearborn (Skip):** Dearborn is Old English, and means the 'place of the deer'. It is also a 'four-wheeled carriage with curtained sides'. I derived the name Skip from a skep, or 'beehive', both names implying something held within something else – i.e. something hidden. A 'whited sepulchre' perhaps?

**De Bale:** See **Bale**

**Dracul (Lupei):** Dracul means 'the devil' in Romanian, but it can also mean 'son of the dragon'. Lupei means a 'wolf'. Both names were chosen specifically to indicate evil, or the possibility of evil. They also have revocations of Vlad Țepeș, nicknamed Dracul or Dracula (the 'impaler'), who was three-time Vovoide of Wallachia, and was renowned for impaling his enemies on stakes.

**Flipo:** Flipo is a slang variant of Filipo, meaning a 'friend of horses'. See **Lemelle**

**Gavril:** Gavril is a variation on the name Gabriel, meaning 'God is my strength' or 'one who worships God'. Also 'God's able-bodied one'. The name is used ironically in the context of the book.

**Hervé:** See **Milouins**

**Ixtab:** Ixtab, or 'rope woman', was the Mayan goddess of suicide – in particular, that by hanging, which was considered quite acceptable in Mayan culture. Ixtab was often depicted as a corpse with a rope around her neck, and was deemed a psychopomp (i.e. one who accompanied suicides to their final resting place).

**Joris:** See **Calque**

**Karaev (Anatoly):** The surname Karaev stems from the Turkic term meaning either 'black' or 'dark'. It can also indicate a dirty or foul-tempered person. The Christian name Anatoly implies that the bearer is 'from the east'.

**Koine/Koiné:** Koiné comes from the Greek *koiné diálektos*, meaning common usage. Like **Sabir**, it was a Lingua Franca of the Eastern Mediterranean in Hellenistic and Roman times, and also the language linking Attic Greece to the Byzantine era.

**Kol (Driver):** Kol means 'coal town' – it also means 'dark' in Norwegian. I chose the name to imply someone who works for a living in a confined space.

**Lamia (de Bale):** Lamia was the daughter of Poseidon and a mistress of Zeus. Hera was so jealous of Lamia that she stole away her children and deformed their mother, giving her the upper body and breasts of a woman, while her lower body was transformed into that of a serpent. This hybrid version of Lamia then lured victims to her domain and devoured them in her grief – her name derives from the Greek word *laimos*, meaning 'gullet'. In ancient Rome she was viewed as a bloodsucking witch. She was also Queen of Libya (even the personification of Libya), and alleged to have become a child-murdering daemon. Lamia was cursed with the inability to close her eyes so that she would always obsess over the image of her dead children – but Plutarch maintained that Lamia also had the gift of being able to pluck her eyes out and then replace them at will.

**Lemelle (Philippe):** Lemelle is a nickname for the 'blackbird', or of someone who lives near a medlar tree. It can also derive from the Latin, *lamina*, meaning a 'thin plate of metal', which transmogrified into the Old French *lemelle*, meaning the 'blade of a knife'.

**Lemma:** From the Latin *lemma*, meaning a theme, title or epigram – something taken as given. Also a proposition used to prove another proposition. It can also be the argument, theme, or subject of a written work, or the motto or legend below a picture. The name continues the theme of language and understanding which imbrues all three books.

**Lenis:** Lenis means soft-voiced. Someone who articulates with little tension. It is the opposite of hard-voiced (i.e. *fortis*).

**Luca:** Luca originally means someone who comes from Luciana in Italy. It also derives from the Latin, *lux*, meaning 'light', or 'the bringer of light'. It is a variation on Lucius.

**Macron (Paul):** Macron comes from the Greek, *makrón*, meaning large, and describes the horizontal bar over a letter indicating that it is long (a long syllable). Paul, of course, means 'small' or 'humble', thus presenting something of a paradox in a two metre tall man.

**Maja:** Maja is an Arabic girl's name meaning 'splendid' – also 'great' and 'mother' in Greek. I chose the name because of Maja's emphasis on motherhood and fatherhood as signs of a well-spent life.

**Markovich (Cosmin):** It means 'gleaming'. It originally derives from the name Mark, meaning 'dedicated to Mars, the god of war'. Cosmin means 'in solidarity with life' or 'praise'. I chose the name to imply someone who wished to go on living.

**Mastigou (Madame):** Mastigou means to be 'tympanized' (i.e. to be stretched on the rack) or 'tortured'. It can also mean 'suffering'.

**Mateos-Corrientes (Emiliano Graciano):** Mateos means 'offered up to God', and Corriente is a 'very basic Spanish wine', the implication being of someone of the lower order – the bottom of the barrel. Corriente also means a 'current', implying someone who is swept along by events. Emiliano means a 'rival' or 'emulator' – i.e. someone who copies. Graciano is meant paradoxically, and means 'pleasing'.

**Milouins (Hervé):** A milouin is a 'wild diving duck' – a winter visitor to France. Hervé means 'eager for battle'. Apposite, I felt.

**Nawal (de Bale):** Central American folk belief has it that the Nawal is a witch who is able to transform herself into an animal (most commonly a donkey, a turkey, or a dog). She can use her power for either good or evil, depending on her nature. In animism, each person will have a familiar animal to which their life force is linked – this is often the first animal that has wandered or flown into a notional circle drawn round the child's cot. In Nahuatal (Aztec), the Nawal is always linked with harmful magic, and can transform herself, usually at night, into an owl, a bat, or a turkey, sucking blood from unsuspecting victims.

**Nuelle:** Nuelle comes from the Hebrew, and means 'a peaceful soul'.

**Oni (de Bale):** In Japanese folk belief the Oni were demons similar to the devils spoken of in medieval sorcery. They are usually depicted as hideous, gigantic, creatures with sharp claws, wild hair, and two long horns growing from their heads – sometimes with extra fingers and toes. Their skin is often red or blue, and they are frequently portrayed wearing tiger-skin loincloths and carrying iron clubs. They are considered virtually undefeatable. It was said that they could cause disease, disasters, and a plethora of other unpleasant things, should they be so inclined. Thus Oni.

**Picaro (Jean):** A Picaro was a 'rogue', a 'bohemian', or an 'adventurer' – also known as a picaroon. Also the main male character in a picaresque novel. Jean means 'God is gracious'.

**Radu:** Radu is of Slavonic origin, and means 'the happy one' or someone who is 'joyful'. In Chinese it can mean 'the leg of the dragon'. Chinese dragons are both potent and auspicious, unlike Western dragons.

**Rocha (de Bale):** Rocha means a 'ewe' or 'something that is to be sacrificed'. In Portuguese it means a 'rock'. See **Achor**.

**Rudra (de Bale):** Rudra is the Indian demon-God of storms, the hunt, and fierce winds – he is also associated with the forces of death. A skilful archer, he can bring disease with his arrows. His

631

name can also be construed as the 'roarer', the 'howler', or the 'terrible one'. He is sometimes linked with the god Shiva, and some know him as 'the red one' or 'the wild beast'.

**Sabir (Adam):** Sabir comes from the Portuguese *sabir*, meaning to know. Sabir was also the earliest known pidgin, or Lingua Franca, based on a European language, and used from the time of the Crusades (eleventh to thirteenth centuries) until the early twentieth century, for communication between Europeans, Turks, Arabs and other Levantines in the Mediterranean. The name, in its Arabic form, can also mean 'long-lasting', 'enduring', 'patient', or 'persevering'. In ancient Byzantium the Sabir people, who lived on the east coast of the Caspian Sea, were renowned as 'reliable'. The name Adam, of course, can also mean 'the earth', or 'red earth', or simply 'man'.

**Samana:** Samana is a Creole language, used on southern plantations, and later, post-1820, in the Dominican Republic. It can also mean 'heard' or 'asked of' God. In Sanskrit, Samana is one of the five main pranas, and means 'equality'.

**Tepeu:** Tepeu comes from K'iche' Maya, and means 'sovereign', or 'one who conquers' or 'wins out'. In the Popol Vuh the name means 'Sovereign Plumed Serpent'.

**Valah:** Valah is of Romanian origin and means 'one who is singled out'. The Valah were Latin speakers and traditional herders of sheep.

**Vaulderie (de Bale):** Vaulderie is a French expression used by members of the French Inquisition to describe the act of forming a Satanic pact. Named after the hermit Robinet de Vaulse, it became something of a familiar charge during the Middle Ages. It was also linked to the magical flying ointments allegedly used by the witches to 'fly wherever they wished to go… the Devil carrying them to the place where they should hold their assembly.'

**Yola:** From the Old English/ West Saxon *yald*, meaning 'old'. The name was used for the first variant of English spoken in Ireland, circa the twelfth century, with the 'old' emphasis implying a separate evolution. It can also mean a 'violet flower'. I used it to imply ancient heredity.

**Zina (Samana):** The meaning of Zina in Arabic has to do with extramarital or premarital sex. It is considered one of the great sins of Islam. The Greek meaning of Zina is a 'guest' or 'stranger'. It can also mean 'shining' or 'going back'. The 'stranger' meaning fits best with Zina's nomadic character.

# MARIO READING

## THE ANTICHRIST TRILOGY

## HAVE YOU READ THEM ALL?

### TURN THE PAGE FOR A PREVIEW...

# THE NOSTRADAMUS PROPHECIES

Hidden for centuries, the lost quatrains of Nostradamus contain
secrets so powerful that men will kill for them. Scholar Adam Sabir
risks his life among the ancient gypsy clans of France to find the
lost quatrains before they fall into the wrong hands...

ACHOR BALE TOOK NO REAL PLEASURE IN
killing. That had long since left him. He watched the
gypsy almost fondly, as one might watch a chance
acquaintance getting off an airplane.

The man had been late of course. One only had to look
at him to see the vanity bleeding from each pore. The
1950s moustache à la Zorro. The shiny leather jacket
bought for fifty euros at the Clignancourt flea market.
The scarlet see-through socks. The yellow shirt with the
Prince of Wales plumes and the outsized pointed collar.
The fake gold medallion with the image of Sainte Sara.
The man was a dandy without taste – as recognisable to
one of his own as a dog is to another dog.

'Do you have the manuscript with you?'

'What do you think I am? A fool?'

Well, hardly that, thought Bale. A fool is rarely self-conscious. This man wears his venality like a badge of office. Bale noted the dilated pupils. The sheen of sweat on the handsome, razor-sharp features. The drumming of the fingers on the table. The tapping of the feet. A drug addict, then. Strange, for a gypsy. That must be why he needed the money so badly. 'Are you Manouche or Rom? Gitan, perhaps?'

'What do you care?'

'Given your moustache, I'd say Manouche. One of Django Reinhardt's descendants, maybe?'

'My name is Samana. Babel Samana.'

'Your gypsy name?'

'That is secret.'

'My name is Bale. No secret there.'

The gypsy's fingers increased their beat upon the table. His eyes were everywhere now – flitting across the other drinkers, testing the doors, plumbing the dimensions of the ceiling.

'How much do you want for it?' Cut straight to the chase. That was the way with a man like this. Bale watched the gypsy's tongue dart out to moisten the thin, artificially virilised mouth.

'I want half a million euros.'

'Just so.' Bale felt a profound calmness descending upon him. Good. The gypsy really did have something to sell. The whole thing wasn't just a come-on. 'For such a sum of money, we'd need to inspect the manuscript before purchase. Ascertain its viability.'

'And memorise it! Yes. I've heard of such things. This much I know. Once the contents are out into the open it's worthless. Its value lies in its secrecy.'

'You're so right. I'm very glad you take that position.'

'I've got someone else interested. Don't think you're the only fish in the sea.'

Bale's eyes closed down on themselves. Ah. He would have to kill the gypsy after all. Torment and kill. He was aware of the telltale twitching above his right eye. 'Shall we go and see the manuscript now?'

'I'm talking to the other man first. Perhaps you'll even bid each other up.'

Bale shrugged. 'Where are you meeting him?'

'I'm not saying.'

'How do you wish to play this then?'

'You stay here. I go and talk to the other man. See if he's serious. Then I come back.'

'And if he's not? The price goes down?'

'Of course not. Half a million.'

'I'll stay here then.'

'You do that.'

The gypsy lurched to his feet. He was breathing heavily now, the sweat dampening his shirt at the neck and sternum. When he turned around Bale noticed the imprint of the chair on the cheap leather jacket.

'If you follow me, I'll know. Don't think I won't.'

Bale took off his sunglasses and laid them on the table. He looked up, smiling. He had long understood the effect his freakishly clotted eyes had on susceptible people. 'I won't follow you.'

The gypsy's mouth went slack with shock. He gazed in horror at Bale's face. This man had the *ia chalou* – the evil eye. Babel's mother had warned him of such people. Once you saw them – once they fixed you with the stare of the basilisk – you were doomed. Somewhere, deep inside his unconscious mind, Babel Samana was acknowledging his mistake – acknowledging that he had let the wrong man into his life.

'You'll stay here?'

'Never fear. I'll be waiting for you.'

# THE MAYAN CODEX

The prophecies of the lost quatrains are coming true. But there's
one which Adam Sabir can't decipher, and it warns of the coming
of the Third Antichrist. Sabir must make a dangerous journey to
the Palace of the Masks in Mexico. Only there can the secrets of
the Apocalypse be revealed...

SO. IT WAS TIME. THE COUNTESS LAID ASIDE
the document whose ancient codification had caused so
much trouble to the inquisitive police captain – what
had been his name? Clique? Claque? – the one who had
so dogged her footsteps in the run-up to the death of
her eldest son earlier that summer. She knew its entire
contents by heart.

'Who are we?'

'We are the Corpus.' Her children responded as one.

'Which Corpus?'

'The Corpus Maleficus.'

'And what do we do?'

'We protect the realm.'

'And who is our enemy?'

'The Devil.'

'And how shall we defeat him?'

'We shall never defeat him.'

'And how shall we unseat him?'

'We shall never unseat him.'

'So what is our purpose?'

'Delay.'

'And how do we procure it?'

'By serving Christ's dark shadow.'

'And who is that?'

'The *antimimon pneuma*. The counterfeit spirit.'

'And what is his name?'

'The Antichrist.'

'And how do we serve him?'

'By destroying the *Parousia*.'

'And what is the *Parousia*?'

'He is the Second Coming of Christ. He is the brother of Satan.'

'And how shall we know Him?'

'A sign will be given.'

'And how shall we kill Him?'

'He will be sacrificed.'

'And what shall be our reward?'

'Death.'

'And what is our law?'

'Death.'

'And how shall we achieve it?'

'Anarchy.'

'And who are our brothers and sisters?'

'We shall know them.'

'And who are our enemies?'

'We shall know them.'

'And who is the Third Antichrist?'

'We shall know him and guard him.'
'And who is the Second Coming?'
'We shall know Him and kill Him...'

*The Nostradamus Propecies* and *The Mayan Codex*
are available in paperback and eBook at all good retailers.

And why not pay us a visit at www.corvus-books.co.uk